NO
GOOD
DEED

Edited by
Amanda Saint and
Sophie Duffy

ISBN paperback: 978-1-9160693-4-3
ISBN eBook: 978-1-9160693-5-0

Retreat West Books
retreatwestbooks.com

CONTENTS

FOREWORD

In a year of turbulence when people have been taking to the streets all across the world to protest against social and environmental injustice, I am proud to be publishing the third charity anthology at Retreat West Books. This book is supporting Indigo Volunteers, an organisation that helps people all around the world whose lives are impacted by climate change, war, inequality and poverty by connecting volunteers with the projects that need them. They do not charge the volunteers or the projects and rely entirely on donations to support the work they do.

The theme of the anthology is 'help' and we were overwhelmed by the response to the submission call and the hundred and thirty-two writers who sent in their stories for consideration. We enjoyed reading them all. The stories we have chosen to include are a mix of flash fiction and longer short stories that have approached the theme in many different ways. We loved the strangeness and humour of some and were very moved by others.

Our thanks go to all of the authors who have donated

their stories for this book; to Jennie Rawlings at Serifim Design for donating her time to create the beautiful cover; and to Nomad Books for hosting the launch celebration.

One hundred percent of the royalties will be donated to Indigo Volunteers, so if you enjoy this book please do tell all your friends and family to buy one too and leave a review online. Word of mouth is the best way to support indie publishers and help us to keep on bringing new authors and great stories to the world.

Amanda Saint and Sophie Duffy (Editors)

No Good Deed

Liz Drayer

JACKSON FOX WAS a man of his word. And he'd promised to pay for the Color Guard's spring costumes. Before his daughter had joined Guard, he thought it had something to do with the flag. Now he'd learned about side whips, blind forty-fives and trust falls, perfected in practices six days a week. Whatever, he was glad Silver had found something to do after school besides smoking pot behind the Starbucks.

What had Jackson fed up was the music department's endless money-grubbing – the wheedling, the guilting, the outright demands for funds from the parents. Sure, arts education received zero money from the school district, and where else could these groups get their cash? Still, Jackson thought the five hundred he'd dished out at the start of the year was enough for an after-school club. The emails demanding attendance at weekly fundraisers informed him otherwise.

'How much does the music program need?' he'd naively asked at the department barbecue Freshman Year.

The department chair, Harley Biss, puffed out his chest like a Thanksgiving turkey. 'Sir, the marching band needs a new sousaphone AND a bass drum, the latter a victim of the head-butting goat Future Farmers keep on the back field. And what of our jazz trio, favored to win state this year? How do you expect them to get to Pensacola?'

Even worse, soon Jackson discovered that though he'd ponied up the requested five hundred bucks, most parents had not, leaving the program thousands in the red. Public schools couldn't force students to pay for extracurriculars; anyone could take part for free. Of course, if no one paid their fair share, the activities couldn't take place. The result was a few parents subsidized the delinquent dozens, then got hit up again for more cash.

'In what universe is that fair?' Jackson complained to his wife while they cleaned up the kitchen. 'Can't Silver find another hobby?'

'You're kidding, right?' Claire replied. 'All Silver's friends are in Guard. You don't ask a high schooler to give up her friends. Not to mention, she needs to stick with some activity to show colleges she's committed.'

'I should be committed, agreeing to finance this boondoggle. And I'd like to strangle that little creep Biss. All he wants is to win the state championship so some college will recruit him away.'

'Can you blame him?'

Jackson shrugged. 'No one forced him to teach high school.'

'Silver said he rescues bichon frises from abusive homes.'

'Oh, gag me. The public servant, sacrificing for the beasts and the children.'

Now that Silver was in Year Two of Guard, Jackson had determined to limit his suckerdom. He'd secured a seat on the Music Booster Board, tasked with raising money through car washes, auctions, and the monster time suck of them all, the Annual Yard Sale, held behind the school in April, steam rising in waves from the asphalt. Weeks before the event, volunteers drove around collecting junk from anyone willing to donate. The previous year, someone's broken-down Schwinn had smeared grease on the creamy leather of Jackson's Audi, and for this he held Biss responsible. Then came the sorting, tagging, the loading of purchases into buyers' cars, and driving the leftover crap to donation bins. Last year, the sale netted a measly five hundred dollars.

So at the Boosters' fall meeting, Jackson had made an offer.

'I'll pay for the spring costumes if we limit fundraisers to one bug eating contest.'

'Wow,' said the board president. 'That's pretty generous, Jack.'

'That's Jackson.'

'I'm in favor,' said the treasurer, prompting a chorus of "ayes." The group adjourned in high spirits, and Jackson swaggered out to the parking lot, convinced he'd saved himself a crapload of hassles. Plus, he enjoyed playing the big shot – returns from his side hustle, the grow house, now rivaled his software developer salary, and he could afford to help the music department and also gin up good will he could use if he ran for local office, which he threatened to do every year.

The winter months passed, the March meeting arrived and the board convened in the band room, the smell of brass and spit valve condensation perfuming the air. The members wedged into metal chairs attached to tiny desks to wait for Biss, who they all knew was playing computer games in his office, though no one had the nerve to call him on it. Suppose your kid had his eye on first chair in the flute section? It was Biss you needed to stroke.

Finally, he strode in, and slapped a paper on Jackson's desk. 'The costume bill, friend.'

Jackson stared. 'Twenty-four thousand? What are those leotards made of, spun gold?'

'You don't want to cheap out on costumes,' Biss said. 'The judges will count it against us.'

'Cheap out? There are twelve kids in Color Guard. That's two thousand per outfit.'

'You're forgetting the marching band, jazz trio and

orchestra, friend. Do you want them to go naked?'

'I never agreed to buy clothes for the whole department!'

'Really? That's what I heard you say,' Biss said, looking around for confirmation. Heads bobbed in unison.

'Come on!' Jackson said. 'The jazz trio and orchestra always wear black clothes from home.'

Biss waved the air. 'Fine. We can make this the Amateur Hour. Whatever you say.'

'You're taking advantage of me,' Jackson said, 'when I'm just trying to help.'

Biss smirked. 'We don't all drive Teslas and race yachts in Tampa Bay, Fox.'

'I don't own a yacht! Or a Tesla.'

'Whatever,' Biss said. 'Do you want to help, or not?'

'Someone read back the minutes from January,' Jackson demanded. 'I didn't commit to buy hundreds of costumes.'

The secretary scrolled down her laptop. 'It says "File unavailable." That's weird. Guess I can't read back the minutes.'

Biss smiled. 'So, Fox? Do I cancel the order, and crush the dreams of two hundred future artistes?'

Jackson wanted to punch his mustachioed face. He'd look like a jerk if he backed out now, and Biss might take it out on Silver, who knew? Suppose she was up for squad captain, and Biss chose someone else, just to be a huge dick?

'Fine,' Jackson said, slumping in the undersized chair.

The board president rapped his gavel. 'Okay, who's ordering insects for the contest? Half decomposers and half carnivores, this year, please. Last time we had complaints.'

Jackson closed his eyes, wishing Silver had taken up skydiving.

When the meeting ended, Jackson trudged to the parking lot and drove home to his gated community. On the way up the stone path, he felt something stick to his face – a web, he realized, batting the gummy snare. His animal-loving wife refused to knock down spider webs, depriving the creatures of nourishment. 'It's like taking away their car keys so they can't get to Food World,' Claire said. 'Only a monster would do that!'

Inside, he found Silver hunched at the big kitchen table, looking more mopey than usual. His wife wiped her hands on a towel. 'Go ahead,' she said, 'tell your father.'

'Daddy,' Silver sobbed, running to Jackson and hugging his neck.

'What's wrong?'

'I got a D in Spanish.'

'Don't worry, honey. You'll work harder next marking period.'

'Yes. But –' Silver's breath came in snotty bursts.

'Sweetheart, a bad grade is not the end of the world.'

'But, Dad! I'm suspended from Color Guard for the

6

rest of the semester. I promised to get all Cs when I joined. I signed a paper.'

'Is that right?' Jackson stepped out onto the porch, the humid air enveloping him like a sauna. In the distance, crickets chirped, bullfrogs bleated. He'd read about grubs that ate frogs that were supposed to eat them. Upending the order. Nature, it could kick your ass.

Cooking Chicken in Kentucky
Reshma Ruia

PETER AND CAROLINE stand together in their hotel room, elbows on the window ledge, staring at the golden fields. They are in a small village outside Calais.

A gunshot followed by loud shouts breaks the stillness. A plume of smoke curls up from a clump of trees bordering the fields. Caroline frowns as she looks at the smoke that briefly hides the sun.

'I hope everything's okay.'

Peter says he'd read in the papers about a refugee colony near the village.

'Don't worry about it,' he says, his fingers brushing the nape of her neck. His voice is a whisper. 'This weekend is all about us.' They are celebrating their tenth wedding anniversary.

***

THEY DRIVE TO Calais to catch the ferry home, stopping at a petrol station to re-fuel. Peter fills up and goes in to pay while Caroline stays in the car. Through the rear-view mirror, she spots a group of young men huddled together near the hard shoulder of the motorway. Dark skinned and dressed in shiny tracksuits, they look out of place. One of them punches the air with his fist and they scatter in different directions.

The car smells of cheese and cuts of ham, mementoes of their French weekend. Caroline spent the morning in a frenzy of buying camembert and Bordeaux reds from the farmers' market in the village square. The food packed in shiny brown paper bags fills the back seat. The smell makes her retch and she winds down the windows to let in some fresh air. She feels a headache coming on and dozes off.

They make the ferry just in time.

'Lots of shopping, eh?' The border guard glances at the back seat and flicks through their passports with a yawn.

'*Il est notre anniversaire. J'aime beaucoup Le France, aussi ma…*' Peter hesitates, searching for the right word.

'*Femme.*' Caroline finishes his sentence.

'*Joyeux anniversaire.*' The *gendarme* waves them on.

They reach home after midnight. Peter's back is sore from driving and he wants to go to bed right away.

'Don't worry. I'll do the unpacking,' Caroline says, patting his arm.

***

IN THE GARAGE, she fumbles for the light, almost tripping over Peter's golf clubs. Two trips from the car to the fridge and she is almost done, when she returns one last time for the wine in the boot. A soft thud and a small bundle rolls out of the boot and settles near her feet. Does she scream? She can't remember.

The grey bundle uncurls itself and crouches at her feet. It is a small boy with PG Tips brown skin and a head of tightly woven curls. He opens his mouth and she sees the gap between his two front teeth.

'Who the hell are you?' She grabs a golf club, waving it like a flag.

He squats on the floor, dusty toes curled against the cold concrete. Caroline comes nearer and he raises his arms, covering the top of his head, readying himself for the blow. She is about to run upstairs and shake Peter awake when she stops. How dangerous can he be? A little boy who looks lost and confused. The golf club slips from her hand.

Crouching down, one hand pressing his shoulder, she asks, 'Who are you?'

He blinks rapidly and starts rocking back and forth, shivering in his faded blue tracksuit bottom and a striped tee shirt that seems too tight on his body.

A small hoarse voice mumbles something.

Caroline frowns. 'Sorry, I don't understand.'

He sticks out his tongue. It is pale and flecked with white.

She hears his stomach rumble and understands. 'You want food.'

In the kitchen, she quickly cuts him slices of thick white bread, makes him milky tea and pours him water. He eats too quickly, retching once or twice, bringing up the tea. It dribbles down the side of his mouth and neck, a thin brown stream wending its way down his tee shirt.

'Hey, slowly, eat slowly,' she says, glancing towards the stairs to check whether the commotion has woken up Peter.

The boy points to his crotch and she takes him to the downstairs loo. The trickle of his urine rings out feeble and lonely in the silent house. She goes back to the bathroom and flushes the toilet twice, emptying a bottle of Dettol into the bowl.

Afterwards, she takes him into the garden and hands him an old sleeping bag that she spreads in the garden shed.

'Be very quiet,' she tells him as he edges himself inside the sleeping bag. 'Make no noise and only come out when I tell you.'

Caroline can't sleep that night. She imagines the boy prowling downstairs. His small, sweaty hands running like mice through her things. She lies awake, staring at the window, willing the daylight to come faster.

***

NEXT MORNING PETER rushes to work and there is no time for explanations. Caroline can't understand why she, sparrow-timid at heart, hasn't confided in him. She calls in sick at the school where she teaches and stands at the kitchen sink staring at the neighbour's house.

The door opens. It is the boy watching her, his soot-dark eyes alert.

'I told you not to come out, until I call you.'

He stands, eyes fixed on her face.

'H-E-L-L-O and G-O-O-D M-O-R-N-I-N-G. Did you sleep well?' She speaks slowly, pronounces each syllable clearly.

He doesn't reply.

'Don't be afraid,' she says, going up to him and stroking his cheek.

He steps back, his index finger rubbing his cheek.

She tries again. 'What is your name?'

'Ali,' the boy whispers finally. 'Name is Ali,' he repeats.

'Like Ali Baba.' She smiles, but he doesn't smile back. He is looking at the fruit bowl piled high with apples.

She points to her stomach, patting it with her palm. 'Hungry?'

He nods.

'You need to brush your teeth first. Have a shower.' Caroline's voice is brisk and teacher-like. The boy stinks of dried sweat and straw.

Ali follows Caroline upstairs, bare feet padding on the carpeted floor. She turns on the shower. He strips and squats on the floor, head buried between his folded arms. The water beats against his skin like rain. His elbows jut out, thin, bony and needy.

She gives him Peter's gym tee shirt and a pair of old shorts. In the bedroom, she hides her pearl necklace under the mattress.

Ali comes down, drowning in his borrowed clothes, his old ones rolled tight against his chest. He points to the fruit bowl.

She throws him an apple and he lunges forward to catch it and misses. He giggles, his face opening up like a flower.

Caroline pats the empty chair beside her. 'Come and sit.' She hands him an apple.

He sits, swinging his foot, taking quick bites of the fruit.

'Ali, how did you end up in my car?'

He doesn't understand her question, so she mimics the motion of driving a car, her hands going round an imaginary steering wheel.

Ali gets up and edges towards the door.

'Don't worry. I won't tell the police.' She takes his

elbow and leads him back to the chair.

'Where are you from, Ali?' Caroline asks, pretending as though he's a new boy who's just joined her class.

'Somalia,' he answers. 'In Africa.' His voice has a small American twang.

'That's far away,' Caroline says. 'How did you get in my car? Was it in France?'

Ali nods without looking at her.

'And…?' She prompts.

He sighs and starts speaking. Words tumble out haltingly. 'I come in lorry. Lorry with sheep. We hide under the animals.' He screws up his nose. 'Aatch stinking with shit.'

Caroline asks him how long he'd been in the lorry. He holds his fingers up and says four days.

He continues. 'We wait near the petrol station and the driver get angry and screams, get out, get out fast.' Ali snaps his fingers. 'Everybody run. I see your car. You sleeping. I hide inside your car.'

She listens rapt. It's like hearing a fairy-tale. 'Your mother? Was she in the lorry also?' Caroline wants to make sure the boy is not alone. She pictures his mother roaming the streets, calling his name; her eyes wide open in panic.

Ali folds his arms, looks at his feet. He frowns. 'No mother.'

'You speak good English.'

He shrugs. 'I go to UN school in camp.'

Her mobile on the kitchen counter vibrates as Peter's number flashes. Caroline ignores it but Ali's arm shoots out and he grabs her phone. Eyes narrowed, his thumb runs over the screen. 'You have iPhone.' He looks at her approvingly.

'It's just a phone,' Caroline says, 'In fact let's call your mother.' She looks at him expectantly, her fingers ready to punch in the numbers.

Ali says something in a language she doesn't understand.

'English please,' Caroline adopts her teacher's voice. 'We are in England now.'

'Mother has no phone,' Ali replies, switching to English. He rubs away at his eyes with the heel of his palm.

'Where is your father? I can let him know you are safe.'

This time Ali answers straight away, repeating almost parrot fashion, lines he has memorised. 'My father is dead. He was soldier. And my mother.' Ali's hands fold into fists and he places them flat on the table like a sleeping animal. 'My mother very ill. She sits inside the camp and prays to god. My mother wants me to be doctor. If I stay in Somalia, I become soldier. I die like my father. Go to England she says. Live.' He begins to cry, dry sobs jiggling his shoulders.

'Don't cry, please don't cry,' Caroline stands over

him, wringing her hands. She squeezes his arm and hands him a Kleenex. He blows his nose and throws the used tissue on the floor.

After a while, the sobs die out and he looks around the kitchen.

'You are rich.' He states it like a fact.

Caroline feels her cheeks go warm. 'We get by. We have no children so we can save a lot.'

Her fridge is stuffed with French cheese and wine and organic fruits. Hers is a rich life but sitting next to him, she suddenly feels poor.

'You have no girl. No boy?' Ali's eyebrows shoot up in surprise.

'I have plenty of god children, nephews, nieces,' Caroline explains. Her voice turns loud and bright. She changes the subject. 'You must be hungry. Let me make you a sandwich.' She busies herself slicing the bread, slathering it with jam.

A small swell of disgust rises in her as she watches him stuff the bread into his mouth. There is something naked and ugly in his perpetual hunger. 'Eat slowly. It's not running away,' she says.

She glances at the clock. Soon it will be lunchtime and she can hear Ali's stomach rumble again with hunger. Boys have big appetites.

'I am going to cook your food.' Caroline stops herself. She must speak properly so the boy can learn. 'I am going to prepare your lunch. What is your favourite dish?'

'We eat mutton at Eid. My grandfather is killing goat. We eat nonstop.' His eyes shine at the memory.

'What is your best food?' It's his turn to ask.

Caroline shrugs. 'I don't know. Caesar salad, I guess.'

Ali's face is blank but he swivels in his chair and looks around.

'This is big house. Many people live here.'

'It's not that big,' she corrects him. 'We bought it ages back when prices weren't so ridiculously high. I live here with my husband.'

'Your husband is soldier.' Ali leans towards her, examining her face, eyes narrowed, checking for signs of buried grief.

'Oh no, Peter is an accountant.' She smiles. 'But he is a busy man. I will introduce you to him later.'

'He is not dead. You are lucky woman. Uncle Musa also live here. He works in Kentucky, cooking chicken,' he pronounces the name proudly. 'He said he will give me a job cooking chicken in Kentucky.'

Caroline bursts out laughing. 'How cute is that.' She stops to get her breath back and tells Ali solemnly that the correct name of his uncle's employer is Kentucky Fried Chicken.

***

LATER THAT MORNING, while Ali naps, she drives to an

unfamiliar part of town with boarded up shops and council flats. A group of Somali women stand at the traffic light, waiting to cross. Their black robes billow in the afternoon breeze.

Caroline rolls down her car window.

'Excuse me. Can you suggest a good butcher that sells mutton?'

The women look at each other and the youngest one, the one with a silver stud in her nose speaks, gesturing with her hands.

Caroline hears them giggle as she drives away.

Back home she downloads the recipe from the computer. The onions make her eyes sting and the pan sputters with oil. She flings open the window, worried the neighbours will complain as the smells of garlic and onion waft out into the London air. The meat tastes like leather and she spits it out before calling Ali, piling soft mounds of rice and mutton on his plate, until he clutches his stomach saying, 'Stop, I can eat no more.'

'Is it good?' she asks.

'Not good like my mother, 'Ali replies.

He passes the second night in the garden shed.

'Stay quiet. Don't make a noise,' she warns again, pressing a finger to her lip. 'We don't want to disturb my husband. He get very angry.'

'Your husband call police?' Ali's face twists in fear.

She shakes her head and says he is a good man but she

needs time before she tells him.

Tomorrow, she tells herself. I promise I will tell Peter tomorrow.

***

SHE CAN'T AVOID going to work the next morning.

'Make yourself at home,' she tells Ali, bringing out the Tupperware with the left over mutton and switching on the TV, flicking through the channels until a Disney cartoon comes up.

She tweaks his cheek. 'You're a good boy.' Her hand lingers on his face. 'I'm going to hire a good lawyer, sort your papers out …maybe we can adopt you.'

Ali sitting cross-legged on the sofa, chin cupped in his hands, engrossed in the cartoon doesn't hear her.

Returning home from work, she buys a chocolate cake. It'll be a surprise for Ali. Also a sweetener for Peter as she introduces him to the boy. He will like Ali. Her eyes well up imagining their meeting. Peter sweeping Ali into his arms. 'Someone to fill the silence…' he'll joke, winking at her. Didn't he always say the house could do with the patter of little feet? Hadn't he painted the spare room bright canary yellow in anticipation of children to come? So busy is she drawing up plans she almost crashes into the police car with its flashing lights that's blocking her front door.

Caroline runs inside, her handbag and shopping bag

slide from her hand. Peter's in the kitchen, lips clamped tight, white in anger. A police officer is scribbling something in a notebook. Ali stands near them. He is back in his old clothes, his head bowed. He looks up when he sees Caroline, but his eyes are mute.

'Ali,' she whispers, running to him. 'You okay?'

It was the postman. He'd spotted the brown face through the window and called the police.

'We've had a narrow escape. This scoundrel had broken in, trying to make off with our stuff,' Peter says, grabbing her arm.

The police officer agrees. 'He doesn't have any papers on him.'

'You can't do anything to him.' She places a protective hand on Ali's shoulder. 'He is innocent. His uncle works in Kentucky...Ali's a good boy.' Her voice falters and she begins crying, her folded arms pressed tight against her chest.

Peter raises an eyebrow. 'Calm down, Caroline. You're not thinking straight. You've never set eyes on this boy before.'

The policeman turns to Ali. 'Do you know this lady?' He raises his voice. 'Do you know her?'

'I don't know her.' Ali shakes his head and spits on the floor.

***

THEY WATCH THE nine o'clock news. There is a special report on the crackdown on illegal immigration.

'We had a narrow escape. Poor faceless mutt. Thank God you were out and all this melodrama, Caroline. You should know better,' says Peter reaching for his wine glass. He takes an appreciative sip and smacks his lips. 'Good vintage, this. I'm glad we picked it up over the weekend.'

'He is not a faceless mutt. His name is Ali. All he wants is to have a better life,' Caroline says. Her voice is wobbly as though she were treading water and failing to find a footing.

'You're overreacting, darling. You don't know him.' Peter sighs and reaches out to hold her hand.

Caroline pushes his hand away.

****

ALI'S FINGERS HAD grazed hers as he followed the policeman. He whispered words meant for her alone.

'I will work in Kentucky. No worry. I will come and see you.'

Caroline opens the back door and steps outside. Bare feet buried deep in grass, her face upturned to the scatter of stars patrolling the night sky. She lets out a howl.

Needle Cat in a Haystack

Meg Pokrass

WE KNEW THAT Stanley the cat might die. He wheezed when he slept. Male cats almost never got breast cancer.

'Hairballs and male breast cancer at the same time?' Dad used to say. 'Needle cat in a haystack.'

Doing homework, I pretended not to hear such things. I felt angry with Stanley, and then hated myself for it. Mom standing near Stanley's bed. My sister, digging madly at her skin. Help, she'd say. I'd pretend to be watching from an eagle's nest.

Mom would bring my sister a cup of water. She believed in cups of water. My sister, who was born needing help. My mother who seemed to embrace it. This was something I had learned to accept.

Climbing city trees, the ones in our front yard, would be a violation in adulthood. I didn't have much longer. I liked the way they felt underneath me—strong. I needed no help, I told myself. I dreamed about trees, their thick branches and slanted leaves. I was stronger and more agile than anyone else in my family.

Mom always smiled when she could not fathom something. She asked the doctor if my size was an issue. She had to get a bit of help with things. Later she told me she wasn't *worrying* that my growth was stunted, she just wanted to keep a jump ahead.

Adult women glared at my large bosom these days, as though my breasts reminded them of someone else, as though I had stolen them. I tried to remain disinterested. Not fear, just not wanting to know.

'Mom, what did the doctor say?'

'He said your hormones will settle down, your breasts will stop growing. That you're *petite,* not a dwarf. You're just… someone special.'

'Special,' I said. 'Terrific.'

Mom always smiled when she could not cope with something. She had smiled when she got the call that my father died. Then she howled.

I wondered if Dad felt more cat than human during his last minutes on Earth, nobody able to help. His heart seized up at work. He curled up like a hairball and died on the floor.

Needle cat in the haystack. This had become like a song in my head.

Mom came back from the vet with Stanley in his kitty carrier.

'What did he say?' I asked.

'The vet called it "unfortunate" in such a young cat,' Mom said. 'But he said that Stanley is a helluva soldier.' She let Stanley out, and he wobbled up to me as if to tell me that he had indeed received help. As if to say, stop worrying young lady and get on with your life. Who let me know that with just the right care, he wouldn't die on us any time soon.

Star

Clare Harvey

WE WAVE GOODBYE at the window. The outside light is on, illuminating the damp leaves on the front path in the dew-falling autumn night. My husband raises a hand, half wave, half salute; his beige-brown figure catches the light one final time, flaring yellow, then disappears into the darkness.

I switch off the light, plunging the garden into night and tell my boy that it is time for bed. He cleans his teeth and showers. His wet blonde hair spikes and glints as he towels it dry.

He doesn't want a story at bedtime; instead he wants me to read from his new astronomy book, a goodbye present from his dad. Together we learn that the moon doesn't actually shine. She's just a reflection of the sun, that's all. When the sun disappears into the darkness, she shines. But it's not her light; it's his. Stars, however – stars generate their own light. You just can't see them when the sun's there. It's the absence of sun that brings out the stars.

Before I hug him, I switch on his bedside light, an illuminated globe. We find ourselves on the world and trace our fingers along to where Daddy would be by morning time.

My boy turns his face up to say goodnight, and I see him radiant in the globe's reflection, with his halo of hair. It almost looks as if the light is coming from within him. I tell him I love him, leaving him to think and drift to sleep.

I tidy and put away and iron and watch TV and pour myself a glass of wine and drink it too quickly and tell myself not to cry. The late news finishes. I pull on my crumpled old pyjamas and crawl into bed. Maybe sleep will come.

Mummy?

A small figure in the doorway, silhouetted against the light from the bathroom.

Help, Mummy, I swallowed a star. It came in through the window and into my mouth and I swallowed it.

Okay darling. Get yourself a drink of water from the bathroom. Hop into your dad's side of the bed. You can sleep here tonight if you want.

He gets into bed beside me and soon his breaths lengthen and he turns and sleeps. At last I sleep too, but fitfully, and I wake sandy-eyed and un-rested to the cold morning.

My boy is already awake, sitting up.

Mum, it's still there, in my tummy.

He places a hand over his solar plexus and I think I see a flash, a pulse of light between his fingers, but then when I turn on the bedside lamp, it's gone.

At breakfast, he doesn't want toast, just milk.

I give him medicine. I think he must have a virus. His glands must be up in his stomach. But he doesn't have a fever, so I say he has to go to school.

When I pick him up after school his pale skin is vivid and his white hair stands in peaks. He falls into my embrace.

When is Daddy coming back?

Twelve weeks until R&R.

How many sleeps?

We do the maths. He seems satisfied. We drive home together and I ask him about his day. He says it was okay. At home I unpack his school bag and empty his lunch box.

You didn't eat your lunch, sweetheart.

It's the spikes in my tummy, Mummy. They make me not hungry.

I check his temperature again, but he doesn't have a fever. I ask him where it hurts. He points to a spot just below his ribcage. At supper he asks for soup, and soon afterwards slips into bed, splayed out, fingers wide, hair wild, eyes blinking.

He asks me to read his astronomy book again. He nods as I repeat the words about the moon reflecting the sunlight, and the stars coming out when the sun disappears. Then he wants to talk about his dad.

So it's eighty-four sleeps until Daddy comes home?

Yes, just eighty-four sleeps.

He rubs his eyes. In the light from the globe he looks luminous, translucent.

That night he wakes me again, and climbs into his father's side of the bed. I'm too exhausted to care.

THE FOLLOWING NIGHT we get a phone call from his father. I tell my husband that our son is fine, that we're both fine. I say fine so many times that I wonder who I'm trying to convince. I don't mention our boy's bad dream. I call it a dream because what else can it be?

Then I pass the phone to my son. When he talks to his dad the colour seems to return to his cheeks and he giggles, but when the call ends he looks pale and exhausted. I suggest an early night and he agrees.

He wants the astronomy book again. This time I notice him mouthing the words as I read: he is memorising them.

That night he comes into my bed again, stumbling in at midnight with a quivering bottom lip.

THE DAYS PASS. Each morning I make my son's packed lunch with more enticing food: biscuits, crisps, sausage rolls – even a chocolate egg with a toy inside. But every day his food comes home untouched.

The next time my husband calls I repeat: we're fine; we're fine. It's becoming a mantra.

My boy gets thinner and paler by the day. His hair is blonder and his skin has a transparent quality, stretched tight over his slender bones. And inside him there's this pulse, this tic. He can't sit still: expressions flit across his features; his smile flashes.

And still he comes into the bed at night, occupying his father's space, elongating, all limbs and fingers and fine strands of metallic hair radiating out over the pillow.

Someone calls from the doctor's surgery and asks to bring my son in for an appointment. When we go in the GP asks him to get on the scales and makes a note of his weight. Her eyes narrow and she sits down and checks his file. I tell her that he just won't eat. She says have I tried introducing more protein into his diet. I repeat that he's not eating. All children like fish fingers, she says.

On her desk is a picture of her own children: two plump-faced girls with shiny chestnut hair and rosy-apple cheeks. They look like they eat a lot of fish fingers.

I glance back as we're leaving and I see her scribbling something down on a piece of paper and picking up the phone.

EVERY TIME MY husband calls I tell him we're fine, but my son is insubstantial as tinsel.

Days turn into weeks.

One day, there's a ring on the doorbell. The health visitor is there; with her union jack tote bag full of files and her scuffed court shoes tapping at the front step. I ask her in and put the kettle on.

I say that my son has started school now. She smiles and says that children are technically 'hers' until their sixth birthday. She asks how he's getting on. I pass her over her cup of tea and reply that he's fine. We go through to the living room. We sit down. She crosses her legs and places her bag on the floor. When she talks she puts her head on one side and her eyebrows go up in the middle. It's a face that says concern and empathy. Her lipstick is too pink. Some of it has come off on her teeth. I try to concentrate on what she's saying, but I just keep staring at the pink smudge on her buck teeth. I catch words as they pass: diet; nutrition; development; concern. And then she says something that makes me stop and listen.

So we thought it might be useful to talk to a professional...

I'm sorry, what was that?

If things don't improve, then it could be an idea to get a professional involved, given your situation.

The health visitor leaves messages on my phone. I

delete them.

I forget to take my son to the doctor for his weigh-in session.

Then I get another call. It's a social worker. She wants to come round. I tell her she's welcome to drop by, anytime, thinking that she'll make an appointment and that I can just happen to forget about it.

Before I even have time to put the phone down, there's a ring at the door, and I know there's no escape. The social worker is large, with a face like a pudding and thighs squeezed into polyester trousers. She says that our family has been referred to her because of my son's weight loss and because of failure to keep appointments with medical professionals regarding the issue. I look blankly at her, wishing she'd just go away. She asks if she can come in and I say that it's not a good time.

Well, when would be a good time? I'd really like the chance to have a chat with you and your son…

I think for a moment before replying.

Tomorrow.

Tomorrow? And I'll come around teatime, so I can meet your boy as well? You do know that if you fail to meet this appointment then there might be some consequences? Well, I've made a note of that, so I'll see you tomorrow, then.

When I go to collect my son from school I grab him and hold him as tight as I can. The classroom assistant gives me a funny look.

By now my boy knows his astronomy book off by heart. At bedtime he reads to me, telling me with authority about the sun, moon and stars. I look at him as I turn off his light, this sliver of silver, barely denting his pillow with his shining aura. I know that by midnight it will be the same as it has been for weeks: the bad dreams, the tummy ache, and the restless night in my husband's side of the bed.

AND THEN AT last, my husband is back, blasting in from the east, rousing us at daybreak with a shout, hurling himself in through the bedroom door and tumbling onto the bed where we both lay, still asleep.

My son opens his eyes and sits up.

Daddy!

I watch the light pull itself back inside my boy. His hair is suddenly darker, his skin pinker. He falls into his father and lets himself be enveloped.

At breakfast he has two pieces of toast.

It feels as if someone has turned the lights on.

That afternoon my husband picks up our son from school.

The social worker turns up for her appointment and she sees him playing football in the front garden with our boy. I'm cooking fish fingers and chips for tea. My husband introduces himself to the social worker. He says nice things about her hair and makes a joke about my cooking and she laughs. He invites her to stay for tea and she says well, maybe just a few chips, and she eats a huge plateful. My son has four fish fingers, chips and beans and afterwards two yoghurts. My husband tells stories about things that happened while he was on tour: someone got drunk and fell down a toilet; someone accidentally shot himself in the foot; a couple fell in love and got engaged in a helicopter; someone came back from leave with tattoo that was supposed to say 'desert rat' but the tattoo artist misspelled it 'dessert rat'. We all laugh and I put the kettle on. My husband goes through to the living room to watch TV with our boy, and the social worker sidles up next to me as I pour milk into mugs.

Well, there was clearly some mistake. I can't think why I was called in to see you. There's nothing wrong with that child. Maybe he was just missing his dad.

Yes, maybe.

And that night our son doesn't creep into the bedroom. At bedtime he asks his dad to read him a book about pirates and then he turns off the globe next to his bed and snores until morning.

A few days later I see my son as he gets out of the bath, drying himself with the towel as he wanders back to his room to find his pyjamas. I notice the space just below his chest, where there's a faint tracing on the skin, silvery intersecting lines, like you get where a scar has healed.

It's in the shape of a star.

Pure Lucky

Anne O'Leary

SO, WE'RE ON the beach, right? And it's scorching. I mean, like, you can feel your face melting while you're lying there, frying on a towel. I lifts up me sunnies and looks over at Gemma and she's already a lovely bright red. It'll look massive when it goes brown tomorrow, which is what she wants to go with the white stretch-mini she got in Penneys. She's pure lucky, that one.

I'm still like a ghost, course. Me mam says I wasn't meant for the sun and I'll catch cancer if I bake meself in it. But, sure, the sun's there to be used, isn't it? Why'd you want to spend a fortune on sun beds, or smell like a biscuit from fake tan, when you can just lie there and neck Bacardi Breezers and bronze?

It's our first day and we're dropping. We arrived fierce late last night cos the flight outta Cork was delayed. They told us nothing, course, just left us waiting. It was freezing at the gate, and me in a halter neck top – sun holiday here I come, like. And there wasn't even enough seats to sit on.

Me and Gemma and Tracey were the last to roll up cos we likes a good gurry round Duty Free, trying out the perfume and the good make-up, so we'd to sit on the ground like we'd no homes to go to. By the time we got off the shuttle bus at the resort, we were wrecked and had no mind for going out, so we just got into our onesies and sank the tequila we bought on the plane. Better than nothing, like. We said we'd hit the town bigtime after a night's sleep, and the fellas had better watch out.

Gemma's mad keen for a bit of action. Since Trev cheated on her again with Kayla, she's like a girl possessed. Me and Trace has to mind her when we goes out now cos she gets wasted even before we get to the club, and then picks up the first loser that talks to her. They're all the same – they try and get her on her own, ask her to go outside for a smoke, but we're no eejits. Trace says they're trying to separate the weakest member from the pack. She's right. A bit of flirting's good for Gemma so she won't spend the evening roaring in the toilets about how ugly she is, smearing mascara all over her face like the Joker in that *Batman* film. But we watches her, and gets her back on the dance floor whenever it looks like it's getting too heavy with a creep. You've got to keep an eye out for one another in life, like. It's survival.

Me and Trace were mad to get away, and all. I've had it up to here with the tills, and it's no fun since they let Trace go. We used to work the same shifts so at least we could have a laugh, shouting across at one another between customers. It made the day go faster, anyway. Now it's *swipe-swipe-have you a loyalty card, love?* all day long. I'm allergic, I swear. She hates having to sign on, says she'll never find another job, but we tells her to have patience. Something will come along. Them crowd at the benefits office wants her to do a course, but there's nothing she's interested in. I mean, they can't force her, like. She's got rights.

So, in fairness, we're well up for cutting loose, looking forward to sun, sea and whatever.

I'm just starting to feel chilled out, soaking up the hot sun and the blue skies, when I sees something in the water. It's like a tourist boat, but the longer I'm watching it the weirder the shape seems. It's noisy on the beach, a radio playing Beyoncé and kids screeching in the waves, but I can hear a *put-put* sound – a motor under fierce pressure. It gets slowly, slowly closer, and then other people around me starts noticing too.

'Wha's tha'?' says a Dub sittin' on a deck chair near me. Gemma and Tracey are flaked out from the heat and the hangovers so they don't notice, but I stands up for a better look.

Slowly, slowly, *put-put*.

It isn't a boat at all, really, just a big sort of dinghy. And there's so many people sitting in it, and standing on it, and in the water hanging off of it that I think maybe it's some kind of mad bachelor party. But there's no laughing or singing or swigging from cans. Instead, there's a horrible sound of people moaning. Like the end of the world.

People on the beach start running down to the water as the boat tries to land, the waves pulling it and pushing it, in and out. I goes too, though I'm not sure I want to see whatever this is.

When they're pulled up onto the sand by a few big men, the boat people starts roaring and screaming, pointing to their mouths and falling into the waves like they're half dead.

'Water,' someone shouts. 'They need water. Quickly!'

A bunch of us runs back up the beach, picking up any bottles we see. At our towels, I stop and grab our cans of Coke.

'What's going on down there, girl?' Gemma asks, holding her head and squinting.

'There's loads of people on a boat, and they're in trouble,' I shouts, running back down as fast as I can in me sparkly flip flops.

She and Tracey are right behind me, and when I've handed over the drinks – had 'em grabbed out of me hands, like – we stand and stare.

It's pure wrong, the holiday makers in their togs next to the people on the dinghy. All of 'em are covered up to their necks in layers and layers of clothes, even though it's roasting. Someone tells me later that all they own is what they can wear. It's gross, all of our naked backs and white legs and boobs pouring outta bikini tops leaning over 'em. The smell of sweat in the air is rank.

The people are pulled out of the dinghy and lie on the sand, gasping like fresh caught mackerel. There must be 30 of 'em, easy. Mostly young guys, but a few women too, and a bunch of kids. This one girl looks around our age – though it's hard to tell cos her hair's covered with a scarf and her face is all scrunched up from crying, but probably early 20s. She's got a small one in her arms, a little girl about a year old, I'd say. The baby's whinging but half dozy at the same time, brown eyes rolling up into her head and her arms all floppy. When Gemma sees her, she starts crying almost as bad as the mam. Trace and I looks at one another. We know Gemma's thinking about Rhiannon, her own baby, who's being minded back at home by her nana so Gemma can have a cheapo break away. Gemma cries about Rhiannon all the time, like when Trevor says he'll visit her and then he never shows. She wanted to move out, get a flat with Trev and be a family, but now with the whole Kayla thing she knows he's a pure loser.

The woman is rocking back and forward with the little girl in her arms and a man in blue swimming trunks, who says he's a doctor, takes her little wrist between his big fingers.

'We need an ambulance here,' he shouts in this pure posh English accent. 'Has anyone called for emergency services?' A few people are on their mobiles, either calling for help or telling their pals what's happening. One or two people are using their phones to take pictures. He gives the child a dribble of water, and she kind of chokes on it, whining louder. Her mam rocks and cries.

In no time, there's the sound of sirens, and police cars and police vans and ambulances are racing across the sand to where we are. The police wave us back away from the scene, like it's nothing to do with us. One or two of 'em starts sprinting, hands on guns, when a few of the men from the boat try to leg it. But they're too beat out to get very far and fall on the soft sand, jumped on by the cops.

We all back away as the boat people are put in police vans or strapped onto ambulance gurneys.

'What'll happen to 'em?' Tracey asks a policeman.

'They be put with other refugees,' he says. 'Sent home, not sent home. Who knows? Too many.'

Out on the water, there's a big grey boat with Coastguard written on the side. It's moving slow through the waves.

'Bodies,' says the posh doctor, shielding his eyes with his iPhone. 'They're searching for the people that didn't make it. This lot are the lucky ones.'

Tracey doubles over all of a sudden and starts puking, last night's tequila back to haunt her.

We watches the girl with the baby getting in an ambulance. A paramedic is holding a drip up over the small one's head like it's a party balloon. The mam looks pure scared and her eyes are so huge you can see the whites. She's searching around for someone, but the paramedic gives her a shove in through the back doors and they slam them shut before taking off fast up the beach, sand spraying mad behind 'em.

When they're all gone, and the dinghy is dragged off the beach like a sad whale skin, there's a whole bunch of us left standing around. Someone says they came from Syria, and they're running away from the terrorists.

'No,' says a man with pretty good English, maybe French, 'it is about money. They come for a better standard of living.'

'Don't be stupid, mate, says a guy with a Cockney accent. 'No one would risk their lives, and their family's lives, for the chance to shop in Ikea. This is survival stuff, no-choice stuff.'

They've both obviously had a few so it gets heated, the Cockney right up in the other guy's face, pot bellies slapping together. The French fella looks scared, but won't back down. Their wives or girlfriends are trying to calm 'em, and they ease up, but you can tell it won't take much for them to get going again. It's like that time after a nightclub closes, when you're all poured out onto the street, and everyone's wasted, but no one can make the decision to go home. It's the dodgiest time of the night, cos you can't quite believe that's it, over, like. Anything can happen, and it's usually bad things, a fight breaking out or seeing your fella heading off with someone else.

Gemma grabs my arm and nods towards the resort. Me skin's all goose bumpy cos this part of the beach is in shade now and the heat's going, so the three of us collects up our stuff and heads back to the apartment.

We showers off the sun tan lotion and changes into our onesies. Tracey turns on the telly, flicks through the channels. On one of 'em, *Dirty Dancing* is just starting. It's dubbed, but we knows it off by heart so that doesn't matter. Baby's dad is telling the slimy manager and the creep waiter that Baby's going to change the world.

We settle down, get as comfy as we can on the hard sofa that pulls out into a bed of nails. We're not going out tonight. Not tonight.

The Promise of Pakoras
Susmita Bhattacharya

IN THE END, it is a question of survival.

The gnaw of hunger is an unbearable sensation. From the stench of the open gutters, the freewheeling of flies and mosquitoes, giddy on blood and shit, from the fug of sweat and fear-laden air, a wisp of aroma enters her nostrils. She remembers this smell. The smoke of mustard oil. The popping of nigella seeds and the sizzle of batter when sliced onions are dropped into the oil. Is she hallucinating? Conjuring up smells and memories? Or is this for real? She walks where the aroma leads. The earth muddy from last night's unwelcome rain. The tents damp and the ground too wet to sleep on. She has not slept well ever since she arrived here. All of them, competing for space like the flies they're swatting away. But it is useless. Kill one and ten more come to take its place. Where is that smell again? She stumbles after it, sandals slapping her cracked heels. She is lucky to have those sandals. She pulled them off her mother's feet when she fell dead on the long walk to here. Oh, she'd kill for a taste of those fried onions. Maybe dip them in the chutney her mother used to make with the tamarinds from their tree. Their tree – which was now in another country.

Their country, now torn in two. She is alone. She is afraid. The wound on her shoulder has healed. She sees the gun fire, her father pulling the trigger. His eyes are blinded by tears. She sees her sisters fall. One by one. All four of them. And she falls with them. It is safer to be dead than to be alive. It is better to have one's honour intact than to be defiled by the enemy. Is it a miracle then that she lives? Why? The question pounds her brain constantly. Why is she alive when they are all dead? Why is she hungry? What has she done to deserve this?

In the end, the answer is in front of her eyes. Those hands that reached out and helped her up. Who hid her under his shawl while the crazed thugs hunted out the women for their pleasure. Who claimed that she was his wife when she had to register at the camp. Who married her and gave her the flesh and blood that she craved so desperately. Who she celebrated with on their wedding day – feeding everyone in the camp onion pakoras – the only food they managed to prepare out of the meagre camp supplies. Everyone contributed to the ingredients and feasted on this wedding fare.

A plate of pakoras appears in front of her. There is laughter as her grandchildren gather round to help themselves. Their chubby hands grab the pakoras and they stuff them into their eager mouths. She picks one, looks at the oil oozing out – a gleaming thing of beauty, this onion pakora. Perfectly crisp. Perfectly satiating. She bites into it and closes her eyes. Her life rewinds like a cinema reel. Back through the ages. Back to her childhood home across the border. Where her sisters are sitting together, laughing and helping mother to prepare the evening meal. Their father and brothers returning home from the fields to sit in the front yard and eat their food. The soft swish of the tamarind tree and the lowing of the cow, her suckling calf. The strong smell of mustard oil sizzling on the stove.

When she looks out into the distance, she sees her future. She sees the love of her own daughters. The liveliness of her granddaughters. Her husband. She is lucky to be alive.

She has known hunger. She has known fear. But now, she knows what it is to watch her daughters mature into women. To grow old with the man she has made a life with. She is lucky to have all of this. Her bad shoulder aches, reminding her of what could have been. And she smiles, offers him a pakora. They eat in silence. Fully aware of the gift that they've been given: their lives. And the freedom to live the way they choose to.

Citroen Sid
Briony Collins

LEANDER HUCKABY'S FACE mashed further into the palm of his hand as his eyelids drooped, lulled to sleep by the wisps of hair that fluttered free from Ms. Bochart's ponytail. All he had to do was survive ten more minutes of Science and he was home-free. As he became aware he was falling asleep, his head snapped up and he snorted. Ms. Bochart's steely stare fell heavy on his head like an axe on a chopping block.

'I trust you slept well, Leander,' she rasped.

Mumbling an apology, Leander tried to refocus his attention on the class. Next to him, Trisha Yellowwood popped pink bubbles under her breath from some forbidden bubble-gum. It was against the rules to chew gum, but she did so often that it was almost an accessory to her school uniform. Leander stole a glance at her and half-wondered if she might be pretty, but shivered the thought away. Trisha was a *girl*.

'Your homework for next week is on trees. We'll be

looking at summer branch drop,' Ms. Bochart said. 'Sometimes in the summer, older branches will break off trees, but the cause for this is still unknown. They just fall away with no obvious explanation.'

When the last bell of the day rang, Leander began the long walk home. It was down past Willoughby Way where Robbie Bakerfield picked him up by the ankles and shook pennies from his pockets. It was beyond the old stone steps down to the canal. Sycamore trees grew over the pathway, buckling under the weight of seeds that spun in the wind like helicopters. Did these trees lose their branches when they were old? His house was even further than Conkers Creek, a secret spot behind the houses on Oak Avenue where he knew his brother took girls to *kiss*. Leander thought of Trisha Yellowwood again and her pout that glazed her gum with saliva as bubbles pushed through her wet lips. Who would kiss *that*?

Leander's street – Poppy Drive – was different to the surrounding rows. First of all, it wasn't a street at all, but rather a large alleyway between Maple Road and Blossom Street. It wasn't paved, so it was subjected to new dips and bumps after each rainfall. Only four houses lined Poppy Drive – two on the left side and two on the right – and each was responsible for maintaining the section of road outside their property. The second reason Leander's street was different to the others was that it was where Citroen Sid lived. As Leander rounded the corner of

Blossom Street onto his driveway, he saw Sid at his usual 3:45pm antics.

Sid was lying in the middle of the road face down, panting. With each exhalation, dirt from the ground blew up in clouds. Leander thought about whether Sid sucked any into his mouth when he breathed in. He was eyeing up the rocks along his section of the driveway. He moved them exactly half a centimetre forward every morning, slowly expanding the boundary of his land five millimetres at a time. Abruptly pushing himself to his feet and saying a word Leander knew not to repeat, Sid brushed himself off and noticed Leander staring at him.

'You tell your [CENSORED] mum to stay off my mother[CENSORED] property,' he snapped.

Leander's eyes widened. He watched Sid go into his house and slam the door. It wasn't the first time he'd heard that word, but normally when somebody said it around him they immediately looked at the ground and apologised. Nobody had ever, *ever* said it so proudly. Leander decided that he liked the word. It sounded strong and grown up which, so his father told him, was exactly why he couldn't say it. He wasn't old enough to swear yet. At what point then, he wondered, would he be old enough to say…[CENSORED]? Going inside, Leander dumped his bag on the kitchen counter.

'No, no, no. Not *there*. Put it over *there*,' his mother said, gesturing that his bag belonged on a hook with the coats and not, in fact, in the way of everything.

She was kneading dough on a pastry board. White flour speckled the curls in her hair. Unruly butter slid up her fingers. Their dog, Rosco, sat at her feet hoping that, in her clumsiness, she would drop the pastry altogether.

'Mum,' Leander said, helping himself to some apple juice from the fridge, 'Citroen Sid said you need to stop meddling.'

'For the last time, stop calling him that. He's just Sid.'

'Mum, Just Sid said you need to stop meddling.'

'You know what I meant.'

She began pushing a rolling pin over the dough before pulling out a ruler and making nicks in it with a knife.

'Why you doing that for?' Leander asked.

'Why *are* you doing that? Speak properly.'

'Okay, why *are* you doing that?'

'To make sure it's the right size for the casserole dish.'

'What did Cit – *Sid* – mean by meddling?'

'I was moving those blummin' rocks back.'

'Why?'

'Because the further out he puts them, the closer people drive to our property.'

'So?'

'So I don't want the road moved right by us, with traffic smashing into our hedges and leaving potholes along our driveway. I want the road where it is.'

'Why don't you tell on him?'

'I tried,' she said, placing the dough into the dish and folding the edges up. 'I told the Reeves next door, but they went on again about how Sid's been here forty years. They don't care. Bloody useless.' She threw the pastry trimmings in the bin and Rosco began to whine. 'Take the dog for a walk, Lee.'

'But, Muuuuum!'

'Take him. You both need some fresh air and he's driving me barmy.'

'I just had a walk! I walked home from school!'

'Two won't kill you.'

Leander sighed and grabbed the leash, snapping it to Rosco's collar. He grabbed his keys from the front pocket of his schoolbag, put the backpack on its correct hook in the proper place, and went back outside.

It was obvious to everyone that Sid earned his nickname from the dozen Citroen cars that littered his yard. They were his prized possessions, but he didn't treat them like they were important. Instead, they rotted and fell apart in the overgrown grass. Their metal corpses filled with rust. Weeds tangled themselves in the tyres. Birds flew through smashed windows to peck stuffing from the seats. Every now and then, Sid would acquire another car for his graveyard at an auction, dump it with the others, and never look at it again. Rumours about this odd behaviour went around the school. Some said that Sid bought a Citroen every time he murdered someone and the bodies were buried in the yard under the cars. Leander shuddered as he walked past them. He doubted this was true, but even murderers have to live somewhere, right?

At least his mother refused to put up with Sid. Every morning she'd take Rosco for a walk before she went to work and on the way back home she'd kick all the rocks into the hedges. Then Sid would come out at 7:45am and put them all back a little closer to Leander's house, measuring the distance as accurately as he could after they had all been booted out of place.

'If he took care of those cars like he does those blasted rocks, his yard wouldn't be such a tip,' Leander's mother said.

The walk with Rosco went quickly. Leander didn't hate walking the dog, he'd just rather be doing something else like watching his favourite cartoon, *Marco and Rodney*, a show about two space cowboys who went on intergalactic adventures. It was definitely for grown-ups, because they used some pretty bad language like what Sid said earlier. Leander's parents didn't know. They just figured it was a cartoon, so it was appropriate for him to watch. As long as Leander used his headphones, his mum and dad were none the wiser.

When Leander walked past Citroen Sid's house coming home, he noticed something strange. The front door was open, but Sid wasn't anywhere to be seen. The detail that made it weird was the *type* of open the door was; it wasn't cracked or ajar, it was all the way open. In the years Leander had been living on Poppy Drive, Sid never left the door open. Overpowered by curiosity, Leander tightened his grip on Rosco's leash and crept a little closer to Sid's house. He could see right through the living room in the front to the kitchen in the back. There was no movement, only the flickering of Citroen Sid's kitchen light and his cemetery of cars. Leander gulped.

Sneaking closer – treading the ground underneath him from the back of his heel to the tip of his toe – Leander craned his neck to see more. Still there was no one. The carpet in the living room was thick and dark. It looked brown – though it could have been red – but it was hard to tell as all the curtains were pulled shut. The sofa was against the far wall, but all its cushions were on the floor by a tall, ominous bookcase. Nothing matched. Leander tied Rosco to the fence post and drew in a deep breath. It didn't look like Sid was home. If he went inside, he'd be known at school as the boy who went into Citroen Sid's house. He'd have the inside scoop. He might even be popular. Maybe Robbie Bakerfield would stop stealing his pocket money and want to be friends instead. The compulsion to go inside became too strong. As Marco and Rodney would say in their cartoon, *buckle up and [CENSORED] it.*

Leander stood in Citroen Sid's doorway, his eyes adjusting to his surroundings. As he stepped inside, he was immediately hit with a smell he couldn't identify. It was like old bananas, but burnt; similar to custard, but with a sour note. Leander had no idea where it was coming from, but the whole house reeked of it.

Everything was covered in dust and it was clear that nothing had been disturbed in years. In the corner, there was a big square radio with huge black CDs. Leander had never seen anything like it. He sat down cross-legged in front of a large box full of the CDs and flicked through them. As the first one fell forward, it shot dust out into his face and Leander coughed. Pulling his school shirt up over his nose, he browsed the rest of them. They were all names he'd never heard before: *Fats Domino, Ella Fitzgerald, Duke Ellington...* They looked old anyway and, as Leander's schoolmates made him blatantly aware, nothing old was good. New was undoubtedly always better. Maybe that's why trees dropped their old branches; they were just making room for better ones.

Suddenly, the door behind him closed. Leander shot up off the floor. He spun around. Citroen Sid towered above him, palm spread flat against the front door.

'A visitor,' Sid said.

Leander needed to explain that he came in because the door was open and wanted to check on him, but as he went to speak it occurred to him how stupid that would sound. Not only was it a lie, but an open door wasn't an invitation and Leander knew it. Instead, he kept his mouth shut and stared at his mysterious neighbour.

'I didn't know you were comin' today. Please, sit...' Sid gestured to the sofa, but noticed all the cushions were on the floor. 'How did they get there? Have you been makin' a mess again?'

Leander wondered what Sid meant by 'again' as he watched him put the cushions back.

'How about a cuppa, eh?' Sid smiled. His hands shook as he beckoned to Leander. 'Why don't you help me?'

Cautiously, Leander followed him into the kitchen. Sid flicked the kettle on and took two cups down from a cupboard.

'I wondered when you were comin' over. You always say 'soon' on the phone, but it feels like forever,' Sid said.

'I-I've never phoned you.'

'Then what was last night all about?'

'What?'

'Don't be stupid,' Sid snapped, slamming his hand on the counter and making Leander jump. 'Has your mother put you up to this? Plannin' some joke on me?'

'My mum?'

'Just because she has custody don't mean I'm some extra in your life!' Sid shouted.

Leander began to tremble. Nothing Sid was saying made any sense and he got angry so quickly. *Does he know who I am?* he thought. *How could a person forget someone they see every day?* The boiling water shook the kettle violently before it finished. Sid drew in several deep breaths and then smiled at Leander.

'I haven't seen you in so long. But I have a surprise for you.'

'A surprise?'

'Yeah. Remember that car you said you loved? That nice Citroen we saw at the fair a couple of weeks back?'

'C-Citroen?'

'I know you're far too young, but I bought one. Thought maybe you'd enjoy going for drives with me in it until we can get you your own one day.'

'You bought a Citroen for me?'

'Of course. You're my boy.'

Leander's mouth was dry. He heard a faint bark and remembered that Rosco was still tied up outside. Sid put the cups back into the cupboard without making any tea and Leander glanced over at the front door, visualising the distance between this kitchen and his own.

'Can I go have a look at it?' Leander said.

'Sure, and then we can go for a drive.'

'G-great! It's cold out,' Leander lied, 'You should get your coat. I'll meet you outside.'

They smiled at each other and then Leander tried to walk outside as normally as possible. He ran to Rosco who leapt up when he saw him. Leander grabbed his leash and fumbled with the knot. Finally he wrenched Rosco free and they ran back home together. He shut the door so hard that the ceiling light shook and then he bolted it. He lowered the blinds in the window. Dragging Rosco into the kitchen and throwing his bag on the counter, he was barely able to catch his breath.

'Hey, hey!' His mother began to chastise him for leaving his bag in the way again, before noticing that something was wrong. 'Leander? Are you okay?'

Leander shook his head.

'What happened?'

'I was at Sid's.'

'*Sid's*? Why the bloody hell were you at Sid's?'

'His door was open.'

'So you just walked in? Leander Huckaby, do you have any idea how irresponsible that is? Not only could you have been in danger, but it was extremely…'

Leander could hear her telling him off, but he wasn't listening. He tuned her voice out, nodding at the right times and keeping his gaze low, trying to look ashamed.

Later, he sat on the sofa with his mum watching the television. Rosco lay across Leander's feet so he could feel the dog's warm belly move with each breath over his toes. It was hard to focus on the programme. Whatever it was, it lacked the snap and spirit of *Marco and Rodney*, and nobody at all said [CENSORED]. Besides, his thoughts were still with Sid. Leander turned his attention to the window next to him, looking across the street to Sid's house. The moon highlighted the tops of the rocks with which Sid lined his stretch of Poppy Drive and glinted across the sloping roof. Everything else was cradled in the soft black of the warm night.

'Lee...' his mum said, coaxing him back into the room. 'I'm sorry for getting so cross earlier. I was worried.'

Leander nodded and watched her face. Her lips were small and puckered, pulling a few extra shadows across her skin by the orange glow of the table lamp. Rosco sighed deeply the way dogs do when they're just about to drift off to sleep. Leander felt Rosco's heart beat drumming along the bones in his foot. He pictured his feet like the inside of a piano; Rosco's pulse was the hammer that hit the strings, but in this empty evening neither one of them made a noise.

'Sid isn't very well,' she said eventually.

'He's sick?'

'Sort of. But it's not his body. It's his brain. He doesn't remember things very well.'

'He needs a doctor.'

'He has one, Lee. But even doctors can't fix everything.'

'Can we help him?'

He felt her hand brush the back of his. For a moment, Leander saw her glance out the window. Then she tugged her feet out from underneath Rosco's bottom and stuck them into the pair of slippers she'd left by the end table.

'No. We can't help him,' she said, picking up the remote and turning off the television.

'So what do we do?'

'We carry on as normal, Lee. Now get to bed; you've got school in the morning.'

He kissed the top of Rosco's head the way he did every night and stole one last look at Sid's house. An overwhelming heaviness rose in his chest, but Leander couldn't define it. Somehow his world felt different tonight. There wasn't any medicine to fix Sid, his Citroens decaying with his memory as he waited for a day that would never come. What if Leander's brain caught a cold like Sid's and he couldn't remember anything? Maybe Sid was like a piano too and something else was playing on him. It certainly felt like it and that, Leander decided, was truly...*fucked*.

Bufo Bufo

Johanna Robinson

WE ARE THE second shift: ten till midnight. We are hatted and hooded, layered and booted. Our fingers splay as we pull on the one-size-fits-all, thin, blue rubber gloves: we chase wrinkles over our knuckles and shock our wrists with a let-go. Orange buckets are passed like batons between the two groups. We keep our goodbyes and hellos low and quiet, as though we shouldn't be here, yet our neon yellow vests declare us to drivers, their head-lamps slicing us into reflective quarters. We watch where we put our feet. This is my second time.

'Go for me,' Dad said from his hospital bed last week, still high on morphine. 'Take my place. Come home, just for a while.'

'Not many so far,' says a woman from the eight-till-ten shift, peeling the blue skin off her hand. Her real skin glistens under the light of my head-torch. 'Mind you, not many cars either.' She holds her bucket out to me. 'How's your dad?'

I take the bucket and place it on the kerb. 'Should be home soon. We hope.'

The rain has stopped and the sky has cleared from grumble-grey to black. The night smells both old and new. We cannot see beyond the other side of the road, but we know it's the meadow. The toads know it too, girding to go home, back to where they were born. Lunar cues, auditory, celestial or magnetic – we don't really know what pulls them, what pushes them, what lures them, drives them. Evolution. Revolution. Dad used to try to tell me, to explain, but I only half-remember. I was only ever half-listening.

A toad stirs next to my foot, and I crouch and reach. I'm careful to hold it and not-hold it. It's a new sense, to grip but not squeeze. Not too hard; not too soft. Its eyes don't move, as if this is the moment it's been waiting for. It's on its own: no mate yet. Body soft but bony and skin glowing like topaz. Dangling legs every now and again pumping the air, like an electrical fault. Its throat pulses, stretches, shrinks, stretches, shrinks. I hold it up, between finger and thumb. Behind it, a star catches my eye. No, not a star.

'Look.' I turn the toad a little. 'That's the ISS.' The toad blinks. The space station disappears behind the reptile's rubbly silhouette, and re-emerges, on a trajectory to a horizon we can't see.

I lower the toad into the bucket, and look for the next

one, which turns out to be two. The male clamped to the female's back, a joint migration, getting ready to start all over again. I place the bucket down and cup my blue hands around them. 'Sorry,' I say, because it seems appropriate. But they don't seem to mind, continuing their quiet copulation in the brash orange bucket.

A car's headlights turn us all into rabbits, the glare diminishing all the stars. It passes and we wait for our eyes to readjust. The drivers are used to us; they slow down, but a slow car kills the toads just the same as a fast one. When the red taillights have vanished, I cross the road with the bucket and set it down. The first toad sits on my palm for a moment, before pushing off with its back legs. The two-as-one don't budge so I scoop them up, placing them on the slope of the verge, my boot slipping a little on the soil, sending clods tumbling.

Dad asked me to help out last spring too, as we sat in his garden one night, watching the bats. I'd said no, given him excuses, engagements. In fact – although on this I kept quiet – it seemed frivolous to me, this toad-patrol, such a tiny, futile gesture among the enormous terribleness of the world. It was too dark to see his face, but I heard the disappointment in his voice, not just at the fact that I wouldn't come, but that I wouldn't understand. He'd changed the subject. At least I thought he had. 'There's nearly five thousand satellites up there,' he said. 'And each of them has a ground track.' I looked up into the sky that seemed to hold nothing. 'What's a ground track?' I asked, as we both knew I would. 'It's the invisible line a satellite's orbit projects onto the surface of the Earth. A million invisible paths. A hypothetical web.'

I turn and watch my group; buckets swing and dip, neon vests merge and blur and herd, and separate out again, the odd one wandering across the road. I cross back over, and I'm not careful enough. My heel skids on guts and viscera, and I refuse to think of an eye popping, a deflated throat; one we didn't save. On the other side, I rasp my heel against the kerb, and am grateful for the dark. I bend down and lay my hand, palm up, on the grass. A toad jumps on and eyes me, seed-like pupils as black as the sky. Its spindly feet tickle, and before it can jump off again, I tip it into the bucket.

Ten years ago, there was no road here. No B-road traced across a map. Ten years ago, two satellites collided, above Siberia. Dad had been dismayed and intrigued. 'Two thousand pieces of debris,' he'd said, shaking his head, looking to the sky as though he might see the fragments, ricocheting, falling. But ten years ago, I was fifteen and didn't care. He'd hugged me anyway, not too hard, and not too soft.

Last night, a man told me, as he ran his finger down the creature's spine, that someone somewhere has extracted morphine from the skin of toads. Our shift saved thirty-four tonight, the tally marks chalked up on an A-frame blackboard. I take a photograph of the lines and text it to my dad. Tomorrow, I hope, I will bring him home.

What We Talk About When We Talk About Owls

Judy Darley

AFTER WE'VE EATEN the last of the trifle, Natalie pushes back her chair and excuses herself.

'You ok?' I ask, looking at the shadows under her eyes. Is she getting enough sleep? Maybe the anxiety is rearing up again.

'Think I ate too much, Cal.' She grimaces, one hand on her belly. 'Just going to have a lie down.'

I watch her leave. Her hair is twisted into a chignon. It reveals the small islands of bone that protrude at the top of her spine.

I helped her with one the night she met Darren.

DARREN AND I clear the table together but I leave him to load the dishwasher while I settle to building a Lego house with Sammy.

'Did you know apes don't live in an apiary, Auntie

Cally?' my niece asks. 'Bees do.' Her face is full of wonder.

'Is that so?' I select a blue tile to add to the roof amid the red ones, keeping one eye on Sammy to see how she reacts.

She shakes her head before I can slot it in place. 'We need it to fit with the others.'

'You're the architect,' I say, relinquishing the tile. 'I'm going to check on your mum.'

UPSTAIRS, NATALIE IS stretched out on the eiderdown. Beside her lies a small egg so plump it's almost round. It glows with creamy white perfection.

'Oh, cool!' Sammy runs in for a closer look. 'Where'd you find it?'

Without waiting for a response, she dashes off.

I stare at my sister. Her face is as pale as the egg's shell. My mouth opens, but I don't know what to say.

She laughs softly, her face mirroring her daughter's earlier awe-filled expression. 'I thought I had indigestion.'

Sammy's back before I can take in her words.

'That's a tawny owl egg,' Sammy declares, holding up the egg identification chart I gave her at Easter. 'Did you know tawny owls are ferociously defensive of their young? If it's just been laid it'll hatch in thirty days. Can I have it?'

'No!'

Natalie's voice is so loud that it makes us jump.

'Sammy, go and play, will you? I need to speak to Cal.'

Sammy glowers, but growls her way out of the room.

I sit down beside my sister. Despite what she said, she's silent, her gaze fixed on the egg.

'Did you…' I begin. 'Were you expecting…?'

'Not that I knew. I mean… I've been feeling a bit off. Haven't been sleeping much at night.' She sniffs suddenly. 'Cal, do you know if…? Could this be some kind of hereditary thing?'

'Mum never said anything. Perhaps it skips a generation.'

'Yes! Like twins.'

'Or maybe Darren… Has he mentioned…?'

'No. Oh my god, what's he going to think?' Natalie strokes the egg tenderly. 'What if he doesn't want it?'

I try to seem certain. 'Of course he will. It's part of your family.' I look her in the eye, seeing her glance skirt from mine. 'You two ok? You barely spoke over lunch.'

'I… We're worried about Sammy, about the stigma of being neuro-nuanced.' She swallows. 'Would you believe we haven't told her yet?'

'Oh?'

'Darren doesn't want her feeling different.'

'Sammy *knows* she's different,' I say. 'Wouldn't it help

her to understand why?'

Natalie shrugs, lips pursed.

I look at the egg resting quietly between us. 'She's a great kid, and she's going to love whoever hatches with her whole heart. But right now we should call someone.'

'Like who? A shrink?'

'I was thinking an ambulance, or a midwife,' I say, and manage a wry, head-tilt grin. 'Or maybe the RSPCA.'

I reach out my hand, it hovers, uncertain, in the air between us. After a moment, Natalie nods her permission, and I run my fingers over the egg. It's smooth and warm. My sister and I blink at one another.

The Case of Baby Shaw

Joanna Campbell

ON A DANK Monday evening in October 1973, while eighteen-year-old Lesley Shaw was watching *Man About the House* in the hospital rest-room, her new-born baby disappeared.

After the closing credits, her stitches itching, Lesley Shaw hobbled back to the ward, glancing through the window of the night nursery. Baby Dean's cot was empty, the white sheet folded back in a neat triangular shape.

Assuming a nurse was changing Dean's nappy in the adjoining room, Lesley returned to bed and leafed through *Jackie* magazine. The alarm was not raised until the child had been missing for an hour, the last sighting marked by the six o'clock feed entered on Baby Shaw's notes.

The nurses couldn't recall seeing Baby Shaw during the flurry of visiting husbands in rain-spotted overcoats from the buses converging at the hospital stop at twenty-five past six. Some waved at their new offspring through the nursery window. Others held their babies while the mothers had a quiet smoke. Lesley Shaw's young husband had gone out of his way to find fresh flowers and arrived too late.

Nurse Christine Duncan left her shift at six-twenty. No one saw her exit the ward and she was not at her maisonette in Tower Street, seven minutes away by bus. The conductor could not recall her auburn hair and russet coat, but his bus was jam-packed. He couldn't be expected to take note. Nurse Duncan had recently suffered a miscarriage.

The announcer on the wireless said the police search was closing in.

***

AT FIVE O'CLOCK that wet October Monday, Geoffrey March was stewing apples. They took seven minutes to release their tart, green fragrance. He was waiting for his timer to stop ticking. Its alarm had seized up. All Geoffrey could do was listen for the silence.

His daughter's key turned in the lock. Her feet made their brief shuffle on the doormat.

"All right, Susan?" he called, scraping the softened apple into a dish. Tinny music erupted from the wireless, some new pop-group turning all the teenagers wild.

Geoffrey's wife had left them five years ago. She met a man at a cheese-and-wine party and eventually married him. She moved into his bungalow in Bayswater where they kept tropical fish.

After her departure, the house stiffened, seizing up in the grip of her absence. Susan spent hours in her bedroom, arranging and rearranging the dozens of cloth dolls her mother had made her over the years.

Susan worked at the fishmonger's, her seventh job in three years, but her dream was to be someone's perfect wife.

"How was today?" Geoffrey asked, peering at the braising-steak, the orange-tinted Cook-In sauce crusting in the oven's roaring heat.

Susan chattered about the fishmonger, who leered at her while she swabbed the floor. "Thinks he's God's gift and all that," she said, peeling off her overalls. Geoffrey imagined her mop slapping the cold tiles, gathering shed herring scales and mucky footprints.

They ate in the kitchen. Susan passed the salt and Geoffrey poured the tea. They liked it brewing as soon as the meal was served, the teapot between them, fat and warm in its cosy.

Geoffrey washed up while Susan got ready for her walk. She sometimes went to the park and sat on the little swing where her mother once pushed her to and fro, or to the field where there was once a horse. Now its old, grey droppings disintegrated underfoot.

She used to seek company in a strip-lit coffee-bar in

town, where lively teenagers drank coffee from thick glass cups, but the manager had barred her. Geoffrey imagined her pressing her nose to the steamy window, watching the young people dig their spoons into the sugar.

Her rubber boots made a soft sigh as her legs slid inside them.

"See you later," she said.

***

NURSE CHRISTINE DUNCAN was traced to her mother's flat in Ealing. She was sorry for disappearing. She was escorted back to her maisonette, where she huddled by an electric heater and peered at the policemen with the black stare of a hooked fish.

A policewoman made tea and perched on a vinyl pouffe. "Who was with you when you had the miscarriage, Christine?"

"No one," Christine said, her cup jittering on its saucer. "He cleared off soon as he knew."

Nothing was amiss at the maisonette. The police found the man Christine had been courting. He could barely remember the moody bitch. He did a runner one morning as soon as she left for her shift. Packed his belongings in a Lipton's carrier bag and scarpered. He'd only taken what was his.

The investigation continued.

***

WHEN SHE WAS nine, Susan had seized Geoffrey's hand and pressed it against the grill. Her toast was not brown enough, she said, pressing his fingertips to the blistering whiteness of maximum heat.

She claimed it must have warmed up the moment he touched it. She had not meant to hurt his fingers, only guide them to the metal coils. She wrapped gauze around his hand. She knew not to put a knob of butter on a burn. "It fries, you see," she said. "Just sizzles away."

For a long time the kitchen retained the smell of scorched flesh.

The night Geoffrey's wife packed her bags, Susan wept on the floor outside the bedroom. When the door opened and the suitcases were rolled out, she gripped her mother's legs, scratching ladders in her nylons, clawing until she drew blood.

Afterwards, she often disappeared and was discovered crouching in the junior school grounds, or beneath the slide in the play-park, or in the car park of the hospital where she was born.

A psychiatrist said insecurity made her impulsive. This might be inconvenient at times, but professional help wouldn't help as much as love. Mr March should try to see the problem as a faint shadow over her life, a shadow without which she would not be Susan March.

When she was eighteen, Susan was brought home by the police for disorderly behaviour at the railway station. During morning rush hour, she had attempted to engage the interest of a young man on Platform One. When his train arrived, she peeled off her mackintosh to reveal her naked body. Such was the young man's distress, he had to let the train depart without him and missed a vital meeting in the city.

Cheerfully, as if he'd enjoyed her chatter in the car, the policeman who dropped her off said, "Behave yourself now, Miss."

"Please, there's something awfully wrong," Geoffrey whispered at the door, grasping the policeman's shoulder as he turned to leave.

"She wants watching, Sir, that's all," the policeman said. "Nice girl. Just needs a bit of attention."

Geoffrey had to let him go.

"The desk sergeant thinks he's God's gift and all that, but guess what, Daddy?" Susan said from the stairs. "He's going to ring me up. Dead dishy, he is."

The telephone remained silent. After her shifts at the fishmonger's, Susan withdrew deeper into her bedroom, talking to the new dolls she made herself from scraps and stuffed with her mother's discarded nylons. The house was unsettled, as if the foundations were loose sand.

Geoffrey wondered when he would hear Susan's key turn in the lock, or her tread on the stairs, without bracing every muscle.

***

DURING THE LATE evening of the dank October Monday, while Susan was still out walking—without an umbrella, although Geoffrey had suggested it—the downpour intensified.

He tried to watch the news, the screen fizzing with interference, as if the rain were pouring into the television set.

Young Lesley Shaw was sobbing between her mother and her tearful husband, Shane. Her hair hung in limp strings around her face, still the face of a child. Shane— said to be twenty-two, but looking about fourteen— sandwiched Lesley's hands between his own.

It was a long time before the next news story, about the Dalai Lama's visit. A long time before Baby Shaw's picture disappeared from the screen.

Last August Bank Holiday Monday, Susan had gone to a fête. Although it was an attraction for children, she insisted on riding the miniature pony, her feet dragging through the grass. The pony had to be bedded down in deep straw for the rest of the day. Geoffrey donated a sack of fresh carrots for Susan to take in apology. But cupping the pony's plush nose in her hand made her cry for when she was little, for the time her parents had walked either side of the donkey she rode at the seaside.

"The wind kept snapping at Mum's pink frock," she said. "And she laughed so much the seagulls copied her."

A few weeks after that, reading in the local newspaper about laundry stolen from washing-lines in their street, Geoffrey rummaged through Susan's chest of drawers, her sewing basket, her ottoman. He looked behind the painting-by-numbers of Conwy Castle on the wall above her divan, inside the Petite typewriter under her bed, beneath the row of rag dolls propped against her pillows. After searching for evidence he could not find, he left the room in its state of devastation, to let Susan know.

Now, while the October gale lifted the roof tiles, Geoffrey lay in bed waiting for the rasp of her key, the squeak of the door. He had left a pan of cocoa on the stove, the lid on to keep it warm.

He remembered the pair of guinea-pigs taken from a hutch in April and left to wander along the main road, where at least they had the sense to stay close to the kerb. The dog released from its tether outside the launderette in May, who bounded up to a horse and almost unseated the rider. The toddler coaxed away from a front garden in June and left in the precinct with a note stating his address and a vanilla ice-cream cornet.

Nothing was ever proved. The note was typewritten and the toddler incapable of a sworn statement. But the shadow over Geoffrey's house lengthened.

***

WHILE SUSAN SLEPT all morning after the wild October night, her hair a damp, straggling fan around her head on the pillow, Geoffrey telephoned her mother in Bayswater. Susan's mother claimed the Shaw case was overexciting his imagination. After she hung up, the drone of her fish-tank pump kept humming in his ear.

"You were out late," he said when Susan came downstairs in the afternoon.

"That bloke from the off-licence chatted me up in the park. Thinks he's all that and then some."

She talked about all the men she fancied. She was making a list of the pros and cons of marriage to each one. She knew she mustn't over-think things, but this wasn't thinking. This was planning.

"God's gift he thinks he is," she said, referring now to the fishmonger, or perhaps the librarian. Geoffrey had lost track, suddenly weary.

***

THE NEXT MORNING, a man foraging for mushrooms discovered a baby in an abandoned trough under the sheltering branches of a horse-chestnut. Inside a candle-wick bedspread cocoon lay little Dean Shaw.

The news report stated Baby Shaw would survive his ordeal. Next time, Lesley Shaw vowed, she would give birth at home. The hospital had never let Shane come near her in Delivery. They said men got in the way. Shame they didn't keep a closer eye on the nurses. She would never trust them again.

***

TWO DAYS LATER, Nurse Christine Duncan was found on the floor of her maisonette. She had taken an overdose of painkilling drugs. Her death was reported because she had been a person of interest in the case of Baby Shaw. The blurry picture of Christine Duncan stayed in Geoffrey's head, sharpening whenever he stewed apples, when the acid-green aroma filled his kitchen.

***

GEOFFREY TELEPHONED THE police the next afternoon and quietly gave an account of Susan's movements that October evening, how she was out for hours with no witnesses to attest for her whereabouts. He mentioned the field where horses were once kept.

He remembered Susan's tears when she stroked the pony's soft muzzle. His wife had asked him dozens of times if Susan could come to Bayswater. Geoffrey insisted she didn't want to. And he told Susan her mother had washed her hands of them both.

He'd thought it would help, imagining the confusion Susan would suffer with two houses to live in, two places in which to organise and reorganise her room. And her poor, puzzled heart, divided in half. Now, his hand still nursing the receiver in its cradle, he thought for the first time about what Susan had lost.

He telephoned the police again, to say sorry for wasting their time. He had suddenly remembered it was another evening when Susan went out, a different time altogether. Yes, he would vouch for her.

Susan was getting agitated with her dolls, tossing them across the room. He went up there and helped her return them to the right positions, smoothing their dresses the way she liked them. He persuaded her to lie down while he cooked her tea, folding back the sheet in a careful triangle, the way she liked it, ready for her to climb in.

From her window he saw the bus hissing slowly through the puddles to the stop outside his house. The bus served the hospital, arriving there at six twenty-five. Always punctual.

He went down to fry the liver. It was vital to listen to liver. In the second before it stubbornly gripped the pan, it tended to sigh. Always the same.

Susan's shiny boots stood on the doormat. He must get round to cleaning the dried mud and clogged grass, the desiccated droppings, from his own shoes, hidden carefully under his bed.

Between the Cracks

Laura Besley

THE BUS STOPS and sighs, as if the tilt to the pavement is the hardest thing it's had to do all day. Six people get on, four get off. No prams or wheelchairs, and the bus sighs again – in wasted effort, no doubt – before it leaves. Opposite, the café doesn't huff and puff like the disgruntled bus, but sits quietly, almost like a grandmother knitting, between a newsagent's and a second-hand book shop. Its large front windows are steamed up and a small boy wipes patterns in the condensation. He gives a gaptoothed smile. His mother, presumably, peers at me over his shoulder and pulls him away. When they leave a few moments later, neither of them look at me.

Customers ebb and flow throughout the day, as do the waiting staff. The only person who is there the entire time is a man. He's taller than average with a thick white beard which doesn't match the colour of his hair, making it look as though he's just stuck it on for fun, or is pretending to be Santa.

The rain stops. Sunshine pushes through the patch-work clouds, playing with the dormant puddles, and momentarily blinds me, so I don't see him approach. I notice his shoes; not trainers like the other, younger, waiting staff, but proper leather shoes. They stop just in front of me.

'You've been sitting here a long time,' he says.

His voice is surprisingly soft. Won't make a good Santa after all.

'Why don't you come in for something to eat? Warm up?'

'I can't pay,' I say.

He nods. 'It's fine. Come on, before the rain starts up again.'

I stand, smile for the first time today.

I don't even mind that he'll notice my missing tooth.

The Opera Singer

Terry Sanville

EVERY AFTERNOON MRS. Story sang intricate voice exercises and rehearsed arias, stood behind a music stand, wearing a sleek silk gown. On an end table, a square glass holding scotch over ice rested within easy reach. The cocktail hour came early in her solitary household.

Outside her picture window, a steady parade of children climbed Calle Poniente on their way home from Harding School. The small kids had flyers pinned to their shirts which fluttered in the wind like colorful whirligigs. The bigger kids rode bicycles.

Mrs. Story stopped singing and scanned the street. A pair of boys followed by a clot of smaller ones rounded the corner. Johnny, her paperboy, was easy to pick out. Red-faced and dripping as he puffed up the hill, pushing his fat-tired bicycle. His sodden T-shirt stretched across his bulging belly, his pink midriff showing.

Johnny's friend, Paul, circled him on his Schwinn, grinning stupidly. The smaller boys ran up and poked

Johnny in the butt or stomach. He mouthed something and took a swipe at one of them. They scattered but continued their taunting.

Mrs. Story grabbed her scotch, tossed it down, then stepped to the window. Pulling her crimson hair back from her face, she presented her best Rubenesque profile and waved at Johnny. She kept waving until she knew he had seen her. His face transformed with a smile and he sucked in his stomach, straightened his back. She had no children, didn't much like them. And her ex-husband was off shtupping his twenty-something bimbo. Good riddance. But she felt something for Johnny and figured a little kindness couldn't hurt.

She returned to her music and continued singing until the sun dropped below the ridgeline of Santa Barbara's Westside hills and something clattered against the side of her house. She went to investigate and found Mr. Hobson swaying in his driveway that adjoined her property.

Dressed only in his underwear, he fingered a can of Brew 102 and yelled, 'Will you stop that infernal racket? How many times do I gotta tell ya ta shut up.'

His Japanese wife, Minako, hurried to his side and tugged at his arm. The shouting stopped and he staggered away. Mrs. Story often thought about complaining to the Police. But seeing as Harry Hobson *was* the Police, his bosses probably wouldn't do anything.

Ever since the divorce, Mrs. Story had become the

neighborhood outcast. The wives stopped inviting her to their weekly coffee klatch. Maybe they were afraid she'd come after their husbands since the men seemed to appreciate her more than their spouses. And the kids made fun of her singing, mimicking her operatic voice in high falsetto then laughing. Teenagers turned up the radios in their cars as they passed, drowning her out with Elvis Presley, Ricky Nelson, Chuck Berry. Opera was no doubt too hoity-toity for the adults and too square for the kids.

As the oak-covered hills surrounding Calle Poniente darkened and turned a warm black, Mrs. Story closed the curtains and poured herself another drink. She took out a Swanson's TV dinner and popped it in the oven, then set up the metal tray stand in front of her favorite chair and watched the evening news. She was nearly through her sliced turkey and mashed potato dinner when someone thumped on her front door.

Then the yell, 'Paperboy. Collecting!'

Pushing herself up, she stepped to the hall mirror and arranged her gown and hair before answering the door. Johnny stood under the buzzing porch light, shifting from foot to foot while staring at his feet.

'Oh, Hello, Johnny. Come on in.'

'I…I can wait here if ya want. That'll be four dollars for the month.'

'Don't be ridiculous. Come in and sit while I find my

TERRY SANVILLE

purse.'

'Thanks. I have change if ya need it.' Johnny lowered himself carefully onto the sofa, as if he might break it.

Mrs. Story figured he was eleven or twelve, but already as tall as she and as heavy as many of the men she knew. She hurried from the room. In the kitchen she slid a half dozen Oreos from their package onto a plate, grabbed her purse from the sideboard next to the phone and returned to the living room.

'Here, have some of these while I dig out the money.'

Johnny grinned. He took each Oreo, pried the chocolate halves apart and licked the cream filling before crunching the rest.

'Er…sorry for being a pig. But I can beat my pal Paul at licking the icing off in one or two swipes.'

Mrs. Story smiled. 'I'll bet you can.'

Johnny's face reddened and he fumbled with the payment book as he tore off the little square receipt.

'You have any problems findin' your paper, Mrs. Story? I know I threw one on your roof a while back, but I had an extra.'

'No, you do a good job. You're a very responsible young man.'

Johnny face flushed even more. Mrs. Story handed him a five-dollar bill. Johnny reached into his collection bag and pulled out a rumpled dollar for change.

'You keep it, Johnny.'

'Gee thanks, Mrs. Story. That's really swell. Most folks give me a dime or a quarter.'

'You know, Johnny, I see you coming home from school most days. Do you hear me singing in the afternoons?'

'Sure do.'

'So…so what do you think?'

'Whatdaya mean?'

'Do you like what you hear?'

Johnny paused then looked away. 'Well, my Mama always says if ya can't say somethin' nice don' say nothin' at all.'

Mrs. Story laughed. 'Your mother is a very wise woman.'

'Yeah, I guess.'

'When I see you coming up the street after school it looks like the other kids are picking on you. What's that about?'

'Ah, it ain't nothin'. I'm just…just fat and they make fun of me because I'm slow and can't catch 'em.'

Johnny crossed his arms and rocked back and forth slowly while studying the carpet.

'Yes, well there are a lot of famous people that are…are big. Wasn't Babe Ruth a big guy? And what about all those football players?'

'Yeah, yeah. And I like to watch wrestling on Channel 5 and there's always a lot of big guys like me. But…but they usually lose to the guys with more muscles and less…' He tapped his belly and frowned.

'Wait here for a minute, I got something to show you.' Mrs. Story rose, moved to a bookcase and took down a leather-bound volume. She sat next to Johnny and opened the book.

'So, look at these guys. They're world famous opera singers and many of them are big. Nobody makes fun of them.'

'Yeah, but I can't sing.'

'You won't have to. I've seen your family. You're all big and tall, all over 6 feet, right?'

Johnny smiled. 'Yeah, my Pop's 6'6" and Russ, he's my brother, is 6'5". Even Mom is tall'.'

'You've got a lot of growing to do, Johnny. And when you do, nobody's going to make fun of you anymore.'

'Yeah, I suppose. But that's gonna take a long time.'

'Well, in the meantime, think about all the famous people that are big. You have nothing to be ashamed of.'

'Thanks.'

Sat side-by-side they stared at portraits of opera stars as Mrs. Story turned the pages. The silence got awkward.

'I gotta get goin' – got thirty more collections to make.'

'Sure, Johnny. Say hello to your mother for me. We should have coffee one of these days.'

'I'll tell her, and thanks for the tip.'

Johnny disappeared into the night. When she could no longer hear his footsteps she flicked off the porch light and returned to the living room. She picked up the book and shelved it. Her fingers danced along the spines of the other volumes until she came to a leather folder. She removed it and returned to the sofa. Opening the folder she turned the pages of the photo album her mother gave her before she died.

There she was, baby Jacquelyn, cradled in her mama's arms. Another snapshot showed her as a tiny child, climbing the steps for her first day at Nursery School. What followed were photos of a sullen-looking girl in Junior and Senior High with a puffy face, double chin, floppy arms, wearing a dress that hid her true girth. It had taken her years and lots of tears to feel good about herself, about what she had accomplished. She hoped it would not take Johnny as long.

YEARS LATER, IN a locker room in Green Bay, Wisconsin, the Packers' left tackle John Lockhart prepared for the game. He opened his locker and stared at his wife's picture pasted to the inside of the door, right above photos of huge male opera stars. His teammates kidded him about those photos, but not for long. Because Johnny would answer with a thundering attempt to sing an aria, an event that usually cleared the room.

Fly By Night

Anne Hamilton

THEY CAME BY night and they would leave by night. Three times it had happened and she knew it was only the beginning – or maybe the end – of something. It was the secrets she hated most. And the darkness. And the secrets were worse in the darkness.

Where they were right now, Elena still didn't know. A week had passed since that storm-that-wasn't-a-storm-but-was-gunfire had disturbed her and the fighting had started. The men came to their street, pointing guns, shouting through loud-hailers; ordering everyone to get out immediately – or else.

Elena ran. They all ran, and kept running until a white car with shattered windows slowed down. 'Help us. Please,' begged Aunt Irini, and the driver shouted at them to get in. He didn't speak any other words. Neither did they. They just drove until he stopped and pointed at a village huddled under the brow of the hill. Uncle Anthony knocked at the first house. 'Help us. Please,' begged Aunt Irini for the second time, and they were ushered in. The next day they went to another house; the next day, another.

In the day they kept inside, in the kitchen or playing in the cellar if the house was bigger. They weren't hiding, Aunt Irini said, not really, just being careful.

'But where are we?' Elena asked the first time, and the second.

'In the village,' someone, Irini or one of the local aunties, would answer quickly before they asked Elena or Krista to wash the vegetables or put out the tea things. Elena's, 'what village?' was never heard in the general hubbub of preparing the endless food. It was Uncle Anthony who took her aside and whispered, 'Best not to know, Elena. These people could get into lots of trouble by helping us. I'll explain why one day, I promise, but for now just be a good girl and pretend everything's okay.'

So, the third time – *now* – she waited and she pretended.

First, Aunt Irini took Krista, whose eyes were popping with excitement. Then, minutes or maybe an hour later, she came back for Sofia who barely stirred, burrowing into their aunt's shoulder as she was lifted up. Elena cuddled her knees and wished Mama was beside her. Outside, it was a hot, breathless night but the worn flagstones on which she sat were cold and smooth. Elena remembered being little, how the tin pitchers of milk, then as tall as her and fatter, were lined up like marching soldiers. Four times four times four, they stretched into the place Mama called the pantry at home but the dairy to the neighbours who bought milk from them. Elena, leaning against the churns, had pretended to sip her hated beaker of strong goat's milk, pouring teasing little puddles just beyond the old cat's whiskers so he had to stretch and twist his neck to lap them up.

'Elena? Elena, are you ready?' Aunt Irini made Elena jump. 'Shh.' She put her forefinger on Elena's lips. Her finger was dry and cold, soft.

Hand in hand they walked slowly across the yard. Elena half-expected they would crouch in the shadows, darting from bush to bush when clouds crossed the moon, fearful that the bushes would rise up as militiamen and shoot them dead. But Irini's gait was leisurely, they might have been returning home from an evening stroll, ready to pass the time of day with villagers old and young. Only the tightness of her grip indicated that Aunt Irini was 'being careful.'

This time it was a truck, spattered with stinking cow dung and chicken shit, parked on the road, with its back wheels angled onto the field. Uncle Anthony leant against the grey-green cab, an unlit cigarette balanced on his lower lip. He gave Elena a thumbs-up and jerked his head towards the back of the truck, where crates of stunned hens blearily peeked out from underneath a loosely tied canvas. It took him only a minute to hoist her into a gap between the cab and the chicken boxes. It was lined with another tarpaulin, but it did little to break her fall and Elena winced as her knees and elbows clunked against the corrugated metal. She rolled, uncomplaining, under the plastic sheets and shuffled into the hidey-hole formed from a careful arrangement of straw-filled crates and horse blankets.

'Mind my hand, daydream girl,' hissed Krista, even as she helped pull Elena into the space. 'That's your place there. You're to stay awake and keep me company.' Kicking her leg in the direction of Sofia, she added, 'She's no good.' Sofia opened her eyes sleepily and half-smiled before her lids drooped again.

'We should try to sleep, too.' Elena repeated Aunt Irini's clipped advice. 'It might take hours to get to the mountains. Lots of the roads are closed and it's better that we avoid the checkpoints. We can't be sure they'll help us.'

'I won't sleep.' Krista paused. 'Because I'm scared *shitless*.'

Elena ignored her; Krista was just practising until she was brave enough to say that to Aunt Irini. Anyway, she didn't look scared. Krista's eyes were still bright and she buzzed with energy. Elena wriggled herself more comfortable and crossed her arms over her chest, muffling her thumping heart. Tentatively, she reached out and touched her sister's hand and, when it wasn't snatched away, she curled her fingers around Krista's thumb. With her foot touching Sofia's, Elena took comfort in the closeness of her sisters. 'Holy Mary, Mother of God, help us,' she prayed, willing the miles would bring them closer to Mama.

Later – she had no idea how long, but the pick-up now bucked and spun over a road that had clearly stopped being a road so she knew they were heading for the dirt tracks that spiralled like spider's webs out of the foothills of the mountains – Elena jerked from a half-dream. She gagged and spat out the hair, it might have been hers or Krista's, which was tangled with them under the blanket. Suddenly came the pressure of the brakes as Uncle Anthony applied them too fast and too late; Elena pictured the telling-off look on Aunt Irini's face. She felt a surge of hope that they were arriving, claiming the sanctuary of the magic forest where Red Riding Hood had outwitted the wolf and they all lived happily ever after.

Breaking the rules, she crawled to the edge of the makeshift tent and wrenched at the string that fastened the tarpaulin to the side of the truck. It loosened slightly and she forced her head out. Her mouth made a round O, gulping like Krista's goldfish used to when food was sprinkled over its bowl. The new day was racing their journey and winning, clean light suspended in streaks from the sky where it met with a smoky haze. A strong scent of wood-smoke caught at the back of her throat, reminding her of charred souvlaki on an open grill. Her stomach heaved and rumbled at the same time. Straight ahead was the sign for some townland, destroyed by red graffiti that ran like blood over the letters and into a pool on the uneven ground. They were not in the mountains at all, not even in the forest, but in an open clearing with a proper concrete road.

Elena heard a sound from the other side of the truck and twisted round. Aunt Irini and Uncle Anthony must have stopped to pee or stretch their legs. They were stumbling back to the pick-up from the direction of the hedgerow, both looked pale and Aunt Irini had a handkerchief to her mouth. She was saying something, saying it over again: 'We have to help them, Tony. We have to.'

Uncle Anthony's face was strained, almost angry. 'They're beyond help. And they're not ours. *Not ours*, Irini. You know what that means.'

'That *we* did this to *them…*' Her voice rose.

'Get in the truck. Now!'

Elena saw him shove her aunt towards the cab. Her eyes slid over them, to the hedgerow a few feet away, and she frowned. What–

'Oh, my God.' Aunt Irini's head whipped round. Her eyes locked with Elena's. 'Get down,' she cried out. 'Get down, Elena and stay down.'

She shot back into the stinking hell-smell of the tarpaulin and squeezed her eyes shut. But the blackness didn't dull what she'd seen above the hedge: the lines of wire strung from one telegraph pole to the next and a line of scarecrows hanging from them. They were flapping and twisting their horrible faces, groaning in the wind. A baby song, one of Sofia's filled her ears: *I'm a dingle-dangle scarecrow with a dingle dangle head, I can wave my arms like this, I can wave my legs like that…* It was a trick of her imagination, of course. They hadn't been scarecrows. Not so many, not so close to the road, but why, then, would someone hang their washed clothes there, in public, and so far from the laundry?

They wouldn't. Elena opened her mouth to scream but nothing came out. She was still crying silent baubles of tears when the truck stopped again, and Irini reached in and grabbed her, lifted her to the cab, and held her close as Anthony roared off once more.

'I'm sorry, I'm so sorry, Elena,' Irini whispered. 'We'll send someone to help them, I promise.'

'You can't help them.' Her mind cleared and her voice rang out strong, coming from the depths of her hollow insides. 'They were dead. They were dead men hanging down, weren't they?' Elena challenged Irini into an unwilling nod. 'So only God can help them now.'

Uncle Anthony snorted. 'If there was a God, he should have fucking helped them before they were fucking strung up–'

'Anthony!'

'Sorry.' His hands tightened on the steering wheel and he stared straight ahead.

Elena thought she might be sick. *I'm a dingle-dangle scarecrow...*

High up in the mountains they would be safe, Aunt Irini tried to reassure her. There were people waiting, good people, who would care for them. Look, they were already past the monastery and climbing through the forest; higher and higher, safer and safer.

Finally the car bumped over what felt like giant marbles, and came to a halt at the entrance to a cluster of small cottages. A crowd of people surged to meet them. Elena froze between the firm hands lifting her down, watching other strangers scrabbling to rescue Krista and Sofia until the sisters were all being hugged and squeezed breathless by people they had never seen before.

A stranger pulled off Elena's sweater and swept back the hair from her face, tying it deftly under a headscarf in a style she had never used before. Someone else was doing the same to Krista who was scowling and squirming, and to Aunt Irini who was sobbing. 'We couldn't help them,' she was sobbing. 'They were boys, some of them. Boys. And we did nothing.'

'They deserve nothing.' One of the men, hard-faced, with a rifle, spat on the ground and the crowd rumbled its approval. 'They bring war here; they invite death. We celebrate it.'

But the old lady holding Elena tutted loudly and clucked Elena's chin, pulling her away. She offered her cold water and Elena drank cup after cup until her insides felt loose and swimming. Then she and Krista and Sofia were sat on little wooden stools in the shade, and the grown-ups plotted and wailed out of earshot.

Elena looked around. It was another village, but this one was different. She knew she had never been anywhere like this before, ever. At home, the houses were small and white-washed with flower boxes on the windows and the shops and cafes made a big square that led up to the church. At the seaside, where they were before the men came, the shiny hotels rose high above them, new protectors of the sandy beaches. But here, the tiny buildings were made of stone, close to the ground, six of them in a half circle. Nothing else. The road was a track and there were no colours; Elena checked, none at all. It felt… she struggled for the word, an odd one because of all the people, but it felt… abandoned. And cooler; a breeze ruffled her new headscarf and dried the sweat on her neck.

An old man with thick black-rimmed glasses and a billowing white shirt, took them into the first house, through one big empty room, and into the yard. Someone had tidied up tractor parts and bicycles, stones and rubble, into a messy pile to make room for a long table piled with meat and salad; souvlaki roasting over a homemade fire. Elena felt sick again and was grateful that the elderly lady who had tied back her hair saw it and put a hand to her forehead.

'You are hot, child,' she said. 'Come, all of you, wash your hands and faces and then we will give thanks and eat.' She nodded towards a tin bath filled with water.

'In there?' Krista looked disbelieving. 'Where's the bathroom?'

'Krista–' Aunt Irini's voice held a note of warning, and Krista curled up her top lip but obediently splashed her hands and face.

Elena, intending to do the same, stopped. She thought she might faint – if she knew how. Above the trough, pegged by its long legs to the string washing line was a rag doll. It was a Jemima doll; Sofia had one but it got left behind in the running away. But this Jemima-doll was dirty and her apron was flapping. Her head was hanging, almost chopped off. *I'm a dingle dangle scarecrow with a dingle dangle head...* Pictures flashed through Elena's head from left to right like signposts at a station when you were on a fast train: shiny Jemima, Aunt Irini with a handkerchief to her mouth, scarecrows in a field with their dingle dangle heads, torn patchy overalls on washing lines, a whole row of washing lines then another then another then another...

Elena knew she felt sorry for screaming, guilty that she wasn't being calm, but she knew she had to scream, she had to force out the pictures from her head. 'Help,' she screamed. 'Help! Help us!' She did it methodically, one scream after another, but it wasn't strong enough. She watched herself kneel down on the sandy ground and lean over the trough that was half full of dirty water and bits of hay. And there was her reflection, all out of focus, her hair missing, her eyes wide and staring, her mouth open. She looked like a witch. She was a witch. The pictures flashed behind her, in front of her, and the words, *I can wave my arms like this, I can wave my legs like that,* echoed all around her.

Elena did the only thing she could do to make it all go away. She grasped the sides of the bath and banged her head on it. Over and over and over again. Her skin and bones made a dull thump against the blunt metal, the sweat stung her eyes and left a greasy mark behind.

Then she watched Uncle Anthony prising her hands away, and she bit him, and she was sorry she bit him. As he laid her down on the path she clamped her lips together so she wouldn't bite anymore; dogs bit, not people. She opened her eyes and saw Aunt Irini there too, the old lady handing her a big bottle, but Elena's mouth was tight shut and she couldn't open it for the medicine. So her head was forced back, and something brown and burning poured into her nostrils, which were pinched tight shut as Elena gagged and bucked and coughed down the liquid.

And then she disappeared.

She slept on and off throughout the afternoon, vaguely aware of Aunt Irini and Uncle Anthony swapping places to sit beside her. The shadows had grown very long when she awoke properly. Sofia was slumped on the end of the daybed, picking at a scab on her knee and lining up dead pieces of skin on her leg. Elena looked around the room. It was small and square with a low ceiling and whitewashed walls patterned with black cracks. There was a table covered with a flowery plastic cloth; above it a shelf of old books, their titles in a foreign language. The same letters Elena saw on a wall calendar that had been stuck up crookedly, its edges curling from damp.

Elena's gaze wandered onto Sofia who was flapping her hands crossly to gain attention.

'Is this home now?' It took Elena a minute to understand her, because Sofia had her toy lion clamped tightly under her arm and her face buried in its fur. 'Elena, is this home now?'

Was it? She didn't know where home was any more. She wished Mama was there with them. She wished them back at school. Doing chores. Playing checkers. Laughing. Being ordinary but whole. Instead they were all slowly becoming flat like Fuzzy Felt sticker people. That is, if there was a Fuzzy Felt called In the War. There probably wasn't; there would have to be pictures of killing people and killing people was wrong.

Elena was suddenly weary; ten years old and exhausted to her bones like the old village aunties used to complain. 'It's not home,' she told Sofia, finally. 'But these people are our friends. They're helping us to stay safe.' *Help,* she thought bleakly. She kept hearing that word, a nice one turned horrible. She didn't want help; they shouldn't have to need it. It wasn't fair.

Nothing was fair anymore.

This time they had come by day, and who knew when they would leave, but the darkness was never very far away.

Climbing Wall

Rosie Garland

SHE PRIDES HERSELF on being a supportive friend: a shoulder to lean on, a listening ear at the end of the phone. A tall woman, only forbidding at first glance, she likes the feeling of people scaling her defences so much that she makes it easy, attaching colourful grips of moulded plastic for them to clutch. They are so grateful. Call her their best friend ever.

In return, their weight holds her steady. Mother always stressed the importance of service to others. Besides, it's only a matter of time before they take their own initiative. As soon as they climb to the top of her wall and see the amazing view, they'll rush back down to construct their own.

It's not hard. She did it.

So she doesn't understand why they seem content to cling. Not that she minds, but surely they'd prefer to be independent. She must be doing something wrong. She puts up notices printed in block capitals, *THIS WAY*

DOWN. Waits for the highest to abseil back to the ground.

But next morning, the crowd of climbers is just as dense. They grin through the windows of her eyes, waving hello. She tries to get her fingernails underneath one and prise him loose, but he's fastened tight as a limpet. Surely, she's running out of room; but still they swarm, two or three deep in places, clambering on each other's shoulders and hanging on.

She's exhausted from carrying the extra load. Leans dangerously. When was the last time she slept through without waking at 4am, forced to eavesdrop their muttering whine? And that other sound: a hundred thumbs being sucked at once.

Please, she says. Maybe just one or two of you could go?

You said you'd always be there, they moan. *You promised.*

She can barely breathe. She unscrews the bright plastic handhold closest to her mouth and takes in a lungful of air, the first for weeks without sucking in someone's fingers, or a ponytail. There's a thud. She doesn't know if it's the handhold dropping to the floor, or one of the hangers-on. She doesn't want to look.

Oh, they cry. *How can you do this? We thought you were our friend.*

She's a fool. She should never have made it so easy; should unbolt the handholds closest to the ground, dissuade them from starting to climb. Too late now. She's buckling but can't bear the idea of prising their fingers loose, the thought of their limp bodies piling around her ankles.

Whining in her ears. High-pitched, unending.

She sleeps fitfully. Dreams of empty walls.

The Helpline

Rose McGinty

TED LIFTED THE telephone handpiece from its cradle and wiped it carefully. He started around the edge of the earpiece with considered swabs and worked his way inwards towards the small square formation of holes in the centre. He repeated the same precise movement with the mouthpiece and then in four long swipes cleaned the handle between the two ends. He paused after those four soft strokes and then ran the wet wipe along the cable, stretching out its tight coils.

There was absolutely no need to clean the telephone like this as it was as pristine as the day it was unwrapped and placed on the desk, and no one had touched the telephone since last Monday when he cleaned it previously, or in fact forty Mondays ago when he first started cleaning it. A meaningless routine, but for Ted it was the only activity permitted and it was everything, those four long caresses.

The telephone sat silent and solitary on the desk.

When he first took up this role a binder containing two neatly typed pages of The Protocol sat on the desk beside the telephone, along with a notepad and biro. The end of the biro was chewed. Ted had picked it up with his handkerchief and transferred it into the bin, where it dropped in with an embarrassed twang. Not one of the biros back at the hospital had been un-chewed. But somehow a chewed-up biro didn't matter then, and Ted didn't actually have time to notice what with the constant stream of calls. He had been the switchboard manager, the most important cog in the clinical wheel, he liked to boast.

Other than his desk, chair and bin there was only a pin board in the office. A poster of The Product was tacked to it. Ted scrunched up the wet wipe, deposited it in the bin and sat down. He suppressed a sigh, the expulsion of air through his teeth, slight though the noise was, made him notice the silence all the more. He didn't want to notice the silence. It made him remember the silence after the screech of tyres. He fixed his eyes on the telephone and waited.

AT THE JOB centre this position had been the first that had popped up on the touchscreen after Ted entered his qualifications. He clicked to register his interest and found himself the following Monday at The Firm being given directions by a receptionist on how to locate his new office – second floor, turn right, seven doors down on the left. She didn't look up from her computer to acknowledge him, but handed over a box. He opened it once he was in his new office. It contained a cellophane wrapped telephone. He unwrapped the phone and plugged it in. He turned his attention to The Protocol, read it through twice, memorising the opening greeting it stipulated should be given to callers.

Ted checked his watch three times during his first half an hour, expecting his supervisor to arrive and give him The Firm's induction. He was keen to enquire about promotion potential, after all he had been the hospital switchboard manager and then there was his array of skills and accolades from his charitable works. But no one came, so he dialled 0 for reception and was informed that he would find adequate instruction to perform his role in The Protocol.

By eleven o'clock Ted had read The Protocol fifteen times, each time more slowly, savouring particular words. He had to, there was no other reading material and he needed each word to ward off the crushing boredom of his stark, silent office. He hadn't heard so much as another footstep, let alone voice from the corridor or other offices. Ted called the receptionist once more.

'Hello, it's Ted Harris here, I started this morning.'

'How may I help you Ted?'

'Well, the telephone, it hasn't rung once.'

'Yes, Ted.'

'What am I expected to do?'

'Wait for it to ring.' The receptionist hung up.

'Wait for it to ring.' Ted repeated into the silence.

This wouldn't do. He couldn't just sit still and wait. He'd never had to wait for a call at the hospital switch. It was the other way round, a line of callers waiting for him and his team to put them through to their desired extension. Ted didn't do waiting and had never waited for anything. He was a do-er, always on the go, chasing his ambitions. Up with his alarm at six a.m. for a quick shower and slice of toast before he nipped next door to make sure Mrs Mirza had got through the night and to make her a cuppa. Off to the hospital, picking up his deputy, Beryl, along the way, who would cling onto her seatbelt, pleading with him not to drive so fast. But he liked to go at a lick and get to the hospital early so that before his shift started he had time to visit a ward, taking requests for the hospital radio show that he would host later that evening. Then full tilt at the switchboard, button jabbing without pause for seven and a half hours.

Ted ventured out into the corridor. He crossed to the door opposite, put his ear to it, strained to hear even a breath on the other side. But nothing. He tried the handle, it gave without a squeak. The door opened and before him he saw a urinal. The men's toilets and no one there, and not so much as a tap dripping. He closed the door and moved along to the next one. Again he listened, tried the handle, this one gave open to a cupboard kitted out with a sink, tap, kettle and shelf of white porcelain mugs. He looked at the mugs, none had a coffee stain or a chip. What was it with The Firm? Ted shut the door. He continued down the corridor but the next door he tried was locked, and the next and in fact all the nine other doors. He returned to his office, sat down at the desk and stared at the phone.

He tapped his fingers on the desk, but the sound echoed and made him feel irritable. Some minutes passed, he whistled. That was worse, the tune bouncing off the walls was eerie. He opened The Protocol binder again but he could not bear to read it, the words almost stung with their over-familiarity. He closed his eyes. A snooze, why not? The telephone would wake him after all, if it rang.

As soon as his eyelids closed the thoughts started racing around his mind. What was his team doing now? Gone to a utility company call centre. Bet they weren't waiting on a phone to ring there, no time to even go to the loo at those places he'd heard. Inconvenient as it sounded, Ted was envious. And how would dear old Mr Appleby be coping without his daily chat with Ted? He rang every day at three for a quick catch-up. The new automated system wouldn't have an option for tips on the riders and runners at Cheltenham. The new automated system didn't have an option for Ted and his team, other than a meagre redundancy pay-out that had given him heartburn and pains in his arm. Ted snapped his eyes open and glowered at the telephone. Ring, damn it.

At twelve-thirty Ted took his ham sandwich out of his rucksack and retraced his footsteps down to reception.

'Excuse me, could you tell me where the canteen is please?' he asked the receptionist.

'There isn't one,' she replied, again without looking at him.

'Where am I meant to eat my lunch?'

'Most people eat at their desks, or there is a picnic table where the sandwich van parks.' She nodded vaguely to an unknown spot beyond the revolving doors.

Ted dodged his way out the revolving doors to the industrial estate beyond. He hadn't gone many paces when rain started to spit. He hadn't brought his umbrella with him. He put his head down and pushed forward, hopefully the rain would ease off as he couldn't face going back to his office and the silent telephone, not yet. He needed to see another soul. The rain came down harder. He reached a bus shelter with a bench. He sat in there and ate his limp sandwich, watching the rain hit the pavement.

In the hospital, on the rare occasion he had time for lunch, the canteen was always loud and thronging. An elbow in your face wasn't uncommon as a nurse wolfed down her beans and chips beside you, before tearing back to the ward. Two thousand people worked at the hospital. Ted had probably spoken to most of them, when they called up for HR, or rang in sick, or needed to get hold of payroll. And that was without the patients, millions of calls he must have taken over his thirty odd years at the switch. All those voices, some raspy with disease, or shrill with urgency, then the ones that were little more than a scared whisper. Others though were joyful, waiting to get through to maternity to hear the baby's name or to get the much anticipated all-clear. And the accents, every region, every nationality. They filled his ears, his head with inflections, rhythms, tones and cadences. How grateful in the end he was for their noise after the accident. A perpetual play list that squeezed out any threat of silence, of hearing those other voices, long lost.

The rain had stopped and with it went the cacophony of his memories. Ted realised the rain was the only sound he had heard all day. He put his hand out from the shelter, desperate for a last drop, but the sky was clear and his lunch hour was nearly over. He trudged back to The Firm. The receptionist did not raise her eyes as he spun back into the foyer. Back in his office, the telephone didn't ring all afternoon.

The next morning Ted picked up a book at home and put in in his rucksack along with his sandwich before he set off for his second day at The Firm. He felt tired, even though he had barely done a thing the day before and in fact had come home and after his tea had fallen asleep on the sofa immediately. This was a novelty. Ted's evenings, like his days, were always packed. Two nights a week he hosted his radio show, another he went to the elderly care ward to call the bingo, hospital choir once a week, on a Friday it was the fundraising committee for the baby unit and the weekends were no less busy, as he helped out both nights at the soup kitchen and during the day busied about town running errands for his causes. He was the hospital hero, the town's hero. The local paper loved him, everyone did and Ted loved the adulation, the shiny medals collecting in his sock drawer. It was addictive, that glimpse of a gong or perhaps a nomination for the position of Mayor.

A nap was a foreign concept to Ted, as for a duvet day! He'd not had so much as a day off sick in all his working life. Beryl used to joke that no germ could catch Ted. No one could catch him, least of all his own family. Ted did have a family – a wife, two daughters and a son. Ted's wife once used to make his sandwiches, wrap them in foil, hand them to him, with a kiss that never caught his cheek as he dashed off for another busy, noisy day.

Ted whirled through the doors to The Firm and headed towards the stairwell, when the receptionist called over to him.

'No unauthorised reading material permitted.'

'Sorry?'

'Your rucksack, please bring it to the counter.'

Startled, Ted did as he was requested.

'Open it, please.'

Ted unzipped his rucksack. The receptionist peered in.

'Please remove that book.'

Ted drew it out and she took it from him, placing it under the counter.

'You may collect it when you leave this evening.'

'But it's like being in Limbo. There's nothing to do and that phone is never going to ring, is it?'

'Please proceed to your office. You are required to staff The Helpline.'

'But no one ever calls. Why does The Firm even need The Helpline?'

She looked up at Ted for the first time.

'The Helpline requires you.'

But why, Ted wanted to shout.

'WHY?' HIS OLDEST daughter, yelled at him as his wife had bumped one, two, three, four suitcases down the stairs, tears bumping down her cheeks.

'Why?' his other daughter cried, grabbing their coats from the stand in the hallway. Ted had spent the rent money on his rotary club regalia, even though there were rumours of redundancies at the hospital.

'Why does everyone else always come first? It's so unfair,' his son whispered, as he closed the door behind them. Unfair? He was a whisker away from becoming chairman of the rotary club. Them leaving was unfair. But you couldn't help some people, they were just selfish. He shouted it after them, into the silence after the screech of tyres.

Ted returned to his office, waited.

HE WAITED WEEK in, week out for forty weeks for The Helpline to ring. In all that time it was the same, as soon as he got home, had his tea, he fell asleep, shattered on the sofa. His days and evenings were no longer busy, not even his weekends as he found he just slept and slept. At least he thought he did. Once he left The Firm at five p.m. he couldn't recall anything. In his office, he no longer tapped, or whistled, or sighed or did anything that caused any unnecessary noise. He merely wiped the telephone every Monday morning, as he had just this morning done, and waited. His head, once so frantic with plans, lists and schedules and so noisy with all those voices he used to know, had slowed. The lists had drifted away and the voices were distant echoes. It wasn't like this after the accident, then he had thrown himself into work and his philanthropic activities with even greater gusto, as if he had to prove himself for once and for all; get some reward. He never even had time to go to the graveyard.

Ted ate his ham sandwich at his desk every day. He saw no point in going out at lunchtime, there was no one else about to pass the time of day, and after that first day it had never rained again, so he didn't even have the raindrops for company. Today though as he pulled his sandwich out from his rucksack a soft sound caught his attention. Surely not? He looked at the window, it was true, his ears hadn't deceived him, there was the evidence – a splatter of rain and then another. Ted stuffed the sandwich in his pocket and raced downstairs and out into the industrial estate. Rain, its tap, tap, tap on the pavement, calling back those beloved voices to him. He must do something. He decided he would go in search of the sandwich van and its picnic table, perhaps someone would be there? He followed the path, past the bus shelter, and onwards. The rain fell. After he had passed ten office blocks, all as anonymous as The Firm, he was puffed out, that sharp pain that had gripped his arm, then his heart, on the day of his redundancy came back. He checked his watch, his lunch hour was nearly over. The van and bench couldn't be much further, could they? How big was this estate? It seemed endless.

The rain eased and silence descended. It was so unfair, he just wanted to reach the van and spend time with another soul. So unfair. The silence cracked and the voices came clear and loud to him now, like never before. How often he had heard those words, from his son when he wanted help with his homework, but he had a dinner to go to and be toasted at; from his daughters when they wanted him to go camping of a weekend but he had scout troops to ferry about; or from his wife, when she rang him, begging him to come home and spend some time with the four of them, and he let it go to voicemail. If only he had answered her calls, just once.

If only he hadn't stood on the stairs that night in his rotary club regalia and let his wife bump the four suitcases down the stairs. If only, as she drove the four of them away that night, it hadn't been raining, there hadn't been a lorry, a blaze of headlights. If her eyes hadn't been blurred with tears, if she hadn't been dialling on her mobile the council's emergency housing helpline.

Ted wiped his eyes. Somehow the road he had followed about the industrial estate had brought him back to The Firm. He pushed through the revolving doors, crossed the foyer, with every step cursing his own narcissism, his need for adulation. He didn't even know who or what causes he was helping most of the time he realised.

'Yourself, that was who you were helping, your ego,' called out the receptionist, her angel wings blazing behind her. It was true.

'Forgive me.'

Ted reached his office, sat down in the chair. He fished out the wet wipes from his drawer and dropped them into the bin. He settled himself for the eternal wait.

The helpline rang, four soft rings. Ted reached for the hand piece.

Say When

Nicola Humphreys

EMILY. FIVE YEARS ago.

Her nails were a dirty scrabble of cracked and missing french tips. What a waste of a manicure not even a day old. By daybreak, her wrinkled fingerprints couldn't identify anyone, and her softened, scabbing knuckles were a spongy moss, that leaked clear fluid whenever she stretched her hand. Swollen, purple skin strained around her rings. How exactly do they cut them off? Her head itched in the tender patch where he'd dragged her across the room before the force scalped a clump clean out. Fight, flight then freeze. One fist under her chin, sucking her thumb, she lay there coiled, with grazed, raw knees almost touching bruised elbows. More alive than she'd ever been, yet as discarded as a chicken carcass on day two in summer. Whoever found her now, determined her fate. No-one could see her, when her eyes were closed, except a friendly dog sniffing round to play. Every passing car had him in it. Some first date this had turned out to be. She now knew why they say you should always take spare socks when you go camping.

EMILY. FOUR YEARS ago.

Hands thrust deep into her pockets, her scarf covering her mouth, she huddled at the bus stop. A teenage girl smiled and stood behind her for protection. The unwritten rule of not having to keep watch. Emily would never be second in the queue again, because how she lived now was the only way to make going through all that worth it. Thank God City lost tonight. A dozen somber, sober fans brought the night air with them. When they win, they want to talk to anyone.

Crowded buses at night still scared her but she didn't get a choice sometimes. Once, a freshly-showered man, with pink, shiny cheeks sat across the aisle. His upper arms bulged through a crisply ironed shirt. Musky body spray catching in the back of her throat. She had to get off at the next stop to force breaths out hard through the nausea and walk the rest of the way home. Keep a rhythm. Strong peppermints. 'Get a grip, woman. This is nothing.'

THE DAY AFTER the bus, she walked up to three young men in the park and said 'I've lost my travelcard. Do you know where can I get a bike?' As brazen as that. One youth got up, said nothing and lolloped off. The one perched on the back of the bench said 'Are you police?' She shook her head. Then, cockily, with his chin jerking slightly up, he said, 'Show us what you got.' Laughing, he fist-bumped youth number three, who smiled, laid-back through a fug of weed. She turned and started to walk away. He shouted 'Where you going, girl?' but she didn't look back. After a couple of minutes the first lad glided past on a ladies racer bike then skidded right in front of her, blocking her path. Squaring up, in her space, in her face, he lingered over his pat-down. He rubbed and squeezed her body in places she'd rather he didn't touch, jerking the lining out of one coat pocket and the contents out of the other. He kept the £20 that he found in there for his trouble. She thought they might frisk or rob her, so all she brought with her was twenty quid for the score and the usual half packet of mints. He left the bike and mints on the ground in front of her, stared straight into her eyes, sucked his tongue between his top teeth, puckered his lips, then, almost shoulder bumping her, sauntered on back to his mates.

WITHIN TEN MINUTES, Emily had blagged her way into the halls of residence. Those kids were mollycoddled. Naive. They were way too trusting. They'd learn. She figured that as Millie Holmes had just started university, she wouldn't be needing her driving licence, passport or

National Insurance number for a while. What did she expect, anyway, leaving her room unlocked, the silly cow? She should be grateful that her laptop and phone were still there.

EMILY. THREE YEARS ago.

On days when she was on earlies, there would be a quiet hour to have a bath without interruption. She might even be lucky and find a nice Whoops! meal in the supermarket, or the treat of an oven-baked, not micro-waved jacket potato. A seven-thirty bedtime. Maybe more than four hours tonight, but probably not. She'd wake up paralysed again, with him crushing her chest. A fox was a terrified woman. A bird on the window ledge or a pizza leaflet through the letterbox was someone trying to break in. Next door's telly was her neighbour being hurt by her alcoholic son.

THE GRINDING EXHAUSTION of merely existing, but constantly being on hyper, gripped her neck tightly. The only time her shoulders dropped was when the self-loathing of regret forced its hand inside her mouth and ripped out her lungs. Now she was deliberately speechless and voiceless. Her throat swelled so she couldn't breathe or swallow the growing lump. Silent screams into the pillow. Punching the mattress. Crying quickly to get it over with in a cold shower. Shock herself out of it. Relief was short-lived. That calm never lasted. No-one can ever know. She's done the hard bit. No way was she doing time. It was just a matter of getting used to it. She just got soap in her eyes.

EMILY. TWO YEARS ago.

She paced, fiddling with her ring. Her finger was still not right. It creaked when rain was forecast but the black nail had long since grown out. Not concentrating, Emily caught her inner wrist on the oven shelf and almost dropped the baking sheet. Another burn to prove her cook status.

HOLDING HER ARM in the stream of cold water, back teeth clamped, she chuntered under her breath, 'That's just freaking marvellous. I am going to strangle that muther fudgeing, conning student with her own head-phones cable. I'll flatten those big elephant ears out with her straighteners. She won't be able to see a mascara brush when I've finished with her. If she thinks this is a game, she'll soon fracking find out that I never lose. How dare that wench have the nerve. It had better be all there or she'll regret it.'

WHY ARE PEOPLE so stupid? No-one would leave £500 on

the table in a café while they went to the toilet, but they'll leave their phone. Emily had the chance to make the call and put the phone back without anyone noticing. Block, delete. Millie Holmes wouldn't go to the police. What would she even say? 'I think some woman is impersonating me so I stole four grand out of her bank account, but then she phoned me to tell me to put it back or she'd hurt my sister?'

WHILST CLEANING HOLIDAY caravans on the North East coast, Emily found a gold chain with the letter M on it, so kept it. Perk of the job. It made a change from used underwear in the bed or dried vomit down the side of the toilet. Everyone called her 'Em' anyway, so it stuck. The least anyone knew about her the better. No-one cared anyway. They all spent more on cans of cider this week than they did for the newspaper tokens for this holiday.

Then onto a fusty call-centre, just outside Leeds, that sold gardening equipment. For four months, she endured a wheezing, obese woman, with halitosis and a bladder problem, who wittered on constantly about her grandkids. Obviously they were all either exceptionally talented or had special needs because no-one wanted to be ordinary these days. That old dear actually thought they were friends, bless her little heart. Fish factory line operative in Grimsby was one way to keep the men well away.

Cooking fry-ups and changing beds in a guesthouse near St Ives. People were scum. The things they did to their sheets and towels then leave for someone else to sort out. Night office cleaner everywhere. Sleeping all day was an honest reason to avoid any friendly housemates. She tried not to interact unless she had to. They usually fell into three categories: Polish women doing three jobs who were home at odd hours, the lonely ones who didn't have jobs who stayed in their rooms and graduate assistant managers of chain restaurants who had £50,000 of student debt and couldn't go home for some reason. She did actually work in the laundry for a chain of London hotels for a bit. That's where her gran always thought she was. A Christmas card or Facebook message every now and then kept her happy.

THAT NANNY JOB was great. Emily loved that baby. Live-in, nice food, cash-in hand, Sky TV, loads of books. She only left because they kept trying to make her do a fear of flying course, so they could all go on holiday, but it was too risky. One time, the mum asked Emily what perfume she was wearing, and she said 'page 37 of your Vogue magazine. A few days later, the mum gave her a fancy gift bag tied with ribbon. Inside was a heavy glass bottle of Chanel, plus the body wash and lotion. They even trusted her to house sit one weekend when they went to a wedding. She didn't deserve their kindness. This was the first job she'd ever had where she didn't steal anything. Well, she bought stuff online with the mum's credit card from the same shops. Selling them on was easy money, but she never nicked any jewellery or cash. You never know these days, they probably had a nanny cam.

EMILY. LAST YEAR.

She'd washed up for two months without complaint, in a wholefood café in Bristol. The owner called her 'a good little worker' and put her onto the catering gig. An old ambulance, painted purple, and converted into a vegan burger van that went all over the UK to festivals from May right through to October. Physically hard, twelve-hour days, bone-tired, sleeping in a caravan. The freedom to wander round the site and just be. Everyone was on holiday from their normal lives at places like these. Not on alert, constantly scanning. Even the men at festivals smelled of woodsmoke, BBQ and sweat. Then tour catering for a couple of indie bands until March, where she somehow, naturally, became part of the crew. She'd found her people. One night, a momentary leap of faith due to the bravado of drink, made her climb into the guitar tech's bunk on the tour bus, in whose arms she felt safer than she had done in a long time.

PHILIP. LAST MONTH.

'Yeah mate, no worries about the ticket. My treat, for, y'know. To welcome you back. You've got a lot of catching up to do,' Neil said.

'Cheers. Thanks. I appreciate it,' Philip replied.

'Here.' Neil tapped and swiped the tablet screen and passed it to Philip. 'Have a look at these.'

Phil put down his mug and carefully took the tablet. These were photos that he should have been in. Basecamp at Kilimanjaro. Swimming with dolphins. A wedding of someone he vaguely once knew at school. Surfing off Costa Rica. Off-roading. Champions League in Barcelona. Las Vegas. Sausage festival. Cider Festival. Oktoberfest. Stag do in Prague. So many big nights out with the lads. One photo caught his eye and he felt his chest prickling. It was like an electric zap to his lungs and he could suddenly hear the sea. He was looking at a picture of Neil in the queue for a food van, at some music festival in Somerset, thumbs out Fonzie-style, with the caption, 'Worth waitin' in line for a famous #VegasBaby burger'.

'I'M SORRY,' PHILIP said. 'I need a fag.' He slid the patio door open, walked outside with his mug of tea and smoked two roll-ups in quick succession. So much to process. He wasn't expecting this. In his head, he was back in the anger management classes. 'Take a timeout. Don't hold a grudge. Get some exercise. Get some rest. Eat properly. Remember your breathing. Avoid trigger situations.'

'I CAN'T GO round like I'm enjoying myself though, can I? What if someone sees me?'

'Take no notice. You've done your time. You're entitled to go wherever you like,' Neil said. He misread the situation and continued, 'If they've read it in The Mail then it must be true, that's all they care about. They don't know that you talked that con down and gave that screw the kiss of life. None of them lot have ever saved anyone else's lives. You've saved three. Three! Saving plastic bags is as close to what some of them lot ever do.'

ALL A PERSON had when they were Inside was their word. Philip never stopped expecting a letter, but his Personal Officer said that maybe she just wanted to put it behind her and get on with her life, and that it wouldn't look good for him if he tried to find her when she clearly didn't want to be found. Once he realised that he wasn't as important to her as he thought he was, it was too late to do anything about it. Whilst you were holding the fish, you still had a chance to throw it back, but then you'd never see it again. Five years to learn the hard way to accept he may never get any answers, and all of the mantras in the world meant nothing. But at least now he knew she was okay. It wasn't over yet.

PHILIP. TODAY.

He still couldn't relax. He tried to be here now in the moment, and listen to the Social Anthropologist speaker on 'The Good Intent Stage' talking about how this festival reminded him of his recent visit to a Syrian refugee camp, but without the weather and not enough tents or food. How groups of people thrown together form communities and self-regulate in a confined space. That the unifying power of music made people pay to be enclosed in these metal walls for three days. Philip stopped listening after a while and let himself imagine how close she was to him right now. If he opened his eyes, she'd be there.

VEGAN FOOD WASN'T Philip's thing, but even Neil was surprised that he didn't have to be more persuasive. Then again, if all you'd eaten was canteen slop for five years, you'd try anything new.

'Spicy bean with apple slaw please. Um… is Emily working today? asked Phil.

'Emily? Nah, mate. There's no Emily working here. Sorry.'

Philip showed the burger van man the photo on his phone.

'Sorry mate, I've never seen her before. I wasn't here last year, but I know she doesn't work here now.'

After their burgers, Neil looked at the running order of the bands in the festival newspaper.

'Ah no. Airmail and Kickbacker are on at the same time,' said Neil. 'Which one do you want to go see?'

'Airmail will probably be on iPlayer so if we watch Kickbacker, then we'll be all set for The Inertia Creeps,' Philip replied.

'Down the front like we used to, back in the day?'

'Yeah why not? Sounds like a plan.'

MID-SET, BETWEEN SONGS, Airmail's guitar tech, was fiddling with some leads on stage, when the singer suddenly said 'Jimmy, my man. C'mere pal.' He put his arm around Jimmy's sweaty shoulder and addressed the crowd. 'Ladies and Gentlemen. Please put your hands together for our good friend Jimmy and our very talented chef M, who got married yesterday, right here on site! Not only that, they're going to have their very own Vegasbaby!' The crowd erupted in unison with a huge cheer. Modestly blushing, the shaggy-bearded, bald-headed roadie, wearing skinny black jeans and a t-shirt that said 'Kim is the real deal' took a bow. He kissed his hands, waved them high in the air like a proper rock star, and jogged offstage. The cameras caught him beaming a smile of pure joy as he locked eyes with, then hugged, a tanned, strong-limbed, young woman watching from the wings. Anonymous in this crowd, she wore the standard uniform of seasoned festival-goers. Hiking boots, denim cut-off shorts, an armful of wristbands, an AAA Airmail lanyard and a vintage Nirvana t-shirt, except hers was ever-so slightly stretched over her belly.

PHILIP. FIVE YEARS ago.

If he'd phoned her twenty minutes earlier, everything would have been different. He remembered Emily screaming on the phone, and knew she would be dead before he got there. Emily's statement said that the man held a screwdriver inside her ear and told her not to move or he'd push it into her brain. She never told the police that when Phil jumped on the man's back, she'd grabbed the screwdriver and within a couple of seconds had stabbed the man's neck. Philip never thought that the last thing he would ever say to her was 'RUN!'. There was a brief struggle but the man grew paler and his crackling breath rasped slower and slower. Philip stroked the man's head in his lap and said 'everything's going to be alright' over and over again, until it wasn't. Trembling with shame, Philip knew the one thing he could do was protect her now.

Seedlings

W. T. Paterson

IT WAS A silly thing to say, he meant nothing by it really, but his daughter found the idea to be horribly wretched.

'But Dad, I already swallowed a watermelon seed,' Heidi said, her ten-year-old eyes swelling with tears under the late June sun. The neighborhood barbecue was teeming with people stuffing their faces with juicy hotdogs, sizzling burgers with slices of cold yellow cheese, and cans of soda popping open like arthritic knuckles.

'Uh oh, Heidi,' Louis told her. 'Looks like you're going to have a watermelon grow inside of you.'

Louis should have told her it was a joke, he later realized. Kids didn't know any better, but also wasn't that a bit of the fun? A single father raising a daughter wasn't exactly the job he had hoped for, but it was the job he had been handed after his wife Alma had died of an unexpected aneurism on a flight back from London a year ago. She was the one who had done the bulk of the childcare while Louis was off consulting with growing businesses on how to create stable employee infrastructures. On days when he was home, more often than not, Louis felt like he was less of a father and more of a casual acquaintance to Heidi, his own daughter.

They had been invited to a neighborhood barbecue after moving out of Chicago and into the suburb of Evanston, Illinois. Neighbors saw the moving trucks and slipped an invite – a bright green photocopy of the fun details – under their door. Louis mentioned the party to their therapist who loved the idea and recommended getting back out there, that new friendships were often the key to overcoming tragedy because on the whole, people were welcoming.

It was true. An hour into the event and Louis had already gotten the phone number of three separate single mothers and was on his way to a fourth when Heidi butted in slobbering on a piece of watermelon, her lips bright pink and shiny with juice.

'Are we going to do anything for Mom's birthday?' she asked. It was an innocent question, they had discussed potentially heading to the cemetery with cake and flowers, but out of context it made Louis look like a dirty dog. The single mother scoffed, folded her arms across her bosom, and walked away mumbling about how all men were the same.

'Don't swallow any seeds,' he told Heidi, slightly annoyed. 'You don't want a watermelon to grow in your tum-tum.'

In truth, he felt that Heidi was a little too old to believe that a watermelon would actually grow in her little belly. She'd already debunked Santa Claus and the Tooth Fairy that year when she'd caught Louis in the act as he put sloppily wrapped presents under their Christmas tree, or loudly came clomping into her room with a fistful of singles to slip under her pillow. But for some reason, the idea of swallowing a seed stuck and the little girl looked as though she'd been handed a death sentence.

Heidi lowered the remaining chunk of melon and rind back towards her small paper plate and placed it on the chipped wooden table beside them. She placed a hand over her stomach and looked up at Louis.

'I don't feel well,' she said.

'It's probably already starting to grow,' Louis joked, looking to see if there were any other women around without husbands that he could schmooze with. It wasn't as though he was glad his wife was gone, it actually pained him horribly, severely even. It was that getting attention from someone new made him feel like he was in high school again where the idea of romance instead of pain was as wild and magical as sitting on the hood of an old beater car watching the sunrise with the captain of the girl's varsity soccer team.

Heidi rubbed her eyes with the back of her wrist and wandered over to a tree to sit by the gnarled stump in the shade.

'Not feeling well?' a woman asked, walking over holding a silver tray with a pyramid of rice crispy treats. She had close cropped black hair with angular bangs swooped across her face and tucked behind her right ear. A low cut maroon v-neck revealed an array of beaded turquoise necklaces against perfectly mocha skin. Gold and silver bracelets dangled off of her arms, one of which had a dream-catcher tattooed just below the crook of the elbow.

'She's fine,' Louis said. 'Stress of the move.' He craned his neck to look at the plate of treats and felt the sides of his tongue begin to water.

'Take two,' the woman said. 'I'm Navi.'

'Louis.'

Navi held out the shining metal plate while Louis took two squares that were stuck together. He nodded a quick thanks before shoving the first into his mouth and chewing without closing his lips. Crumbs sprayed out like sand from the back of a shoe after a day at the beach.

'So where are you from?' Navi asked. She placed the tray down on the chipped wooden table and politely sat on the accompanying bench. Louis instinctively followed. The day was unusually warm, something more in line with late August than early June.

'Chicago,' he said, licking his fingers of the excess sticky marshmallow. It reminded him of the time that he had lost his mother before Heidi was born, back when

Alma was new to the picture. Hesitant, he broke the news in an awkward phone call so filled with pain that he could barely keep his thoughts together.

'My mother is gone,' he said, startled by the pain of saying it out loud, let alone to someone he been dating for only a few months.

'Gone how?' Alma asked.

'To get cigarettes, like those dads that go get cigarettes and never come home,' he said, wincing at his own spiraling narrative. *She's dead*, he needed to say. *Just tell her she died. People have strokes all of the time.* But the words wouldn't come.

'That's weird,' Alma said. 'I didn't know she smoked.'

Louis thought about smoking, and then imagined his mother getting cremated. It broke something inside. The deep roots of strength that he believed existed at his core were nothing more than seedlings poking through the ground during the first rain of hurricane season.

'I'm not doing this right,' he said, and his throat let loose a primal groan that seemed more appropriate for a zombie movie than a phone call with bad news.

'Oh…Oh lord,' Alma gasped, realizing what he was trying to say. 'I'm at a gas station right now, but I'll come over right away. Work can do without me for an evening.'

Fifteen minutes later, Alma showed up at Louis' door with a thin plastic bag bustling with chips, candy bars, ice cream and soda. Louis fell to his knees and allowed himself to cry, to really accept the loss, and to let Alma see him as the broken man that he always knew he was.

Instead of passing judgment, Alma sat with him on the couch running soft fingers through his hair while the Chicago Blackhawks played on TV. They ate the junk food together burning through bags of salty chips, gooey chocolate, and fizzy drinks. They split a rice crispy treat, but as Louis ate his half, he caught Alma watching him.

'Take my half too.' She smiled. Louis took the piece from Alma's tender hands. He knew at once that he was deeply, madly, crazy in love and refused to imagine a future without the two of them together.

Now at the barbecue, the June sky hosting cotton candy clouds as a gentle wind skipped across the green grass chasing butterflies, everything began to sink back in. Life had continued to push forward even as he silently begged for it not to.

'I love Chicago,' Navi said. 'You ever go to Second City?'

'Can I ask you a question?' Louis said, interrupting. 'If a person swallowed a watermelon seed…'

He started to trail off realizing the lunacy of his question. Navi looked at Heidi who had moved to a different side of the tree. Neighborhood kids had gathered and were giggling, interested in befriending the new girl.

'My father is Native American,' Navi started. 'He honestly believes that we cycle through life experiencing the same events in different ways until we learn what we're supposed to learn. Then, once we learn that lesson, life will change and start a new series of cycles.'

'My mother died of a stroke, my wife because of an aneurism, and I made my little girl's head explode because I told her that eating a seed...' Louis paused again. Saying true things out loud was harder than lying. Being vulnerable wasn't something he came by naturally.

Heidi got up from the side of the tree as a trail of kids followed behind. She was clutching her stomach like she was carrying something heavy underneath.

'Daddy, you were right,' she said, lifting her shirt to show a swollen belly. It looked like the little girl was pregnant. The protruding rounded skin was solid and turning green. Red veins traced the sides like tiger stripes. Louis shot upright, shocked.

'What did you do?! How did this happen?' he asked, the same way he did when he found out Alma was pregnant. Alma was smiling while Louis was terrified that their life together would be irreversibly changed. He was right, just not in the way he had feared.

'I ate the seed,' Heidi said. The girl seemed far less concerned than Louis.

'Children find ways of making real the things we say,' Navi said, reaching forward and tickling Heidi's bare belly with the tips of her fingers. Heidi chuckled and stepped back.

'You don't see…' Louis started, pointing at his daughter's engorged, green stomach feeling horribly confused. 'I feel like I should get her to a doctor.'

Heidi shrunk away at the idea and turned to rejoin her new friends as they scampered back to the shade of the tree. A dog barked in the distance. Someone threw a yellow flying disc to their friend.

'Am I insane?' Louis asked.

'You're shouldering a lot of responsibility,' Navi said. 'It's natural to feel disconnected from time to time.' She pulled one of the treats from the tray and bit into one of the corners. 'What do you do for work?'

'Consultation for growing businesses. We help them build infrastructures. HR, accounts receivable, logistics, support, things like that.'

'That sounds helpful,' Navi said.

'For a growing business, absolutely. Otherwise it's chaos. People get very bitter.'

'So it's important that these growing businesses listen. It's important that they believe you.'

'That's the idea,' Louis said. Something about Navi reminded him of Alma. Maybe it was the dark hair and mocha skin. Maybe it was the way she listened without judgment and had an uncanny way of putting him at ease.

'My wife quit her job at a packaging plant to work for my company,' he said. 'She was our intake extraordinaire fielding phone calls, scheduling consultations. It was perfect. We sent her to conferences, let her work from home to be with Heidi. But that's what killed her. It was a work trip abroad and…pop.' He made a bursting motion with his fingers near the back of his head.

'Did you tell her that you loved her?' Navi asked, taking another slow bite of the rice crispy treat.

'Not nearly enough,' Louis answered.

'And your daughter?'

'She knows,' he said, and watched as the children began marching back over to the bench. Heidi was holding something in her arms that was wrapped in a beach towel. The children cooed and whispered with hands cupped to their mouths.

'Look Dad,' the little girl said, unfolding the towel. 'I had three watermelons. Aren't they cute?'

Louis was so startled that his whole body jolted backwards. The small watermelons were the size of chocolate Easter eggs, but more than that they appeared to be breathing and nuzzling against each other.

He grabbed the bottom of Heidi's shirt and lifted it to look at the girl's belly. It was no longer swollen and green, but rather back to the ten-year-old pudge it had always been.

'They're beautiful,' Navi said. 'You must be proud.'

'This is Nina, this is Pinta, and this is Santa Maria,' Heidi said. She looked at the small watermelons with large, loving and eyes.

'Who gave you those?' Louis asked. His voice was stern. 'What have I told you about strangers?'

'I know you're scared, Dad, but I swallowed the watermelon seed. It is I who must bare the consequences.'

Louis stood up ready to snatch Heidi and leave the barbecue. Whatever game she was playing, it wasn't funny. That phrase, *it is I who must bare the consequences,* was something that Alma had said over and over when making big decisions. He overheard her say it when she spoke with her boss on the phone when she left the packaging plant, at the OBGYN when she discussed the legacy of hemophilia in her family, and when she told Louis that she was in love with him. It was possible that Alma had also said it to Heidi, but he had never once heard her utter that phrase after their daughter's birth. He wondered if all that time away had done something irreparable to his relationships because he constantly found himself in the land of not knowing.

Navi extended a gentle arm and blocked Louis from stepping forward.

'Such a strong girl to go through this all by yourself,' Navi said to Heidi.

Heidi looked at her father and frowned. 'Sometimes we have to,' she said, and then walked back over to the shaded roots of the tree. The other children joined her.

'The first language a child learns is story,' Navi said. 'The second language is games, things like risk/reward, probability and chance, and *what if*. Their third language, which is spoken, becomes their native tongue.'

Louis felt crazy. Was no one else aware of the bizarre game his daughter was playing, let alone how she was pulling it off? Shouldn't he be putting in an emergency call to their therapist instead of sitting on a bench eating homemade desserts? He looked at Navi who didn't seem concerned at all and so he drew in a long, deep breath and exhaled.

'Did it hurt?' he asked.

'I'm not an angel, if that's what you're implying,' she said.

'Your tattoo,' Louis said, pointing to her arm.

'Oh, I thought you were using a pick-up line. You know, fell from heaven. Sorry.'

'I've always wanted one but could never commit to one design. I'm too afraid I'll regret it somewhere down the road.'

'The thing about permanence is that we adapt. Our choices become our lives and so imagining a life without those choices is fruitless,' Navi said, looking at Heidi. 'The things that are actually important to us, we don't wear them on our bodies.'

After Alma died, Louis had considered getting a tattoo of her name on his shoulder so that she'd always be with him. He'd gone so far as to show up to a parlor and talk with an artist – a woman with tattoos up and down both arms and neck – but backed out when it came time to make a deposit.

'She's with you regardless,' the woman said, un-offended by the last second cancellation. 'Be well.'

Shocked, Louis left the parlor wondering how many of his life perspectives had been misaligned, misinformed, and shaped by pain. That night, he swung by a pizzeria and grabbed a deep-dish pepperoni so that he didn't have to cook. He and Heidi ate it on their living room floor sitting side my side and leaning against each other for support. They put on a movie so that they could both share something else, and twenty minutes in, Heidi fell asleep in Louis' lap. He pushed some strands of hair out of his daughter's sleeping face and felt the terrifying pressure of raising a child alone. Alma had left him with such an enormous responsibility, but in watching his daughter sleep, he saw that she was still a part of them both in ways that he could have never imagined.

'Thank you for talking to me,' Louis said. Navi stood up and brushed a few renegade crumbs from her hips and knees.

'You're a good man, Louis,' she said. 'I hope you're able to see it, too.'

'Hey, you wouldn't want to maybe go out sometime, would you?'

'The cycle continues,' Navi said, this time with a hint of a frown. 'Heidi doesn't need a *mother* right now.'

They looked over and the young girl was walking back. She was carrying a full sized watermelon like a football.

'This is the only one left. It grew up faster than I was ready for.'

'Yeah, that's kind of how it goes,' Louis said.

'I'm sorry I ate the seeds, Daddy. I didn't know this would happen.'

'There was no way to know. It's impossible to know.'

'I'm in charge of this watermelon now, and I can't pretend I'm not.'

Louis pulled his daughter into an enormous hug. Scents of barbecue were locked in the fabric of her shirt and the back of her hair. The sun beat down casting their shadows in slender stretches behind them. Louis felt the seedlings inside of him start to sprout and blossom in spite of the hurricane. He needed his daughter as much as she needed him, and that was how they would both survive the storm.

'I love you,' he whispered so that only she could hear. 'You know that, right?'

'Yeah,' she said, the watermelon pressing into both of their bellies. 'It's just nice to hear it sometimes.'

The Storage Unit

Hilda Sheehan

FRANCES, I HAVE moved my final marriage contents into one of those Big Yellow Cupboards. It means all my life can be activated by a pin code and is individually alarmed if I call for help in my loneliness of old books and expired National Trust cards.

Like a panic room?

Yes, with 24/7 externally monitored CCTV. Staff on site seven days a week during trading hours.

Sounds like a psychiatric unit. Is it a psychiatric unit?

No, it's a storage unit with fire and smoke detection systems.

Are you planning a cry for help using fire and smoke, Martine?

No, Frances, I'm just moving into a storage unit, cheaper than a flat and with all my home comforts in a modern purpose-built store this side of Bristol.

There are no windows, Martine, and you can't lock it from the inside. What about your other storage unit neighbours? Will they intrude on your new uneventful life of stacked cushions and flat-packed love letters?

They'll never know I'm there. I'm taking my funeral arrangements and a well-chosen coffin.

Blue Swing

Matty Bannond

IT WAS LATE August and Louisa was five months pregnant when I told her I was going to steal part of our neighbours' swing. We'd just moved into our house and were staring at the TV, balanced on an upturned plastic crate, the screen filling up with red and green as the camera zoomed in on a rhubarb tartlet.

Louisa's wrists were swollen and her jawline had softened, but I could still see her tendons constrict. 'And now *this*,' she said. 'Who's *this* for?'

'It's for their little lad.'

She reached back to grab her ponytail, pulled it taut.

My voice was strained and unsteady when I spoke again. 'He plays on it nearly every day after school – I see him when I get home,' I said. 'He goes on the swing next to the part that's been painted blue and his mate, that scruffy blond boy, sits on the one by the unpainted bit. The poor lad must know it didn't get finished because his parents have separated, Louisa. And the top beam isn't painted either.'

A rush of heat tightened my throat so I opened the second button on my polo shirt. It popped off and landed in her mug on the coffee table. A great shot. I fished it out. Louisa's eyes narrowed.

I made her another cup of tea.

'So why does that mean you have to sneak into their garden and damage it?'

'I'm only going to chip a bit off. To take to the DIY shop and get a matching shade of paint. Then I'll sneak in again and paint it. The dad's not going to do it, is he? Somebody should help them.'

'So you're going to break in *twice*?'

She turned back to the TV.

I loaded the dishwasher and then headed upstairs, where I put a pair of black jeans and a navy jumper on top of a stack of boxes on the landing before setting my alarm for 3:15am.

WHEN IT RANG, I slid out of bed and got dressed in the bathroom, half-lit by streetlight ghosting through the small window. Then I went downstairs and put on my smartest shoes – the only black ones I've got.

The soles clattered against the pavement as I made my way to the house with the swing, an end terrace on the other side of the street about five doors down. The garden gate was locked so I placed my hands on the metal posts and swung myself over. My shoes slapped the paving stones. A rabbit thumped its back feet in a hutch that was positioned against the side of the house, haloed by speckles of black mould on the white wall.

Using the heavy spatula I'd brought from the kitchen, I chivvied a shard of wood free from the painted part of the swing. I think it's probably called a stanchion: two wooden posts dug into the ground to form a triangle. My dad never taught me any practical stuff like that, and I don't own any tools. That's why I was using a spatula.

During my lunchbreak the next day a friendly woman in the DIY shop put the piece of swing under a scanner and got me the right blue paint. She told me I needed special stuff for wooden things that are kept outside. I bought a cheap brush and some glue to reattach the fragment I'd stolen. It was bigger than I'd planned. Then I decided to go back into the garden that night because it was forecast to stay dry.

Louisa was in a great mood: she laid my clothes out on the stack of boxes after dinner (calling it my ninja costume) and put my painting stuff and the glue in a tote bag for me so it wouldn't rustle like a plastic bag. I hadn't thought of that. Maybe she felt partly responsible because she'd told me that the couple with the side garden had broken up. She'd heard it from one of the student lads who live next door. They'd had to intervene one night when the husband was standing on the drive and bellowing up at the bedroom window.

The gate was unlocked this time. I put my bag down, opened the tin of paint and removed my brush from a plastic wrapper that crackled loudly. Then I got to work, sweeping strokes this way and that. The grass was long and a few blades at the base of the stanchion clung to the paint like wet hair, but mostly it went well.

I imagined my mum whispering words of encouragement. She was always building me up when I was a kid, whooping and punching the air if I finished a paint-by-numbers or a sandwich or a bowel movement, but then disappearing for what felt like weeks at a time to sell affordable IT equipment to schools that couldn't afford it. That left me with Dad, who was always there but usually facing the wrong way. I'd run towards the touchline with my arms aloft and he'd be scowling into the distance beyond the corner flag, straining to identify an osprey or a goshawk or some other feathery trollop. Or I'd look out from the front of the school assembly hall, a certificate fluttering in my trembling hands, to see his eyes trained down, inspecting the workmanship where the parquet floor had been repaired.

I had to do much better.

I was enjoying myself until I realised I couldn't reach the top bar supporting the two swings. I jumped a couple of times and managed to dab the tip of the brush against the underside, but it wouldn't be enough. A cluster of metal chairs were leaning against a small round table beside a shed with a half-collapsed roof. I pulled one away and placed it beneath the swing before standing on the seat and resting the bottom of my paint pot on the top of the seatback as I stretched upwards. *All or nothing.*

As I bent down to dip my brush into the pot something caught my eye: streaks of orange streetlight bouncing off the panels of the husband's leather jacket as he leant on the garden gate watching me, his heap of curly hair backlit like a crown of tumbleweed. He was thinner than I remembered, and taller too. His nose, lips and jaw were clearly defined but swollen, like the slightly melted face of a handsome action figure. He opened the gate and walked in, setting a slim suitcase down on the metal table before removing his rucksack and dropping it on the ground.

'What's she been doing to get you painting the bloody swing in the middle of the night?' he said. 'Don't you live around here? Aren't you the one with the wife who's *pregnant*?'

They were fair questions. I felt the chair wobble.

He moved towards me and I stumbled off, dropping the paint pot onto the floor before quickly scooping it up.

'Shhhhh! Yes, Louisa is pregnant. But I've never even spoken to your wife. I just wanted to paint the swing. To help. As a favour.'

He glared at me and then snorted a laugh, his hand rising to cover his mouth. Then he grabbed one of the metal chairs from beside the shed and sat down. 'Alright. You go for it, mate.'

I told him my name and he introduced himself as Molly, short for Malcolm, in a watery Scottish accent. His back was slightly hunched and I saw crooked teeth as he popped a cigarette between his lips. He went to put the packet back into the front of his rucksack but then held it out towards me. I told him I didn't smoke.

'Of course you don't,' he said. 'Have you still got enough paint, Dave?'

My hands fumbled on the ground for the paint pot. It was still about three-quarters full. I nodded, climbed back onto the chair and started painting again.

'Tell me about yourself,' I said, performing a dismissive wave of my brush. 'What do you do for a living? How long have you lived down here?'

'I play the bass guitar. Jazz.' He shrugged. 'I've been living here for about twenty years, but I travel a lot. That'll be why we've never been introduced.' He seemed shy about it. I told him I thought it was great.

'I don't know anything about jazz but it must be amazing to play in front of big crowds all the time. What are you doing living around here if you're famous?'

'I'm not famous and there are no big crowds.' He sounded annoyed. 'Nobody listens to jazz except smelly old men and people who want their friends to think they're more intelligent than they really are. Sometimes there are more of us on the stage than in the audience. So you can imagine, Dave, that it doesn't pay too well. Not that I don't like it here.'

The first half of the swing's top beam was now slick and glistening. I picked up the chair and planted it alongside the second swing, where Molly's son usually sat. I had an idea.

'Can you play something now?' I asked. 'My wife wants our baby to play a musical instrument. Maybe if I know more about it, I might be able to help.'

He shrugged again and said he didn't want to wake his wife or son. I kept asking him – I'm like that – until he unpacked a laser blue bass guitar from its case. It wasn't plugged in, but I could hear what he was playing. His left hand clasped the neck of the instrument while the fingers on his right hand plucked, flapped and slapped away at the strings. His shoulders rocked from side to side and his chin seemed to pulsate.

'What do you want to hear?'

'I don't know any jazz songs. Just play what you normally play. What about some of the songs you did tonight?'

I turned away and started painting again. Maybe it would be easier for him if I wasn't looking – Louisa always stops singing in the car if I turn to face her, but if I ignore her, she really goes for it. Banging her hands on the steering wheel and everything.

Now that I'd already been caught, I took my time. I made sure the paint was even around the fixtures where the chains joined the top beam. Molly kept playing his jazz music until I had to say something.

'Are these really *songs*? With a start and a middle and ending and a *tune*? Because it sounds like you're starting a new song every five seconds. Is that how it's supposed to be?'

Molly rested his palms across the strings at either end of the guitar. 'I'm following a pattern, but I'm improvising,' he said. 'Making it up as I go along.'

It was only then that I noticed that he didn't have a music stand. I asked him if that was why he wasn't playing any real *songs*. Or was it because he just played the bass line and the other instruments were supposed to do the melody? But he was playing a lot of notes for a bass line. Even I knew that.

'I don't need any sheet music.' He laughed a little bit. 'I can just play whatever I want.'

'Isn't that basically like a toddler punching the keyboard on a piano?'

He shrugged. 'Not really. It's a mixture of skill on your instrument, knowledge of how music is put together, and just… experience of composing melodies on the run.'

Our voices had got louder. I turned back to my painting. He spoke again, this time more softly.

'Anyone can do it. You can do it. *Now.*'

I dipped my brush into the pot and shook my head. 'I don't know anything about music, Molly. Even less than I know about painting.'

His eyes narrowed. He looked tired but like he wasn't ready to give up, like a very drunk person ordering another pint. He asked me to name a song I knew. I couldn't think of one – I'm not a big music person – so he picked one for me. *Happy Birthday.*

'You know how *that* goes, right?'

I nodded.

He began playing the song very slowly. He went through it three times and then started adding a few extra notes. When he went around the fifth time he added even more. Each time he got to the start of the tune, he'd add more notes and leave out more of the normal notes from the song. Eventually, he was playing something completely different, except somehow I could still tell it was *Happy Birthday.* He'd probably done this trick on other people thousands of times before. He had me going, anyway.

'Now it's your turn.' He kept playing, long notes that followed the shape of the song from start to finish. 'Just hum or sing "la" or whistle. Whatever you like. Not too loud. Just do whatever comes into your head.'

I reached up to press the bristles of my brush deep into a small hollow in the top beam. Molly was still playing the shape of the song, nice and slowly. The smell of the paint was sharp, almost like lemon.

I began to hum the tune quietly. 'Hmf-hmf-hmmf-hmmf… hmmf-hmmmmf.'

I hummed until I got to the end of the song, then started from the beginning, this time adding a few extra hums in the space after "to you". We went around again and I kept building in more and more new bits. Molly somehow changed what he was playing until it sounded like something Bob Marley would do – a sort of reggae version of *Happy Birthday*. I kept going, just humming whatever came out. I made little shapes that seemed to tie together. The notes were in my ears before they were in my mouth. Rising runs, long notes, sounds that stopped suddenly or that wavered in pitch and faded until I couldn't hear them but could still feel them in my ribcage.

I noticed that Molly was playing his bass more and more slowly, so we ended our song together with a long note. He slumped forward in his chair, cuddling the bass as his hunched back folded over towards the dry grass. I giggled and sniffed. My eyes were damp.

'That's it, Dave. You're a natural born improviser,' he said, clapping his right hand against the body of his guitar.

I stepped down from the chair and shook his hand. He wiped his palm against his jeans. Then he packed his bass into its case, stood up, and pulled a set of keys out of the front pocket of his rucksack. I noticed the curtains in one of the upstairs windows twitching, but I didn't mention it. We said goodbye and I scurried off home pretty quickly. To tell you the truth, I needed a moment to myself.

Anyway, I think Molly's moved out for good since then and his son doesn't go on the swing now it's winter, even though the blue paint looks gorgeous against the cool sky. Since our daughter, Juliana, was born just over a month ago, I've been helping Louisa as much as I can and helping Juliana with baths, changing nappies and hundreds of other things. I cut all the remaining buttons off my polo shirts, for example, so the hard plastic doesn't scratch her face when she cuddles into my chest.

And when she cries at night, I pick her up and walk up and down the landing. I peek out through the bathroom window at the blue swing and sing her a song that starts off like *Happy Birthday* but changes into something new. Something better. Maybe it'll help her develop a gift for music or perhaps she'll help Molly by becoming part of a new wave of young jazz fans.

In the weak light, I sometimes imagine myself sitting in the front row at school concerts, the shadowy outline of a young woman taking deep breaths as she waits for the stage lights to come on. And when they do, I'll be there. Always there, every time. And always facing the right way. Ready for anything.

Dancing Crimson
Claire Hinchliffe

EGGS.

Eggs, potatoes, onions, spices, oil, tomatoes and ham. Cheese, optional.

Eggs.

Eggs, potatoes, onions…eggs.

It's a long list. Miranda can remember the first three items but not the rest. She copies from '*Meals for One*' cookbook onto the notepad, making sure to write in quite large letters so it will be legible in the shop. Last week she didn't do this and when she stood in front of the supermarket aisles with a page of scribble, it was no good. No good at all.

She starts looking. Loads of cupboards, too many. The first is full of plates, all the same. The second is much more interesting. There's a strange silver bowl covered in tiny holes, like rain and sprinkles and Blackpool. On the beach she kissed a man and the waves, the waves, the wind and sand in her eyes. The bowl's so cold she moves on to cupboard number three. Jackpot! Potatoes and onions are in the same place – the big drawer underneath the knives and forks. It takes four minutes to distinguish potatoes from the other veg. There's so many different kinds she has to check the list for broccoli or carrots.

No broccoli. No carrots.

It's boring and she's tired and aching.

The silver bowl with holes and the man she kissed until she was sprinkling and coming apart.

She takes the potatoes and onions and places them on the table, next to the list. She places a large tick against their names, so that later on she'll be clear about what to buy. But should she cross the items out altogether? If she deletes, she won't have to spend ages considering in the shop but then again if she leaves them, she can use the list to show Mum. Too many decisions, it's too many and anyway she can't show Mum. Not until visiting time.

Miranda sits on the tall pink plastic chair. Only a few ticks of a lamb's tail. 'I'll just tick.'

Tick-tock-tick-tock… Because potatoes and onions were fairly easy to find she goes back to the big drawer and hunts for the other items. Perhaps everything will be here? 'Come to Momma!' If she can find them quickly and get to the shop, she should be able to rush back and spend a lot of time getting ready.

Cheap thrills and Da-da-da-da-daa!

The silver bowl, the kiss and Mum in the care home

now. She sits again but tick-tock-tick-tock.

It takes another ten minutes, two minutes longer than her time guide for keeping calm. After the eight-minute threshold, sprinkles start coming through the holes in the bowl. She got told off for kissing the man, thirty years ago. All she wants is to kiss again but there are eggs and potatoes and too many things. Wants, wanted, will want. All the wanting. Too much for one crappy kitchen.

'No sodding tomatoes!' she shouts. It doesn't matter, there's nobody in her flat to hear. 'Why isn't there?'

The leaking sprinkles turn into rage, or anger but who cares. Is there any difference?

After the shoulders, rage can sometimes – often – move onto volatile behaviours such as throwing, but today Miranda is able to stop this advance. 'Stand up straight,' she says, just the same as Bill the therapist. 'Hands out. Round and round.'

It's boring and she's cold and tired. Fuck sake. On the beach that day she had so much energy she could have climbed to the moon. Maybe that's what she should've done.

By the time the index finger on her right hand makes circles on her left palm, Miranda's shoulders are starting to slip down past the point of no return. On some days this can take a long time. On other days Bill's skills are a fucking waste of time. Maybe Bill should try kissing?

Sprinkles, kissing.

Today, there's a very good reason to concentrate. She has a juicy carrot and an incentive. It's enough to start writing again: lipstick, eyeshadow, perfume. She thinks about perfumes and cost – her budget for the meal is a tenner – however, first impressions are very important and anyway she wants them. She wanted the man on the beach too but police and chasing and Mum was crying. It was only a ripped skirt. She sits on the plastic chair and strokes its bold edges.

She crosses out eye shadow but underlines perfume and lipstick.

Finding the items is taking up a lot of energy so a cup of tea might be a good idea. As she opens the fridge, Miranda hits the jackpot again because there, right in front, are tomatoes and ham. 'Mamma Mia!'

She yanks them out and plops them onto the table next to the list, where she notices there's only three items left to find, three items with no tick.

Tick-tock-tick-tock.

Eggs, spices, oil.

She makes the tea because she's thirsty, and dehydration would not be good for the forthcoming events of the day. Not very good at all.

Eggs, spices, oil.

She knows not to leave the fridge door open. Wasting the world's resources is something she often worries about, and that includes leaving on lights and hair straighteners. As she pushes the fridge door shut, she sees the empty plastic box with little pods like space beds.

No eggs.

'Fuck.' She writes eggs on the list, which is looking, not long, but more complicated than she would have liked. Fuck, like the man on the beach.

Eggs, perfume, lipstick.

Fuck.

She cannot look away from the deleted eyeshadow.

She has no sodding clue where oil and spices are. What are spices? Does she like spices? Will it interfere with her new perfume? There was The Spice Girls and dancing in the club.

You can't make omelette without all the ingredients, so she resumes her search. On the window ledge a few small jars of dust are arranged. Paprika, chili, salt and pepper. Pepper is labelled as spice. She snatches it up and onto the table it goes, thank you very much.

Suddenly she remembers the olive oil! Mum always likes a lot on salad but Miranda doesn't. It's in a huge carton with potential for spillages. It's kept in the washing machine room. Mum only sits still now. Big scary eyes. Did she drink too much oil? Is that why her brain went south? She needs a good pinch.

Miranda's ready, and in a very good mood. So far everything has gone well! Mum'll be pleased. The achievements include copying a recipe and more exciting – a decision to buy lipstick and perfume!

All this leads to a few stomach flutters of anticipation about this afternoon.

After putting on her coat, she re-writes eyeshadow and then sets off.

***

ON THE WALK to the supermarket, she's plagued by worries about the afternoon. To some extent a potential new lipstick eases this discomfort, as does ticking off the landmarks of the journey.

Lamppost.

Garden gnome.

Red door.

It is a short walk encompassing three kinds of pavement and a crossing with traffic lights. The number 67 bus and the tram follow this route.

Red door.

Why is the red door open? The red door is never open.

Mum hardly ever used to sit down.

Open legs, slutty slut.

Fuck. Miranda has to stop at the red door because it's open. She has no eggs for the omelette, needs new lipstick for the afternoon but now her plans are screwed because she has to stop. The red door is never open.

Fuck!

The red door is a gate into the garden of number 55 Penistone Road. It's always closed. Always. It needs to be closed before she can go on.

She looks up and down the street. Cars zoom by and a number 67 bus approaches. No people. The landmarks in the direction of home can easily be seen from this point – lamppost, garden gnome. By turning in the opposite direction, the going away landmarks are also visible. Pizza place, hairdresser, bus stop and tram cables.

Except for the red door, all is OK.

The red door is always closed. Keep your hand on your h'penny.

'Stand up straight!' she says loudly, not quite a shout. Closing the red door would be easy. It would not be against the law. It would make everything a lot easier. Making circles on her palm is enough to prevent the need to shout swear words.

Briskly, she closes the red door and continues on with her journey to the shop, heart hammering. Twice she looks behind to check if anyone is following to reprimand her.

Pizza place.

Hairdresser.

Bus stop.

Tram cables.

She must stop for the tram cables, as always. The complicated network is far too interesting to ignore. It's integral and vital. Up above, wires crisscross and converge because it's a junction. Trams go into the depo and also come out, on their way to town centre. Beneath the rubber casing, wiring sends electronic messages to some centre point of knowledge. Miranda would really love to visit that centre, but not today because she needs the eggs and the lipstick.

Not tonight, Josephine.

With difficulty, she walks away from the junction and on towards the shop, looming now at the far end of the street. Near enough to know she's going to make it! Two weeks ago, a lorry had broken down, making it impossible for pedestrians to make their journeys. A man dressed in bright yellow had tried to explain she needed to cross to the other side. Needed to cross to the other side and Mum needed to go in the care home, need is a bloody fuck. It did not go well. It did not go well at all. You can stick your need up your arse.

But today there's nothing to prevent Miranda from buying the eggs and the lipstick. Buying the eggs will enable her to make the omelette and the lipstick will help her get ready for the afternoon.

Kissy-kiss kiss.

Bang bang.

***

THE MAKE-UP AISLE is gorgeous. She wants to stay there a

long time. Rows of colours are arranged into shades and numbers, little brushes, pallets and tubes, planets and seas and rolling in the hay. Thankfully, nobody has messed up the categories or left whole rows empty. People can be such bastards.

She can't choose between Dancing Crimson or Bewitching Scarlet. Dancing is dark red, almost purple, Bewitching is more girly pink. She can be both. Can't she? Whichever she chooses, she won't have to dance or bewitch because the words are only marketing.

She might though. She might bewitch like the man on the beach and then tee-hee-hee.

It's not an easy decision. Miranda wants both. It's all she wants. If she buys both, she'll be very happy. Mum would want that. To help decide, she finds the list and is shocked to see she also needs eggs, eyeshadow and perfume with a question mark. Bloody hell! She remembers the afternoon and the time, tick-tock.

Date.

Both. Yeah. She makes a decision to buy both lipsticks, although she won't be able to wear them both this afternoon. Will she?

Genius idea and the silver sprinkles spinning – she could wear Bewitch on the top lip and Dancing on the bottom but not her bottom arse.

Tee-hee-hee.

Both. There's no time to look at eyeshadow and perfume and anyway those things no longer matter because she of two lipsticks.

She places the precious lipsticks carefully, so they don't fall through the holes in the basket. Things have fallen out before and it wasn't very good. No good at all. Falling out like the baby did and then where did it go?

Woosh. Gone. Baby all gone. Sad face.

Eggs.

Once she gets the eggs, she'll pay using the money Sheila Helpsout put in her purse. Then she can put her purchases in her bag and leave. The walk home will take fifteen minutes. Miranda will be able to make the omelette and try out the lipsticks. There'll be lots of time. No need to think about the baby and shoulders down.

Eggs.

Miranda has no fucking clue where the egg aisle is and this is very stressful. Not as much as the baby. She walks briskly up and down the aisles. Left-right-left-right… Goods rush past, people pushing, buggies and kids everywhere. Why don't the shop owners label eggs at the entrance? Stupid fucking arseholes.

Eggs.

She sees a shop worker and decides to approach. This won't be easy. 'Stand up straight!' She does Bill's technique three times. She has to put the basket on the floor. Her hands are sweaty. She marches to the worker and asks him without looking, 'excuse me please where are the eggs please?'

Eggs.

'Just there, love.' He points to the adjacent row. 'Don't forget your basket. You left it up there on the floor.'

Oh my god! Miranda rushes back for the basket with the lipsticks but she's almost done. Triumphantly she makes her way to where the worker pointed.

It says eggs, in large letters. A label says eggs, yes, and the shelf is right there but it is empty of eggs. There are absolutely no eggs, not one. On the floor is a mop and bucket and a sign saying *wet be careful.*

Silver bowl – potatoes – tomatoes – lipstick – kissing and they called it sex – lights – lights – fucked up – no good – slutty – waster – loser.

Baby.

It was there and then it wasn't.

No eggs.

No baby.

'No eggs!' Miranda shouts. 'No eggs – no eggs – no eggs!'

She shouts some more, and more. It pours out a tornado tsunami and sprinkles of herself. Not much left after the baby.

The worker is pulling her arm. Sorry, miss, I forgot. We're waiting for the eggs. We had an accident.'

'No fucking eggs!' She can't stop it. They took the

baby, her baby, took·it forever and ever.

Overtakes. The rage overtakes and then she punches out and someone pushes her and lays on top. They don't bring back her baby. The basket overturned. Dancing Crimson rolls away under the shelves, into the dust with the baby.

Forever is a long time but it never leaves her head.

***

THE POLICE LADY, Barb, hands a cuppa tea. The tea in the station is always good. They know to add sugar and lots of milk. She might even be offered a biscuit, like last time, or even a mini-meal like the time with the punching. 'Here you go, Miranda. They run out of eggs?'

So tired. Miranda shakes her head wearily. All burned out, burned out to the ground. 'I wanted to make an omelette. For my date. He's called Simon and he likes cars and trains. I met him at the centre. It's our first date but I won't have another baby.'

'Oh, love.'

There won't be any date now because she didn't get the eggs and time has run out. Dancing Crimson is probably still under the shelves and god only knows where the baby is. Miranda has fucked up. Miranda always fucks up. Miranda will always fuck up. She can't cook an omelette and Mum has lost her brain.

'You're not allowed back in the shop. Not for a while.

OK? I'll go and talk to the manager, he'll come round in a few weeks. Just don't go back, love, not until I tell you. I'll take you home.'

'OK.' It doesn't matter now. Nothing does. 'I want my baby.' The words don't come out right.

'Oh, love. Here.' Barb hands something over. You can't always take gifts because of danger like fireworks, that time. It's Dancing Crimson, still shiny and new. Brilliant and beautiful, a shooting star in a dark day. The baby's gone but Dancing Crimson is here in her hand. One day it will slip through her fingers like everyone else even though it feels solid. 'Thought you'd want it.'

It's not enough. 'But I didn't pay.' It never will be. Not all the lipsticks in the world will bring the baby back. Tiny fingers all wrinkled up waiting to be loved.

'Yes?'

In the sun, Dancing Crimson looks like crystals and diamonds. She isn't going to say yes, she isn't. 'I didn't pay.'

'Fuck that. I paid. A little prezzie. I knew you'd want it.'

Miranda's hand wobbles up and down like Mum's, all shaken up with silver sprinkles and the open door. No eggs. There are no open doors, not anymore. 'Thank you.'

'If we get a rush on, you can still do it, Miranda! We can make the date. Then you can tell your mum all about it. Eh?'

'No eggs.' No eggs, no mum, no baby, open door, too much life left, stretching on and on and on.

'Oh, love. Fuck eggs. I bet Simon doesn't even like eggs and they give you bad breath.' Barb breathes forward in Miranda's face and laughs. 'And farts. You don't want him going home farting, do you?' Miranda laughs too, thinking of farting at dates. 'I'll make sarnies while you doll yourself up. It'll be fine, my love. We'll make you look gorgeous. Eh?' Barb squeezes her hand like Mum used to, before they took her away. 'What do you say?'

'Yes.'

A Longing for Clouds
Amanda Huggins

MAGGIE SPRAWLED IN the dust, drowning in the pungent scent of overripe mangoes. A familiar voice repeated her name, and there was something hard pressing into the small of her back. When she opened her eyes, Vishal's hand reached out to pull her to her feet.

'Lady Margaret? Let me help you.'

She could see the unspoken question in his eyes, and she snatched her hand back and flapped him away, the silver bangles on her wrists jangling like wind chimes.

'I'm not drunk!' she snapped. 'I slipped, that's all. On this rubbish. I don't need your help.'

She waved her hands again, indicating the rotting fruit and vegetables strewn around the stall, and rubbed her grazed elbow as she walked out of the market. Vishal ran after her, and handed over two forgotten bags of spices and tomatoes. She took them from him without a word, and placed them inside the door at the foot of the steps leading to Amit's bar. She just needed one quick drink before she went home and then she'd be fine.

Why was everyone always telling her she needed help all of a sudden? Since when had they started seeing her as elderly or frail, or somehow incapable?

'Let me help you carry these things, Lady Margaret.'

'Take my arm, Lady Margaret.'

'I will bring a chair for you, Lady Margaret.'

When did they all decide she was a lady? And why couldn't they call her Maggie as she asked?

She felt the heat as a tangible weight, coating her with its heavy, slippery skin. She sat outside on the balcony, watching rickshaws and handcarts wind their way along the street below, and Vishal's scales glinting in the sun as he weighed out jeera and turmeric. Amit nodded to her as he squeezed fresh limes into a chilled soda. He brought it across to the table with a bottle of vodka. She added a large measure to the glass and ran her finger down the condensation on the outside, pausing for a moment before she drank, anticipating the citrus tang and the slow fire of the spirit.

There were voices and laughter on the steps; a couple appeared on the balcony and sat down at the next table. They filled every inch of space with their youth, their sprawling limbs and their tanned faces. The girl tipped out the contents of her shopping bags, and examined the scarves and spices she had bought. The man got up to fetch an ashtray from the bar. As he brushed past her,

Maggie caught the scent of sandalwood on warm skin, and she thought of her father.

She could picture him, freshly shaven, knocking on her mother's bedroom door, dressed for dinner in a starched shirt and bow tie, and her mother, standing at the long mirror in a nile green gown, fastening diamond clips to her ears.

As the man returned with the ashtray, she caught sight of her reflection in the glass door. Frayed at the edges; a face reddened and coarsened by one too many days in the sun and one too many bottles of cheap vodka. She felt crushed beneath the weight of her tiredness, a weariness that increased year upon year in the oppressive heat. Every summer she prayed for the monsoon to come early, and after the rains she was grateful for the brief lull and the warm, musty damp. Maggie couldn't even remember why she'd stayed on in India any more. It was years since her friends had left, one by one, heading back to England as their money ran out. Most of them were virtuous, clean-living citizens now, their hippie days long since left behind.

She called over to Amit and asked him for another bottle of vodka. The couple were laughing too loudly and she needed to leave. She placed the bottle in her bag and headed down the stairs, taking the short cut through the alleyway. At the other end of the street the town gave way to countryside. A group of women were working in the distance, their covered heads bobbing like vivid flowers in the expanse of fresh green shoots. Even in the heat the red earth smelt rich and fertile. The only sound she could hear was the faint tinkle of the tiny bells on the women's bracelets and ankle chains.

The noise reminded Maggie of the dress she wore to Deepak's wedding; cerulean blue with bells around the hem. It conjured the warmth of the soft Jaipur dusk; the air heavy with incense and sandalwood attar, the gate adorned with flowers. Bright saris, silk scarves billowing like jewel-bright parachutes. The bride, nervous and pale, beautifully gift-wrapped in red and gold.

Deepak had promised to protect her, to love her always, yet he was taken from her by a shy temptress and family tradition. The prince took his princess; a startled fawn with dark, wide eyes, and Maggie was left on her own as the words of the ceremony floated across the lawns.

'We have become partners. I have become yours. Hereafter, I cannot live without you.'

She reached the house, her rambling rose of a house with its leaking roof, its stained pink walls and wild, abandoned garden. Sanjay jumped up from his rope charpoy, and reached for the bags of shopping. She walked past him and sank onto the couch beneath the ceiling fan. He fetched a tumbler for the vodka, followed by bowls of rice and daal.

'You must eat, Lady Margaret,' he said.

'What would I do without you, Sanjay? Your superb cooking, and all your help.' There it was again. The 'help' word. She didn't need help, she had always managed everything quite well on her own. Yet she knew that Sanjay was doing more and more. She still brought home spices from the market, fooling herself that she was doing the shopping, yet it was Sanjay who did all the heavy work, who organised the meals and the laundry.

She watched him move quickly around the kitchen. He had been with her so long, had grown old with her. She knew so little about him, yet had given so much of herself away over the years. Careless words while under the influence. And Sanjay had never married, yet she could see that he was still an attractive man.

He looked at her now from the kitchen doorway, and she was scared to meet his eyes in case she saw pity. Yet when she did he was smiling.

'It is nothing, Lady Margaret, I am doing the job you pay me to do. You have always been good to me.'

'I hope we are friends, too, Sanjay?'

He stared at her unblinking, unsure, almost like a startled gazelle, then turned away as he answered.

'That would not be right, Lady M.'

She felt snubbed for a moment, wrong-footed, but she didn't let him see her discomfort. Instead she lay back on the couch and picked up the photograph of Michael.

Michael, the son she had left behind, the boy she didn't understand; the boy that wanted something from her that she didn't know how to give. She'd betrayed him, and she knew it was too late for atonement. The only time anyone had ever asked Maggie for help was when Michael's father asked her to go home, to take responsibility, had said he couldn't cope without her. And she'd said no.

And now she had nothing left, nothing except for the house, the heat, and the unending wait for the rains. Sometimes she wondered if she could take that one final journey. More and more, she ached with a longing for clouds; for the grey clouds of suburbia. A longing for home. And only Michael could save her.

'Sanjay, could you bring me some writing paper please?'

***

THE MONSOON WAS late. For weeks now, Maggie had searched the sky for clouds, praying for rain to dissolve the unbroken blue.

She sat down at her usual table on Amit's balcony, peeling wisps of damp hair from her forehead. Vishal had closed his stall early and was sat in the shade of the doorway below, chatting with his friends, sipping cold lassi. Amit placed a jug of fresh lime soda on her table and a tall tumbler, followed by a new bottle of vodka, the seal still intact.

'I am thinking the rains must come today, Lady Margaret,' he said. He leaned over the balcony as though to seek proof.

She didn't answer, but poured herself a glass of neat vodka, ignoring the soda.

Footsteps thudded up the wooden stairs, and a young couple appeared in the bar. They whispered in Spanish and stepped outside to sit at the next table. The girl smiled at her, but didn't speak. The man ordered two beers.

She watched them for a minute before she finished her drink. Then she put the bottle of vodka into her bag, next to the envelope containing her air ticket and the letter from Michael; the hoped for, but unexpected reply to her own letter, offering a journey to salvation and a home in which to end her days. 'Her proper home', he said in the letter. It appeared they wanted to help her, he and his wife, Alice, and they accepted that the past was water under the bridge. They were welcoming her with open arms to the mock-Tudor avenues of suburban north London, to the tired, distant drone of the M1.

She had considered their offer of help. A help she didn't deserve, born out of duty, nothing else – she accepted that. The kind of help that could – that would – turn to bitterness and resentment if she proved a burden. Yet in a way that was better – she couldn't bear the weight of kindness when she herself had been so seldom kind.

And what was the alternative? Sanjay's help. A help that was bought with money. And stupidly she had let her guard down, had fooled herself that they were friends, that he cared about her. So now she had no choice but to leave.

She picked up her small suitcase and went out into the street. Amit called down to her.

'Lady Margaret! Memsahib! There are clouds. I tell you, the rains are coming!'

She looked up and saw it was true. She could feel the hint of a breeze on her bare arm. And as she reached the taxi stand the sky opened wide, spilling fat raindrops that danced on the car bonnets like jumping beans. The water ran in rivulets beneath her feet, turning the dusty earth to mud.

She opened the taxi door and put her suitcase on the seat.

'Airport, miss?' asked the driver.

Maggie told him to wait a moment, and took the vodka out of her bag, thrusting it into a nearby bag of rubbish. She looked down at her shoes, caked with red earth, and saw the rain dancing on every surface, dripping from leaves like molten glass, hammering on the corrugated roofs. Every year the rain washed away her self-pity and despair, and she could breathe again. The tension left her body. India was beautiful.

What had she been thinking? How could she possibly

leave?

She retrieved the vodka, and pushed Michael's letter to the bottom of the rubbish. Then she lay down in the road, a rain-starved flower, and let the torrent of water bring her back to life.

A pair of worn leather chappals appeared at the side of her, level with her face. She examined the long toes, the neatly cut nails.

'Come back to the house, Lady Margaret.'

She looked up at him. 'Why have you followed me?'

Sanjay paused, his clothes drenched, water dripping from his face.

'Because you are my friend,' he said at last.

'Well call me Maggie then, Sanjay, for goodness sake.'

'Come home ... Maggie,' he said shyly.

She held out her hand and let him help her up. He retrieved her case from the taxi and they walked home together, arm in arm.

Charity Ends at Home

Louise Mangos

MONSIEUR GIRARD'S GRIP on my ear tightened as we rounded the hedge bordering the garden. My blood pounded between his thumb and forefinger, and heat bloomed in my chest as I gazed at the lawn. The neighbour's dog had left his calling card on my freshly mown lines again. Everything I touched was turning foul.

Girard balanced the cardboard cake box on his left palm like a waiter, and dragged me up the gravel driveway towards the house. Milly, our cleaner, was waving her feather duster at an invisible cobweb behind the living room window. Her face ghosted briefly and then disappeared, leaving the curtain swaying. My heart sank when I saw Mum's Jag parked haphazardly at the foot of the steps. Not because she was there, but the way she'd parked conveyed volumes of stress.

Blue-and-white striped apron stretched across his bulging midriff as he puffed his way up to the porch, Girard stood for a comical moment, as though searching for another arm, and finally let go of my ear. If it hurt before, the return of blood to the lobe was now excruciating. I rubbed it vigorously, my eyes watering with relief and shame. Girard shook some life back into his fingers before pulling the brass knob next to the door. I admired the endurance it had taken to hold my ear all that time as we walked from the high street.

I stared at the ledges around each of the door panels, examining the grainy wood where the paint hadn't soaked in properly. The painter did a lousy job. What was I doing anyway? It was so dumb to be waiting outside my own front door. The *ding-dong* of the bell was muffled in the hallway beyond.

Mum would be in the kitchen, juggling the little pastries she often made for Women's Institute meetings. They'd all be arriving soon. Mum insisted on baking *something* herself so she could boast to the group that her offerings were 'mostly' homemade. A buttery aroma seeped under the door. She'd be clattering about in the cupboards, and couldn't possibly have heard the bell. Milly would be on her way.

The sun-soaked slabs of our porch brought to mind the musician from earlier, playing his guitar outside Tesco's on the market square. His fingers flowed perfectly over the strings. The intro to *Stairway to Heaven* had me hooked. His voice had the same raspy twang as Robert Plant. It was awesome sitting there, through all thirteen minutes of the classic, the sun reflecting off the terracotta paving onto my face, imagining I was on a street in California, not loitering in Flitworth town centre on a boring school holiday afternoon. The errand I'd been tasked with was forgotten.

A few people stopped to listen to the guy play. As the last *'he-ea-ve-en…'* warbled off the busker's tongue, I clapped enthusiastically, and the others either looked away, or absent-mindedly nodded in appreciation.

A man in a suit with his tie pulled away from his collar waved a packaged sandwich at the guitarist as he told him he played quite well, then asked where he came from.

'I'm a citizen of the world,' said the busker.

How cool was that?

He added he was passing through and had been hungry for days. The suit, who was about to unwrap his sandwich, put it in his briefcase instead.

The musician looked around at the pathetic gathering and asked whether anyone would be willing to donate some coins for the entertainment he'd provided. He was brave. There wasn't much cash in the open guitar case lying at his feet. He'd have made a killing at the Lyceum, but this crowd didn't have a clue.

A couple of blue rinses turned away. One of them shifted her gaze to a dress in a nearby window. It was obvious she was ignoring him. *'Hey lady!'* I wanted to yell.

'You're getting free entertainment!' But I kept quiet.

An overweight guy snorted and mumbled something unintelligible. He finished his burger, a blob of mayonnaise shining on his fat lip, and sauntered away.

The suit chucked a twenty pence piece into the guitar case. Sheesh, the generosity!

I looked down at the ten quid clutched in my hand. Mum had given it to me, saying, 'Pop along to the *Confiserie Parisienne,* Danny darling, and buy a box of those yummy French macarons with fresh cream.'

Without thinking, I thrust the note towards the musician and told him to get himself a decent dinner.

I didn't normally give money away to begging bums, even spare coins, but he truly deserved it. His eyes shone with gratitude as he started strumming another number, Neil Young I think it was. I grinned like a stupid kid.

MILLY FUMBLED WITH the latch, and the wood grain dissolved in front of my eyes as the door swung inwards. I smiled weakly, and lowered my head in an appropriate vision of shame.

'Oh! Mrs Middleton! You'd better come quick. I think there's been a bit of trouble with young Daniel,' Milly said.

We stepped into the hallway and Mum walked briskly towards us, skirt swishing against her legs, with a bunch of freshly cut roses in her hand. One eyebrow creased into a horizontal question mark as she noted my glistening eyes. She looked from me to Girard, and back again.

'Didier! *Quelle plaisir!* Danny, what are you doing? What took you so long?'

Mum loved to practice her French on Monsieur Girard. She was probably one of his best clients, always ordering cakes and canapés from him if she and Milly couldn't cope with guest numbers. She reached past me and took the box of macarons from Girard's hands.

'Daniel, darling, go and pop these in the fridge. We don't want them to sweat in this heat. Chop-chop.'

She thrust the box at me. Blood rushed to my head.

Girard's mouth hung open in a gaping U, his arm outstretched, a hand still holding the air where the box had been. Mum registered the oddity of Didier Girard standing in her hallway, and for a moment the only movement came from the feathers on Milly's duster, ruffled by a breeze from the open door. I slunk away towards the kitchen.

MUM'S WOMEN'S INSTITUTE meetings were important to her. I didn't want to mess up her afternoon. She always worried she wouldn't have enough sweet things on offer to fill those pouting lipsticked mouths.

After I'd given the cash to the busker, I pulled out all

the loose change I had in my jeans pocket. How many French macarons would that get? Not many. Walking into the *Confiserie*, I counted the coins. Not even a quid. Five macaroons would be insultingly worse than none.

It seemed so easy once I was inside the shop. My mother had invested a fortune in this place over the years. Girard was bending down behind the counter. Right in front of me sat a box of freshly made mixed macaroons on display. A stealthy grab, a quick turn, and I hurried towards the door.

But the bulk of a large body blocked my escape. The burger eating guy I'd seen earlier appeared in the doorway. Coming to get a stack of extra calories for dessert. The sun bounced off the pavement behind him as he straightened up and crossed his arms, a triangle of light shining through the space between his legs. I thought about bolting through the hole, but knew I wouldn't fit.

'Have you paid for those, laddie?' Glutton-head asked.

Girard stood up from whatever he was doing behind the counter. He looked from the box in my hands to my face, and our eyes locked as he registered my intention to scarper.

IN OUR HALLWAY, Girard cleared his throat, and I held my breath behind the kitchen door.

'Madame Middleton. I zink you do not understand.

Les macarons, votre jeune homme Daniel did not pay for zem.'

'Oh my goodness. I'm so sorry, I was sure I gave him some money. Did he think he was just picking up an order? Wait, please, one moment. Milly, take these, they need to be in water in the next two minutes.'

She thrust the roses at Milly, who walked quickly down the hallway towards the kitchen. Mum glanced at her watch. 'Heavens, is that the time?' she asked no one in particular.

I should own up. It wasn't fair. Mum was retrieving her purse from her handbag on the hall sideboard.

I came out from behind the door as Milly entered the kitchen. Shielded by the roses, she didn't see me. She squealed and jumped to the side with surprise. In a clash of arms, her feather duster caught the underside of the box of macarons and it spun round in front of our eyes. My hands grappled for it. The box landed on the kitchen floor and skittered across the tiles.

It landed lid side up. The Gods were with us. Milly's round eyes showed genuine fear, but I held my finger to my lips and she remained silent. I glanced back to the front door where my mother was thrusting a ten-pound note into Girard's hand.

'*Mais, vous ne comprenez pas…* You don't understand, Madame Middleton. *Votre fils…* Your son…'

'Oh Didier, chérie…'

Chérie? My mother had surely taken this French business too far. Her voice rose a tone, indicating impending panic.

'*Je n'ai pas le temps…* I don't have time to deal with all this now. The ladies are showing up at any moment. Look, oh dear, here comes Jennifer, that's her car. I have to go. I'm so sorry. *Je m'excuse. Une autre fois.* Another time…'

I breathed a sigh of relief as I realised Girard had retreated down the steps.

'Jennifer! Darling! How lovely to see you…' Mum trilled.

As I carefully opened the macaroon box, Milly took a sharp breath beside me. The tops had all slipped off to one side. Milly placed the roses next to the sink, and passed me a porcelain serving-platter. I organised the macaroons, squishing all the tops carefully back onto their rightful place without too much overspill. Desperate to try and fix *something* that day, I made sure they formed a random colourful masterpiece on the platter: vanilla, chocolate, lemon and strawberry. A culinary palette of colourful blobs. Their smooth matt tops reminded me of hamburger sliders. I popped a green one into my mouth, and relished the delicate crush of meringue between my tongue and the roof of my mouth followed by a delicious burst of pistachio cream.

I heard Mum escorting the first arrivals through the

living room to the patio at the back of the house.

As Milly arranged the roses in a large crystal vase, I took the platter of macarons from the counter, and a plate of dainty sandwiches Milly pointed to with her chin. I went out into the bright sunshine and placed them on the table between the teapot and the cafetière.

'*Merci* Daniel!' My mother smiled proudly, and the ladies fixed me with their sweet, patronising smiles.

And there was the moment where I finally felt good. But I didn't go as far as pouring the tea.

I excused myself and disappeared upstairs to the sanctuary of my room. It was a relief to escape the wafts of cloying perfume, female chatter, and tinkling laughter.

I knuckled my pillow and jumped onto my rumpled duvet, pulling my earphones over my head. Clicking on my iPhone playlist, I scrolled down to another of those old Zeppelin numbers, and considered whether I should train to be a French pastry chef or take up playing the guitar.

AUTHORS
(in order of appearance)

Liz Drayer

Liz Drayer is arbitrator in Clearwater, Florida. Her short fiction, poems and essays have appeared in the Tampa Bay Times, Orlando Sentinel, Prick of the Spindle, Foliate Oak, Fourth River, New Plains Review, Construction, and other publications. Her story "Spring Tide" was nominated for a Pushcart Prize.

Reshma Ruia

Reshma Ruia's first novel, 'Something Black in the Lentil Soup', was described in the Sunday Times as 'a gem of straight-faced comedy.' Her second novel manuscript, 'A Mouthful of Silence,' was shortlisted for the 2014 SI Leeds Literary Prize. Reshma's short stories and poems have appeared in various British and International anthologies and magazines and commissioned for Radio 4. She is co-founder of The Whole Kahani – a writers' collective of British South Asian writers. Born in India, but brought up in Italy, her writing reflects the inherent preoccupations of those who possess a multiple sense of belonging.

Meg Pokrass

Meg is the author of five flash fiction collections, an award-winning collection of prose poetry, and a novella-in-flash from the Rose Metal Press. Her latest book is a flash fiction collection called *The Dog Seated Next To Me*, published in 2019 by Pelekinesis Press.

A new novella in flash *The Smell Of Good Luck* is due to be published in 2019 by Flash: The International Short Short Story Press. Her work has been recently anthologized in two Norton Anthology Readers: *New Micro* (W.W. Norton & Co, 2018) and *Flash Fiction International* (W.W. Norton & Co., 2015), *Best Small Fictions, 2018* (ed. Aimee Bender), *Wigleaf Top 50*, *Nothing Short Of 100*, *Flash Non-Fiction Funny*, *Flash Fiction Funny*, and has appeared in 350 literary magazines both online and in print including *Electric Literature, Tin House, McSweeney's, Five Points, Smokelong Quarterly, Tupelo Review*.

She currently serves as Flash Challenge Editor at *Mslexia Magazine*, Festival Curator for Flash Fiction Festival UK, Co-Editor of Best Microfiction, 2019, and Founding/Managing Editor of New Flash Fiction Review. Meg teaches ongoing flash fiction workshops both online and in person, in the UK and Ireland.

Clare Harvey

Clare Harvey is an ex-army wife who writes historical fiction novels. *The Gunner Girl*, her debut novel, was inspired by her mother-in-law's experience during WWII and written while her husband was on active service in Afghanistan. It won the Exeter Novel Prize in 2015 and the RNA Joan Hessayon Prize in 2016. She has since written *The English Agent* and *The Night Raid*. She lives in Nottingham with her family.

Anne O'Leary

Anne O'Leary lives in Cork, Ireland. She won the Molly Keane Award 2018 and From the Well Short Story Competition 2017, was runner-up in the UCC/Carried In Waves Short Story Competition 2015, shortlisted for the Colm Tóibín International Short Story Award 2016 and highly commended in 2017, and longlisted for the Irish Novel Fair 2016 and RTE Guide/Penguin Ireland Short Story Competition 2015. Her work has featured in The Ogham Stone, Spelk, The Wellington Street Review, Fictive Dream, The Drabble, Jellyfish Review, Dodging the Rain, The Nottingham Review, Spontaneity and The Incubator.

Susmita Bhattacharya

Susmita Bhattacharya is the author of the novel, The Normal State of Mind (2015) and Table Manners (2018), which won the Best Short Fiction Collection prize at the 2019 Saboteur Awards. Originally from Mumbai, India, Susmita now lives in Winchester, UK where she is a Creative Writing Lecturer for Winchester University; the Creative Writing lead at SO:Write Young Writers workshops; and a mentor on the Middle Way Mentoring Project.

Briony Collins
Briony Collins is a writer based in North Wales where she attends Bangor University. She won the 2016 Exeter Novel Prize and was the 2018 recipient of Literature Wales' Under 25s Bursary. Her poetry has also been published through Black Bough, Agenda Magazine, and Nightingale & Sparrow. Currently, she is writing her third novel.

Johanna Robinson
Johanna is a proofreader from the northwest of England. She has been writing for four years and has had stories published in Mslexia, SmokeLong, Strix, Ellipsis, Reflex and Rattle Tales. Her historical novellla-in-flash, Homing, was runner up in the 2019 Bath Award and was published in June 2019.

Judy Darley
Judy Darley is a British writer who can't stop writing about the fallibilities of the human mind. Judy has shared

her stories in magazines and anthologies, on BBC radio, as well as in cafés, caves, an artist's studio and a disused church. Her second short fiction collection, *Sky Light Rain*, is due out in late 2019.

Joanna Campbell

Joanna Campbell has been shortlisted eight times for the Bridport Prize – her flash fiction placed second in their 2017 anthology. She also has stories in two Bristol Short Story Prize anthologies. She was second in the 2011 Scottish Writers Association's contest and won the Exeter Writers competition. In 2013, she had a story in the Salt Anthology of New Writing and won local prize in the Bath Short Story Award, who included her novella-in-flash, *A Safer Way To Fall*, in their trio of novellas, *How To Make A Window Snake* (Ad Hoc Fiction). In 2015 she won the London Short Story Prize. In 2018, Royal Academy Pin Drop Award featured her story in A Short Affair (Scribner). She has a story in 24 Stories of hope for survivors of the Grenfell Tower Fire, edited by Kathy Burke, and two stories in the 2018 Stroud Short Stories anthology. Her novel, *Tying Down The Lion*, is published in paperback by Brick Lane. Her story collection, *When Planets Slip Their Tracks*, published by Ink Tears in hardback, was short-listed for The Rubery International Book Award and long-listed for The Edge Hill Story Prize.

Laura Besley

Laura Besley writes short fiction in the precious moments that her children are asleep. Her fiction has appeared online (Fictive Dream, Spelk, EllipsisZine) as well as in print (Flash: The International Short Story Magazine, vol.9 No.1) and in various anthologies (Adverbally Challenged Vol.1&2, Another Hong Kong, Story Cities).

Terry Sanville

Terry Sanville lives in San Luis Obispo, California with his artist-poet wife (his in-house editor) and two plump cats (his in-house critics). He writes full time, producing short stories, essays, poems, and novels. Since 2005, his short stories have been accepted more than 350 times by commercial and academic journals, magazines, and anthologies including The Potomac Review, The Bryant Literary Review, and Shenandoah. He was nominated twice for Pushcart Prizes and once for inclusion in Best of the Net anthology. His stories have been listed among "The Most Popular Contemporary Fiction of 2017" by the Saturday Evening Post. Terry is a retired urban planner and an accomplished jazz and blues guitarist – who once played with a symphony orchestra backing up jazz legend George Shearing.

Anne Hamilton

Anne Hamilton is an author, editor of fiction, and creative writing tutor, who has a PhD in English and Creative Writing from the university of Glasgow. She's had a number of short stories published in anthologies and on-line, and is now working on a novel. Her 2010 travel memoir, *A Blonde Bengali Wife*, inspired the charity Bhola's Children, and the royalties still help to support it.

Rosie Garland

Poet, novelist and singer with post-punk band The March Violets, Rosie Garland's work appears in Under the Radar, Spelk, The Rialto, Ellipsis, Butcher's Dog, Longleaf Review, The North and elsewhere. Her latest poetry collection is *As In Judy* (Flapjack Press). She's authored three novels: *The Palace of Curiosities*, *Vixen*, & *The Night Brother*, which The Times of London described as "a delight…with shades of Angela Carter."

Rose McGinty

Rose McGinty is the author of *Electric Souk*, published in 2017 by Urbane Publications and Spokenword Audio. Rose lives in Kent and is a creative writing tutor and editor at Retreat West. She works for the NHS and has lived and worked overseas, including the Middle East.

Nicola Humphreys

Nicola Humphreys is a part-time writer with a full-time job to pay the bills. She's lived with her partner for half of her life, and they've moved house eight times in nearly 25 years. She writes short stories on the themes of nostalgia and the potential of connection, on her blog, aramblingcollective.wordpress.com and all of her dresses have pockets.

W. T. Paterson

W. T. Paterson is the author of the novels *"Dark Satellites"* and *"WOTNA"*. A Pushcart Prize nominee and graduate of Second City Chicago, his work has appeared in over 50 publications worldwide include Fiction Magazine, The Gateway Review, and The Paragon Press. A number of stories have been anthologized by Lycan Valley, North 2 South Press, and Thuggish Itch. He spends most nights yelling for his cat to "Get down from there!"

Hilda Sheehan

Hilda Sheehan's debut poetry collection is *The Night my Sister Went to Hollywood* (Cultured Llama Press, 2013). She has also published a chapbook of prose poems, *Frances and Martine* (Dancing Girl, 2014) 'Joyously funny... comic writing with a bite' David Caddy, *Tears in the Fence*. Her most recent pamphlet is *The God Baby*

(Dancing Girl Press, 2017). Hilda's work is subversive, and engages with both surreal and absurdist traditions. She is the Director of Swindon Poetry Festival.

Matty Bannond

Matty Bannond grew up close to Manchester, UK. He is thirty-three years old and lives in Germany. Alongside writing fiction, he plays the tenor saxophone in a six-piece jazz and funk band. He is currently working on a novel.

Claire Hinchliffe

Claire Hinchliffe has been writing for six years and is about to begin an MA in Creative Writing. She works as a Community Facilitator and has also been a teacher, youth worker and probation officer. As a teenager she was obsessed by The Brontë's and then moved on to Jean Rhys and Sci-fi. For a long time, she tried to write like neuro-typical people but it did not really work and so now she's giving herself free reign to write in the same way she thinks.

Amanda Huggins

Amanda Huggins is the author of the short story collection, *Separated From the Sea* (Retreat West Books), and the flash fiction collection, *Brightly Coloured Horses* (Chapeltown Books). Her stories also appear in the Ink Tears showcase anthology *Death of a Superhero*. Amanda's travel writing has won several prizes, notably the BGTW New Travel Writer of the Year in 2014 and in 2018 she was a runner-up in the Costa Short Story Award, and was also commended in both the Bath and InkTears flash awards, shortlisted for the Walter Swan Poetry Prize, the Colm Toibin International Short Story Award, and the Fish and Bridport flash prizes. She was also a finalist in this year's Bradt Guides New Travel Writer of the Year Award. Her short story collection, Scratched Enamel Heart, publishes in 2020 with Retreat West Books.

Louise Mangos

Louise Mangos grew up in the UK but has spent more than half her life in Switzerland. Her debut psychological thriller "*Strangers on a Bridge*" was a finalist in the Exeter Novel Prize and long listed for the Bath Novel Award. Her second novel "*Her Husband's Secrets*" was published in June 2019. She lives on an Alp with her Kiwi husband and two sons, and when she's not writing you can find her on the cross-country ski trails or wild swimming in the lake, depending on the season. She also writes short stories and flash fiction which have won prizes and been published in various anthologies. She has recently completed her MA in crime writing at UEA.

Read more from some of the writers featured here, plus many other talented authors, in other Retreat West Books.

WHAT WAS LEFT, VARIOUS
20 winning and shortlisted stories from the 2016 Retreat West Short Story and Flash Fiction Prizes. A past that comes back to haunt a woman when she feels she has no future. A man with no mind of his own living a life of clichés. A teenage girl band that maybe never was. A dying millionaire's bizarre tasks for the family hoping to get his money. A granddaughter losing the grandfather she loves.

AS IF I WERE A RIVER, AMANDA SAINT
Kate's life is falling apart. Her husband has vanished without a trace – just like her mother did. Laura's about to do something that will change her family's lives forever – but she can't stop herself. Una's been keeping secrets – but for how much longer?

NOTHING IS AS IT WAS, VARIOUS
A charity anthology of climate-fiction stories raising funds for the Earth Day Network. A schoolboy inspired by a conservation hero to do his bit; a mother trying to save her family and her farm from drought; a world that doesn't get dark anymore; and a city that lives in a tower slowly being taken over by the sea.

SEPARATED FROM THE SEA, AMANDA HUGGINS

Separated From the Sea is the debut short story collection from award-winning author, Amanda Huggins. Crossing oceans from Japan to New York and from England to Havana, these stories are filled with a sense of yearning, of loss, of not quite belonging, of not being sure that things are what you thought they were. They are stories imbued with pathos and irony, humour and hope.

IMPERMANENT FACTS, VARIOUS

20 winning stories from the 2017 Retreat West Short Story and Flash Fiction Prizes. A woman ventures out into a marsh at night seeking answers about herself that she cannot find; a man enjoys the solitude when his wife goes away for a few days; and a father longs for the daughter.

THIS IS (NOT ABOUT) DAVID BOWIE, FJ MORRIS

Every day we dress up in other people's expectations. We button on opinions of who we should be, we Instagram impossible ideals, tweet to follow, and comment to judge. But what if we could just let it all go? What if we took off our capes and halos, threw away our uniforms, let go of the future? What if we became who we were always supposed to be? Human.

This is (not about) David Bowie. It's about you. This Is (Not About) David Bowie is the debut flash fiction collection from F.J. Morris. Surreal, strange and beautiful it shines a light on the modern day from the view of the outsider. From lost souls, to missing sisters, and dying lovers to superheroes, it shows what it really is to be human in a world that's always expecting you to be something else.

REMEMBER TOMORROW, AMANDA SAINT

England, 2073. The UK has been cut off from the rest of the world and ravaged by environmental disasters. Small pockets of survivors live in isolated communities with no electricity, communications or transportation, eating only what they can hunt and grow.

Evie is a herbalist, living in a future that's more like the past, and she's fighting for her life. The young people of this post-apocalyptic world have cobbled together a new religion, based on medieval superstitions, and they are convinced she's a witch. Their leader? Evie's own grandson.

Weaving between Evie's current world and her activist past, her tumultuous relationships and the terrifying events that led to the demise of civilised life, Remember Tomorrow is a beautifully written, disturbing and deeply moving portrait of an all-too-possible dystopian world, with a chilling warning at its heart.

RESURRECTION TRUST, VARIOUS
A collection of funny, dark, mad, bad, upbeat, downbeat and fantastical short stories about living sustainably from the University of Southampton's Green Stories writing competition.

From eco communities to singing buildings, and sharing economies to resetting the earth back to prehistoric times, these stories showcase a myriad of different ideas about how humans can live more harmoniously with nature, and each other.

SOUL ETCHINGS, SANDRA ARNOLD
Death, motherhood, the nature of reality, and the gender expectations of cultural conditioning are woven through these biting little stories in Sandra Arnold's debut flash fiction collection. Sometimes sad, surreal and sinister, they're also shot through with love and a deep under-standing of humanity.

In gorgeous, spare prose that paints a vivid picture, Sandra Arnold gives voice to characters that are often unheard. From Daisy in Fireworks Night, willing to do whatever it takes to protect her little sister; to Martha in The Girl With Green Hair who has her body in the world we live in and her mind in the one that not many people see; and Ruby in Don't Mess With Vikings who finds strength in a diagnosis of illness to stand up to bullies. With the stories in this collection, Sandra Arnold etches marks on your soul that will last.

http://retreatwestbooks.com

North Country Walks 3

By Keith Watson

**Dedicated to my sons and daughter,
Andrew, Simon and Gemma**

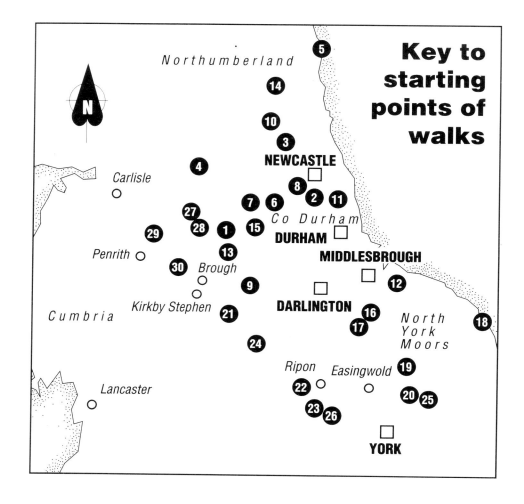

Key to starting points of walks

Northumberland

NEWCASTLE

Carlisle

Co Durham

DURHAM

MIDDLESBROUGH

Penrith

Brough

Kirkby Stephen

DARLINGTON

Cumbria

North York Moors

Ripon *Easingwold*

Lancaster

YORK

Publisher's note

While every care has been taken in the compilation of this book, the publisher cannot accept responsibility for any inaccuracies or omissions. The countryside changes all the time – paths are sometimes diverted, hedges and fences can be removed, stiles disappear.

The maps in this book are based upon the Ordnance Survey Outdoor Leisure and Pathfinder maps with permission of the Controller of Her Majesty's Stationery Office. © Crown Copyright

Published by The Northern Echo, Priestgate, Darlington, Co Durham DL1 1NF
© Keith Watson/The Northern Echo
ISBN 0 9515288 4 X North Country Walks 3 (pbk)

Contents

Introduction

This third guide in the North Country Walks series published by The Northern Echo covers a much wider area and takes you further afield with walks dispersed throughout six counties of the North of England and, for the first time, includes walks in Cumbria, Cleveland and Tyne & Wear.

Like before, the walks have been mainly selected from my popular week-to-week walks of 1991, with eight of my earlier walks from previous years brought up to date and also included.

The walks described cover a total distance of 237 miles. They have been carefully chosen for a variety of tastes from four miles to twelve in length.

Some are quite short strolls and others longer, but all of them are easy to follow and suitable for most people of average fitness with moderate walking powers.

All walks are circular with convenient parking points and all are served by public transport with details given with every walk.

The illustrated maps enhance the text and show the route, but they are no substitute for the recommended Ordnance Survey Maps listed for each walk.

Boots or stout footwear are best and always carry waterproofs, extra warm clothing, first aid and a compass.

This guide will take you on tours afoot into the undiscovered countryside of the North-East, so sample some of the short strolls with a seven miler to Lacy's Caves and Long Meg with her petrified daughters in Cumbria; amble around the famous Aysgarth Falls in the heart of Herriot Country; dawdle through the Derwent Gorge at Kirkham Priory; discover the delights of the Derwent Valley at Blanchland with the Gibraltar Rock of the North or step back in time to the world's oldest railway bridge Causey Arch and see Beamish Open Air Museum.

The longer walks promise stunning views from the Simonside Hills south of Rothbury; the tough trek over the bleak Bowes Moor into Baldersdale, once the home of Hannah Hauxwell, or the monumental view from Penshaw Monument with its famous River Wear Trail.

Walks from Craster and Ravenscar offer some of the finest coastal scenery in the country.

May I hope, with these walks, you will see the undiscovered North Country from new and different angles.

Remember the safety code and observe the Country Code.

Pleasant Walking!

Keith Watson

(Keith Watson was born in Ferryhill, County Durham, in 1940 and now lives in Norton, Cleveland. He has been keenly interested in walking since the age of 18 and has extensively walked throughout northern England. He is the author of four books – North Country Walks, North Country Walks 2, Walking in Teesdale and County Durham Walks for Motorists – and writes a weekly walks column for The Northern Echo's 7 Days Plus magazine. He is married with two sons and a daughter.)

Acknowledgements

This third volume could not have been produced without the encouragement, enthusiastic support and patience of Sue Kendrew, publications editor of The Northern Echo. Once again, my congratulations to Mike Brough, Petra Stanton and Paul Wick, graphic artists with the newspaper, for the splendid presentation of the excellent maps.

I am deeply indebted to David Adams, Val Barlett, Stuart Booth, Eric Brown, Ian Gregory, Ian Hall, The Rev. Neil Lee, Gwen Raine and Audrey Walker for their advice, vehicular support and being such good companions. And I must give special mention to Alan Earle of Norton for being an excellent driver and companion who walked with me on most of these walks. Finally, I thank my wife Jean for her support, helping me check the manuscript and tolerating my Friday forays.

Keith Watson

Country Code

- Avoid damaging fences, hedges, walls.
- Fasten all gates.
- Guard against all risk of fire.
- Safeguard water supplies.
- Go carefully on country roads.
- Keep dogs under proper control.
- Keep to the paths across farmland.
- Leave no litter, take it home.
- Protect wildlife, plants and trees.
- Respect the life of the countryside.

Your enjoyment of all the walks in this book and in the weekly series in The Northern Echo can be further enhanced if you purchase some of the excellent range of cards and leaflets available in villages and churches, including the Local History Cards series by Gatehouse Prints and North York Moors Waymark leaflets.

Colour photographs: Cover views by David Frater
(front, Kirby Hill near Richmond; back, Hartforth)
All others by Tony Bartholomew, Mike Gibb, Andy Lamb, Keith Watson
and Nigel Whitfield

1. St. John's Chapel

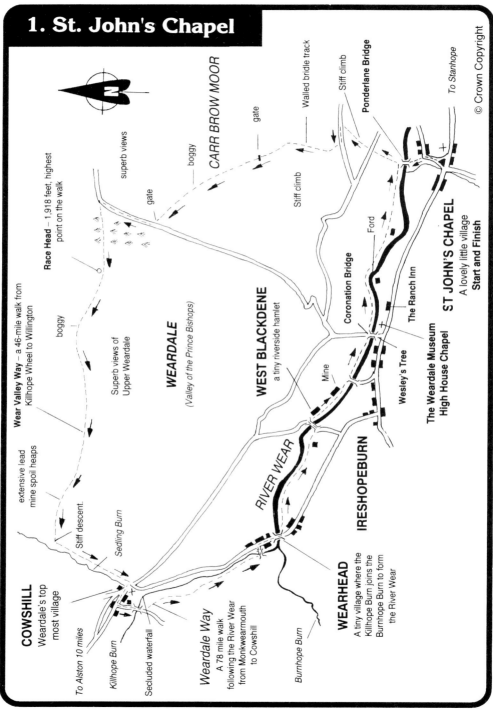

N

© Crown Copyright

CARR BROW MOOR

superb views

Walled bridle track

Stiff climb

Ponderlane Bridge

To Stanhope

gate

boggy

Stiff climb

gate

Race Head – 1,918 feet, highest point on the walk

Ford

ST JOHN'S CHAPEL
A lovely little village
Start and Finish

Wear Valley Way – a 46-mile walk from Killhope Wheel to Willington

boggy

Superb views of Upper Weardale

WEARDALE
(Valley of the Prince Bishops)

Coronation Bridge

The Ranch Inn

WEST BLACKDENE
a tiny riverside hamlet

Mine

Wesley's Tree

The Weardale Museum
High House Chapel

extensive lead mine spoil heaps

Stiff descent.

Sedling Burn

RIVER WEAR

IRESHOPEBURN

COWSHILL
Weardale's top most village

To Alston 10 miles

Killhope Burn

Secluded waterfall

Weardale Way
A 78 mile walk following the River Wear from Monkwearmouth to Cowshill

WEARHEAD
A tiny village where the Killhope Burn joins the Burnhope Burn to form the River Wear

Burnhope Burn

1. St. John's Chapel

Location: *St John's Chapel, a lovely little village which derives its name from the church of St. John the Baptist founded 1465, rebuilt 1752, is 7 miles west of Stanhope (A689)*
Route: *St. John's Chapel – Race Head – Cowshill – Wearhead – Ireshopeburn – St. John's Chapel.*
Distance: *Over 7 miles (11km). Moderate/strenuous. Allow 4/5 hours.*
O.S. Maps: *Landranger 92 Barnard Castle & Richmond; 91 Appleby. Outdoor Leisure 31 Teesdale.*
Parking: *Market Place, St. John's Chapel.*
Public Transport: *Weardale Motors Services Ltd. Service 101/102 Bishop Auckland-Cowshill.*
Refreshments: *The King's Arms Hotel; The King's Head Hotel; Golden Lion, Blue Bell Inn, St. John's Chapel. Cowshill Hotel, The Calf House, Cowshill. The Ranch Inn, Ireshopeburn.*
Note: *Brief description. Carry the relevant O.S. Map. Dogs must be on a lead at all times.*

This high and low level walk from St. John's Chapel offers superb views of Upper Weardale. Leave St. John's Chapel by the lane behind the Town Hall and at the terraced cottages, turn left and cross the bridge over Harthope Burn. At the Public Footpath signpost, turn right and follow the path to cross Ponderlane Bridge over the River Wear. Walk forward up the fieldside to climb the steep railed steps and up the next field, aim diagonally for the signposted stone wall stile to come out on to the road. Almost opposite, take the signposted path, diagonally up the next two stiled pastures for a stiff climb up to the next road with unfolding views of Upper Weardale. Turn left along the quiet hillside road and at the faded Public Bridleway signpost, turn right up the walled stony track which twists left, then right as it climbs fairly steeply for a mile or more. There are some good views of Ireshopeburn and Burnhope Reservoir from this elevated bridleway, once used by lead miners and carrier galloways. At the top of the track, go through a facing metal gate and out on to the open Carr Brow Moor which can be boggy.

Go up the moorland path into a walled grass track and exit through a gate to reach the Middlehope Road. Turn right up the road and where it swings right, turn left up a rutted track by the plantation. You have now joined the Wear Valley Way, a 46 mile long distance walk from Killhope Wheel to Willington. Go up the track strewn with fluorspar specimens, pass through a gate out on to the open moor for a 2 mile walk westwards to Cowshill. The route climbs steadily and traverses Race Head (1,918ft), the highest point on the walk. From here admire the wonderful views of wild Weardale. Go through a gate by some sheep collecting pens, hug the wall on your left and be prepared for some bog hopping to avoid the ink oozing bog.

Head westwards along the ancient galloway track below the rear of Black Head (1,977ft) via Sedling Rake with the remains of the heavily mined Sedling Vein on your right. The winding track descends steeply revealing the extensive spoil heaps of the Burtree Pasture Mine, part of the bygone world of Weardale's lead mining industry. In the valley bottom, turn left and follow the mine road by the Sedling Burn to Cowshill, Weardale's topmost village. Cross the A689 and take the lower road through the village, past the church and post office. Turn down the road to Burtreeford and cross the bridge over the Killhope Burn, where, yards beyond, turn left through the footpath signposted gate. Go along the track by the wall and note the secluded waterfall on Killhope Burn below. Ignore the gate on your right, go through the adjacent open gateway and turn right by the sycamore tree and follow the high level track along by the wall. Where the track ends at the corner wall, turn down the hillside path and aim for the white painted kissing gate seen below. Follow the path through the stiled/gated meadows for a very pleasant walk by the Killhope Burn with lovely little waterfalls to reach the village of Wearhead. Go down the Front Street, cross the rebuilt Wearhead Bridge, where upstream the Burnhope Burn joins the Killhope Burn to form the River Wear. At the bridge end, turn left and take the signposted path for a stroll by the River Wear through the pleasant stiled pastures, past Waterside Farm to reach the road.

Turn left along the road, cross the bridge (built 1841) and enter the hamlet of West Blackdene. Turn right, pass the riverside cottages and follow the signposted path by the River Wear with cascading waterfalls. Pass the fluorspar mine buildings on your left, fork right and follow the gravel path under the concrete bridge for a very pleasant riverside walk to Coronation Bridge, which you must cross for a dual detour to see the Thorn Tree, where John Wesley preached on his first visit to Weardale on May 26, 1752, and to visit Weardale Museum, founded by local enthusiasts in 1985. Re-cross the bridge, turn right and follow the signposted path downstream to reach the ford and a delightful waterfall. Go up the cobbled track, cross a stile, turn right and follow stiled fields above the wooded riverside. The route passes behind Island House Farm and proceeds eastwards through the gated/stiled fields to reach Ponderlane Bridge and return by the outward route to St. John's Chapel.

7

2. Causey Arch

CAUSEY ARCH PICNIC AREA Start and Finish

Tanfield Railway
originally opened in 1725 as a horsedrawn waggonway.
The oldest existing railway in the world

CAUSEY ARCH
The world's oldest surviving railway bridge, built by Ralph Wood in 1725-26

To Sunniside

Causey Arch Inn

footbridges

Beamish Park Hotel

A6076 Causey Road

Beamishburn Road

Causey Burn

Causey Burn

Coppy Lane

Alternative short walk

COPPY
A tiny hamlet

Oxpasture Hill
Views of Pontop Pike and Penshaw Monument

follow waymarks

Starling Bridge

BEAMISH
North of England Open Air Museum

Boghouse Lane

Beamish Burn

Beamish Hall
built in 1813

The Tiny Tim Drop Forge Steam Hammer built 1883 90 ton – 35 feet high (Museum entrance)

Beamish Park Golf Course

Home Farm

Blue Bell Inn

Hellhole Wood

The Shepherd and Shepherdess
Georgian pub

Methold Cottages
(Almhouses)
Built and endowed by John Eden 1863

STANLEY

THE CONSETT AND SUNDERLAND RAILWAY PATH – follows the track of the Stanhope and Tyne Railway

Eden Place Picnic Area

Beamish Shorthorns
(A herd of grazing cows crafted from scrap iron by Sally Mathews)

8

2. Causey Arch

Location: *Causey Arch Picnic Area is 6 miles from Newcastle (A692, A6076); 7 miles from the A1(M) at Chester-le-Street (A693, A6076) and 11 miles miles from Durham (B6532 Sacriston to Stanley then A6076)*

Route: *Causey Arch Picnic Area – Causey Hall – Coppy – Beamish Museum – Eden Place Picnic Area – Consett & Sunderland Railway Path – Blue Bell Inn – Causey Arch.*

Distance: *7 miles (10km) Easy. Allow 3 hours. Some unavoidable road walkimg.*

O.S.Maps: *Landranger 88 Tyneside; Pathfinder 562 (NZ25/35) Washington & Chester-le-Street; 561 (NZ05/15) Consett.*

Parking: *Causey Arch Picnic Area alongside A6076 opposite the Causey Arch Inn. 1 mile from Stanley. GR 205562. N.B. Police Warning – Car thieves operate in this area.*

Public Transport: *Go-Ahead Northern Services X29/X30 & 704 to Causey Arch Inn.*

Refreshments: *Causey Arch Inn; Beamish Park Hotel, Causey Arch. The Shepherd and Shepherdess, Beamish. Blue Bell Inn, South Causey Hotel, Stanley.*

Step back in time, deep into Durham's past for an exciting seven mile stroll from Causey Arch, the world's oldest surviving railway bridge to Beamish Museum, England's first open air museum. This walk offers industrial history and includes the Consett and Sunderland Railway Path with its Celestial Road and Sculpture Trail.

Leave Causey Arch Picnic Area, left of the information kiosk and take the steep path down into the wooded Causey Gorge. At the bottom, a sign 'To The Culvert' offers a short detour to a man made railway embankment with 100yds of culverted stream. There were no bulldozers in those days, just men, shovels and horse drawn wagons. Retrace your steps and go upstream, past the high sandstone cliffs via three bridges to the world's oldest surviving railway bridge, the Causey Arch which is the centre piece of the picnic area. It was built in 1725-26 and the massive arch has a span of 100ft rising to 80ft above the gorge and cost £12,000 to build. The suberb craftmanship was the work of local stonemason Ralph Wood who, fearing that his stone bridge would collapse like a previous wooden structure, committed suicide by jumping from the top of the arch. More than 250 years later the bridge stands safe as ever. It was restored by Durham County Council in 1981.

Go up the steep path and cross the bridge. In its heyday a wagon went by every 20 seconds and some 930 horse drawn wagons a day crossed it in each direction. There is a replica of a 18th century coal wagon built by trainees of the Dragonville Skill Centre and display boards explain the history of the wooden wagonways. Cross the Tanfield Railway, (originally opened in 1725) the oldest existing railway in the world. It runs from Sunniside to the new halt at Causey Arch.

Follow the fenced path which converges with the wagonway (temporary path) and at the sign 'Causey Mill 1 mile', turn left and follow the waymarked field route up to the top of Oxpasture Hill with extensive views of Tyneside, Tantobie and Tanfield plus Pontop Pike and Penshaw Monument. Go downhill, cross the busy A6076 to foot-

path signpost opposite. Descend the steps, cross the stile, turn right and left then walk forward by the holly hedge on your left. Cross the signposted corner stile, bear half left and by Causey Hall Farm, turn right downhill to cross the footbridge over Causey Burn. The Causey Mill Picnic Area, created on the site of an old drift mine is away to your right. Head straight up the waymarked stiled pasture to the Beamishburn Road. Go down the road for 25yds and cross the hidden signposted stile on your left by the entrance to Thorntree. Go diagonally up the rough scrubland, where at the top corner there are two signposted stiles. Cross the stile on your right, walk forward, pass the gate entrance immediately on your left and go straight along the field edge with the hedge on your left. Go diagonally down and follow the waymarked stiled path through the next two fields and up an enclosed path by Peacock House to the tiny hamlet of Coppy.

To shorten the walk, turn left up Coppy Lane for under a mile to the Beamishburn Road. Turn right along the road, left down by the Causey Arch Inn, cross the A6076 and return to the picnic area.

For the main walk, go down Coppy Lane to come out opposite Beamish Hall (built 1813), where you turn left and right along the road with fast tourist traffic for more than a mile, giving a free view of the award winning Beamish Museum. The impressive Tiny Tim Drop Forge Steam Hammer is the entrance to the museum. If you have time, pay your admission and take a trip into the 'living' past. Beyond the museum is the Georgian pub, The Shepherd and Shepherdess with its romantic figures of a shepherd boy and girl. The pub is an ideal stop for refreshments.

Opposite the pub, go through the red barrier gate, bear left and follow the path through the wood to Eden Place Picnic Area created on the site of the former Beamish 2nd Pit with its winding engine rebuilt at Beamish Museum. At the map board, go round the edge of the second car park and down through the barrier gate to the Sunderland & Con-

(Continued on page 10)

9

(Continued from page 9)

sett Railway Path which follows the track of one of the country's oldest railways – the Stanhope & Tyne Railway. Turn right along the 24 mile Railway Path. Pass four grazing Beamish Shorthorns, but don't feed them, they were made out of scrap iron by Sally Matthews and are part of the fascinating Sculpture Trail. Another interesting item is John Downie's 'The Celestial Railroad', a novel you can't read without travelling the length of the railway route as each chapter is printed on display boards marking each mile. Follow the railway path westwards for a mile and as you approach the eastern edge of Shield Row, (part of Stanley), turn left through a barrier gate and go right by the sports

field. Go under the railway path to a residential estate and before house no 46, cross the stile on your right, turn left and follow the path by the fenced gardens. Go half right and forward over the rough pastures to the road by the Blue Bell Inn. Turn right, pass the South Causey Hotel and at the bottom of the road, turn left into the unsignposted Boghouse Lane at the end of the wood. Go along the wooded path, cross a stile and turn left into a hedgerowed lane which winds uphill through high vegetation. At the top, cross a stile and go along a final field to the A6076. Turn right along this busy road back to Causey Arch Picnic Area for a quick finish or use the outward route via Oxpasture Hill to complete a classic Causey Arch circuit.

3. Belsay

Location: *Belsay, a tiny village, well known for its 14th century castle, ruined manor house and neo-classical hall is 14 miles north of Newcastle (A696).*
Route: *Belsay – Bolam – Shaftoe Crags – Ferney Chesters – West Tofthill – Saugh House – Belsay.*
Distance: *Over 10 miles (16km). Allow 5 hours. Moderate.*
O.S. Maps: *Landranger 81 Alnwick & Morpeth; 88 Tyneside. Pathfinder 535 (NZ 07/17) Ponteland; 523 (NZ08/18) Morpeth West.*
Parking: *Layby, north of Belsay Village. Limited parking. GR 100791.*
Public Transport: *National Express: Newcastle - Edinburgh (daily)*
Refreshments: *The Blacksmiths Coffee Shop, Belsay. Belsay Hall, Gardens and Castle-refreshments in The Old Kitchen. None on route.*
Note: *Pathfinder map recommended. Keep dogs on a lead and under strict control. Please close all gates.*

Discover a bit of bygone Britain in rural Northumberland with a fascinating walk on little known paths from Belsay to the lost village of Bolam with its lovely little church and charming country park. This interesting excursion includes the strange shaped Shaftoe Crags and offers extensive views of Northumberland. The return route passes Shortflatt Tower, one of the best examples of a Pele Tower in the area.

From the layby, north of Belsay, walk northwards along the road for 440yds to the road junction, where almost opposite, look for the hidden Public Bridleway signpost, marked 'Bolam Church'. Go through the green metal gate for a two mile field path walk to Bolam. Go down the rough track strewn with thistles in the first field and at the bottom, go through a facing wooden gate. Go up the edge of the next field and cross a wooden footbridge over the infant River Blyth, noting the views eastwards to Blyth Power Station, while westwards pick out the half hidden hamlet of Harnham. Go up the rutted enclosed track strewn with thistles and at the top, go over a cross track and through a facing gate and keep northwards by the field edge. Half way up the field, bear half right and keep to the left of a telegraph pole, where down in the dip, cross the railed footbridge over How Burn and straddle the step stile. Turn left and right up a sunken path by the field edge. Go through a gate and away to your right is the fine house of Foulmartlaw, half hidden in the pine plantation. Go up the track by the arable field and turn left and then right alongside the same field with a tiny wood on your left. At the end of the field negotiate the high vegetation and go through the corner gate. Turn left, pass through a white gate and turn right over a slab bridge and walk up the final field with fine views. Exit through a signposted gate 'Belsay 2 miles' and turn left along the road for 440yds to the lost village of Bolam which was once a thriving township of 200 houses, but all have vanished, except the Hall and little church. You must visit the latter, St. Andrew's is a gem of a church with a purely Saxon Tower. Inside see the inscribed window recording the amazing fact that a German bomb entered the church, but did not explode.

From the church, turn right and walk westwards along the road, noting the sunken boundary by the wall which is a fine example of a ha-ha, so named because of the expression of surprise upon meeting them. The purpose of a ha-ha was to prevent livestock from straying from the parkland of Bolam Hall. Opposite the road junction, cross the unsignposted wooden stile and enter the beautiful 100 acre Bolam Lake Country Park centred around a 25 acre artificial lake created by John Dobson in 1817. There are scenic walks, idyllic lakeside picnic sites plus wildlife-rich woodland. The park was bought by Northumberland County Council in 1972 and developed as a Country Park. Follow the woodland path via the information centre and car park through Boathouse Wood to Bolam Lake, where you turn right along the lakeside into Pheasant Field with its lakeside picnic area which is a very pleasant spot. Pass through the picnic area and follow the Boardwalk through West Wood to come out on to the Scots' Gap/Belsay road.

Turn right along the road for 880yds to Bolam West Houses, where a footpath sign, 'Shaftoe Craggs 1 mile' directs you along a stony lane by the terrace cottages. As shown on the O.S. Map, you cross the course of the mysterious Devil's Causeway Roman Road without even knowing it. Go through a gateway with a cattle grid, turn right, hug the wall and at the top of the field, go through another gate. The strange shaped Shaftoe Crags are on your left. The grass mounds are the remains of ancient camps and earthworks. Keep straight on and drop down into Salters Nick, a mini gorge of craggy outcrops. In front of a gate, turn left along the bracken track, pass Shaftoe Grange and go down the farm road that skirts the weathered crags. From the trig point top, 650ft high, there is a fine view of the Simonside Hills and the villages of Kirk-

(Continued on Page 13)

11

3. Belsay

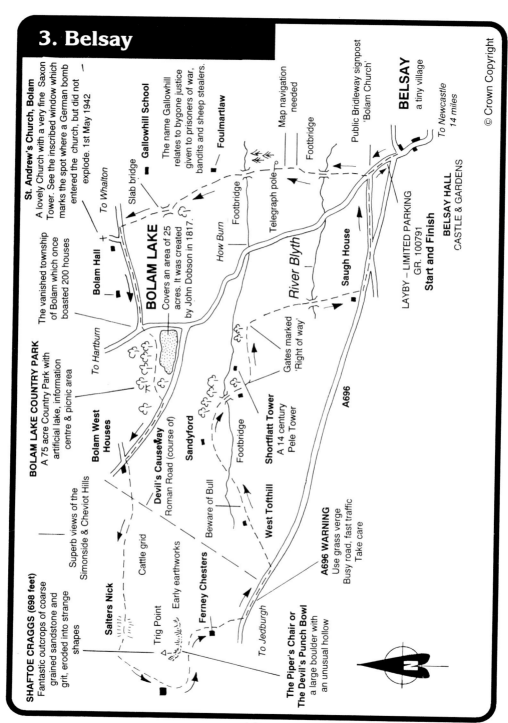

SHAFTOE CRAGGS (698 feet)
Fantastic outcrops of coarse grained sandstone and grit, eroded into strange shapes

Superb views of the Simonside & Cheviot Hills

Salters Nick

Cattle grid

Trig Point

Early earthworks

Ferney Chesters

To Jedburgh

The Piper's Chair or The Devil's Punch Bowl
a large boulder with an unusual hollow

BOLAM LAKE COUNTRY PARK
A 75 acre Country Park with artificial lake, information centre & picnic area

The vanished township of Bolam which once boasted 200 houses

Bolam West Houses

Devil's Causeway
Roman Road (course of)

Beware of Bull

West Tofthill

Sandyford

Footbridge

Shortflatt Tower
A 14 century Pele Tower

Gates marked 'Right of way'

A696 WARNING
Use grass verge
Busy road, fast traffic
Take care

St. Andrew's Church, Bolam
A lovely Church with a very fine Saxon Tower. See the inscribed window which marks the spot where a German bomb entered the church, but did not explode. 1st May 1942

To Whalton

Slab bridge

Bolam Hall

BOLAM LAKE
Covers an area of 25 acres. It was created by John Dobson in 1817.

To Hartburn

Gallowhill School

The name Gallowhill relates to bygone justice given to prisoners of war, bandits and sheep stealers.

Foulmartlaw

Map navigation needed

Footbridge

How Burn

Footbridge

Telegraph pole

River Blyth

Saugh House

A696

Public Bridleway signpost 'Bolam Church'

BELSAY
a tiny village

To Newcastle
14 miles

LAYBY – LIMITED PARKING
GR. 100791
Start and Finish

BELSAY HALL
CASTLE & GARDENS

N

(Continued from page 11)

whelpington, Cambo and Scots' Gap, plus the stately Wallington Hall. You will pass the towering boulder called The Piper's Chair, better known as The Devil's Punchbowl (697ft) with an unusual hollow on top, which was filled with wine during the wedding celebrations of Sir William Blackett of Wallington in 1775. Below the boulder is a crude cave called Shaftoe Hall. Remember, if you explore these rocky outcrops, they are steep and dangerous. The huge fallen boulder, split in two by frost, is nicknamed The Tailor and His Man.

Turn right through a open gateway and follow the track up past Ferney Chesters and down to the A696. Turn left along the busy road with fast traffic, for about 440yds. Turn left into the narrow gated road signposted 'Toft Hill' and follow it for over a mile past West Tofthill, where you might encounter a grazing bull. Pass the turn off to Sandyford and where the road curves right, leave it and branch left on a faint path at first in the direction of Shortflatt

Tower seen in the distance. Use the plank bridge over How Burn, cross a stile marked 'Right of Way' and turn right up the track to the cottage and go through the adjacent gate, also marked 'Right of Way'. The route through the next few fields is easy to follow as most of the gates have been marked with a 'Right of Way' label. Follow the path up by the wall which curves left through a corner gate. Keep eastwards by the walled field edge, noting the fine view of Shortflatt Tower, one of Northumberland's best pele towers. Go through another gate and the renovated building, used to support a water tower (1887-London). Eastwards, pass through an open gateway with a wood on your left and at the end of the field, turn right in front of a facing gate. Go down the edge of the next two gated fields on little used paths and cross the footbridge over the River Blyth. Turn up the field, pass the ivy clad Saugh House to reach the A696. Turn left up the main road for 440yds and at the cross roads, take the road signed 'Bolam 3 miles' for over half a mile to return by the outward route back to Belsay.

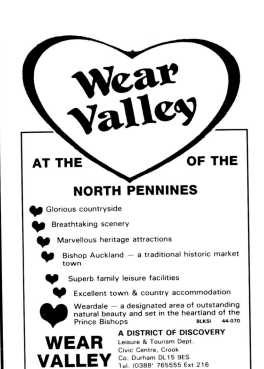
13

4. Hadrian's Wall

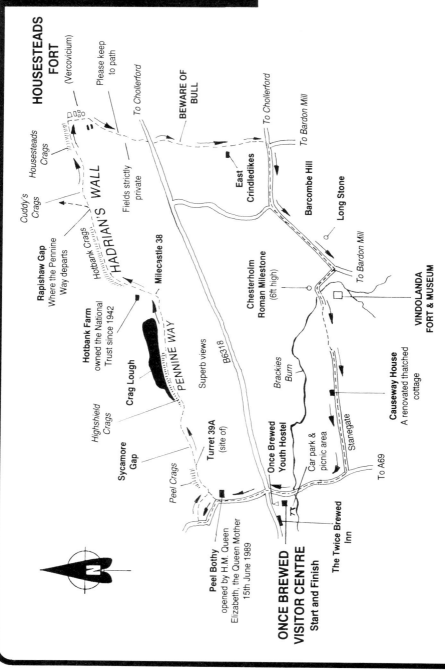

HOUSESTEADS FORT (Vercovicium)

Please keep to path

To Chollerford

BEWARE OF BULL

To Chollerford

To Bardon Mill

East Crindledikes

Barcombe Hill

Long Stone

To Bardon Mill

Housesteads Crags

Cuddy's Crags

HADRIAN'S WALL

Fields strictly private

Rapishaw Gap
Where the Pennine Way departs

Hotbank Crags

Milecastle 38

Hotbank Farm
owned the National Trust since 1942

PENNINE WAY

Crag Lough

B6318

Superb views

Chesterholm Roman Milestone (6ft high)

VINDOLANDA
FORT & MUSEUM

Highshield Crags

Brackies Burn

Sycamore Gap

Turret 39A (site of)

Peel Crags

Once Brewed Youth Hostel

Car park & picnic area

Stanegate

To A69

Causeway House
A renovated thatched cottage

Peel Bothy
opened by H.M. Queen Elizabeth, the Queen Mother 15th June 1989

ONCE BREWED VISITOR CENTRE
Start and Finish

The Twice Brewed Inn

N

14

4. Hadrian's Wall

Location: Once Brewed Visitor Centre car park is 3 miles west of Housesteads; New-castle – 33 miles, Carlisle – 24 miles (B6318)
Route: Once Brewed – Peel Crags – Highshield Crags – Hotbank – Housesteads – East Crindledikes – Vindolanda – Once Brewed.
Distance: 7 miles (12km). Allow 4-5 hours. Moderate/quite strenuous with a number of steep climbs.
O.S. Maps: Landranger 87 Hexham & Haltwhistle; 86 Haltwhistle; Pathfinder 546 (NY 66/67) Haltwhistle & Gilsland.
Parking: Once Brewed Visitor Centre Car Park. GR 753668
Public Transport: No bus service, but Service 890 Hadrian's Wall Tourist Coach, Rochester & Marshall provides a special rail link bus service with Haltwhistle and Hexham stations from July 20 to September 1.
Refreshments: The Twice Brewed Inn.
Note: Stout footwear essential. Paths slippery and muddy in wet weather. Watch your way carefully along Highshield Crags with 200ft sheer cliffs to Crag Lough below. This walk is not recommended for Bank Holidays or at the height of the tourist season. Please keep dogs on a lead.

Step back in time for a roller coaster ramble which visits Housesteads Fort and returns via Vindolanda and is without doubt one of the finest historic walks in England, if not in Europe.

From Once Brewed, turn left, cross the busy B6318 (Military Road) and go northwards up the road for half a mile. Pass Peel Bothy, opened by H.M. Queen Elizabeth the Queen Mother on June 15 1989 and note the memorial seat to Major James Scott Kingham RE killed in action in the Gulf War, February 14 1991. Continue up the road to the path sign 'Crag Lough/ Housesteads', and here you join the Pennine Way. Turn right for a 500yd walk along the top of Hadrian's Wall. As requested, leave the Wall via some railed steps, turn right and the path to Housesteads (2 miles) drops down by the Wall into Peel Gap. Cross the railed bridge and note the extensive repair work carried out by the National Trust on the nearby Wall. Scramble up the stony staircase to the lofty Peel Crags (913ft) with exhilarating views westwards to Winshield Crags (1,260ft) and a bird's eye view eastwards to Cuddy Crags with Crag Lough shimmering below High-shield Crags. Cross a stile, keep by the Wall and an explanatory panel tells you that Turret 39A is the only known example of a narrow gauge turret. Turn right and then left for an uphill climb with a section of the Wall missing. Descend the stepped path into the dip known as Sycamore Gap. The old tree there is dying and to make sure the name carries on for another 100 years, the National Trust planted a replacement in 1989. Beyond Sycamore Gap, go uphill and follow the waymarked route by the Wall and scramble up the sharp rise over a ladder stile to the massive Highshield Crags. Go along the top of the crags with superb views and the shallow lake of Crag Lough below. Take care, as it is a dangerous spot especially in windy weather. Go down the path through the small wood of Scots pines and exit over a stile. Cross the signposted stile on your right and a few yards along the farm road at Milking Gap, cross the ladder stile on your left. You now follow one of the finest stretches of Hadrian's Wall for 11$^{1}/_{2}$ miles to Housesteads Fort. Go along the grass path and note the explanatory panel saying that the ruined Milecastle 38 was constructed in 122-126 AD by the Second Legion. Pass Hotbank Farm and ascend the steep hill of Hotbank Crags (1,074ft), the highest point on the walk. The lakes of Greenlee Lough, Broomlee Lough and Crag Lough are all visible. As requested, keep by the Wall and dip down into Rapishaw Gap. Climb up by Cuddy Crags and skirt the remains of Milecastle 37. Follow the path along the top of Hadrian's Wall through the wood to reach Housesteads Vercovicium Roman Fort, best known of all the forts along the Wall. Turn right and walk down past the West Gate of the five acre fort and pay your admission at the museum.

Below the fort, turn right at the 19th century well and follow the farm road by the Education Room/ Museum. The fields are strictly private and visitors should keep to the footpath. Follow the surfaced farm road to the B6138 and almost opposite, cross the ladder stile left of the gate with a bull warning symbol. Follow the narrow path straight down the rough pasture and go up the col between the hillocks and downhill on a track to East Crindle-dikes. Pass through the gated farmyard with blue waymarks and follow the road up to the Stanegate Road which pre-dates Hadrian's Wall. Turn right and follow this road downhill for a mile. After you pass the roadside coach parking area, turn right down the narrow lane to Vindolanda Roman Fort and Settlement circa 78-400 AD. There are remains of successive forts on the site together with at least two large settlements. For the last leg of the walk, see if you can spot the six foot high Chesterholm Milestone as you climb for a mile up the Stanegate Road. At the road junction, turn right and follow the road for half a mile back to Once Brewed.

15

5. Craster

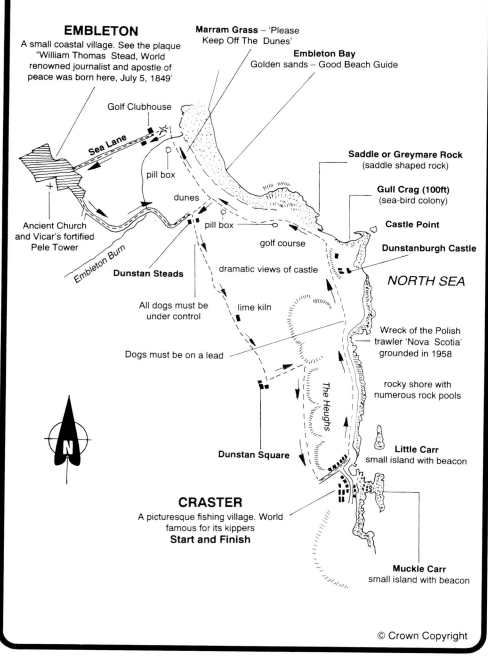

EMBLETON
A small coastal village. See the plaque "William Thomas Stead, World renowned journalist and apostle of peace was born here, July 5, 1849'

Marram Grass – 'Please Keep Off The Dunes'

Embleton Bay
Golden sands – Good Beach Guide

Golf Clubhouse

Sea Lane

pill box

dunes

Ancient Church and Vicar's fortified Pele Tower

Embleton Burn

Dunstan Steads

pill box

golf course

All dogs must be under control

lime kiln

Dogs must be on a lead

Dunstan Square

Saddle or Greymare Rock
(saddle shaped rock)

Gull Crag (100ft)
(sea-bird colony)

Castle Point

Dunstanburgh Castle

NORTH SEA

dramatic views of castle

Wreck of the Polish trawler 'Nova Scotia' grounded in 1958

rocky shore with numerous rock pools

The Heughs

Little Carr
small island with beacon

N

CRASTER
A picturesque fishing village. World famous for its kippers
Start and Finish

Muckle Carr
small island with beacon

© Crown Copyright

5. Craster Coastal Circuit

Location: Craster, a picturesque fishing village with a miniature harbour, is world famous for the smoking of its delectable kippers. 7 miles north-east of Alnwick, off the B1339.
Route: Craster – Dunstanburgh Castle – Embleton – Dunstan Steads – Dunstan Square – Craster.
Distance: 6 miles (10km) Easy. Allow 3/4 hours.
O.S. Maps: Landranger 81 Alnwick & Morpeth; 75 Berwick upon Tweed. Pathfinder 477 (NU21/22) Embleton & Alnmouth
Parking: Public Car Park, Craster. GR NU 258199
Public Transport: Northumbrian Motor Services. Service 501 Newcastle-Berwick via Seahouses.
Refreshments: Bark Pots; Jolly Fisherman; Craster Restaurant, Craster. Dunstanburgh Castle Golf Club; Blue Bell Inn; Grey Inn; Dunstanburgh Castle Hotel, Embleton.
Note: Dogs must be on a lead and under strict control. Stout footwear advisable. Special mention, not one stile on this walk!

Enjoy an easy bracing walk along a beautiful stretch of coastline, north of the picturesque fishing village of Craster in Northumberland. The walk offers some of the finest scenery on the Northumberland coast and leads to the gaunt ruin of Dunstanburgh Castle with an inland return via the small coastal village of Embleton, birthplace of William Thomas Stead, world renowned journalist and former editor of The Northern Echo.

From Craster car park, turn right along the road to the fishing village of Craster and at the sign 'Dunstanburgh Castle' overlooking the tiny Memorial Harbour, turn left by the neat cottages for 400yds to the road end. Go through the kissing gate signposted 'Dunstanburgh Castle' with a couple of requests – 'Keep to the path' and 'Dogs must be on a lead'. The route, an easy sea edge walk along the coastal path, requires little description. Just remember to keep the North Sea on your right!

The most demanding aspect of this walk is trying to avoid the number of visitors during the summer season. After a mile, pass through a third kissing gate, where, if the tide is out, you might be lucky to see the wreck of the Polish trawler Nova Scotia driven ashore in 1958. The small bay is named Nova Scotia.

If you visit the ruined Dunstanburgh Castle, expect a stiff climb up to the 11-acre ruin perched on the Great Whin Sill outcrops of Castle Point. The castle was completed by Thomas, Earl of Lancaster, in 1314 and enlarged by John of Gaunt in 1356. It is in the care of English Heritage and open to the public.

Those not visiting the castle should bear half left from the kissing gate and follow the inland path past some craggy outcrops and curve round below the dramatic castle mound dominated by Lilburn Tower. Pass through a kissing gate by the National Trust sign 'Dunstanburgh Links' and rejoin the coastal path with superb backward views to the black basalt cliffs of Gull Crag, named after its large sea bird colony.

Follow the path to the right of the golf course

Dunstanburgh Castle

and proceed with care when golf is being played. Keep to the marked path parallel to the rocky shoreline and note the strangely shaped rock known as Saddle or Greymare Rock. It is an outstanding geological feature of folded limestone strata and should interest the amateur geologist.

Keep on the undulating sand dune path and pass a couple of Second World War pill boxes to reach the magnificent golden sandy beach of the curved Embleton Bay.

At 100yds beyond the second pill box, you have the opportunity to shorten the walk by turning left through the deep gap between the dunes and following the access path with caution over the fairway to a signposted gate with an illustrated National Trust map board. Go up the enclosed lane to the large Dunstan Steads Farm, where you join

(Continued on Page 18)

17

(Continued from page 17)

the main route. For the main route, the right of way is northwards over the high sand dunes, but a notice states 'Marram Grass – This area has been planted with Marram Grass in order to repair the erosion and stablise the dunes. Please keep off the dunes'. So avoid the high dunes if you can and walk along the excellent beach of Embleton Bay with attractive views towards Newton by-the-Sea. Alternatively, there is a path by the edge of the golf course, where beyond a pill box, pass a footbridge, walk by the beckside and turn left over a plank bridge. Follow the white posted path over the golf course and pass the club house which is open to the public for meals. Go up the paved Sea Lane to the small coastal village of Embleton which boasts a couple of pubs and a hotel.

Go down the Front Street, pass the United Reformed Church (1833) and at The Old Manse there is a wall plaque dedicated to Willam Thomas Stead, 1849-1912: 'World renowned journalist and apostle of peace was born here, July 5, 1849.' He was the editor of The Northern Echo from 1871-1880 and regarded as the one of the greatest journalists of all time. While in Embleton, visit the 13th century Holy Trinity Church and see the old vicarage, a fine example of a Vicar's Pele Tower

which is a reminder of the days when the Border Counties were less peaceful than they are today. In 1975 the old Vicarage was sold and replaced.

Leave Embleton at the top of Sea Lane, go past Grey's Inn and at the road junction by the Blue Bell Inn, follow the Craster road. At the double signs indicating Dunstan and Dunstanburgh Castle, turn left and follow the road for a mile to Dunstan Steads with three houses and a large farm.

At Dunstan Steads Farm entrance, a Public Bridleway signpost directs you right through the farmyard to a gate with notices 'All dogs must be under proper control' and 'No Motors'. Follow the concrete road southwards for a mile to Dunstan Square with dramatic views of Dunstanburgh Castle. You pass an old lime kiln and an unusual Second World War pill box of cement filled sandbags. When you reach Dunstan Square Farm, turn left through the metal gate signposted 'Craster 1 mile' and follow the track down through a facing gate at the bottom of the pasture. Fifty yards further on, turn right through a kissing gate by a large gate and follow the pasture path at the base of the gorse covered craggy outcrops called The Heughs. At the end of the pasture, go through another kissing gate and follow the well worn path through the scrub woodland to come out opposite Craster car park to complete a classic coastal circuit.

6. Allensford

Location: *Allensford Park, a delightful riverside picnic area by the River Derwent in North West Durham, is one mile north of Castleside on the east side of the A68*
Route: *Allensford – Shotley Bridge – Panshield – Newlands – Ebchester – The Derwent Walk – Shotley Bridge – Burn House – Bulbeck Cottage – Allensford.*
Distance: *5 miles (8km). Easy. Allow 2 hours. Or 10 miles (16km). Moderate. Allow 5 hours.*
O.S. Maps: *Landranger 88 Tyneside Pathfinder 561 (NZ05/15) Consett.*
Parking: *Allensford Park. Free parking. Open dawn to dusk.*
Public Transport: *OK Travel 869 Bishop Auckland - Hexham to Allensford Road End (Tues only): Go-Ahead Northern X11,X12,744, 747,748 to Castleside (1 mile).*
Refreshments: *Allensford Park Tourist Information Centre for soft drinks. Rose Cottage Tea Gardens open weekends. The King's Head; The Crown and Crossed Swords, Shotley Bridge. The Chelmsford; The Derwent Walk Inn, Ebchester.*
Note: *Please keep to the paths. Please keep dogs on a lead.*

Far too few walkers know the delightful Derwent Valley as well as it deserves to be known. This two-in-one-walk from Allensford Park in North West Durham takes you along both sides of the Derwent Valley and includes The Derwent Walk.

From Allensford Park, walk westwards via the picnic area along by the banks of the River Derwent to the A68. Cross Allensford Bridge over the River Derwent into Northumberland and walk up the A68 to the white-washed Allansford Mill Farm. Turn right, do not enter the farmyard, but bear left along an unsignposted path above the farm and cross a small stone bridge over the Wallishwalls Burn into a wood. Fork right, turn left and hug the fence until a broad path descends through the wood to the River Derwent. Turn left and follow the wooded riverside downstream with little direction needed. The River Derwent is a haven for river birds, especially the heron which patrols this part of the river. Five weirs and a pumping station (disused brick building on the river bend) controlled the river and water was pumped to Consett Steel Works.

Downstream pass Forge Cottage and do not cross the nearby footbridge over the river. Cross a white footbridge over the Letch Burn and opposite you will see the ruined Shotley Grove Paper Mills, famous for fine cartridge paper which was supplied to Her Majesty's Stationery Office. The Mill closed down in 1905. This is the best part of the walk, where the delightful Derwent passes through a rocky gorge of millstone cliffs. It's a picturesque place and a popular spot with locals. At the end of the riverside path, cross the footbridge over the River Derwent for a brief return into County Durham. Turn left and follow the road via Derwentdale and Riverside (A694) into the large hillside village of Shotley Bridge, once famous for its seventeenth century swordmakers from Solingen in Germany. At the sign 'Shotley Bridge Picnic Area', fork left down the road, pass The King's Head and note the nearby pub called The Crown and Crossed Swords, originally owned by William Oley, a descendant of the famous German family of sword-

making fame. Cross the bridge over the River Derwent into Northumberland. At this point, you have to decide whether to take the shorter walk which is described on the return route. Go along the B6278 and opposite the cottage called The Bothy turn right along the enclosed path (signposted 'Panshield/ Newlands') above the River Derwent with views of Shotley Bridge. At the end of the fenced field, leave the river and turn left through the broom bushes to a half hidden footpath signpost. Bear right up into a young conifer plantation for a level walk northwards. Exit out of the wood, where a waymark guides you up the fenced edge of a rough field. Cross a waymarked wooden stile, turn right through the farmyard and pass Panshield Farm on your left. Go through the gate and follow the farm track (waymarked) for 100yds, where the track ends in front of two gates.

As directed by the waymark, turn left through the gate and follow the track which curves right along the field and ends in front of another two gates. Cross the ladder stile and walk straight on along the edge of the field. Watch out for the path that forks left between the growing crops of the same field. Go through the handgate into a cleared area of woodland with excellent views over the Derwent Valley down to Ebchester. Follow the track downhill and as it swings left, go down into the wooded burn which is a pretty spot with wild flowers. Cross the footbridge over Mere Burn, noting the waterfall. Turn right and in yards go up the stepped path by the woodland edge and look for a ladder stile in the fence on your right. Ten yards further on there is a waymarked handgate in the wall. Use either and walk along the field with the fence on your right. As you approach the next wood, bear half left for the far corner gate by the wood. Go through the gate, follow the fenced path down into the wood and cross the stone bridge over Small Burn. It's a delightful spot with an unexpected mini gorge and impressive drop waterfall. Follow the

(Continued on page 21)

19

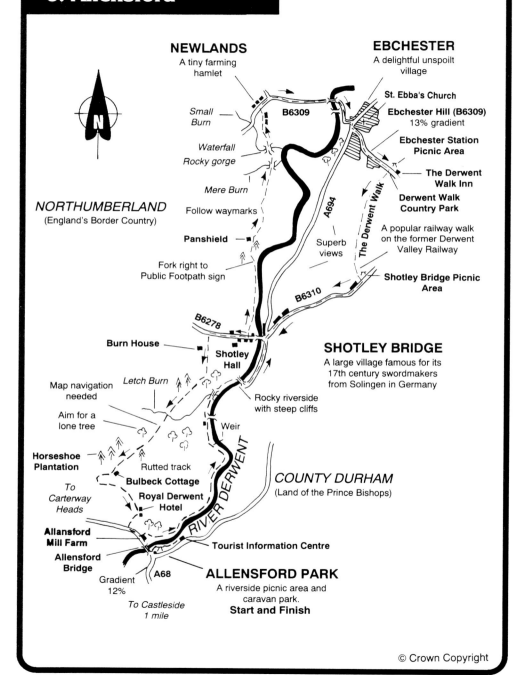

NEWLANDS
A tiny farming hamlet

EBCHESTER
A delightful unspoilt village

Small Burn

B6309

St. Ebba's Church

Ebchester Hill (B6309)
13% gradient

Waterfall
Rocky gorge

Ebchester Station Picnic Area

Mere Burn

The Derwent Walk Inn

NORTHUMBERLAND
(England's Border Country)

Follow waymarks

A694

The Derwent Walk

Derwent Walk Country Park

Panshield

Superb views

A popular railway walk on the former Derwent Valley Railway

Fork right to Public Footpath sign

B6310

Shotley Bridge Picnic Area

B6278

Burn House

Shotley Hall

SHOTLEY BRIDGE
A large village famous for its 17th century swordmakers from Solingen in Germany

Map navigation needed

Letch Burn

Rocky riverside with steep cliffs

Aim for a lone tree

Weir

Horseshoe Plantation

Rutted track

COUNTY DURHAM
(Land of the Prince Bishops)

To Carterway Heads

Bulbeck Cottage

Royal Derwent Hotel

RIVER DERWENT

Allansford Mill Farm

Allensford Bridge

Tourist Information Centre

Gradient 12%

A68

ALLENSFORD PARK
A riverside picnic area and caravan park.
Start and Finish

To Castleside 1 mile

(Continued from page 19)

path up and out of the wood to a track which leads you past two sets of cottages into the farming hamlet of Newlands. Turn right and at the road junction, go down the busy B6309 (signposted 1 mile) and cross New Bridge (built 1973) over the River Derwent to re-enter County Durham. Continue along the road, note the Old Bridge (built 1864), and pass Ebchester Woods owned by the National Trust. Climb the steep Chare Bank into the unspoilt village of Ebchester which occupies the site of the Roman fort of Vindomora. The Church of St. Ebba dates from Norman times and was partly built of stones from the fort. The Chelmsford offers food.

At the road junction, turn right and go left up the B6309 (Leadgate) and ascend the steep Ebchester Hill for a mile to reach Ebchester Station Picnic Area and join the very popular Derwent Walk. From the picnic area, turn right for an easy stroll along the Derwent Walk, part of the former Derwent Valley railway line which once served Swalwell to Consett. The railway opened in 1867, closed in 1962 and ten years later was developed as a footpath, bridleway and cycle track. Follow this redundant railway route for a mile to Shotley Bridge Picnic Area with delightful views over the Derwent Valley. Turn down Snows Green Road (B6310) for a mile into the village of Shotley Bridge and look out for the attractive Swiss Cottage (1840) and the beautiful old Town Hall, formerly Lloyds Bank. Re-cross the bridge over the Derwent to join the short walk. Go up the

B6278 for 880yds and look out for the Lough Scuptures at the lodge entrance to Shotley Hall. Just before the sign 'Stanhope B6278', turn left at the signpost 'Public Footpath Bulbeck Cottage 1 mile' and go down the lane past Burn House. Fork left, go up the track by Hall Wood and at the end of the second field, go through the gap by the gate and walk down the field edge with a wood on your right. At the bottom, stride the stream and go up the muddy enclosed path with wide views over the Derwent Valley to Shotley Bridge and Consett. Cross a stile by a gate and go downhill by the field edge. Once over Letch Burn, cross a stile by the gate into a field of growing crops and avoid the well-worn path to your left. Walk forward in single file, with no path visible and aim half right for a lone tree in the middle of the field. From the tree, aim for a large holly tree and pass through a couple of gateposts into Horseshoe Plantation. Follow a faint path through the scrubland and turn up the rutted track by the woodland edge. Near the top, bear left, pass Bulbeck Cottage and emerge from the wood into a walled lane. Follow this for a short distance, turn sharp left through two large gateposts and follow the broad, winding, sandy track downhill. The view across the Derwent Valley includes Consett and Castleside with the Victorian viaduct of Hownsgill dominating the skyline. Pass the impressive Royal Derwent Hotel with Hole Row Farm concealed within the hotel complex. Go down the driveway to the A68 and follow the outward route back to Allensford Park.

7. Blanchland

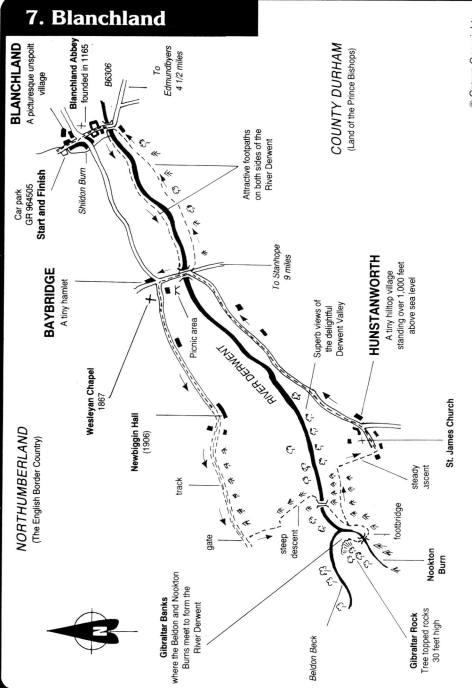

BLANCHLAND
A picturesque unspoilt village

Blanchland Abbey founded in 1165

B6306

To Edmundbyers 4 1/2 miles

Car park
GR 964505
Start and Finish

Shildon Burn

Attractive footpaths on both sides of the River Derwent

To Stanhope 9 miles

BAYBRIDGE
A tiny hamlet

Wesleyan Chapel
1867

Picnic area

RIVER DERWENT

Newbiggin Hall
(1906)

track

gate

steep descent

Superb views of the delightful Derwent Valley

HUNSTANWORTH
A tiny hilltop village standing over 1,000 feet above sea level

steady ascent

St. James Church

footbridge

Nookton Burn

NORTHUMBERLAND
(The English Border Country)

COUNTY DURHAM
(Land of the Prince Bishops)

Gibraltar Banks
where the Beldon and Nookton Burns meet to form the River Derwent

Gibraltar Rock
Tree topped rocks 30 feet high

Beldon Beck

22

7. Blanchland and Gibraltar Rock

Location: *Blanchland in Northumberland is a picturesque, unspoilt village 4^1/$_2$ miles north-west of Edmundbyers (B6306) and 10^1/$_2$ miles south of Hexham.*
Route: *Blanchland – Baybridge – Hunstanworth – Blanchland.*
Distance: *Under 5 miles (8 km). Moderate. Allow 3 hours. Very steep descent. Gradual ascent. Some road walking.*
O.S. Maps: *Landranger 87 Hexham and Haltwhistle. Pathfinder 560 NY85/95 Allendale Town and Blanchland; 570 NY 84/94 Allenheads and Rookhope.*
Parking: *Blanchland Public car park (free). 200 yards north of the village. GR 964505.*
Public Transport: *OK Travel Service 869 Bishop Auckland – Hexham via Blanchland (Tues only). Northumbria Motor Services 773 Consett/Townfield via Blanchland. Tyne Valley Coaches 969 Acomb via Hexham – Blanchland. Schooldays only.*
Refreshments: *Lord Crewe Arms Hotel; The White Monk Tearooms, Blanchland. None on route.*

This short stroll explores the upper Derwent Valley and discovers the romantic cliff called Gibraltar Rock where the River Derwent is born. If you like quiet and solitude, this walk will appeal strongly.

From Blanchland car park, turn back into the village and visit the old Abbey Church founded in 1165 or chance a drink in the haunted Crypt Bar of the Lord Crewe Arms Hotel. At the bottom of the village, just before the bridge, turn right by the end cottage (AD 1862) and fork left through the wall gap. Go over the grass path, cross the Shildon Burn by the footbridge and turn right along the River Derwent. Keep by the river for a very pleasant walk upstream to Baybridge. It's generally an easy walk, though you will have to cross two double sets of ladder stiles and it does get rather muddy in places. After half a mile, as you approach the old arched Bay Bridge, leave the river and fork right along a duck-board railed path to reach the road. Turn right along the road and pass Baybridge Picnic Area – the perfect place for a break. To continue the walk, go along the road into Northumberland and enter the tiny hamlet of Baybridge. Where the road bends back to Blanchland, turn left through the entrance gates with signs 'Newbiggin Hall', 'Private' and 'Baybridge Chapel'. There is also a hidden footpath signpost on your left telling you that Hunstanworth is 1^1/$_2$ miles away. Go up the tarmac lane, pass Baybridge Chapel (1867), for a stiff but steady climb rewarded with some delightful views of the Derwent Valley. As you pass the entrance to Newbiggin Hall (1906), the tarmac lane deteriorates into an unsurfaced track. Follow the track which bends right, goes up past a detached house and turns left and levels out. Go through a facing wooden gate marked 'Shut This Gate' and continue westwards along the track with Long Plantation on your left and open meadow country dotted with plantations on your right. At the far end of the field, where the wood ceases on your left, go through a facing metal gate and ten yards along the track turn left through an unsignposted metal gate with good views across the valley to the Victorian village of Hunstanworth, half hidden in the trees. The path drops gradually down the field. At the bottom, cross a newly erected stile over the wall. Turn left and go along by the wall above the scrubland. Prepare yourself for a steep and slippery descent into the valley bottom, as the path hugs the plantation perimeter on your left. Take your time on this downward route and at the bottom, disregard the stile on your left, unless you fancy fording the Derwent. Turn right for a few yards, cross the footbridge over the River Derwent and you are now in County Durham. Turn right along the meadow track and cross the corner wooden stile at the narrow end of the field. Here it's worth making a detour to see the birthplace of the River Derwent so follow the riverside path upstream, cross the footbridge over the Nookton Burn and go right to the apex point of Gibraltar Banks where the burns of Nookton and Beldon join to form the River Derwent. Behind you is the 30ft high rocky cliff called Gibraltar Rock. Revel in the sylvan beauty and enjoy the quiet and solitude of this heavily wooded, secluded spot. It's a haven for heron, dipper, kingfisher, and red squirrel.

Retrace your steps along the riverside, pass the corner stile crossed on the outward route and keep within Nookton Wood for a stiff but gradual climb on a good path up the thick dark wood with precipitous drops on your left. At the top, cross a ladder stile and go straight up the sloping meadow with backward views into the Derwent Valley. The path goes through a signposted gate beside the church into the hilltop village of Hunstanworth. In 1863 the entire village including church, vicarage, schools and houses were re-built, most of them in Burgundian style by Samuel Teulon. Go along the short street where the Church of St James is worth a visit. In the churchyard are the ruins of a pele tower which had an under vault to hide goods and cattle from the raiding Scots. By Corner Cottage turn left down the quiet road with superb views of the valley and Newbiggin Hall among the woods.

At the Baybridge/Stanhope road go straight over the road to the footpath signposted gate for a delightful woodland walk high above the River Derwent. You come out by a couple of terrace cottages, turn down the road and cross the bridge over the river into Blanchland.

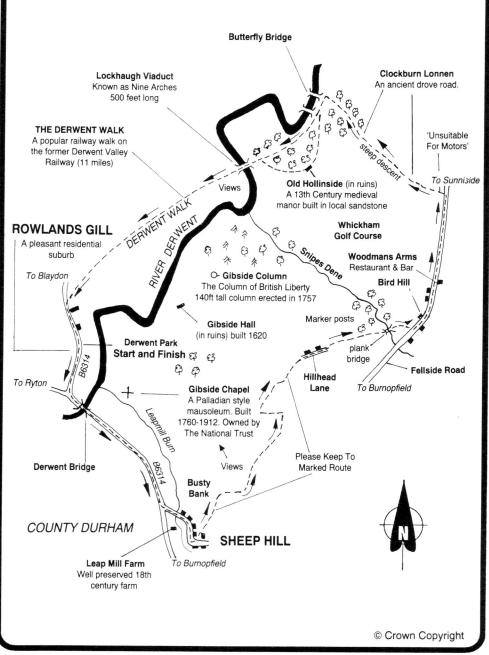

Butterfly Bridge

Lockhaugh Viaduct
Known as Nine Arches
500 feet long

Clockburn Lonnen
An ancient drove road.

THE DERWENT WALK
A popular railway walk on
the former Derwent Valley
Railway (11 miles)

'Unsuitable
For Motors'

steep descent

To Sunniside

Views

Old Hollinside (in ruins)
A 13th Century medieval
manor built in local sandstone

DERWENT WALK

RIVER DERWENT

ROWLANDS GILL
A pleasant residential
suburb

**Whickham
Golf Course**

Snipes Dene

Woodmans Arms
Restaurant & Bar

To Blaydon

O- **Gibside Column**
The Column of British Liberty
140ft tall column erected in 1757

Bird Hill

Marker posts

Gibside Hall
(in ruins) built 1620

plank
bridge

**Derwent Park
Start and Finish**

B6314

Fellside Road

To Ryton

**Hillhead
Lane**

To Burnopfield

+

Leapmill Burn

Gibside Chapel
A Palladian style
mausoleum. Built
1760-1912. Owned by
The National Trust

Please Keep To
Marked Route

B6314

Derwent Bridge

Views

**Busty
Bank**

COUNTY DURHAM

SHEEP HILL

Leap Mill Farm
Well preserved 18th
century farm

To Burnopfield

N

8. Rowlands Gill and Gibside

Location: *Rowlands Gill is a residential suburb high above the scenic Derwent Valley in Gateshead District, 3 miles south of Blaydon, 1 mile north of Burnopefield (B6314).*
Route: *Rowlands Gill – Busty Bank – Hillhead Lane – Bird Hill – Clockburn Lonnen – The Derwent Walk – Rowlands Gill.*
Distance: *6 miles (10km). Fairly easy. Allow 3/4 hours. Some road walking with a steep climb up Busty Bank. Field paths with gradual climbs. One steep descent. Railway walk.*
O.S. Maps: *Landranger 88 Tyneside. Pathfinder 561 (NZ05/15) Consett; 548 (NZ 06/16) Blaydon and Prudhoe.*
Parking: *Derwent Park, Rowlands Gill. GR 168586. At junction of A694 and B6314 in Rowlands Gill. Free. (68 spaces) Park gates close each day at 6pm, October – April.*
Public Transport: *Go ahead Northern, Services 607 Newcastle – Blackhall Mill; 608 Newcastle – Consett; 715 Stanley – Rowlands Gill.*
Refreshments: *MaQuires Fish and Chips; Townley Arms, Rowlands Gill. Woodmans Arms on Fellside Road.*
Note: *Please keep to waymarked route. Please keep dogs on a lead. Reserve this ramble for Easter if you want to visit Gibside Chapel or Leap Mill Farm.*

Six of the best miles around Rowlands Gill rewards this ramble, which encircles the 18th century parkland of the Gibside Estate with scenic views of the delightful Derwent Valley.

Leave Rowlands Gill by the B6314 and follow the Burnopfield Road via the Derwent Bridge over the River Derwent into County Durham. Proceed up the road and on your left note, the access lane to Gibside Chapel. Climb steadily up the B6314 and at the 'Burnopfield' sign, turn left along the road for a steep climb up Busty Bank, named after the bygone Busty coalseam outcrops. As you climb to Sheep Hill, look down to see the Leapmill Burn which marks the boundary between Tyne and Wear and County Durham. Located in this little valley is the well preserved 18th century Leap Mill Farm. In Sheep Hill, turn left into Westwood Close and at the end of the cul de sac, take the unsignposted path between 29 and 16, with a request 'Please Keep To Marked Route'.

Go up the fenced path by the side of the wood and at the top pass through a small waymarked gate. Admire the extensive views of the Derwent Valley. Turn right up the field edge and at the upper end of the field (waymark post) turn left along the same field and exit over a corner stile by a gate. You get your first full view of the Gibside Estate with the handsome domed Gibside Chapel, a mausoleum masterpiece prepared by James Payne for the Bowes Family in 1760 and finally consecrated in 1812. It is the finest example of Palladian architecture in the North-East. Nearly always visible on the walk is the Gibside Column or Monument. This fine Doric stone pillar, 140ft high and surmounted by a 12ft high figure sometimes called 'Lady Liberty', was erected as an ornament to the grounds, not to commemorate some event or person.

Stay on the track, veer right to cross a stile left of a very muddy open gateway. Make sure you follow the yellow directional waymarks. The fields ahead were opencasted for coal and have been restored to agricultural use. Turn immediately left over another stile, follow the field path through a hurdle fence (waymarked) and follow the field edge path which curves down the field. Do not cross the large stile at the bottom, but turn right along the field, fence on your left, to cross the next signposted stile. Turn right, cross two more stiles for a short walk along Hillhead Lane and where it turns right, walk forward, cross the stile and follow the waymarked stiled route via marker posts to skirt the edge of the delightful wooded Snipes Dene. At a triple waymark post, turn down into the Dene, cross a plank bridge, detour round a fallen tree and aim for the hillside marker post for a final climb up to Fellside, which, at 540ft above sea level, is the highest point on the walk. Turn left along the paved Fellside Road to pass Bird Hill. If you fancy a break, call in at The Woodman's Arms for refreshments. Go down the main road past Whickham Golf Course and turn left into the lane marked 'Unsuitable for Motors'.

You have now reached Clockburn Lonnen, an ancient drove road between Scotland and Durham used by Cromwell's armies during the invasion of Scotland in 1650. Today it is part of the Heritage Way, a 70 mile footpath route around Tyne and Wear. Descend the bridle track steeply into the wooded Derwent Valley and as you approach the railway bridge leave the main track and fork right to join the Derwent Walk. Turn left and follow part of the former Derwent Valley railway line which once served Swalwell to Consett. The line was developed as a footpath, bridle way and cycle track in 1972. Follow this route which traverses Lockhaugh Viaduct, known locally as Nine Arches, for a quick return of a mile and three quarters to Rowlands Gill. But, if you have plenty of time, use the signposted stepped path up to Old Hollinside, a medieval manor house.

extensive views
of Baldersdale

Join the Pennine Way

Goldsborough (1,274 ft)
A flat-topped hill
with gritstone outcrops

Pennine Way

Public
bridleway
signpost

Yawd Sike

MoD
Danger Area

map navigation

Pennine Way
(undefined)

boggy

Follow marker posts

COTHERSTONE MOOR

stile/gate

Race Yate
An old boundary stone
dated 1729

Hazelgill Beck

Levy Pool
A ruined heather
thatched house – (1736)

map navigation

gate

Deepdale Beck

ford

**MoD
Danger** poisonous gas
area keep out

Single railed footbridge

West Stoney Keld

BOWES
An ancient village
Start and Finish

boggy

**MoD
Danger** poisonous gas
area keep out

car park

Ravock Castle
The ruins of an
old shepherd's hut

cairned route

Pennine Way

Pennine Way

**Notice
'Manor of Bowes'**
Dogs must be
kept on a lead

Pasture End

A66

River Greta

GRETADALE

God's Bridge
A natural
limestone bridge

Lady Mires

West Gates

West Mellwaters

Pennine Way

East Mellwaters

West Charity Farm

West Pasture

Cardwell Bridge
named after
Stan Cardwell MBE
of Darlington

GILMONBY
A hidden hamlet

N

9. Bowes and Baldersdale

Location: *Bowes, an ancient village, is 4 miles south-west of Barnard Castle.*
Route: *Bowes – Cardwell Bridge – God's Bridge – Race Yate – Goldsborough – Levy Pool – Bowes.*
Distance: *12 miles (19km). Allow 6 hours. Strenuous. Exposed moorland.*
O.S. Maps: *Landranger 92 Barnard Castle and Richmond. Pathfinder 598 (NY81/91) North Stainmore and Bowes.*
Parking: *Car park opposite village hall, Bowes. GR 996134.*
Public Transport: *OK Travel (X74) Darlington – Carlisle – Keswick. Barnard Castle Coaches Ruralride 72 Barnard Castle-Bowes. United 78 Darlington-Bowes Saturday only. Primrose Coaches X69 Newcastle-Bowes Bypass.*
Refreshments: *The Ancient Unicorn Hotel, Bowes. None on route.*
Note: *Brief description. Map and compass skills essential. Dogs must be kept on a lead. This is a strenuous ramble over bleak moorland, often wet and boggy. Be warned: It is arduous and tough going. Stout footwear is needed. Do not attempt in doubtful weather.*

Although the Pennine Way is a linear walk, it is possible to plan a circular walk by using the alternative loops which leave and rejoin the Pennine Way. One such circuit from the village of Bowes starts and finishes with the Bowes Alternative and combines with the Pennine Way for a rough ramble.

From Bowes car park, go down the road to Gilmonby and at the sign 'Lady Mires 1 mile', turn right and follow the 'No Through Road' westwards along Gretadale. Pass West Gates and midway between the farms, West Pasture and Lady Mires, the Bowes Alternative Loop comes down from Bowes, fords the River Greta and joins the farm road. Beyond Lady Mires, follow the track through a couple of gated fields where a double Pennine Way signpost directs you down to West Charity Pasture Farm. Another similar sign points left to the Cardwell Bridge, named after Stan Cardwell MBE of Darlington. Cross the footbridge over Sleightholme Beck. Walk forward, go up and keep by the wall on your left with the River Greta below. Pass through a gate and half left across a field to East Mellwaters. Within the farmyard, turn right, go left between the out buildings, left again and right by the sheep pens and out through a gate. Follow the gated track to West Mellwaters (1773) and just beyond the farm go diagonally downhill to God's Bridge, a natural limestone bridge over the River Greta. Rest at this spot and note the lime kilns.

Leave the Bowes Alternative Loop, cross the bridge and follow the main Pennine Way northwards up to the A66. Cross the road and go over a stile on to the open Bowes Moor where a Notice 'Manor of Bowes' requests that 'Dogs must be kept on a lead'. Follow the Pennine Way northwards, first by the wall, and stride out over the bleak Bowes Moor on a broad bridle track. After a mile, the track climbs up to the ridge (1,250ft) with a large heap of stones on your left – not a cairn, but the ruins of a shepherd's hut, known locally as Ravock Castle. There are extensive views north to Deepdale and back to Gretadale and Swaledale. The cairned track, wet and boggy, descends into Deepdale.

Cross the footbridge over Deepdale Beck. Continue to climb northwards for another mile by the boundary wall for an undulating walk to the summit ridge of Race Yate, where the wall and fence meet. At 1,400ft it is the highest point on the walk.

Cross the corner stile or go through the gate. Make a short detour of 250yds to your left and inspect the boundary stone dated 1729 which marks the division between the moors of Lartington and Cotherstone. Marker posts guide you down the boggy moor into Baldersdale, where Hannah Hauxwell used to live. As you descend, you can see the flat topped Shacklesborough and Goldsborough as well as the reservoirs of Balderhead, Blackton and Hury. Leave the Pennine Way at the minor road near Clove Lodge. Turn right along the unfenced road for three-quarters of a mile until a Public Bridleway signpost with acorn symbols is reached on your right. Rejoin the Pennine Way – Bowes Alternative Loop and turn up the tractor track, veer left and follow the marker posts in a south easterly direction, skirting Goldsborough. On the south side of this flat topped hill, note the great gritstone outcrops and head south-east over the reedy moor. Fork right when you see the tractor tracks that ford Yawd Sike and aim half left, south-east again, for the top corner wall seen on the horizon. Go through the gate and follow the Pennine Way southwards by the MoD danger area with its warning notices.

Keep by the fence/ wall on a good path, go over a cross track and prepare for a stiff scramble, down and up, across Hazelgill Beck. The path ahead is undefined down to the forlorn Hazelgill Plantation and fork south-west for the ford on Deepdale Beck. Cross the step stones over the beck which might be difficult after heavy rain. Go up the muddy track, pass the ruined Levy Pool, a heather thatched house dated 1736, and follow the gated track to come out near West Stoney Keld Farm. Follow the uphill road past the MoD – Danger Poisonous Gas Area, for nearly two miles back to Bowes.

10. Scots' Gap

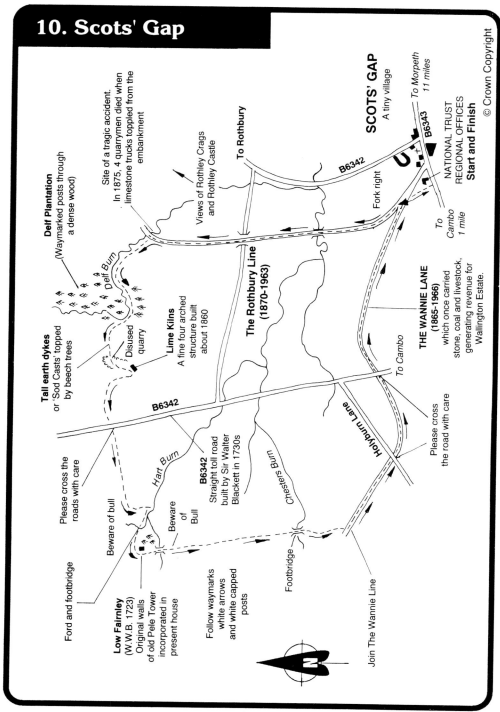

© Crown Copyright

SCOTS' GAP
A tiny village

To Morpeth
11 miles

B6343

NATIONAL TRUST
REGIONAL OFFICES
Start and Finish

To Cambo
1 mile

Fork right

B6342

To Rothbury

Views of Rothley Crags
and Rothley Castle

Delf Plantation
(Waymarked posts through
a dense wood)

Site of a tragic accident.
In 1875, 4 quarrymen died when
limestone trucks toppled from the
embankment

Delf Burn

Tall earth dykes
or 'Sod Casts' topped
by beech trees

Disused
quarry

Lime Kilns
A fine four arched
structure built
about 1860

The Rothbury Line
(1870-1963)

THE WANNIE LANE
(1865-1966)
which once carried
stone, coal and livestock,
generating revenue for
Wallington Estate.

To Cambo

Please cross
the road with care

B6342

B6342
Straight toll road
built by Sir Walter
Blackett in 1730s

Please cross the
roads with care

Hart Burn

Chesters Burn

Holyburn Lane

Beware of bull

Beware
of
Bull

Ford and footbridge

Low Fairnley
(W.W.B. 1723)
Original walls
of old Pele Tower
incorporated in
present house

Follow waymarks
white arrows
and white capped
posts

Footbridge

Join The Wannie Line

N

28

10. Scots' Gap – Wannie Line Walk

Location: The Wannie Line Walk starts and finishes at the National Trust Regional Office car park at Scots' Gap. 12 miles south of Rothbury, 11 miles west of Morpeth.
Route: Scots' Gap – The Rothbury Line – Delf Burn – Low Fairnley – Chesters Burn – The Wannie Line – Scots' Gap.
Distance: 7 miles (11 km). Easy. Allow 3 hours.
O.S. Maps: Landranger 81 Alnwick and Morpeth; Pathfinder 523 (NZ08/18) Morpeth West.
Parking: Limited parking in Scots' Gap Village. National Trust overflow car park .
Public Transport: Northumbria Motor Service or Vasey's Coaches; service 419 Morpeth/Scots' Gap/Cambo (Wed/Fri).
Refreshments: None on route.
Leaflet: Use the excellent leaflet Wallington Estate Walks – Wannie Line Walk available from the National Trust shop at Wallington, price 45p.
Note: Please note that this walk is open only from **June 1 to October 31** in order that the vitally important calving and lambing seasons are undisturbed.

This waymarked walk through the beautiful countryside of the Wallington Estate in Northumberland was devised in 1987 by the National Trust. It uses two disused railways connected by footpaths and gives an insight into the industrial archaeology, history and natural history of the area.

Start by crossing the stile within the overflow car park by the National Trust regional offices at Scots' Gap. Walk forward, aim for a waymarked post, veer right via a sleeper bridge and over a stile down to the disused railway line. Turn left along the track bed, cross a stile and yards beyond the bridge abutment the line splits. Take the railway route on your right and follow the old Rothbury line which ran through here between 1870 and 1963. Note: the line on your left is the old Wansbeck Railway, better known as the Wannie Line which gave its name to this walk. The 25-mile line operated between 1865 and 1966. Both railways carried produce from the Wallington Estate. It is part of the return route.

The route crosses a couple of railway bridges over Hart Burn and an unclassified road. A white post signals a spongy section, so keep on the right side of the rail trail. Wild flowers, including the spotted orchid, can be seen in abundance. After two miles the track curves right. At the waymarked post descend the steep steps, cross the stile and turn right, then left along the delightful Delf Burn. Cross the stile signposted Delf Burn, turn left into the dense Delf Plantation for a woodland walk westwards. Keep by the burn and follow the waymarked white posts upstream for more than half-a-mile, but watch your way carefully. Ascend the steep stepped path above the Delf Burn and keep by the plantation edge. Exit over a stile, note the medieval field strips on Toot Hill and bear half right up the field to the tall beech trees planted on earth dykes faced with dry stone walling. These 'sod casts' are a good example of an 18th century field boundary. The trees are probably 250 years old. Near the top of the field turn right, cross a wedged ladder stile between the trees into the adjacent field. Turn left up the field and down some unexpected steps into an abandoned quarry. Straddle the wire fence, cross the waymarked stile – both on your left – and go through the old limestone quarry. Waymarks guide you up past a fine four-arched group of lime kilns built in the 1860s to replace a single pot kiln.

Walk to the waymarked corner wall and turn right up by the wall edge of the same field. Turn left and go down the old quarry road noting the views northwards of the Simonside Hills. Cross a stile labelled 'Please cross the road safely' and go over the busy B6342 Rothbury road where opposite, cross a waymarked stile. Go down the track with the wall on your right and cross a stile over the barbed wire fence. Bear right and follow the field boundary (another medieval field system) dotted with ash trees. At the field end, turn left down the edge of the same field by the 'sod casts' with waymarked posts. Turn right, cross a cattle grid with a Beware of the Bull symbol and follow the farm road via a ford and footbridge over Hart Burn to Low Fairnley which is the only habitation on the route – a rarity indeed on any walk.

Pass Low Fairnley and turn sharp left by the garden fence, as directed by a flat waymarked stone which you can easily miss. Pass the former fortified pele tower dated WWB 1723 and head southwards down the open field. Cross the bridge over Fairnley Burn and at the end of the plantation on your left, aim up the field for the corner waymarked stile with a Beware of the Bull symbol. Cross the stile and follow the waymarked posts down the edge of the stiled fields with more 'sod casts' on your right. Cross the bridge over Chesters Burn with its own name plate. Aim for a waymarked post by a plantation, turn right, cross a stile and turn left southwards following the stiled route by the side of a couple of plantations. Go up the rough pasture, pass a huge rock pile, cross a slab bridge over Holy Burn and aim for the waymarked, stiled railway embankment. You have now reached the Wannie Line for a two mile return route to Scots' Gap.

11. Penshaw

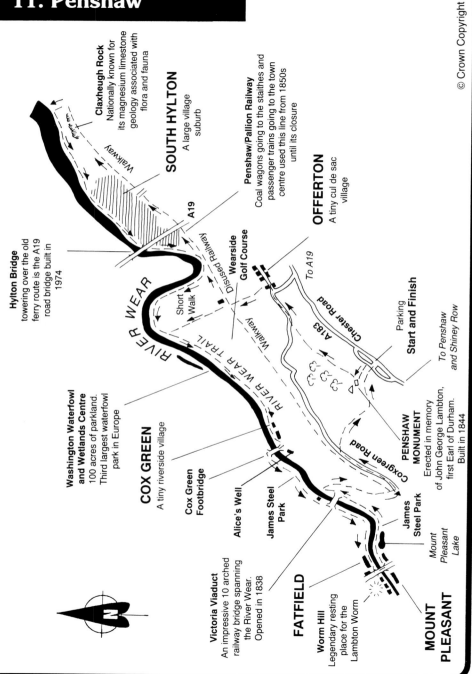

Hylton Bridge
towering over the old
ferry route is the A19
road bridge built in
1974

Claxheugh Rock
Nationally known for
its magnesium limestone
geology associated with
flora and fauna

SOUTH HYLTON
A large village
suburb

A19

Walkway

Penshaw/Pallion Railway
Coal wagons going to the staithes and
passenger trains going to the town
centre used this line from 1850s
until its closure

OFFERTON
A tiny cul de sac
village

RIVER WEAR

**Wearside
Golf Course**

Disused Railway

Short
Walk

To A19

RIVER WEAR TRAIL

Walkway

Chester Road

A183

Parking

Start and Finish

*To Penshaw
and Shiney Row*

**Washington Waterfowl
and Wetlands Centre**
100 acres of parkland.
Third largest waterfowl
park in Europe

COX GREEN
A tiny riverside village

**Cox Green
Footbridge**

Coxgreen Road

**PENSHAW
MONUMENT**
Erected in memory
of John George Lambton,
first Earl of Durham.
Built in 1844

Alice's Well

**James Steel
Park**

**James
Steel Park**

*Mount
Pleasant
Lake*

Victoria Viaduct
An impressive 10 arched
railway bridge spanning
the River Wear.
Opened in 1838

FATFIELD

Worm Hill
Legendary resting
place for the
Lambton Worm

**MOUNT
PLEASANT**

N

30

11. Penshaw and River Wear Trail

Location: *Penshaw Monument, a well known landmark, is open at all times and is cared for by the National Trust. It is 440yds east of Penshaw Village, off A183.*
Route: *Penshaw Hill – Offerton – South Hylton – Claxheugh Rock – Hylton Bridge – Cox Green – Fatfield – Mount Pleasant – Victoria Viaduct – Penshaw Hill.*
Distance: *11 miles or 6 miles. Easy/Moderate. Allow 3/5 hours*
O.S. Maps: *Landranger 88 Tyneside; Pathfinder 562 (NZ25/35) Washington and Chester-le-Street.*
Parking: *Disused stretch of old Chester road, off A183 Sunderland to Chester-le-Street road , 440yds east of Penshaw Village.*
Public Transport: *Go- Ahead Northern Services 775/778 Consett-Sunderland*
Leaflet: *Use the excellent River Wear Trail Leaflet produced by the Borough of Sunderland for points of interest. Available from Tourist Information Centres.*
Refreshments: *The Hycroft; The Golden Lion, South Hylton. Oddfellow Arms, Cox Green. The Biddick; The Riverside; The Havelock, Fatfield.*
Note: *Keep dogs on a lead. Please keep to the paths.*

You will have seen Penshaw Monument on the skyline from a dozen different angles throughout the North East of England. Now here is the opportunity to climb up 'Pensher' for great views in reverse. This easy walk combines a visit to Penshaw Monument, one of the North-East's most famous landmarks with the popular River Wear Trail inaugurated in 1990 by the Borough of Sunderland and offers a rewarding ramble, full of history and legend by the famous River Wear.

From the old Chester Road take the signposted, stepped path straight up Penshaw Hill to Penshaw Monument, the Grecian style temple erected in 1844 in honour of John George Lambton, the first Earl of Durham. From the trig point hill (446ft), admire the wonderful views of Wearside, Washington and Tyneside. Head right (eastwards) down the green track, cross a waymarked stile, bear half left over the corner field and cross another stile into Penshaw Wood. Turn immediately right, follow the stiled/waymarked perimeter path by the wood and along the stiled field edge to join the road. Turn right and follow this to the cul-de-sac village of Offerton. When you see Offerton Lodge on your left (path sign missing), go down the lane to the former Penshaw-Pallion Railway. If you don't fancy going into the suburbs of Sunderland, continue down the lane to the River Wear for the shorter walk.

For the longer walk, turn right along the old Penshaw-Pallion Railway which carried coal to the Sunderland staithes and passengers to the town centre from the 1850s until its closure in the 1960s. Follow the walkway which is the alternative route of River Wear Trail via special waymarkers for two miles eastwards. Go through the A19 underpass, stroll past the village of South Hylton and emerge out of a deep limestone cutting overlooking River Wear on the industrial edge of Sunderland. When you reach a trail waymarker, opposite Sunderland Motor Auctions, go down to the riverside and join the River Wear Trail. Turn left and follow the riverside path below the dramatic Claxheugh

Penshaw Monument

Rock with its impressive magnesian limestone cliffs, well known for flora and fauna. Opposite the water sports centre there is an excellent illustrated information board, one of many on the Trail, giving particular points of interest. Keep by the railed riverside and a quick glance down river reveals the wreck of the concrete tug 'Cretehauser' built in 1919, gutted in 1935 for use as an emergency breakwater and deliberately beached in 1942.

The next section of the Trail, adopted by a South Hylton Primary School, is fairly easy to follow, but marred by burnt out cars, despite the vast improvements at Hylton Riverside Park with a delightful picnic area. The Golden Lion (1705) better known as 'The Big Steaks Pub' is the perfect place for a much needed stop. Go under the impressive Hylton Bridge which is the A19 road bridge built in 1974. The route requires little direction, as it snakes by the River Wear through unattractive flat fields, but improves as you progress westwards. There are distant views of Penshaw Monument. After two miles, join the short walk from Offerton and follow the delightful riverside path by the Wearside Golf Course, where

(Continued on page 32)

(Continued from page 31)

bench seats offer a grandstand view across the river to the superb 100 acre Washington Waterfowl Park and Wetlands Centre with more than 1,200 wildfowl of various kinds. Follow the woodchip path for a delightful tree lined walk westwards by the River Wear, but watch out for a steep stepped path. After a mile, you reach the tiny riverside village of Cox Green, once a thriving port exporting timber, sandstone and coal. Ships were repaired and built here until 1862. The Oddfellows Arms, a riverside pub with rear beer garden offers refreshments. There is a picnic area and map board by the pub. Twenty yards beyond the footbridge, you must see the inscribed Alice's Well, rebuilt 1885 which was Cox Green's only supply of drinking water until the Second World War. Cross Cox Green Footbridge over the River Wear and turn left into the James Steel Park, a popular country riverside park named after Sir James Steel, Lord Lieutenant of Tyne & Wear from 1974-1984. The park extends on both banks of the river from Princess Anne Park to the Waterfowl Park. An illustrated map board gives details of paths/places and a stone plaque commemorates the handing over to the Woodland Trust on July 6 1987 of the surrounding woodlands created by Washington Development Corporation. Go through the park following the signposted/stiled route along the north bank of the river and pass behind a white washed farm with a request 'Please

keep dogs on a lead'. Beyond the farm, the riverside route passes under the impressive ten-arched Victoria Railway Viaduct 128ft above the river. It was opened in 1938 on the day of Queen Victoria's coronation. Somewhere between the Victoria Viaduct and Fatfield Village is the site of Girdle Cake Cottage, once renowned for its cakes. In Fatfield, behind The Biddick pub, is the conical Worm Hill which the mythical Lambton Worm is said to have wound itself around. There is a great view of Penshaw Monument from this hilltop with a bench seat and World War One memorial.

Cross Fatfield Bridge over the Wear to the terrace village of Mount Pleasant and turn immediately left along East Bridge Street into James Steel Park and pass the man made Mount Pleasant Lake with a replica of Penshaw Monument. Follow the wooded riverside path and 30yds beyond Victoria Viaduct, turn right in front of the Trail Map Board and go up the woodland track, where waymarks guide you through the railway arch and over the old Penshaw-Pallion Railway in the direction of Penshaw Village. When you reach the Cox Green Road, turn left by the pigeon crees and follow the road for about a mile. Cross the unsignposted stile, it's the second right of way on your right, for a climb up the field edge and at the top, cross a waymarked stile into a lane. Turn left and then right round the base of Penshaw Hill and fork right down a narrow path back to the old Chester road to complete a walk with monumental views.

Man-made Lacy's Caves near Little Salkeld, Cumbria

The village of Nunnington

12. Guisborough

Location: *Guisborough, ancient capital of Cleveland, is 10 miles South East of Middlesbrough on the A171.*
Route: *Guisborough – Charlton – Aysdale Gate – Quakers' Causeway – Commondale – Gisborough Moor – Guisborough.*
Distance: *Over 11 miles (17km) Moderate/strenuous. Allow 6 hours.*
O.S. Maps: *Landranger 94 Whitby Pathfinder NZ61/71 Guisborough and Loftus. Outdoor Leisure 26 North York Moors (Western area)*
Parking: *Ample parking in Guisborough.*
Public Transport: *Tees and District Service X256, X56 Middlesbrough-Whitby; Service 281 Redcar-Stokesley; Service 258 Middlesbrough-Lingdale. Cleveland Transit Service 71 Saltburn-Guisborough.*
Refreshments: *Pubs, cafes in Guisborough. The Cleveland Inn, Commondale.*
Note: *Map and compass essential. Do not attempt in doubtful weather.*

I am often asked what is my favourite North Country Walk. For me the Guisborough to Commondale circuit via the Quakers' Causeway is a firm favourite which includes pleasant fields, moorland dotted with bronze age burial mounds, thickly wooded hills and extensive views.

Leave Guisborough by walking east along Westgate into Church Street and pass the ruined 12th century Guisborough Priory endowed by Robert de Brus in 1119. Turn right by St. Nicholas Church and follow the flagged path past Prior Pursglove College, former Guisborough Grammar School founded in the reign of Queen Elizabeth AD 1561. Go through the kissing gate, fork right and follow the paved path across the fields to the A171. Cross the busy road, turn left along the footway for 30 yards and turn right at the footpath signposted entrance to 'Foxdale Farm Only'. Walk up the farm track for 200yds and where the track bends, look out for a waymarked footpath signposted stile in the fence on your left. Cross the stile and follow the yellow waymarks eastwards over the next four stiled fields. There are fine views of Gisborough Hall and the Guisborough Woods. At the A171 road, turn right, pass the entrance to Little Waterfall Farm and go up the footpath signposted lane to Spawood Auto Spares. As you climb, note the Waterfall Viaduct built in 1860 to serve the ironstone mines of Spa Wood. Pass the 'graveyard' of old cars, go up and turn left to pass a brick built house on a level path. Cross a waymarked stile into Spa Wood.

Follow the waymarks for an up and down walk over the tree covered spoil heaps. The walk meets the Cleveland Way and follow the signs which eventually lead you down to the road. Leave the Cleveland Way, turn right along the road, pass the terraced houses of Charlton and follow the old road to reach the A171. Continue along the main road to the bottom of Birk Brow, where a Public Bridleway signpost by Aysdale Gate Farm directs you right through a waymarked open gateway. Expect plenty of mud. Aim through a handgate by two metal gates. Climb the spur for a stiff ascent up a couple of stiled fields. At the top, go through a waymarked

Guisborough Priory by Barry Lawson

gate (gatepost inscribed 'ITW') on to Stanghow Moor. Walk straight on and follow the cairned moorland path for a mile to reach the Quakers' Causeway or Trod, a popular paved path used by the Quakers in the 1660s. Keep on the Trod and admire the views over Lockwood Beck Reservoir to Liverton and Loftus. After another mile the Trod finishes by the Bronze Age burial mounds known as Black Howes. Continue on the moorland path to Smeathorns Road where you leave Cleveland County and cross into North Yorkshire. Turn right along the road and just beyond the road barriers fork right down the unsignposted moorland path which converges with a water channel and some interesting inscribed boundary stones. Pass the plantation on your right and on reaching the road go down Sand Hill Bank into the village of Commondale which was once an important brick making centre. The Cleveland Inn is a convenient halfway house for refreshments.

For the return route, go up the road in the direction of Kildale and beyond the last cottage a Public

(Continued on page 37)

35

12. Guisborough

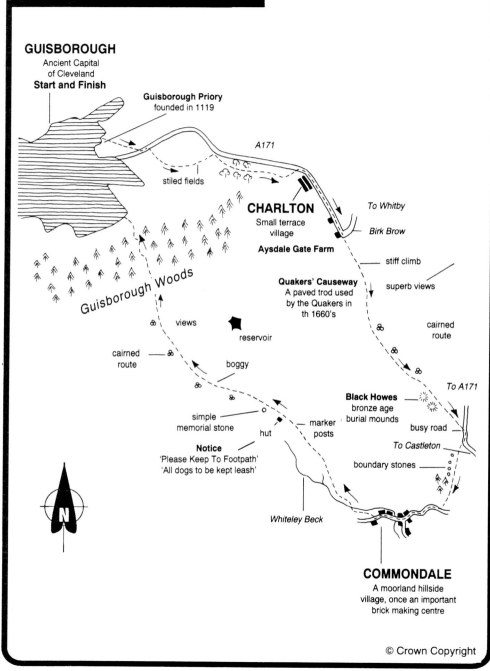

GUISBOROUGH
Ancient Capital
of Cleveland
Start and Finish

Guisborough Priory
founded in 1119

A171

stiled fields

CHARLTON
Small terrace
village

Aysdale Gate Farm

To Whitby

Birk Brow

stiff climb

superb views

Quakers' Causeway
A paved trod used
by the Quakers in
th 1660's

Guisborough Woods

views

cairned
route

reservoir

cairned
route

boggy

To A171

Black Howes
bronze age
burial mounds

simple
memorial stone

marker
posts

busy road

hut

To Castleton

Notice
'Please Keep To Footpath'
'All dogs to be kept leash'

boundary stones

Whiteley Beck

COMMONDALE
A moorland hillside
village, once an important
brick making centre

N

(Continued from page 35)

Footpath sign directs you down a track (paved trod) to Whiteley Beck. Stride the beck, climb uphill and follow the moorland track as it contours left, northwards above a little valley with North Ings Farm nestled below. Pass a couple cairns, plus a marker post (arrow missing) and cross a rough plank bridge over a deep ditch. Go up the track, pass a green painted hut (converted railway wagon) with a Notice 'Please Keep To Footpath' – 'All Dogs To Be Kept On Leash'.

Yards further on, leave the track at a way-marked post and follow the cairned moorland path northwards to reach a simple memorial stone to comemorate two local guardsman, Robbie Leggott and L.S. Cockerill killed in World War One. Cairns guide you up the soggy moor between standing stones and grouse butts (avoid during grouse shooting season). Go over a broad cross track (large cairn), re-enter Cleveland County and head northwards up the cairned Gisborough Moor for $1^1/_2$ miles to Guisborough Woods with grand views to the North Sea. Enter the extensive Guisborough Woods and constantly check the O.S. Map. Walk straight on down the forest drive. Go over a cross track and continue downwards where a double Cleveland Way sign directs you left along the drive which gradually winds down to another Cleveland Way sign. Turn right, steeply downhill, and if you want to avoid the deep mud use the side path between the trees on your left. Rejoin the main route which winds right then left to cross another cross track. At the bottom, exit over a stile and walk along Belmangate back to Guisborough.

© Crown Copyright

Gibson's Cave
'No access beyond this point'

Summerhill Force

To Middleton-in-Teesdale

Bowlees Beck

HOLWICK
A picturesque hamlet

Strathmore Arms
A stone built traditional country inn

TEESDALE
'The undiscovered corner of England'

Durham County Council Bowlees Picnic Area

B6277

PENNINE WAY

Wynch Bridge

Low Force or Salmon Leap

Holwick Lodge

Holwick Scars

CAR PARK
Start and Finish

To Ettersgill

Holwick Head Bridge

stepped climb

HIGH FORCE HOTEL

Nature Reserve sign

Superb views

HIGH FORCE
England's largest waterfall

juniper bushes

private track no access

THE GREEN TROD
An ancient drove road from Holwick to the Eden Valley

Quarry Warning
Bleabeck Force

marker posts

Quarry

stepping stones

footbridges

stiff climb

Warning
Hidden grouse butts

RIVER TEES

Skyer Beck

Dry Beck

Noon Hill
(1,739 feet)

marker post

Nature Reserve Sign

N

13. High Force

Location: *High Force Hotel car park on the north side of B6277 is 5 miles NW of Middleton in Teesdale; 14 miles NW of Barnard Castle*
Route: *High Force car park – Holwick Head Bridge – Blea Beck – Bracken Rigg – Dry Beck – Holwick – Wynch Bridge – Holwick Head Bridge – High Force car park.*
Distance: *Over 7 miles (11.2km) Moderate/ Energetic. Allow 4 hours.*
O.S. Maps: *Landranger 92 Barnard Castle and Richmond. Pathfinder 588 (NY82/92) Middleton in Teesdale. Outdoor Leisure 31.*
Parking: *High Force Hotel pay car park.*
Public Transport: *United: Service 75 Darlington-Langdon Beck. Sunday only. Service 76 Paul's Mini Bus Middleton-Langdon Beck.*
Refreshments: *Strathmore Arms, Holwick; High Force Hotel.*
Warning: *Quarry Blasting. Continuous siren: Stay Clear. 3 Short Signals: All Clear. Avoid this walk during grouse shooting season which begins on August 12. The return route involves a climb between a row of hidden grouse butts. No warning notices.*

This walk in wild rugged country shows the best of the waterfalls in Upper Teesdale. It takes in part of the popular Pennine Way; uses an old drove road called The Green Trod and provides Pennine panorama. Before setting out, pay your admission for a short stroll to High Force, it's one of the finest and largest waterfalls in England. In flood it is an awe inspiring sight.

Fifty yards down the B6277 from High Force car park, at the signs 'No Footway 600yds/Public Footpath', turn right down the new Crag Path, a beautifully constructed flight of steep steps through the whinstone crag to the River Tees. Follow the pleasant riverside path to Holwick Head Bridge. Cross the rickety cart bridge over the River Tees and join the Pennine Way, the oldest long distance walk in England. Turn right, follow the Pennine Way up the rough stepped path and at the top, cross the stile by the padlocked gate marked 'Danger High Fire Risk' and enter the Upper Teesdale National Nature Reserve, where a board tells you all about the reserve, the largest in the country. Follow the surfaced path for a mile through the biggest ancient juniper forest in England. Young children should be carefully supervised as you approach High Force as the path goes very near the edge of the unfenced steep whinstone cliffs. Admire the spectacular views of High Force as the Tees plunges 70ft into an amphitheatre of whinstone cliffs.

From High Force, follow the Pennine Way westwards along the path by the riverside, where a notice warns you of the blasting operations at the quarry across the river. Cross the footbridge (erected 1967) over Bleabeck with its lesser known, pretty waterfall. Cross a stile, follow the riverside path and cross two footbridges over the Dry and Skyer Becks. Leave the River Tees, cross some stepping stones and climb the duck boarded path up between the boulders and junipers to pass a corrugated barn (covered railway wagon). Aim for a waymarked (P.W.) post on the top of Bracken Rigg at 1,275ft above sea level. At this lofty spot, admire the spectacular views of the wild and rugged coun-

Wynch Bridge

try of Upper Teesdale, dotted with white washed farmsteads. Say goodbye to the Pennine Way and turn sharp left down to the gate in the far bottom corner of the rough pasture. Go through the waymarked, waterlogged gate, grip the wall, stride or use the stepping stones, over the fast flowing Fell Dike Syke. Walk straight on to the National Nature Reserve board, where southwards is the conical Noon Hill (1,739ft) overshadowed by Cronkley Fell at 1,793ft. You have now joined the old drove road, known locally as The Green Trod, used for droving cattle from Teesdale via Holwick to the Eden Valley. Turn left and follow The Green Trod eastwards, where the route ahead fords three becks and care should be taken when selecting a suitable crossing. Expect some boulder hopping, especially if the becks are swollen after heavy rain. After a short distance, Skyer Beck is reached which can be tricky, even by using the stepping stones. Dry Beck is much easier and can be crossed in three parts.

To continue, begin a fairly steep climb up by the wall on your left and at the top go through a row of shooting butts. Heed my warnings above. Pass a

(Continued on page 40)

39

(Continued from page 39)

couple of cairns. The track levels out, giving extensive views up and down the dale. Keep on the main track, go through a metal gate ('Please Close Gate') and along this boggy route, ford the final beck called Blea Beck. Despite the large stepping stones laid by volunteers of the Durham Countryside Ranger Service, this wide beck is still very difficult to cross. Head eastwards, pass a couple of marker posts and turn left along a rough track, once used by lead miners to and from the Silver Band Lead Mine. At the Nature Reserve board, cross a wobbly stile by a gate and follow the track for a mile. As you approach the Holwick Scars, do not turn left, it's a private road to the shooting mansion of Holwick Lodge, where the Queen Mother spent part of her honeymoon. Pass through a nearby small gate and go down the stony track between the dramatic whinstone cliffs into the hidden hamlet of Holwick, once the most northerley village in Yorkshire. For those suffering from pangs of thirst, the Strathmore

Arms at the east end of Holwick offers refreshments. At the west end of Holwick, turn left up the 'No Through Road' and where it bends left through an open gateway, turn right and follow the signposted Public Footpath diagonally down the waymaked, stiled meadows via a tiny restored bridge to reach Winch Bridge, better known as the 'Two Inch Bridge'. You have re-joined the Pennine Way.

An interesting extension here is to cross Wynch Bridge over the Tees, go up the wood and over a couple of stiled fields to the B6277. Turn right and left into the tiny terrace hamlet of Bowlees, call in at the Visitor Centre or from the Bowlees Picnic Area follow the nature trail to Gibson's Cave and see Summerhill Force. Retrace your steps back to Wynch Bridge. Turn left, walk upstream and pass the lovely Low Force or Salmon Leap. For the last leg of your journey, follow the Pennine Way with the Tees as your companion for a couple miles to reach Holwick Head Bridge and return via the outward route back to High Force car park to complete this waterfall walk.

14. Rothbury and the Simonside Hills

Location: Rothbury 'Capital of Coquetdale', a market town 12 miles west of Alnwick.
Route: Rothbury – Whitton – Hillhead Road – Whittondean – Garleigh Moor – The Beacon – Dove Crag – Simonside – Great Tosson – Thropton – Physic Lane – Rothbury.
Distance: 10 miles (16km) or 7 miles (11km) Allow 4/6 hours. Strenuous.
O.S. Maps: Landranger 81 Alnwick and Morpeth. Pathfinder 500 (NU00/01) Rothbury and Felton; 511 (NZ 09/19) Longhorsley and Simonside Hills.
Parking: The Haugh, Whitton Lane, car park south of River Coquet, west of road bridge.
Public Transport: Northumbria Motor Services 415, 515, 516. Newcastle-Rothbury.
Refreshments: Queens Head; The Milk Bar; Sun Kitchen; Pizzera Katrina, The Newcastle Hotel, Rothbury. Three Wheat Heads; Cross Keys. Thropton.
Warning: Beware of Adders on Garleigh Moor and the Simonside Hills.
Note: The walk is open all year round except during periods of high fire danger and when 'shoots' are in progress. Map and compass essential. Do not attempt in doubtful weather. Dogs must be kept on a lead at all times.

'Come, climb the steeps of Simonside
Where stretch for miles below
Snug farms, rich fields and waving woods
The Coquet's winding flow'

The Simonside Hills are special and any visitor to Rothbury in Coquetdale cannot fail to be impressed by the silhouetted sandstone summits seen on the skyline. This splendid walk explores the hills and moors on both sides of Coquetdale, south and north of Rothbury in Northumberland. It includes the Simonside Ridge Walk which offers the finest view in all Northumberland.

From the car park, turn right up Whitton Lane to the hilltop hamlet of Whitton with its historic Whitton Tower, a former fortified residence of the Rectors of Rothbury, built by the Umfravilles in the 14th century as a Border pele. At the road junction, go up the road and turn right by Woodford Juniper and follow Hillhead Lane past the tall tower of Sharp's Folly built in 1720 as an observatory for Archdeacon Thomas Sharp who dabbled in astrology. Half a mile past Sharp's Folly, the lane splits. Turn left along the farm road to Whittondean. Go through the gate marked 'Public Footpath Only', keep to the path by the farm with its lovely garden and aviary and as directed, walk along the valley of Whittondean with its cottage chalets.

A path sign with red arrows points the way through a waymarked gate and just beyond a pair of hawthorn bushes, bear left on a faint path for some bracken bashing and a climb up the hillside. Aim for the trees, ascend the steep path via a marker post and at the top go through the gap in the ruined wall to Garleigh Moor. On this moorland hilltop (879ft) there is a fine prehistoric British camp known as Lordenshaws Camp, but be alert during the shooting season, as grouse butts grace the western flank of this hill fort. There are superb views of the Simonside Hills and Coquetdale. Go up by the ruined wall to a path sign with a short diversion rightwards to an Ancient Monument – a large sandstone rock with cup and ring markings.

These concentric circles are thought to have been carved between 2,000-1,000 BC. Return and follow the track southwards down the moor and through a gateway to the unfenced road, where the walk can be shortened by turning right down the road for two miles to Great Tosson. Cross the road and ascend the moorland track, where a notice tells you to beware of adders! Turn right at a rusty post (waymark missing) for the start of the Simonside Ridge Walk, part of the Simonside Forest Walk – a red waymarked route. Follow the track upwards by the ruined wall for a stiff climb to the cairned summit of The Beacon (1,182ft) with superb views. Stride out for half a mile, straddle a stile and prepare for a very steep climb up to the stony summit of Dove Crag (1,295ft).

Walk westwards for a mile along a fine ridge route which passes the craggy mass of Old Stell Crag, believed to be the site of the Simonside beacon, used as a warning against the invading Scots. Follow the ridge path to the top of Simonside (1,409ft) – the finest viewpoint in Northumberland with views across Coquetdale to the Cheviots. You can see the whole of Northumberland's coastline from Tweed to Tyne, or so they say! Remember there is a steep sided drop on the northern face of Simonside summit.

Select your way down the boulder hillside and turn right along the moorland track with views back to Simonside, popular with climbers since 1902. Pass a small reservoir, turn left at the red/orange marker post and follow the moorland path downhill to enter the extensive Simonside Forest. Turn right and follow the waymarked forest walk downhill. Cross over a broad drive and keep along the path to a second drive near the forest edge. Go up this and, yards on your left, look for a concealed waymarked handgate to exit out of the forest. Bear right down the field track through the gated hillside pastures and follow the waymarks into the tiny village of

(Continued on page 43)

41

14. Rothbury

THROPTON
A large well-kept village
Locals are called 'Tatey Town Folk'
First place potatoes were grown in
the area

green track stiff climb

ROTHBURY
A small market town
'Capital of Coquetdale'

Physic Lane

fine views

Drinking Well
'Drink Rest And Be
Thank Full'

B6341

COQUETDALE

River Coquet

**GREAT
TOSSON**
A small
hillside village

lane

golf course

Car Park

Lady's Bridge

Start and Finish

short walk

WHITTON
A tiny hilltop hamlet

Follow
waymarks

Whitton Tower
A pele tower built
in 14th century

Great Tosson Tower
Ruins of a 15th century
border tower – 42ft by 36ft
with walls 9 feet thick

Hillhead Road

farm

Sharp's Folly
A round tower built by
Thomas Sharp, a local
rector in 1720

Ancient Monument Cup
and Ring Marked Rocks
(Date from 2000-1000 BC)

WHITTONDEAN
A narrow wooded valley
with wooden chalets

Prehistoric settlement
known as
Lordenshaw Fort

Steep drop

To Lordenshaw

stiff climb

Simonside (1409ft)

stiff climb

'BEWARE OF ADDERS'

Old Stell Crag

Dove Crag (1,259ft)
cairned summit

Extensive views including the whole of
Northumberland's coastline from Tweed
to Tyne plus Rothbury, Thropton and
the Cheviot Hills

The Beacon (1182ft)
cairned summit

N

SIMONSIDE HILLS
A massive sandstone ridge
rising to over 1400ft

42

(Continued from page 41)

Great Tosson. Turn right along the village to its extreme east end to see the 15th century Tosson Tower, a Border pele with walls 9ft thick. If you want to shorten the walk, fork left down the road towards Newtown and at the road junction, turn left and then right to the hamlet of Little Tosson. Proceed eastwards along the bridleway, cross Lady's Bridge and follow the riverside route back to Rothbury.

The main walk leaves at the west end of Great Tosson and follows the road down to the T junction, where opposite, turn right through a waymarked field gate. Follow the track down through a couple of stiled fields and after the second stile, turn left, keep by the fence and aim diagonally over a large field for a footbridge. Cross the bridge over the River Coquet, turn left along the riverside and go up to the large village of Thropton with its 16th century pele tower. Walk along the main street and take the only opportunity on route to buy drinks at an old coaching inn, The Three Wheat Heads or from the

cosy pub called the Cross Keys. Beyond the pub, go up the B6341 for 150yds, turn left into Physic Lane and by the cottages, look for the interesting drinking well inscribed 'Drink, Rest and be Thank-full'. Follow the gated lane for a mile which turns right for a stiff climb up to the open moor, where at 700ft there are superb views of the Simonside Hills. From the moor gate, bear half right up the bracken path, turn right along the terrace track which contours eastwards along the moor edge of Rothbury Common for a mile and winds between the outcrops of Ship Crag and the radio mast. There are superb views of Rothbury and Coquetdale. Yards before you reach the wood, a waymarked post directs you southwards down Bilberry Hill and at the bottom of the moor, cross a stile and follow the enclosed path downhill. Go right for a few yards along the road to the 'Pedestrian Only' sign and turn left down the narrow stepped path by Mount Pleasant Villas (1893). Opposite Alexandra Cottage, turn left along the lane and by the Co-op Dairy Depot, follow the narrow alleyway back into Rothbury Town Cente.

15. Stanhope

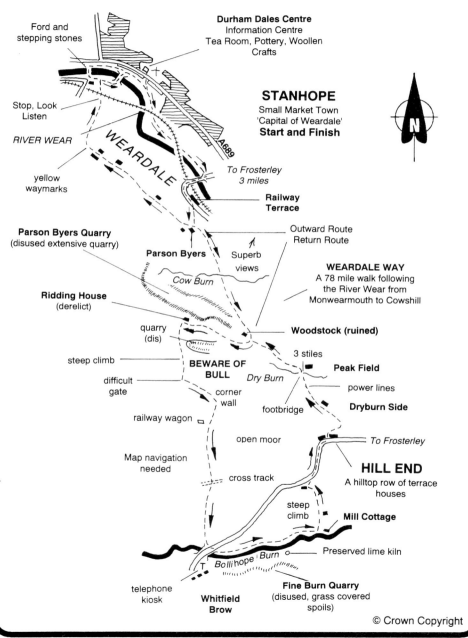

Ford and stepping stones

Durham Dales Centre
Information Centre
Tea Room, Pottery, Woollen Crafts

STANHOPE
Small Market Town
'Capital of Weardale'
Start and Finish

Stop, Look Listen

RIVER WEAR

WEARDALE

yellow waymarks

To Frosterley
3 miles

Railway Terrace

Parson Byers Quarry
(disused extensive quarry)

Parson Byers

Outward Route
Return Route

Cow Burn

Superb views

WEARDALE WAY
A 78 mile walk following the River Wear from Monwearmouth to Cowshill

Ridding House
(derelict)

quarry
(dis)

Woodstock (ruined)

steep climb

BEWARE OF BULL

3 stiles

Peak Field

difficult gate

Dry Burn

power lines

corner wall

footbridge

Dryburn Side

railway wagon

open moor

To Frosterley

Map navigation needed

HILL END
A hilltop row of terrace houses

cross track

steep climb

Mill Cottage

Preserved lime kiln

Bollihope Burn

telephone kiosk

Whitfield Brow

Fine Burn Quarry
(disused, grass covered spoils)

© Crown Copyright

44

15. Stanhope

Location: *Stanhope – 'Capital of Weardale' is a small market town 6 miles west of Wolsingham and 7 miles east of St. John's Chapel on the A689.*
Route: *Stanhope – Railway Terrace – Parson Byers – Ridding House – Bollihope Burn – Bishopley – Hill End – Dryburn Side – Parson Byers – Bushy Field – Stanhope.*
Distance: *8 miles (13km) Allow 4/5 hours. Moderate. Stiff climbs. Road walking.*
O.S. Maps: *Landranger 92 Barnard Castle and Richmond; Outdoor Leisure 31 Teesdale.*
Parking: *Market Place or Castle Gardens, Stanhope.*
Public Transport: *Weardale Services 101/102 Bishop Auckland-Stanhope. British Rail: The Heritage Line Saltburn-Stanhope. Summer Sundays only. Check train times.*
Refreshments: *Durham Dales Centre Tea Room; Bonny Moor Hen Coffee Mill; Chatters; Packhorse Hotel; Sandwich Bar; Grey Bull; The Queens Head, Stanhope. None on route.*

This scenic walk follows little used paths over fields and moorland with extensive views of wild Weardale. From Stanhope Market Place, go down Butts Crescent, turn left along The Butts and follow yellow waymarks along the road. Go through a white kissing gate, cross The Heritage Line railway with care. Go across three fields via white kissing gates and fork right towards the river. Cross the railway again, follow the field path and exit over a stile to the road. Turn right, cross the railway and river bridges, ascend the road and at the entrance to Heather View Caravan Park, turn left along the road to Railway Terrace. Cross the footpath signposted stile opposite and ascend the field with power poles, where at the top, go through a red gate to Parson Byers. At the farm, by turning right, you can shorten the walk, described later. Note, the next part of the walk is also the return route.

Pass the farm on your right and go along the gated track into a large field. Keep on the level path at first, fork half right to a locked gate, so straddle the short fence. Diagonally down the field, cross Cow Beck in the dip and follow the path to the upper end of the field, where the wall stile is in need of repair, so use the nearby gate. In the next field, (check map), keep by the wire fence and cross the short new wooden rail in the same fence. Go over the old tramway, hug the new wire fence on your right by the old quarry and turn up the track to a ruined house. This is the spot where the return to Parson Byers is the same as the outward route.

From the ruined house, go up the gated track which curves uphill to the deserted Ridding House. The right of way goes immediately behind. Go over a fence wedged between the buildings and exit through a wall gap. Turn left along the stony track, go through the isolated gateposts and descend the rough pasture. In the bottom, go through a couple of tied gates between a sleeper bridge for a tough climb by the wall. Scramble over some difficult double rusty gates to Bollihope Common. Turn left and eastwards, follow the moor path by the wall. About 25yds beyond the protruding corner wall, turn right and head for the old railway wagon. Pass it on your right and head southwards, straight over the moor for a mile on a path that appears and disappears. Go over a cross track and the view below

reveals the beautiful Bollihope Burn showing signs of bygone quarrying and lead mining. Drop down into the valley. Turn left, cross over the road and carry on along the stony bridle track by the Bollihope Burn for half a mile via a caravan site, a lime kiln and the disused Fine Burn Quarry. Go through a gate by a sign 'Private Road-Bridleway Only' and yards before Mill Cottage, fork left up the hillside between the holiday chalets. Turn left again, walk through the caravan park, pass High Bishopley and go up the farm road for a very steep climb out of the valley. At the top, rest and admire the views back to the Bollihope Burn. Turn right along the elevated road for half a mile to the hamlet of Hill End. At a footpath sign between the single street terrace, go through the green gate and follow the track downhill which passes in front of Dryburn Side. Go through the gate, turn half right down the rough pasture by a double row of power lines and at the bottom, turn left along the track that leads to a ford and footbridge over a stream near the farm of Peak Field. Go along by the stream, cross three stiles and over a large field to the ruined house already visited.

Now follow the walk back to Parson Byers where beyond the farm, turn left up the track to a derelict house. Cross the stile by a power pole in front of the house, fork right and follow the path by a line of old ash trees. Bear right, then turn left and follow the path by the fence and cross a difficult stile. Go down over a slippery plank bridge and up to a farm. Turn left by the farm, go along the gated track on a level route following the yellow waymarks westwards with superb views of Stanhope. Pass Bushy Field Farm and go up the gated track through a wooded area by some old lime kilns, an old engine house and a cottage. Keep on the track which curves right then left and yards beyond a tiny stone shed, branch right through the trees to a wall stile. Go straight down to the bottom of the field to the corner stone stepped stile, hidden by overhanging tree branches. Descend the stiled field, fork half left and cross the railway line for the last time. Cross a final field (Stanhope Annual Show Field) exit through a kissing gate to reach the River Wear. If the river is in flood, turn right and use the footbridge, otherwise turn left and cross the fifty odd stepping stones back into Stanhope.

45

WALKING
in
ROSSENDALE

THE ROSSENDALE VALLEY IS AN AREA OF
OUTSTANDING NATURAL BEAUTY, APPEALING TO

 WALKERS OF ALL AGES AND
ABILITIES.

WITHIN THE VALLEY FOR THE EXPERIENCED
WALKERS THERE IS, FOR EXAMPLE, THE DEMAND-
ING ROSSENDALE WAY (45 MILES) OR THE
IRWELL VALLEY WAY (35 MILES), WHILE
FOR THE LESS AMBITIOUS OR FAMILY THERE
ARE SHORTER COUNTRYSIDE AND HERITAGE
WALKS.

FOR FURTHER INFORMATION ON THE ROSSENDALE VALLEY,
SEND THE ATTACHED COUPON TO THE TOURIST INFORMATION
CENTRE, 41/45 KAY STREET, RAWTENSTALL, ROSSENDALE,
LANCASHIRE BB4 7LZ.

NCWB1

NAME _ _ _ _ _ _ _ _ _ _ _ _ _ _ _ _ _ _ _

ADDRESS _ _ _ _ _ _ _ _ _ _ _ _ _ _ _ _ _

_ _ _ _ _ _ _ _ _ _ _ _ _ _ _ _ _ _ _

_ _ _ _ _ _ _ POSTCODE _ _ _ _ _ _ _ _ _

Rossendale
leisure services
LEISURE IS OUR BUSINESS

48

Carlton Bank

Refreshments spring from the ground. . .

HOT and thirsty walkers will be delighted to find a source of refreshment — in the shape of a cafe built into the hillside.

Husband and wife team John and Christine Simpson have opened the cleverly-designed building at the top of Carlton Bank, near Stokesley, which is at the heart of three established walking trails, a car park taking more than 70 vehicles, and a picnic area.

The Lord Stone's Cafe on the edge of Lordstone, a former Bronze Age settlement.

The area around Green Bank and Busby Moor is being developed for public recreation with new walks and viewpoints. Already it is an integral part of three designated walks — the Lyke Wake Walk; the Coast to Coast route; and the Cleveland Way.

The cafe, which will seat 44 people inside and about the same number outside, is open seven days a week between 9 a.m. and 5 p.m. John and Christine add that they are quite willing to cater for organised parties outside normal opening hours, including company walks — above 15 in number — if they are told well in advance.

Great care has been taken with landscaping so as not to detract from the local views and natural beauty of the area, and the stone facing of the cafe entrance is designed to blend naturally into the environment.

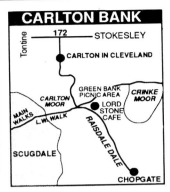

The cafe will be a focal point amidst some 200 acres of land now opened up for people to enjoy. Already the area is a centre for hang gliding and model flying enthusiasts.

49

50

One boy and his dog under the Lochaugh Viaduct, Rowlands Gill

Waterfall along the St. John's Chapel route

The Red Way in Cleveland Forest on the Osmotherley walk

Cattle grazing on the banks of the River Derwent at Kirkham Priory

CARPET SALE

AT UP TO 50% OFF
All our carpets are on the way out

A typical week in The Northern Echo

57

VISIT...
WHITWORTH HALL & GARDENS
PAGE BANK, SPENNYMOOR

Ancestral Home of 'Bonnie Bobbie Shafto'

★ **HALL** ★ **GARDENS** ★ **DEER HERD**
★ **WOODLAND WALKS** ★ **VINEYARD & WINERY**
★ **BREWERY** ★ **CLOCK MUSEUM**

(Tea Room, Wine & Beer Tasting, Gift Shop)

OPEN: WEEKENDS — BANK HOLIDAYS FROM EASTER
(from Spring Bank Holiday — Grounds also open Monday,
Tuesday and Wednesday)
11 a.m. - 6 p.m. (Hall from 1 p.m./Tea Room from 12.30 p.m.)

Adults £3.00   OAPs £2.50   Children £1.00
Season Tickets £15 (accompanying children FREE)

Party discounts available on request

OPEN TO THE END OF SEPTEMBER

(We are situated between SPENNYMOOR and BRANCEPETH
off A688 and A690)

AKWKE

44-070

Maintaining Your Feet Correctly is Essential to the Walker

Not only for the feet themselves, but to reduce effects of wear and tear on other joints e.g. ankles, knees, hips and back

Visit a State Registered Chiropodist for advice or prevention of foot ailments as well as treatment of existing problems

Most State Registered Chiropodists can prescribe and provide individual appliances and Orthotics to compensate for structural imbalance affecting the function of feet and legs

Look after your feet - They're the only pair you get remember - when your feet hurt, you DO hurt all over!

44-260

59

DARLINGTON

DARLINGTON is central to all the glories of the North East. A fascinating Market Town set in the beautiful River Tees Valley, surrounded by countryside full of ancient Castles and Cathedrals, wild sweeping moorlands and sleepy Dales. Home of the world's first public passenger steam railway, pulled by Stephenson's 'Locomotion' in 1825. Darlington is easily reached by bus, train, air or car.

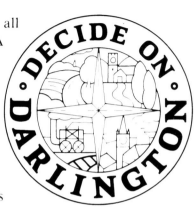

So the next time you are looking for the ideal holiday base, Decide on Darlington for a pleasant surprise.

Darlington Tourist Information staff are waiting to help you enjoy your time.

Tourist
Information Centre
FREEPOST
4 West Row
Market Hall
DARLINGTON
DL1 5PL

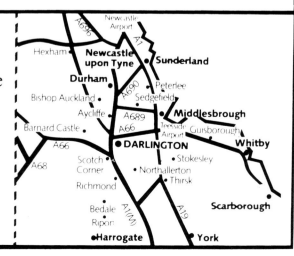

b9

60

62

Darlington & Stockton Times

THE QUALITY PAPER OFFERS MORE DETAILED LOCAL NEWS EVERY WEEK. HAVE IT DELIVERED

QUALITY COLOUR AND ATMOSPHERIC BLACK & WHITE PRINTS FROM £4.00

Have you seen a special picture in **The Northern Echo?** Copies are available for you to purchase as a keepsake, or perhaps as a gift for a relative or friend.

In order to gain the best possible atmospheric effect, some photographs have been captured in black and white only, so please bear this in mind when placing your order(s).

Photographs are available in 8" x 6" at £4 each and 12" x 8" at £5 each (the cost includes postage, packing and VAT).

To order your photograph(s), complete the panel below, and send it, together with a cheque/postal order payable to: **North of England Newspapers,** and a newspaper cutting of the photograph you require, to the address shown.

Name...NE

Address ....

....

Date Appeared	Page Number	Photo Caption	No 8" x 6"	Cost	No 12" x 8"	Cost	Total Payment

Send to: Photo Sale Department, The Northern Echo, Priestgate, Darlington, Co. Durham. DL1 1NF.

AWAVS   29-280

65

16. Swainby

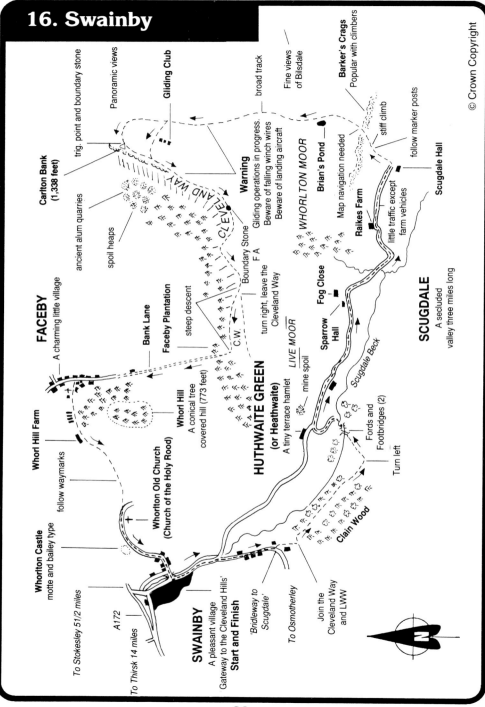

Panoramic views

Gliding Club

trig. point and boundary stone

broad track

Fine views of Bilsdale

Barker's Crags
Popular with climbers

Carlton Bank
(1,338 feet)

stiff climb

ancient alum quarries

spoil heaps

Warning
Gliding operations in progress.
Beware of falling winch wires
Beware of landing aircraft

follow marker posts

Scugdale Hall

CLEVELAND WAY

WHORLTON MOOR

Brian's Pond

little traffic except
farm vehicles

FACEBY
A charming little village

Bank Lane

Faceby Plantation

steep descent

Boundary Stone
F A

turn right, leave the
Cleveland Way

Fog Close

Raikes Farm

Map navigation needed

C.W.

LIVE MOOR

mine spoil

Sparrow Hall

SCUGDALE
A secluded
valley three miles long

Whorl Hill Farm

Whorl Hill
A conical tree
covered hill (773 feet)

HUTHWAITE GREEN
(or Heathwaite)
A tiny terrace hamlet

Scugdale Beck

Fords and
Footbridges (2)

Turn left

follow waymarks

Whorlton Old Church
(Church of the Holy Rood)

Clain Wood

Whorlton Castle
motte and bailey type

To Stokesley 5 1/2 miles

A172

To Thirsk 14 miles

Join the
Cleveland Way
and LWW

*'Bridleway to
Scugdale'*

SWAINBY
A pleasant village
Gateway to the Cleveland Hills'
Start and Finish

To Osmotherley

N

16. Swainby and Scugdale

Location: *Swainby is 5$^1/_2$ miles south-west of Stokesley (A172) and 14 miles north-east of Thirsk.*
Route: *Swainby – Heathwaite – Scugdale Hall – Brian's Pond – Carlton Bank – Faceby – Swainby.*
Distance: *About 10 miles (16km). Allow 5/6 hours. Moderate. Unavoidable road walking along country lanes. Rough moorland tracks. One climb of 250ft. Field paths.*
O.S. Maps: *Landranger 93 Teesside and Darlington. Pathfinder 611 NZ 40/50 Stokesley and Cleveland (North). Outdoor Leisure 26 North Yorks Moors (West).*
Parking: *Small area outside toilets in Emerson Close, off the High Street, Swainby.*
Public Transport: *Tees Services/United 90/90a Middlesbrough/Northallerton.*
Refreshments: *The Black Horse; Miners' Arms; The Blacksmiths' Arms, Swainby. Sutton Arms, Faceby.*
Warning: *When walking along the edge of the Teesside and Newcastle Gliding Club runway beware of falling winch wires, landing aircraft and winding operations.*
Note: *Do not attempt in doubtful winter weather. Map and compass essential.*

This scenic walk from Swainby explores the secluded valley of Scugdale and offers a high level walk along the crest of the Cleveland Hills with superb views. The low level return links the lovely little village of Faceby with the ancient Whorlton Castle and church.

From Swainby walk along the High Street and follow Coalmire Lane southwards (signposted Shepherd Hill) for a mile. Where the lane curves right, walk forward by Baytree Cottage and go through the gate signposted 'Bridleway to Scugdale'. Follow the track, cross a signposed stile and you have now joined the Cleveland Way plus four other famous long distance walks. Turn left along the tarmac path within the edge of Clain Wood and follow this until you reach a Cleveland Way signpost. Turn left, cross the stile and go down the field, where at the bottom exit through a waymarked gate to cross the beck by use of a couple of footbridges or fords. Go up the lane past Hollin Hill to reach the tiny terrace, four house hamlet of Heathwaite. It's shown as Huthwaite Green on O.S. Maps. Leave the Cleveland Way and turn right along the cul de sac lane noting the overgrown spoil heaps of the bygone ironstone mining of Scugdale. In 1880 the Scugdale Iron Mine produced 66,000 tons of ore. Follow the quiet lane through the secluded valley of Scugdale for two miles, where the road ends at Scugdale Hall. It is said that Harry Cooper (Henry), who was nicknamed the Giant of Scugdale, worked for some time as a farm servant at Scugdale Hall. In 1890 at the age of 23 years, he was eight feet six inches tall and weighed 406lb. He joined Barnum's Colossal Show and toured America as the tallest man in the world.

In front of the facing gate by Scugdale Hall, turn left, go up through the small gate and brace yourself for a stiff climb up the bracken path which swings half right via a couple of blue arrow marker posts for a final pull up to Barker Crags. At the top

Whorlton Castle

rest and admire the superb scenes of Scugdale. Climb up to the moor edge (check map) and aim for a small moorland mound by a small pond. From here aim half right for a Public Footpath signpost, seen in the distance to reach a broad moorland track. Turn left along this and pass Brian's Pond on your left, as you stride out for a mile to reach the runway of the Teesside and Newcastle Gliding Club on Carlton Bank, with warning requests 'Beware of Falling Winch Wires and Landing Aircraft'. Avoid crossing the runway and fork right along the broad sandy track which contours round and takes you past the gliding club buildings. Although there is a right of way across the runway, most walkers tend to skirt the edge of the runway and head for the

(Continued on page 70)

(Continued from page 69)

O.S. trig point top and the old boundary stone on Carlton Bank at 1,338ft above sea level. Admire the extensive views over the Cleveland Plain including the twin landmarks of Roseberry Topping and Captain Cook's Monument, industrial Teesside and the distant Pennines. Below Carlton Bank, note the extensive alum workings which closed in 1771. From the trig point top, rejoin the Cleveland Way and head south westwards, skirting the escarpment edge and keeping clear of the gliding club runway. Follow the track and 150/200yds beyond the white boundary stone marked FA and just before you start to climb up the cairned Live Moor, look out for an unsignposted path that leaves the Cleveland Way on your right, and takes you down a sunken bracken path fairly steeply to the foot of the hills.

The path turns left along by the walled wood and over old spoil heaps to reach a gate in the wall on your right. Go through the gate and head steeply down Faceby Plantation into Back Lane, which leads to the lovely little village of Faceby where the Sutton Arms provides refreshments. Backtrack from the pub and leave Faceby by Church Lane on your right and opposite the church, fork left up the path by the garden and cross the corner signposted stile. Diagonally over the field, cross the corner waymarked stile and go up the stiled, enclosed path by four wooden chicken coups with Whorl Hill Wood on your left. At the top, pass above Whorl Hill Farm and cross a stile by a gate. Follow the duck boarded path which curves along the undulating field dotted with bushes. Look out for a concealed stile right of a facing metal gate, cross this, go down the steps and turn left down and around the same field edge. Turn left through a metal gate and over a final field to come out opposite Church House Farm. Turn right along Church Lane and visit the interesting 12th century ruins of Whorlton Old Church with its arched avenue of yew trees. From the church, turn left along the lane for 400 yards and visit the magnificent gatehouse of Whorlton Castle. The Castle is open permanently and admission is free. Go down Church Lane back to Swainby to complete a satisfying high hills walk.

The photograph on page 112 is of Mr Sam Mason's garden gate in High Street, Swainby. Mr Mason built the gate 20 years ago from metal odds and ends. It is made up from 84 different items!

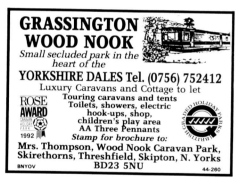

Embleton Bay on the Craster Coastal Circuit

The village of Muker on the Keld and Swale Gorge route

Frozen waterfall at Gibson's Cave on the High Force walk

Causey Arch – oldest surviving railway bridge in the world

17. Osmotherley

Location: Osmotherley, a large picturesque village wedged between the Hambleton Hills and the Cleveland Hills, is 11 miles each way from Thirsk and Stokesley.
Route: Osmotherley – Oakdale – Red Way – Nether Silton – Over Silton – Thimbleby – Osmotherley.
Distance: 9 miles (14.5km). Moderate. Allow 5 hours.
O.S. Maps: Landranger 99 Northallerton and Ripon; 100 Malton and Pickering. Pathfinder 621 (SE48/49) Thirsk. Outdoor Leisure 26 N. York Moors Western area.
Parking: Limited street parking. Do not inconvenience local residents.
Public Transport: Tees and District: 290/90 Middlesbrough – Stokesley – Northallerton.
Refreshments: Queen Catherine Hotel; The Golden Lion; Three Tuns Inn; The Coffee Pot; Fish Shop, Osmotherley. The Gold Cup Inn, Nether Silton.
Note: Brief description. Carry the relevant O.S. Map.

This splendid walk takes you south of Osmotherley via the little valley of Oakdale and explores the lesser-known country around the twin villages of Nether Silton and Over Silton.

Leave Osmotherley by the narrow alleyway inscribed 'Osmotherley Methodist Church 1754' located behind the War Memorial, where North End adjoins South End. Follow the Cleveland Way into Back Lane and cross the signposted stile opposite. Walk eastwards over a couple of stiled fields with views of Black Hambleton. Go down the steep stepped path into the wooded Middlestye Valley. Cross the footbridge over Cod Beck. Walk up the hillside field, cross a stile and aim for a telegraph pole marked 'Footpath' in white paint. Pass White House Farm, go up the track and cross a signposted stile left of the farm gates into Green Lane which was the drovers' winter route. Go down the lane and at the bottom, turn left up the Hawnby Road and cross the signposted stile on your right. Follow the gated/stiled track down into the little wooded valley of Oakdale with its twin reservoirs. Cross a stile by a gate marked 'Keep Dogs On A Lead' and follow the track below the recently renovated Oakdale Cottage.

Proceed along the valley, cross a high ladder stile and enjoy the pleasant walk by the upper reservoir (built 1910). Cross a bridge and strike up the moor for a stiff climb via duck boards and man-made steps. As you climb, look back for views of Osmotherley and westwards to Wensleydale. Pass above a fenced enclosure which protects the Jenny Brewster Spring. Who was the mysterious Jenny Brewster, as no local lore exists on this unknown lady? Follow the moorland path to the road where the Cleveland Way coincides with the famous 'Hambleton Drove Road', an ancient drovers' highway which had its heyday centuries ago. Turn right along the track and follow the Cleveland Way (signposted 'Sneck Yate') and the Hambleton Drove Road southwards. Look for the standing stone marked 'D' and inscribed 'Crayhall Stone' which is another moorland mystery, as there is no name related place in the area. Go through the gate and up the rutted track to the base of Black Hambleton

where a signpost on your right marked 'Bridleway to Nether Silton' gives access through a gate into Cleveland Forest. Having left the Cleveland Way, follow the forest track, an old bridle track called the Red Way which was once the main highway to Nether Silton. At the first junction, turn left and follow the track downhill through an attractive stretch of conifer forest for a mile. At the end of the wood Silton Picnic Area is the perfect place for a stop. Follow the quiet Moor Lane for a mile, with extensive views of the Hambleton Hills. At the T junction, turn left, pass Rose Cottage and follow the narrow lane to another T junction, where you turn right and follow the road for 440yds to enter the unspoilt village of Nether Silton.

Do not miss the opportunity to visit The Gold Cup Inn, a cosy country pub which commemorates one of the earliest flat races in England. The first race was run at Hambleton at the top of Sutton Bank on August 22 1715 for the Gold Cup and a prize of 100 guineas. Beryl and Bjorn Berg welcome walkers and offer a wide menu of choice, plus Swedish dishes and Smorgasbord. Go back along the village to the cottage with a G.R. post box in its wall. A public footpath signpost by the church wall opposite points the way through a white gate by the same cottage. Follow the path between the two cottages and walk northwards up the edge of three stiled fields to reach Kirk Ings Lane. Turn right for a few yards and cross the signposted inset stile opposite. Go up the field edge and visit the isolated 12th century St. Mary's Church. From the church gate, walk westwards over the undulating field, exit over a stile and walk through the tiny village of Over Silton. By Keepers Cottage (1862) turn right and follow the 'No Through Road' out of the village. Beyond the Riding Centre and in front of the Forestry Commission name board, bear left and climb up the edge of Silton Wood. At the top, fork left along a broad forest track and keep on this fairly level route for over a mile.

Eventually the track descends and leads you along a cleared area where the track splits three

(Continued on Page 77)

17. Osmotherley

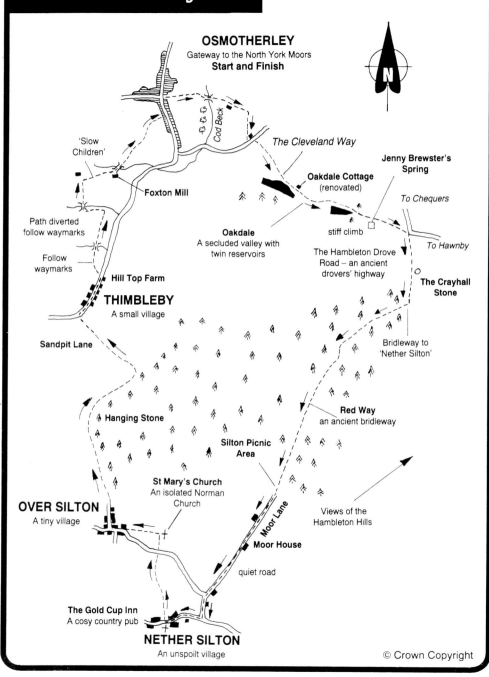

OSMOTHERLEY
Gateway to the North York Moors
Start and Finish

N

'Slow Children'

The Cleveland Way

Jenny Brewster's Spring

Oakdale Cottage (renovated)

To Chequers

Foxton Mill

stiff climb

To Hawnby

Path diverted follow waymarks

Oakdale A secluded valley with twin reservoirs

The Hambleton Drove Road – an ancient drovers' highway

Follow waymarks

The Crayhall Stone

Hill Top Farm

THIMBLEBY A small village

Bridleway to 'Nether Silton'

Sandpit Lane

Red Way an ancient bridleway

Hanging Stone

Silton Picnic Area

St Mary's Church An isolated Norman Church

OVER SILTON A tiny village

Views of the Hambleton Hills

Moor Lane

Moor House

quiet road

The Gold Cup Inn A cosy country pub

NETHER SILTON An unspoilt village

© Crown Copyright

76

(Continued from page 75)

ways. Turn left through the handgate by a chained gate and follow the old bridle path called Sandpit Lane for 880yds. Turn right along the road and walk through the delightful street village of Thimbleby. For a quick finish, you can follow the road back to Osmotherley. At the north end of the village, opposite Hill Top Farm, go through a small gate and bear half right down the field to cross a waymarked stile, double footpath signposted and enter a small wood. Immediatley, another footpath sign guides you out of the wood via a waymarked stile. Turn left, follow the field edge and cross the bridge over Wash Beck. Follow the waymarks along the edge of the next field, but watch out for the curious cows. At the field end, turn left and cross the corner stile. Proceed along the next two fields and cross the footbridge over Brier Beck. Follow the yellow arrows round the railed field and over a stile to come out opposite Boville Park. Turn right along the track and just beyond the sign 'Slow, Children', cross an unsignposted stile on your left. Keep by the fence and enter an enclosed path that bypasses Foxton Mill. Cross the footbridge over Cod Beck. Go along the beckside path, cross a final field and follow the lane back into Osmotherley.

18. Ravenscar

Old Peak

dramatic views to
Robin Hood's Bay

Raven Hall Hotel

RAVENSCAR
The resort that never was
Start and Finish ■

WARNING – DANGER
Steep cliffs

Rocket Post

Blea Wyke Point

Coastal Centre

toilets

Station Rd

To A171

**Foxcliffe
Tea Rooms**

Coast Guard Lookout

ruined military camp

Scenic coastal views

Common Cliff

THE SCARBOROUGH AND WHITBY TRAILWAY

CLEVELAND WAY

NORTH SEA

Beast Cliff

Extensive views to Scarborough,
Filey Brigg and to the chalk cliffs
of Flamborough Head

Trailway or Railway Path
The Scarborough and Whitby railway
opened 16th July 1885 and closed on
6th March 1965. Converted into a
walkway – permissive path

Nature Reserve
A secluded wooded
valley

Staintondale Station
Best preserved former
station. Platforms bedecked
with flowers

Steep
Steps ■

HAYBURN WYKE
A pocket beach of
boulders with
twin waterfalls

Hayburn Beck

**Station
House**

F.B.

Platform remains
of Hayburn Wyke
Station

**Hayburn
Wyke Hotel**

18. Ravenscar

Location: Ravenscar: − 'The resort that never was' − a tiny village perched on imposing 600ft cliff top. Ten miles north of Scarborough off the A171, 2 miles east of the Falcon Inn.
Route: Ravenscar − Common Cliff − Beast Cliff − Hayburn Wyke − Scarborough and Whitby Trailway − Station Square − Ravenscar
Distance: Over 8 miles (13km). Easy/moderate. Allow 4/5 hours.
O.S. Maps: Landranger 94 Whitby; 101 Scarborough and Bridlington. Outdoor Leisure 27 North York Moors, Eastern area.
Parking: Ravenscar roadside car park. GR 980014
Public Transport: Scarborough District. Service 15 Scarborough (Debenhams)− Ravenscar. (Tues, Thurs, Sat.) Infrequent Service. Check Timetables.
Refreshments: Raven Hall Hotel; Foxcliffe Tearooms, Ravenscar. Hayburn Wyke Hotel.
Warning: Danger − sheer cliffs. Part of the cliff path is unfenced.
Note: Brief description. Carry the relevant O.S. Map. Stout footwear essential.

This round trip from Ravenscar highlights the spectacular scenery of Yorkshire's Heritage Coast. From Ravenscar car park, turn left, walk down the road and pass the Ravenscar Coastal Centre which is well worth a visit. Turn right by the entrance of the Raven Hall Hotel and 100yds along Station Road, turn left at the Cleveland Way signpost and follow the unsurfaced track down to the fenced cliff top. There are breathtaking views back to Robin Hood's Bay including the castellated wall gardens of the Raven Hall Hotel.

Turn right and head southwards along the bushy cliff top path which is unfenced on the seaward side. Watch your way as the sheer cliffs are 600ft high. The notorious stretch of coastline below claimed the shipwrecks of the Coronation in 1913 and the Fred Everard in 1965. You will see the old Rocket Post in the first field on your right, with Station Road and the tall terrace houses of Station Square a field away. Skirt round Blea Wyke Point (600ft) with impressive widespread seacapes, including the thin haze of Filey Brigg and the chalk cliffs of Flamborough Head. The path continues along Common Cliff with its wide undercliff and extensive shrub woodland ledge. This clifftop land was bought by the National Trust as part of 'Enterprise Neptune'. After a mile, pass the deserted Coastguard Lookout Station and continue southwards along the great mass of Beast Cliff (500ft) for a mile or more with its large landslip ledge covered in hawthorn, bramble, gorse and woodland.

Local legend states that an English King was shipwrecked on Beast Cliff in the 12th century. Keep along the stiled cliff top path by the thick windswept blackthorn. You will rarely see the North Sea until you reach Petard Point. The enclosed path glides down the coast to Hayburn Wyke, giving good views of Scarborough Castle, Filey Brigg and Flamborough Head. After another mile, turn left over a waymarked stile and descend into the secluded wooded valley of Hayburn Wyke. At first, go down a series of short steps, then along a duck board path between high vegetation and descend with care a second set of steep steps into the 34 acre nature reserve, jointly managed by the National Trust and Yorkshire Wildlife Trust. Ignore the signposted path to Staintondale and cross the wooden footbridge over Hayburn Beck. For an interesting detour, turn left down to the boulder strewn shore of Hayburn Wyke. 'Wyke' is a local term for a small inlet of the sea. Here the beck tumbles down over great gritstone blocks to form a couple of cascading waterfalls before it meets the sea. Enjoy the peace of this inlet haven. It is quiet all the time, as there is no road access. No wonder it was used in the 18th century as a smugglers' cove. The Victorians came by the train load from York and Scarborough to visit this wooded wyke.

Rejoin the main path above the waterfalls, turn left and climb up the woodland to the Cleveland Way sign. Leave this long distance path, fork right and follow the waymarks up the woodland, via man made steps with Hayburn Beck down on your right. At the top, pass the nature reserve map board, cross a waymarked stile and follow the farm track uphill to the excellent Hayburn Wyke Hotel which is your opportunity for buying refreshments.

From this former coaching house, follow the driveway uphill for more than 50yds and turn right along the old coastal railway, now known as the Scarborough-Whitby Trailway or Railway Path. The old railway engineered by John Waddell opened on July 16, 1885 and the line closed on March 6, 1965. Although the return route requires no detailed direction, you pass immediately the Hayburn Wyke platform and Station House and a mile further on is Staintondale Station, one of the best preserved stations on the line. It's a most attractive place with platforms bedecked with flowers, a reminder of when it won the 'Best-Kept Station' awards. Follow this lovely tree lined track with spectacular coastal scenery for 3 miles to exit over a stile into Station Square, where a warm welcome awaits you at the Foxcliffe Tearooms housed in the former Station Hotel before you journey along Station Road back to Ravenscar.

© Crown Copyright

WEST NESS

Ness Bridge

To Malton
9 miles

Caulkleys Lane

Public Bridleway
signpost

RYEDALE

Nunnington Hall
A large 17th Century
manor house, owned
by the National Trust.

Mill Farm

Dogs must be on a lead

Weir

17th Century
arched bridge

trig point (320 ft)

superb views

Caulkleys Bank (1 in 4)
Haunted by a lady cloaked
in white

The Avenue

2 seats

NUNNINGTON
A quiet, unspoilt village
Start and Finish

To Hovingham

All Saints Church

River Rye

follow waymarks

To Hovingham

High Moor Lane

F.B.

stiff climb

Path diverted
follow waymarks

Scarlet Wood

B1257

STONEGRAVE
A small attractive village

Stonegrave Minster
founded 757 A.D.

Dismantled railway

Ryedale Lodge
A small Country
House Hotel

Jubilee Cottages

Waymark
telegraph pole

N

19. Nunnington

Location: *The unspoilt village of Nunnington is 6 miles south east of Helmsley.*
Route: *Nunnington – Stonegrave – Caulkleys Bank – West Ness – Nunnington.*
Distance: *Over 7 miles (11km). Easy. Allow 4 hours. Some road walking. One stiff climb.*
O.S. Maps: *Landranger 100 Malton and Pickering. Pathfinder 643 (SE 67/77) Malton and Gilling East.*
Parking: *Limited roadside parking in Nunnington. Do not inconvenience residents.*
Public Transport: *Yorkshire Coastliner Service 94 Helmsley Malton. No Sunday Service.*
Refreshments: *The Royal Oak, Nunnington. None on route.*
Note: *Brief description. Carry the relevant O.S. Map. Dogs must be kept on a lead and under control.*

Reserve this Ryedale ramble for Easter when Nunnington Hall, a 17th century manor house owned by The National Trust, is open to the public. Starting from the unspoilt village of Nunnington, this is a first class walk and a fine introduction to Ryedale. It takes in stretches of the River Rye; visits Stonegrave village with its ancient Minster and offers a superb ridge walk along Caulkleys Bank.

Leave Nunnington by the rusty gate (Public Footpath signposted), left of Bridge Cottage at the bottom north west corner of the village. Walk westwards for a very pleasant riverside route through half a dozen gated fields over more than 880yds. Keep on the south side of the River Rye, famous for its trout fishing. Cross a single railed bridge over a drainage ditch and leave the river. Turn left along the field edge by Low Moor Plantation and at the notice 'NYCC Path diverted, follow waymarks', go left through the open gateway between the two plantations and turn immediately right along the field with a drainage ditch (posts with blue bags) by New Low Moor Plantation. At the end of the field, you will reach an open track called High Moor Lane. Do not cross over the track and ignore the path going straight on over the ploughed field to the disused railway line. It is not a right of way. Turn left along the lane which swings left by a small wood and turns right up the field to the road. Turn right along the road for half a mile (often busy with local traffic) and on the way you will pass the old railway line and entrance to Ryedale Lodge to reach the brick built Jubilee Cottages, inscribed 'W F Queen Victoria D J 1897'.

Opposite the cottages, turn left into an unsignposted track and follow this (waymarked telegraph pole) which curves along the field edge and when it bends left, fork right and go through a metal gate. Turn left, hug the wire fence and at the far end of the field, cross a stile (waymarked) and climb up the embanked path to the Helmsley/Gilling East Railway. Turn right along the old dismantled railway line for 25yds and fork left down through Scarlet Wood to straddle the railed fence (no stile) next to a chained padlocked gate. Turn left along the busy B1257 for 880yds to reach Stonegrave. Visit Stonegrave Minster founded in 757 AD and see the 9th century Stonegrave Cross, one of the finest Celtic Wheel Crosses in the North of England. Back in the

village, just past the Post Office and telephone kiosk, leave the B1257 and fork left following the signposted bridle track over a waymarked stile by a gate. Go up the rough winding track for a steep climb, and at the top, fork right, cross a stile and you have now reached the long limestone spur of Caulkleys Bank, part of the Hambleton Hills, which used to be a racecourse. Head eastwards, hug the waymarked fence for a level ridge walk. The path forks left away from the fence, joins a track and continues in the same direction, past three dead trees (waymarked) and along a field to cross over the road at the top of the 1:4 hill called Caulkleys Bank. Rest at the seats provided and admire the vast vista. On a clear day, you can see a total of 22 towns, villages and hamlets, as welll as 16 churches from this lofty spot. Do not linger too long, especially in misty weather, as this place is haunted by a lady cloaked in white!

From the seats, turn left along the signposted bridle way by the windswept woodland and stride out with superb views southwards. Head eastwards, pass a trig point, 320ft above sea level, and the rutted track gradually drops down to a Public Bridleway signpost on your left. Turn left, fork right and follow the enclosed Caulkleys Lane which runs downhill to the road. Walk to the crossroads and take the road to Kirkby Moorside to reach the riverside hamlet of West Ness. Just before the white girder bridge, turn left, cross the footpath signposted stile and follow the pleasant path, four fields westwards alongside the River Rye to reach Mill Farm with its four storey mill. Here dogs must be on a lead. Pass between the farm buildings, go over a waymarked stile, proceed by a sunken depression, fork right and aim for the corner stile by a bench seat overlooking the picturesque weir with nearby stepping stones. Leave the river, cross the stile and go diagonally over the next field through a waymarked gate into a final field, with your first glimpse of the impressive Nunnington Hall on the banks of the River Rye. Walk straight on, parallel to the estate wall and cross the concealed stile (footpath signposted) to your right in the corner wall. Turn left along the driveway into Nunnington. This classic circular would not be complete without a visit to Nunnington Hall.

81

© Crown Copyright

Four Faces
A 24 foot high monument with worn stone sculptures. Built before 1727

KIRKHAM PRIORY
Ruins of Augustinian Priory – founded 1122
Magnificent gatehouse

CRAMBECK

RIVER DERWENT

Cram Beck

Todd Wood

Gillylees Wood

Pylons

fast traffic

Ox
Car Wood

stiff climb

Ben Wood

Join The Centenary Way
York to Filey – 100 miles

Impressive views of Castle Howard

East Moor Banks Wood

BEWARE OF TRAINS

fast traffic

A64

▲ **The Pyramid**
Dates from 1728 (Private no access)

marker posts

Monument
Tall column erected in memory of the 7th Earl of Carlisle in 1869-70

Dual carriageway

To York 12 miles

WELBURN
A pleasant village

The Stray

Gate House

Brandrith Wood

Follow marker posts

BEWARE OF BULL

Dogs on lead

Whitwell Hall
Country House Hotel
An impressive Tudor Gothic mansion

WHITWELL ON-THE-HILL

ROUTE DIVERTED
Follow waymarks

Difficult double stile

St Martin's Church
(11th Century)

Monument Plantation

Private No Access

BULMER
A small, dignified estate village
Start and Finish

To Sheriff Hutton

Bull in field

Stiff climb

N

20. Bulmer

Location: Bulmer in North Yorkshire is 3 miles east of Sheriff Hutton, 11 miles east of Easingwold and 12 miles north of York.
Route: Bulmer – The Stray – Four Faces – Crambeck – Kirkham Priory – Whitwell – Monument – Bulmer.
Distance: Over 9 miles. (14.5km) Moderate. Allow 5 hours. Field and woodland paths. Couple of stiff climbs
O.S. Maps: Landranger 100 Malton and Pickering; Pathfinder 655, SE 66/76 Barton-le-Willows.
Parking: Limited roadside parking in Bulmer. Do not inconvenience local residents.
Public Transport: No bus service to Bulmer although the Yorkshire Coastliner Service 81 Malton/York will drop you off at Welburn/Bulmer crossroads, a mile east of Bulmer.
Refreshments: Tearooms in Bulmer; Kirkham Abbey Coffee House.
Note: This walk crosses the York/Scarborough Railway. Beware of Trains. Dogs must be on a lead and under control. A64 is crossed twice. Watch out for fast traffic.

You will remember this ramble for the rest of your life! One of the best in Britain, it highlights Castle Howard estate and follows the Centenary Way to the ruined Augustinian Kirkham Priory. Leave Bulmer at the east end of the village and where the road bends right, fork left by the Parish Council Oak Tree, planted in 1893, and proceed to the bottom of the cul de sac lane. Go through the signposted gate and the route has been diverted, so follow the waymarks. Exit over a stile, go diagonally down the field and through a gate. Cut over the corner field, negotiate difficult double stiles and turn right along the field edge to the road. Go up the road, turn right through an open gateway (footpath signposted), past a hay stack and turn left through a large gap in the hedge. Go up the edge of the field boundary with waymarks, fork right and cross a stile into Brandrith Wood. Follow the track (marker posts) to reach the road called The Stray. Turn up the road which is busy at any time of the year.

Pass through the impressive arched Gate House into the Castle Howard estate and as you turn right, catch a glimpse of The Obelisk, 100ft high and erected in 1714. Walk along the farm road. Despite the notice 'Private Road' it is a right of way. Stride out and savour the surprise rear view of the elegant Castle Howard mansion. You will see the New River Bridge and the Mausoleum in the distance. The Pyramid perched on St. Anne's Hill is to your right. At the staggered crossroads turn right and join the newly created Centenary Way, a 100 mile walk from York to Filey which was opened by Chris Brasher on December 8, 1989, at Kirkham Priory. Follow the signposted route up into East Bank Moor Wood, with a request 'Please Keep Dogs On A Lead'. Turn left along the track (marker posts) for a mile, with an extension to see Four Faces, a 24ft high monument with well worn sculptures. Go downhill, rejoin the main route, and at the bottom of the wooded Cram Beck, cross a stile by a gate and climb out of the wood by the wire fence, noting the old oak trees. Climb again and at the top

Castle Howard

admire the view of Welburn Village seen southwards. Descend the well used field side path which curves down to an open gateway by an old water trough. A waymark gatepost directs you immediately left along to the field end where white capped marker posts (3 in all) indicate the route half left across a very large field with pylons. Aim for the corner of Gillylees Wood, turn right and keep the wood on your left to reach the A64 with fast traffic. Cross this busy road with care. Turn right and then left along the road ('Crambeck Only') for 250 yards. Pass Crambeck Village, a private housing development based on the former Castle Howard Reformatory. Fork right, cross the stile and follow the path to the end of the former school gardens. Over a corner stile, turn right, follow the high level path and admire the views of the lovely wooded Kirkham Valley with the River Derwent and the York to Scarborough Railway below. The mile route southwards is fairly easy to follow along the valley. Proceed to a

(Continued on page 84)

(Continued from page 83)

C.W. sign, turn left and drop steeply down through Ox Carr Wood into the valley.

Cross a lane, note the old Castle Howard Station (private house) seen to your left and enter Ben Wood with a request 'Dogs must be on a lead'. Continue through the wood and out into rough pastures, keeping on the stiled track as it contours round the valley and leads down to the railway. Climb the ladder stile, cross the railway line and observe B.R's warning signs. Go right into Kirkham, via the garden centre, passing the Coffee House, an ideal lunch stop.

For an interesting extension, cross the low arched Kirkham Bridge over the deep River Derwent to the ruined Kirkham Priory with its splendid gatehouse ornamented with heraldic shields. The Priory was built for the monks of the Augustinian Order of Black Canons and founded in 1122 by Walter l'Espec. Leave the Centenary Way, re-cross the bridge and up the road beyond the railway level crossing, turn left into Oak Cliff Wood for a very steep climb. The backward views of the ruined priory are good. At the top, turn right to the cross roads (Malton/York) and left along Onhams Lane to the A64. Cross the busy dual carriageway and walk into Whitwell-on the-Hill. Opposite the telephone kiosk, turn left along the 'No Through Road' and go

right by North Lodge into the signposted path between Pear Tree Cottage. Go up the side of the garden, where you are urged to keep dogs under control. Bear left over a couple of stiles, aim for an isolated tree with a wedged waymark post, noting Whitwell Hall (1835), an impressive Country House Hotel in Tudor Gothic style away to your left. Go diagonally over the same field to cross a corner stile. Keep straight on along the edge of the next two fields, exit through a gate, where a four waymark post directs you left along the track, past Whitwell Grange to the road. Turn up the road to the tall column, a monument erected in memory of the 7th Earl of Carlisle in 1869-70. Beyond the monument, turn left at the Public Footpath signpost and go through the gate into Monument Plantation. When you reach a fence with blue twine, turn right, follow the waymarks and when the track splits, do not turn right but remain on the main track to the end of the wood. Cross a stile, turn up the field and left along its top edge and down the other side of the same field. Exit through a gap in the hedge, before the small clump of trees, into the adjacent field. Go down, pass the trees and along the bottom edge of the same field to cross a corner stile. Go diagonally up the next field for a stiff climb and aim for a stile. Do not cross this, but turn left along the top of the field, pass through a gate and aim diagonally across the stiled fields back to Bulmer.

21. Keld

Location: Keld is the highest village in Swaledale. Kirkby Stephen is 10 miles to the west (B6270). Tan Hill 4 miles to the north. Reeth is more than 12 miles and Richmond more than 22 miles, both to the east (B6270).
Route: Keld – Kisdon – Muker – Ramps Holme Bridge – Swinner Gill – East Gill Force – Keld.
Distance: 5 miles (9km). Allow 3 hours. Fairly easy to moderate. Steep ascent and descent. Gradual gradients. Field paths and stony tracks.
O.S. Maps: Landranger 92 Barnard Castle and Richmond; 98 Wensleydale and Wharfedale. Outdoor Leisure 30 Yorkshire Dales Northern and Central; Upper Swaledale Footpath Map – Stile Publications.
Parking: Limited parking in the bottom of Keld village. Do not obstruct gateways. Farm access – Keep clear. Limited parking also at Keld Green on the B6270 at the upper end of the village. N.B. Problem parking at weekends and Bank Holidays.
Public Transport: United Service 30 Richmond to Keld. Infrequent service. Dales bus 800 Keighley and Dist/Harrogate and Dist Harrogate/Leeds/Keld summer service. Check all timetables.
Refreshments: None in Keld. The Farmers Arms; Tea Shop; Old School Tearoom; The Old Vicarage Licensed Restaurant – Muker.
Note: Dogs must be kept on a lead and under control.

This Keld walk is a classic for spectacular views of Upper Swaledale. It follows the Corpse Way from Keld to Muker with a bracing hill walk over Kisdon which includes a bit of the Pennine Way. The riverside return follows the Coal Road up past Swaledale's former lead mining industry and offers some of the biggest and best views in Swaledale.

Walk out of Keld village and follow the road up to the telephone kiosk at the B6270 junction. Turn left down the main road, pass Hope House, (former Cat Hole Inn) and after 440yds turn left down a rough stony track, signposted 'B.P. Muker' which is the start of the Kisdon Road, better known as the Corpse Way. You now follow the last journey made by the dead along the medieval funeral route from Keld to Grinton. Before Muker Church was built in 1580 there was no consecrated burial ground in Upper Swaledale and the bodies of the dead were conveyed down the dale for a dozen miles for burial in Grinton churchyard.

Follow the track and cross the slab bridge over the Skeb Skeugh. Go through a gate and note the path sign 'Muker' fixed to a tree. Fork right and brace yourself as the track begins to climb, steep and stony, emerging out through another gate. Pity the pall bearers carrying the dead up this steep ascent, although on Kisdon there were two coffin stones, now disappeared, on which the bearers could rest the bodies. They would certainly need them. No wonder it took two days and a night to complete the journey to Grinton.

Follow the old Kisdon Road, a wide open track, climbing steadily along the western flank of Kisdon Hill (1,636ft), to pass through a fourth gate, faintly marked 'Private'. There are fine views southwards of the Buttertubs separating the summits of Great Shunner Fell and Lovely Seat, while backwards you

Swaledale sheep

should see High Seat with Hugh Seat and Wild Boar Fell. Turn half left, cut across the field and go through the corner gate, where a double signpost 'Muker/Keld' points the way over the shoulder of Kisdon. Aim for the enclosed path with ruined walls and watch your way carefully, as there is a large hole in the middle of this track. Out through a gate, follow the track downwards by the wall to the eastern edge of the hillside enclosure, one of the best viewpoints in the Yorkshire Dales, and admire the spectacular views of the Swale Gorge. Go southwards for a steep descent, keeping the wall on your right, to reach the signposted Pennine Way. Turn left and follow this famous walk for only 25yds to Kisdon Cottage, where a triple signpost (BW

(Continued on page 87)

85

21. Keld

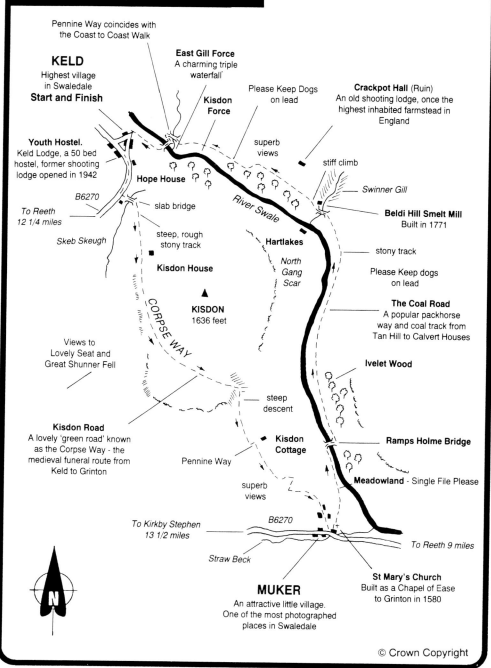

Pennine Way coincides with the Coast to Coast Walk

KELD
Highest village in Swaledale
Start and Finish

East Gill Force
A charming triple waterfall

Please Keep Dogs on lead

Kisdon Force

Crackpot Hall (Ruin)
An old shooting lodge, once the highest inhabited farmstead in England

Youth Hostel.
Keld Lodge, a 50 bed hostel, former shooting lodge opened in 1942

superb views

stiff climb

Hope House

Swinner Gill

B6270

To Reeth 12 1/4 miles

slab bridge

River Swale

Beldi Hill Smelt Mill
Built in 1771

Skeb Skeugh

steep, rough stony track

Hartlakes

stony track

Kisdon House

North Gang Scar

Please Keep dogs on lead

▲
KISDON
1636 feet

The Coal Road
A popular packhorse way and coal track from Tan Hill to Calvert Houses

CORPSE WAY

Views to Lovely Seat and Great Shunner Fell

Ivelet Wood

steep descent

Kisdon Road
A lovely 'green road' known as the Corpse Way - the medieval funeral route from Keld to Grinton

Kisdon Cottage

Ramps Holme Bridge

Pennine Way

Meadowland - Single File Please

superb views

B6270

To Kirkby Stephen 13 1/2 miles

To Reeth 9 miles

Straw Beck

St Mary's Church
Built as a Chapel of Ease to Grinton in 1580

MUKER
An attractive little village. One of the most photographed places in Swaledale

N

(Continued from page 85)

Muker) directs you down a walled lane to an unsurfaced track. Follow this, which becomes surfaced, and you are requested to walk on the road that winds down to the little village of Muker, a Mecca for walkers with its pub, tearooms and shops. Muker Church, consecrated in 1580 as a Chapel of Ease to Grinton, is well worth a visit.

Leave Muker by the same inward route, except take the signposted path ('Gunnerside Keld – Meadowland Single File Please') to the right of Stoneleigh and follow the popular path through a succession of squeeze stiles to reach the riverside. Cross the railed Ramps Holme Bridge over the River Swale. Here you leave the Corpse Way as it journeys down the dale to Grinton. Turn left, climb some steps, join a broad track and follow the signposted 'Keld' path down to the riverside. Stride out and head northwards on a wide track for a very pleasant riverside walk noting the valley views. This riverside route, known as the old Coal Road, was used by packhorse trains with coal loads from the Tan Hill Colliery for Muker. Upstream the track

becomes very stony as it climbs steadily above the river. Across the river, note the isolated round hill of Kisdon and in the valley bottom the ruined farmstead of Hartlakes, known locally as 'Boggles House'. It is reputed to be haunted by Boggles or Barquests – ghosts and hobgoblins. After a mile cross the railed footbridge over Swinner Gill by the ruined Beldi Smelt Mill built in 1771. There is a splendid waterfall tucked in behind these lead mine remains. Go through the gate and prepare for a stiff climb up the zig zag track by East Wood, giving good views back down to Muker. Stay on this high level path which encounters Wainwright's Coast to Coast Walk and passes the spoil heaps of the Beldi Lead Mine, a reminder of Swaledale's lead mining industry. Walk westwards along the gated track above the wooded Swale Gorge with the roar of Kisdon Force below, heard but not seen. Admire the stunning Swaledale scenery. Cross the bridge over the triple East Gill Force where the Coast to Coast Walk intersects the Pennine Way. Take the latter downhill to cross the wooden footbridge over the River Swale. Follow the Pennine Way via Keld Lane back to Keld to complete one the most spectacular and beautiful walks in Upper Swaledale.

22. High Grantley

© Crown Copyright

HIGH GRANTLEY
A charming little village
Start and Finish

Drift Lane

Low Green Farm

Neresford

Skelding Grange

steep ascent

follow waymarks

Sunny Bank Wood

Grantley Hall

Saw Mill

Spa Gill Wood

ruined spa

RIVER SKELL

Skell Bank Wood

Fountains Hall

Fountains Abbey

Green Belt Wood

follow waymarks

busy road

B6265

RISPLITH
A scattered hamlet

SAWLEY
A tiny village

Inn

Gowbusk

Hollin Hill Farm

follow waymarks

stiled fields

Steep, slippery descent

Ravens Crag

Hill Top

Brim Bray Pond

track

EAVESTONE LAKE
A secluded lake

88

22. High Grantley

Location: High Grantley, an unspoilt village, is 8 miles from Masham; 1 mile from Risplith; 5 miles from Ripon.
Route: High Grantley – Risplith – Spa Gill Wood – Fountains Abbey – Sawley – Gowbusk – Eavestone Lake – Skelding Grange – High Grantley.
Distance: Over 10 miles (17km). Moderate. Allow 6 hours. Steep descent and ascent. Some road walking.
O.S. Maps: Landranger 99 Northallerton and Ripon; Pathfinder 641 SE 27/37 Ripon; 653 SE 26/36 Fountains Abbey and Boroughbridge.
Parking: Limited roadside parking at west end of High Grantley near the old school.
Public Transport: United Services 145 Ripon-Grantley Circular. Thurs and Sat only.
Refreshments: The Grantley Arms, Grantley. Blackamoor's Head Inn, Risplith. The Sawley Arms, Sawley. (No Dogs Allowed)
Note: Brief description. Intricate field path walk requires careful map navigation. Pathfinder map recommended. A clarty walk!

This fascinating and intricate field path walk in a little known but well worthwhile walking area south of High Grantley has Eavestone Lake as a noteworthy objective. Combine with a visit to Fountains Hall and Fountains Abbey if you have time.

From High Grantley proceed east and beyond the village hall, go over the road and cross the signposted stile by Grange Cottage. Walk forward, turn right through a waymarked black gate and bear half left for a concealed stile with a yellow metal post where yellow arrows on flat stones direct you down the field edge. Duck under the sloe bushes, cross a stile, and at the bottom of the next field cross not one, but two stiles.

Turn left and follow the waymark arrows round the rough pasture into Sunny Bank Wood and follow the waymarked pines southwards. Cross a bridge, go over the driveway and follow the waymarked route by the wall of Grantley Hall, an Adult Education College. Cross a bridge over the River Skell and scramble up into the timber yard of Grantley Saw Mill. Turn left and by the red shed, turn right and cross a stile by a telegraph pole. Go up the field, hug the wood and negotiate two stiles with difficulty, the first has a loose stepboard. Over the driveway proceed southwards through the waymarked wood and exit over a stile. Go up the road to the hamlet of Risplith and at the road junction turn right, if you need refreshments at the Blackamoor's Head Inn.

For the main route, turn left along the busy B6265 with a 1:5 gradient for a mile. Pass East Lodge and 120yds uphill turn right over a signposted stile by double gates marked 'Fire Road' and enter Spa Gill Wood. Go down the woodland track by the unhurried River Skell and pass the old Spa ruin. After 1.5 miles, leave the wood by a stile, pass a fine arched bridge and follow the track uphill to reach the road. Turn down this, pass the National Trust Shop and the entrance to Fountains Hall and Fountains Abbey, one of the finest monastic ruins in Western Europe. You have to decide whether or not to visit the Abbey or leave it for another day.

Pass the car park, walk up to the road junction and turn right along the Sawley Road for a steady climb with backward views to Fountains Abbey. After a mile you reach a Public Footpath signpost and turn right through a thin belt of trees called Green Belt Wood. Go through the gate, continue round the field on a track, cross a stile by a gate, and in the second field cross a concealed stile, waymarked in the hedge on your left. Turn right up the field edge and cross the corner stile on your right. The route heads westwards through the next five fields via waymarked stiles/gates into Sawley Village. Beyond The Sawley Arms and opposite Green View turn left along the track and between the tiny Parish Hall and the play area, cross the corner signposted stile on your right. Go up the field edge and the old school is on the other side of the hedge on your right. Go through a gate and at the top of the next field cross a waymarked fence stile and turn right along an enclosed path. There are eastward views of the spire of St. Mary's at Studley Royal.

Turn left up the field edge and in the top corner there is an square concrete building on the other side of the fence. Cross the stile and plank bridge, fork right over the enclosed track and cross the corner stile by a gate. Turn right and walk forward along the next two muddy meadows (stiled) and in the third, fork half left uphill and exit through a signposted gate to reach the B6265. Yards up the road, cross the B6265 and follow the signposted track to the two farms of Gowbusk. Opposite the first farm, bear left through a handgate by a black shed and turn right along the track to pass the second farm on your left. Take the open waymarked gateway on the right, pass a caravan and follow the waymarked route round the edge of the field to cross a corner ladder stile. Turn left and follow the waymarks up a very muddy gated track to pass Hollin Hill Farm on your left. Keep on the concrete farm road and where the wall ends on your right, turn right and follow the waymarks along the diverted path. As

(Continued on Page 90)

(Continued from page 89)

requested, keep in single file by the wall along the edge of the fields, until a gate admits you into Fishpond Wood. Follow the waymarks steeply down the woodland and be prepared for a slippery descent and expect a soaking from the overhanging tree branches after wet weather. At the bottom, use the plank path (very muddy), cross the little bridge and walk along the concrete walkway by Eavestone Lake. **Note:** There are warning notices positioned around the lake about the presence of blue/green algae – dangerous to humans and animals. Despite this, it's a lovely wooded walk around the lake which is dominated by craggy outcrops, particularly Ravens Crag. It's best to visit in May and June when the rhododendrons are in bloom. At the west end of the lake cross a slipway and climb steeply up

the woodland path to the road. Turn right and follow the road for more than a mile through the farming hamlet of Eavestone up to Hill Top, where it ends. Go down the signposted gated track between two lovely ponds and follow it uphill above the larger one called Brim Bray Pond. At the top, go through a gate and follow the bush lined track westwards. Once through a second open gateway, turn down a couple of stiled meadows into the wooded valley below. Turn right at the bottom, cross a stile and use the footbridge over the River Skell. Turn right, then left and cross an inset stile for a steep climb up an enclosed path out through the gated meadows to reach a farm road. For the return route, turn right along Drift Lane for a mile back to High Grantley or, as shown on my map, use the field path route eastwards below Skelding Grange via Neresford and Low Green Farm to High Grantley.

90

A bird's eye view of Crag Lough in Hadrian's Wall country

Stride out along the cliffs from Ravenscar

Beautiful old stone buildings in Blanchland

The gatehouse to Castle Howard along the Bulmer walk

23. Ripley

Location: Ripley is 8 miles south of Ripon (A61); 9 miles east of Pateley Bridge (B6165); 3 miles north of Harrogate (A61); 4 miles north west of Knaresborough (B6165)
Route: Ripley – Hampsthwaite – Birstwith – New Bridge – Burnt Yates – Clint – Ripley.
Distance: 8 miles. (13. 5km). Easy to moderate. Allow 5 hours. Field and riverside paths. Some road walking. One stiff climb.
O.S. Maps: Landranger 99 Northallerton and Ripon; Leeds and Bradford. Pathfinder 653 SE 26/36 Fountains Abbey and Boroughbridge; 663 SE/25/35 Harrogate.
Parking: Ripley Village car park. (free) 230 spaces. Located at the southern approach to the village. Check at the entrance, when the car park gates are open and closed.
Public Transport: Harrogate Independent: Service 6 Harrogate-Ripon. Reliant Motors: Service 46 York Station via Ripon United: Service 57 Ripon-Scotton. Harrogate District: Service 23 Harrogate-Pateley Bridge; Service 36 Ripon-Leeds. Check timetables.
Refreshments: The Castle Tearooms; The Boar's Head, Ripley. Joiners Arms; Lonsdale House, Hampsthwaite. The Station, Birstwith. The Bay Horse Inn, Burnt Yates.

This popular Ripley ramble provides a fine introduction to lower Nidderdale. It's an interesting eight miler, packed with history and heritage.

A brief pre-amble of Ripley is recommended if you want to see one of the most remarkable model estate villages in the country. Leave Ripley's Main Street by the cobbled Market Square and walk westwards past the 15th century All Saints Church, with its Weeping and Kneeling Cross. Pass Ripley Castle which dates back to 1450 and has been the ancient home of the Ingleby family for more than 650 years. The castle and grounds have been used for various TV and films. Go down Hollybank Lane which follows the Nidderdale Way in reverse. Cross the bridge over Ripley Beck and see the impressive lake with a grand view of the castle. Follow the bridle track up by the parkland wall and do not turn right when you see a waymark arrow. Keep on the main track through Hollybank Wood and watch out for the deer. Remember, this part of the walk is the return route.

At the end of the wood, exit through a signposted gate into a dead end lane. A few yards along the lane, beyond a green metal gate, (Nidderdale Way sign missing) turn left and follow the narrow enclosed path, a partially paved medieval track, for 880yds. Don't be alarmed, its often very muddy and flooded. Turn down Clint Bank Lane to Hampsthwaite. Before the old bridge and by a bench seat, a plaque tells you that the wall was built and the road widened in commemoration of the Jubilee of H.M. Queen Victoria, June 20 1887. Cross the three arched bridge, (built 1598) over the River Nidd and note the delightful riverside church. Even in Roman times there was an important river crossing here as part of the highway linking Aldborough and Ilkley. Walk into the pretty village of Hampsthwaite for refreshments at the Joiners Arms and the licensed Lonsdale House.

Return to Hampsthwaite church for a short cut through the churchyard. The church, dedicated to St. Thomas a Becket, was founded in 1175. There is an interesting porch erected in memory of William Makepeace Thackeray who suffered at the stake

St James's Church, Birstwith

for the Protestant faith at the end of Queen Mary's reign. Follow an enclosed path and turn right along the busy Birstwith road for 880yds, where the Nidderdale Way turns right by a barn building down to the banks of the River Nidd. Walk upstream, where the stiled path climbs above the wooded riverside and descends to Birstwith Mill, a food factory owned by Lucas Ingredients Ltd. As directed, pass through the mill complex by the old mill race to enter Birstwith village, dominated by the tall spire of St. James's Church. The old school (1879) has an inscribed clock – 'Whilst thou art looking, the hour is flying'. Perched above this picturesque village is the impressive Swarcliffe Hall (1848) where Charlotte Bronte spent an unhappy holiday as a governess.

(Continued on page 97)

23. Ripley

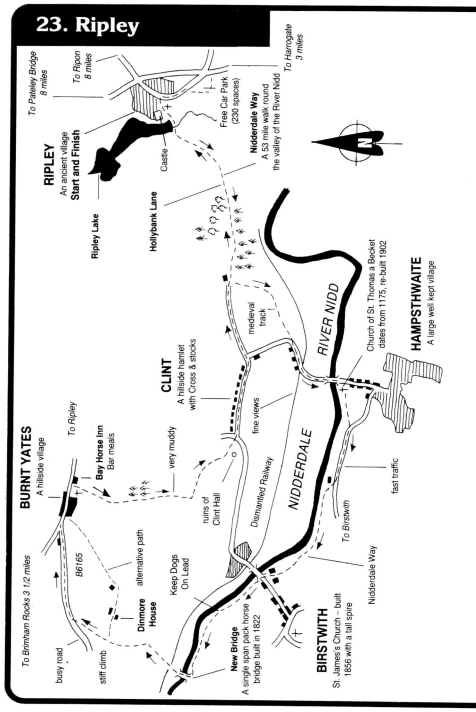

RIPLEY
An ancient village
Start and Finish

To Pateley Bridge 8 miles

To Ripon 8 miles

To Harrogate 3 miles

Free Car Park (230 spaces)

Nidderdale Way
A 53 mile walk round the valley of the River Nidd

Castle

Ripley Lake

Hollybank Lane

N

medieval track

CLINT
A hillside hamlet with Cross & stocks

RIVER NIDD

Church of St. Thomas a Becket dates from 1175, re-built 1902

HAMPSTHWAITE
A large well kept village

BURNT YATES
A hillside village

To Ripley

Bay Horse Inn
Bar meals

very muddy

fine views

NIDDERDALE

fast traffic

To Brimham Rocks 3 1/2 miles

B6165

busy road

stiff climb

alternative path

Dinmore House

Keep Dogs On Lead

ruins of Clint Hall

Dismantled Railway

To Birstwith

Nidderdale Way

New Bridge
A single span pack horse bridge built in 1822

BIRSTWITH
St. James's Church – built 1856 with a tall spire

96

(Continued from page 95)

Make a short detour over Birstwith Bridge for the fine views of the weir and a stop at The Station Inn for refreshments.

Return over the bridge and follow the signposted Nidderdale Way upstream for under a mile, using the stiled riverside path with detailed direction not needed. A couple of notices ask you to keep dogs on a lead. You soon reach New Bridge, a single span pack horse bridge which is the highlight of the walk. Here you leave the Nidderdale Way. Cross the cobbled bridge over the River Nidd. Go up the muddy lane, cross the disused Nidderdale Railway, (Harrogate to Pateley Bridge line, opened 1862, closed 1964) and continue upwards for another climb. Exit through a gate, turn left up the field edge and aim through a metal gate into a walled lane for another stiff climb out of the Nidd Valley. As you climb, admire the views up the dale and across the valley to Birstwith village.

So far up this lane, a stile on your right offers an alternative route to Burnt Yates. As shown on my map, go across a field to Dinmore House with its award winning holiday cottages and eastwards, take the gate below a barn. Walk northwards up the edge of three stiled fields following the course of the Monks Wall to reach the hilltop village of Burnt Yates – the highest point on the walk. For the main route, continue up the lane and at the top, go through a gate and follow the farm road to the B6165. Turn right along this road with fast traffic for a mile to Burnt Yates, which once marked the boundary between the Forest of Knaresborough and Fountains Abbey.

Opposite the tiny school, turn right between St. Andrews Church with its tall spire and the Bay Horse Inn, recommended for meals and go along the lane which swings right to Church Farm and aim left to cross a signposted stile. Follow the way-marked track, cross another stile and follow the field edge downhill by the fenced woodland on your left. At the bottom cross a stile, fork left over another stile and go down the ploughed field edge for a very muddy walk. Exit through a metal gate and turn immediately left along the fenced top edge of the meadow. At the far end of the field, go through a similar gate and aim half right across a final field keeping to the left of the ruined remains of Clint Hall. Out through a white gate, cross the road and pass through the tiny hamlet of Clint with fine views over Nidderdale to Harrogate.

Pass the ancient monument known as Ripley Cross with stocks. Beyond Clint Cottages, turn left and follow the dead end lane to rejoin Hollybank Lane back to Ripley.

© Crown Copyright

WENSLEYDALE

RIVER URE

To Carperby

AYSGARTH
An attractive village

AYSGARTH FALLS
NATIONAL PARK CENTRE
AND CAR PARK
Start and Finish

Aysgarth Church

To West Witton

Upper Falls
(Access Fee)

A684

Eshington Bridge
dated NRY 1883

To West Witton

Burton Bridge
An ancient packhorse bridge

Walden Beck

Upper Cauldron Falls

WEST BURTON
A lovely village with large green,
stocks and cross.
Most photographed village in
Wensleydale

Alternative
return route

BISHOPDALE

Bishopdale Beck

Little Beck

To Hawes

High Lane

Haw Beck

B6160

Superb views

Multiplicity of stiles

NEWBIGGIN
A tiny village

stiff stony
descent

To Thornton
Rust

Folly Lane

stepping stones

Map navigation
needed

Haw Lane
extensive
views

THORALBY
A charming village
with interesting
17th century houses

Street Head Inn
1730 – an old
coaching inn

N

24. Aysgarth Falls

Location: *Aysgarth Falls National Park Centre half a mile east of Aysgarth village (A684).*
Route: *Aysgarth Falls – Aysgarth village –Thoralby – Newbiggin – West Burton – Thieves Gill – Aysgarth Falls.*
Distance: *6 miles (10km) Fairly Easy. Allow 3 hours.*
O.S. Maps: *Landranger 98 Wensleydale and Wharfedale; Outdoor Leisure 30 Yorkshire Dales, Northern and Central Areas.*
Parking: *Aysgarth Falls National Park Centre Car Park. Pay and Display.*
Public Transport: *United Services 26 Richmond-Leyburn-Hawes. Dales Bus 800 Keighley and Dist/Harrogate and Dist. Summer Saturday service from Leeds-Keld: Sunday service Harrogate/Leeds-Hawes. Dales Bus 809 Keighley and Dist. Summer service Tues Keighley-Skipton-Hawes-Settle. Check all timetables*
Refreshments: *Dales Park Cafe; Mill Race Tea Shop; Falls Restuarant and Cafeteria; Palmer Flatt Hotel; Aysgarth Falls. George and Dragon, Yoredale House, Aysgarth village. George Inn, Thoralby. Street Head Inn, Newbiggin. Fox and Hounds, West Burton.*

This amble links Wensleydale with Bishopdale and visits the picturesque villages of Aysgarth, Thoralby, Newbiggin and West Burton and is recommended for the eating and drinking places en route.

Leave the car park at Aysgarth Falls by the signposted path at the south west corner and follow it to Yore Bridge. Cross the bridge over the River Ure with good views of the famous Upper Falls. Yore Mill, built as a cotton mill in 1784, now houses the Carriage Museum and Craft Shop. Go between the museum and Mill Cottages, climb the steep steps up to the 12th century St. Andrew's Church and turn right up the churchyard driveway. At the church gates, cross the road and go through the stile, signposted 'Aysgarth' and follow the parishioners' path through the stiled pastures to Aysgarth. Continue along the main road through the village. At the road junction, fork left and follow the Thornton Rust road westwards for 600yds. There are extensive views to Carperby, Castle Bolton, Wether Fell and Addleborough.

Turn left into the walled High Lane which is double signposted 'Thoralby/Gayle' near a large stone barn. Go up this unsurfaced bridle track and where it splits, fork left and follow Folly Lane southwards. At the bottom of this walled lane, ford Haw Beck or use the stepping stones and go through the squeeze stile wedged by the wall and gate. Go straight up the field by the growing crops and at the top, pass through a facing metal gate. Fork half right over a long meadow bisected by a boundary of boulders, maintain the same direction and aim through a green metal gate. Descend the stony track with expanding views of Wensleydale and Bishopdale dominated by Pen Hill. At the bottom of the track, go through a wooden gate and turn left down the walled Haw Lane and follow this stony track which descends steeply into Thoralby.Turn left along the village. You can shorten the return route from Thoralby by walking east along the village via Eastfield Lane to Eshington Lane and Eshington Bridge to meet the main walk. For the main route, turn right by the Methodist Church and follow

the lane for 880yds to the B6160. Here you can cross the busy Bishopdale road and follow the signposted lane to the tiny village of Newbiggin or turn right along the B6160 for 300yds to the Street Head Inn, an old coaching inn established in 1730. Opposite the inn, follow the road to Newbiggin and turn left along this quiet village to its extreme east end. Turn right by East Farm and go up the unnamed stony lane which curves left and levels out. Cross the stile by the red gate on your right and bear half left up the first field and follow the same route direction, eastwards through a succession of stiles over the patchwork pastures with extensive views. When you pass a stone barn, veer right and keep by Little Beck via more stiles down to West Burton built around a green with stocks and a spire market cross. At the bottom right hand corner of the green, turn right by The Mill and pass Blue Bridge (1860), a packhorse bridge, to the secluded Cauldron Falls. Retrace your steps, turn right and follow the lower road, noting the Lower Cauldron Falls. Pass Burton Bridge, an ancient packhorse bridge, and yards along the road, fork left and follow the Aysgarth road to the point where the paved path ends. Go through the wall stile signposted 'Eshington Bridge 250yds' and as directed, follow the short field path which avoids some road walking. Exit over a signposted stile back out on the same road, turn left and cross Eshington Bridge (1883) over Bishopdale Beck. Turn right along the road for a few yards, cross the stile signposted 'Aysgarth Church' on your left and bear half right, aim for the stile behind the power line pole. Go through the gated stile, turn right, pass through a second stile and the route swings half left up the field with glorious views behind you of Waldendale and Bishopdale. Keep by the wall on your right and follow the stiled path down into the hidden dry beck of Thieves Gill for a steep descent and ascent. As requested, keep in single file across the final meadow to the A684. Cross the main road, go down Church Lane to Aysgarth Church and follow the outward route back to the car park.

KIRKHAM PRIORY
Start and Finish
A ruined Augustinian priory
founded in 1122 by
Walter l'Espec

To Malton

DANGER WEIR

WESTOW
An unspoilt village

Dark Lane
unsuitable for motors

RIVER DERWENT

Kirkham Bridge

follow waymarks

Henlow Lane

The Derwent Way
An 80-mile walk
from Barmby on the Marsh
to Lilla Howe

Dogs must be
on a lead

stiff climb

stile

Spy Hill
viewpoint

field

Westow Hall
A fine early
18th century house

Howsham Wood

To York

Pleasant, easy
riverside walk

man-made pond

Braisthwaite Wood

steep
steps

Howsham Hall

HOWSHAM
A pretty village

N

Weir

disused lock

'Private
Land'

Howsham Bridge

25. Kirkham Priory

Location: *Kirkham Priory is 5 miles south-west of Malton on a minor road off the A64 opposite Whitwell on the Hill.*
Route: *Kirkham Priory – Howsham – Howsham Wood – Spy Hill – Westow – Dark Lane – Kirkham Priory.*
Distance: *About 8 miles (13km). Fairly easy. Allow 4/5 hours.*
O.S. Maps: *Landranger 100 Malton and Pickering Pathfinder 655 (SE66/76) Barton le Willows.*
Parking: *Kirkham Priory car park. (Free). Limited parking.*
Public Transport: *Yorkshire Coastliner 840, 843 Leeds/Scarborough service to Whitwell on the Hill and walk down Onham Lane to Kirkham Priory.*
Refreshments: *Kirkham Abbey Coffee House. Blacksmiths Arms, Westow.*

This Ryedale ramble based on the ruined Kirkham Priory explores the Kirkham Valley between Kirkham Bridge and Howsham Bridge, includes the ancient Howsham Wood and visits the pretty villages of Howsham and Westow.

From Kirkham Priory car park, turn left down the road and cross the Kirkham Bridge over the River Derwent. Opposite Kirkham Abbey Coffee House, turn left and cross a waymarked stile with a request 'Please keep to paths and ensure dogs are on a lead'. The outward route to Howsham Bridge follows part of the Derwent Way, an 80 mile walk from Barmby on the Marsh to Lilla Howe which was pioneered by Richard Kenchington in 1982. Follow the riverside path southwards, pass Kirkham Weir (Danger) and enjoy the excellent view of Kirkham Priory. Keep to the well worn path through Oak Cliff Wood and expect to scramble over fallen trees. Emerge from the wood and follow the path sandwiched between the river and railway. The next two miles are well waymarked. Just keep by the river, beside the stiled fields and over railed footbridges. The wooded slopes of the Forestry Commission's Howsham Wood, an ancient and modern mixture of conifers and deciduous trees on the opposite bank, drop down to the Derwent which is the perfect place for woodcock and kingfisher. Also on the opposite riverbank is the rear of the Jacobean Howsham Hall built by Sir William Bamburgh between 1612 and 1625 with used stone from Kirkham Priory. Today it's a private school.

When you reach a padlocked gate, turn right, cross a footbridge and go up the fenced path by Braisthwaites Wood with signs 'Private Land – Trespassers Will Be Prosecuted'. Go carefully down some steep steps into the wood and cross a footbridge to rejoin the River Derwent. The old Howsham Lock is a reminder that the river was opened up to navigation in Queen Anne's reign. Walk beside the river and at the end of the wood, cross a stile and follow the riverside path to a stile south of an old stone bridge. Turn left along the road, cross Howsham Bridge over the River Derwent and it is here that you leave the Derwent Way which journeys south to Scrayingham. Go up the

road to the sign 'Howsham Only' and turn down into Howsham. George Hudson, who became known as the Railway King, was born in this tiny village. The quaint Church of St. John, (built 1859/60) is worth a visit. Two cottages below the church, (15 Howsham) turn right through the unsignposted double gates and follow the gravel track. Cross a corner stile and walk eastwards along the edge of the next two stiled fields. Go through a gate marked 'Please Shut Gate', turn sharp left and left through the adjacent gate and right down the field edge. At the bottom, turn right through a gate ('Please Shut Gate') and downhill, pass a pond.

Go up the field by the wood with a sprawling oak and cross the stile, right of a gate into Howsham Wood. At first, turn right along the woodland edge and where the path becomes a rutted muddy track, expect a stiff climb up the wood. At the top, turn right along a broad forest track and keep to this route which steadily climbs, levels out and curves to join another track coming in on your left. Turn right along this track with the forest on your left and an open field on your right. Twenty to thirty yards before the track begins to go down into the wood, look out for a step stile in the field fence on your right. Scramble over the stile and bear half left for a stiff climb up to the top corner of the field by the wood. At the top, walk forward through the facing gate (do not go through the gate on your left) and you have reached Spy Hill, the highest point on the walk. From here you can see Kirkham Valley, Howsham, Sheriff Hutton and Castle Howard. Follow the path downhill by the edge of the fields with growing crops and on the way down you will pass the scant remains of a stone building. Turn left up Henlow Lane and as you enter the unspoilt village of Westow, note the 18th century Westow Hall. The Blacksmiths Arms, an excellent pub for bar meals. David Greenwood welcomes walkers and gives you the rare opportunity to eat your own food. Beyond the pub, turn left along the road to Kirkham and at the sign 'Unsuitable For Motors', turn right along the track called Dark Lane to the Kirkham/Firby road junction. Turn left along this road for a quiet return to Kirkham Priory.

26. Knaresborough

© Crown Copyright

KNARESBOROUGH

Ancient Market Town
Gateway to Nidderdale
Start and Finish

St. Robert's Cave
13th century home of
an eccentric hermit

Grimbald Bridge
Two arched ancient bridge

'Dogs must be on a lead'

Plompton Mill Farm

caravan park

Grimbald Crag – lofty limestone
crag with a precipitous drop

caravan park

Birkham Wood
70 acres of ancient
woodland

Crag Top – a limestone
precipitous cliff top

Plaque –
Trinitarian Priors built
a Priory Church near
this spot in 1252

Abbey Road

The House in the Rock
constructed between
1770 and 1786

**Chapel of Our Lady
of the Crag**

14th century
castle

Market Place

Briggate

Mill

very muddy

stile

stile

**Thistle
Cottage**

stile

To Calcutt

fine
riverside views

Low Bridge

Inn

Station

Waterside

Parish Church

High Bridge

Railway Viaduct
(rebuilt in 1851)

RIVER NIDD

**Mother Shipton's
Cave**

Dropping Well

N

26. Knaresborough

Location: *Knaresborough is 3 miles south west of Harrogate on (A59)*
Route: *Knaresborough – Market Place – Briggate – Abbey Road – Grimbald Bridge – Grimbald Crag – Birkham Wood – Low Bridge – Waterside – Market Place.*
Distance: *About 5 miles (9km). Easy. Allow 2/3 hours.*
O.S. Maps: *Landranger 104 Leeds and Bradford; Pathfinder 663 (SE 25/35) Harrogate*
Parking: *Disc parking. Two free hours in the town centre. Discs from shops, banks, council offices, Information Centre. Car parks at York Place, Castle Yard, Fisher Street, Market Place, Waterside, Conyngham Hall and Dropping Well Estate.*
Public Transport: *Regular bus services from Harrogate, Marton, Roecliffe and Wetherby. British Rail: Metro Harrogate Line. Regular services between York and Leeds.*
Refreshments: *Plenty of pubs and cafes in Knaresborough.*
Warning: *Grimbald Crag – narrow, slippery path. Children should be supervised.*
Note: *For the Town Trail, use a Town Map, 'A Walkabout Tour of Knaresborough' and booklet 'Exploring Knaresborough' by Arnold Kellett from Information Centre.*

This splendid waterside walk from Knaresborough follows paths on both sides of the River Nidd and offers spectacular views of the lower Nidd Gorge. Before you set out you must see 'Ye Oldest Chymist Shoppe' which claims to be the oldest pharmacy in England. Established in 1720 during the reign of George I, it is still in use today.

Leave the Market Place along Castlegate by the Market public house and go left into Cheapside. As you pass the Cross Keys, pop into Castle Yard if you want view the 14th century cliff top ruin of Knaresborough Castle and enjoy the famous picture postcard view of the River Nidd. Continue along Cheapside to come out opposite the United Reformed Church. Go down the steep street of Briggate (B6163) and just before Low Bridge, cross Briggate and turn left by the Half Moon Inn along the quiet Abbey Road dominated by limestone cliffs overlooking the River Nidd. This is the start of a delightful riverside ramble, full of historic interest.

Yards along the road, take a guided tour of Fort Montague, the House in the Rock. Carved out of solid rock, work was started in 1770 by Thomas Hill and completed in 1786 by his son, also Thomas. Next to this house is the small shrine Chapel of Our Lady of the Crag, hewn out of rock by John the Mason around 1408. Carry on along the road and when you reach a white barrier gate by Priory Cottage, note a plaque on the cottage wall which proclaims that the Trinitarian Priors built a Priory Church near this spot in 1252. Go up the road, pass Larchfield on your left and where the wall ends on your right, go through the gap and down the rough steps to St. Robert's Cave, home of the hermit St. Robert who lived here in the early 13th century. He tamed wild animals, befriended the poor, gave shelter to outlaws and even gained favour with King John. This riverside cave was desecrated when Daniel Cark, a shoemaker, was murdered and buried by Eugene Aram in the 18th century. At the end of Abbey Road, walk over Grimbald Bridge, turn right, cross a ladder stile signposted 'Public Footpath Calcutt' and follow the farm road along the south bank of the River Nidd. Pass Plomptom Farm with its old mill and attractive weir. Keep in front of the Lido Caravan Park and follow the riverside path to Grimbald Crag, a magnificent rock of magnesian limestone and a splendid viewpoint. Exercise great care on this narrow steep path, as it curves round the craggy mass with a deep drop to the mill weir below. Emerge into a second caravan park and by the van called 'The Creek', go steeply down into the ancient 70 acre Birkham Wood to the River Nidd. Turn left, keep by the wooded riverside with numerous springs and expect plenty of mud, even in summer. At the end of the wood, cross a stone stile and follow the fenced field path (very muddy) westwards away from the river. Exit over a stile, ignore the uphill track on your left and follow the signposted footpath by Thistle Cottage. Keep on the paved path, pass an old lime kiln and climb up through the wood with delightful views of the riverside cottages. Ignore the path to your left, unless you need refreshments at The Union in Calcutt. Keep straight on by the walled gardens and over a stile to come out by Eden Roc. Go along the surfaced Spitalcroft to the B6163 and turn down Blands Hill to Low Bridge. Behind the 17th century Mother Shipton's Inn you can pay your admission to see Mother Shipton's Cave and The Dropping Well.

For the Town Trail, cross Low Bridge and enjoy the spectacular views on both sides of the River Nidd. Turn left along Waterside, pass the car park/picnic area and just beyond Castle Mill you get your first glimpse of the ruins of the 14th century Knaresborough Castle. Continue along Waterside and enjoy the famous picture postcard view of the River Nidd. Relax at the riverside cafe and watch the boats go by, then go under the railway viaduct, rebuilt in 1851 after the original one collapsed in 1848. It is 90ft high, 338ft long, with spans of 56ft 4ins. Beyond the viaduct at the Old Manor House, turn right up Water Bag Bank and pass the thatched Manor Cottage. Go uphill, pass Knaresborough Station, cross the railway line and go up Kirkgate back to the Market Place.

105

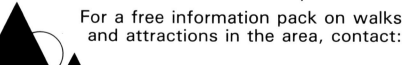

108

FIR TREE COUNTRY HOTEL

TO FIND US:
We are located on the junction of the main A68 road between Darlington and Corbridge in the picturesque village of Fir Tree — the gateway to beautiful Dales Country.

THE FACILITIES:
★ 14 en-suite Lodges with Tea/Coffee making facilities
★ Luxurious Function Room seating 80 guests.
★ Resident's Lounge with colour T.V.
★ Restaurant and Bar Meals available throughout the Inn.

★ Comprehensive Wine List
★ Cocktail Lounge adjacent to Hotel Reception Area.
★ Coffee/Tea and light meals available all day.
★ Hospitality and Friendliness assured.

The resident owner, Barry will be on hand at all times to give details of accommodation and all facilities on offer — all types of private functions are welcome.

Whatever you choose, a weekend break to a large private party, we will endeavour to make your visit to the Fir Tree Inn a pleasurable one.

ETB 👑 👑 👑
COMMENDED -

FIR TREE, CROOK, CO. DURHAM DL15 8DD
Telephone (0388) 762161

Drinking well at Thropton near Rothbury

How many items make up this gate in Swainby High Street?

MILLBURNGATE
S H O P P I N G   C E N T R E
DURHAM CITY

MORE SHOPS . . . MORE COMFORT
MORE CHOICE . . . MORE STYLE

Enjoy a day out combining excellent shopping facilities with a visit to the Historic Cathedral and Castle

Some of the retail names in the centre are:

T. & G. Allan ● Athena ● Dixons ● Dorothy Perkins
Early Learning Centre ● Evans ● Fosters
Hallmark Cards ● Holland & Barrett
Little John Restaurant ● Mothercare
Monument Sports ● Our Price Records ● Principles
Rumbelows ● Safeway ● Superdrug

Plus many more!

MILLBURNGATE SHOPPING CENTRE BETWEEN FRAMWELLGATE AND MLLBURNGATE BRIDGES, DURHAM CITY

Come and shop in pleasant surroundings FREE from traffic and the weather, with undercover parking available for over 500 cars
AN EXPERIENCE TO REMEMBER

MILLBURNGATE
S H O P P I N G   C E N T R E

The First Class Centre in the New First Class County

The Millburngate Shopping Centre is managed by C.I.N. Properties Ltd.
The property investment arm of British Coal Pension Funds

BKLKR   44-073

The Wishing Well

The Friendly Pub

Probably the best night out in the North of England

The Collinge family look forward to seeing you at their excellent pub and restaurant overlooking the beautiful Durham countryside

Set amidst the beautiful countryside, The Wishing Well extends a warm welcome

Tastefully decorated restaurant comfortably seating 150 with friendly atmosphere

The pleasant conservatory - an ideal place to relax and view the beautiful surrounding countryside

Bar lounge where you can relax and soak up the warm and friendly atmosphere

- **A la carte menu • Sunday Lunches • Lounge bar • Free House**
- **150 seater Restaurant • Catering for private functions**
- **Large dance floor**

★ WEEKEND CABARET ★

So why not call and see us soon

The Wishing Well
BURNHOPE
VILLAGE

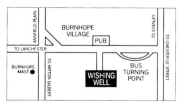

BPRCB **THE AVENUE, BURNHOPE (0207) 529247** 44-073

You don't need the Radio Times or the TV Times...

...You only need The Northern Echo

7PLUSDAYS

7 Days Plus
FREE with The Northern Echo every Friday

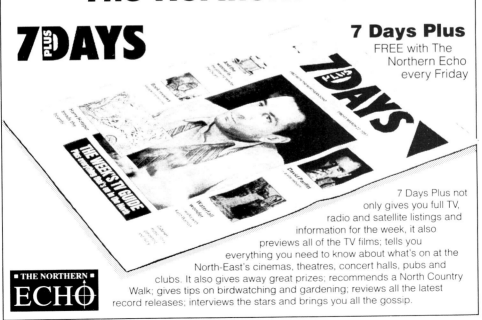

7 Days Plus not only gives you full TV, radio and satellite listings and information for the week, it also previews all of the TV films; tells you everything you need to know about what's on at the North-East's cinemas, theatres, concert halls, pubs and clubs. It also gives away great prizes; recommends a North Country Walk; gives tips on birdwatching and gardening; reviews all the latest record releases; interviews the stars and brings you all the gossip.

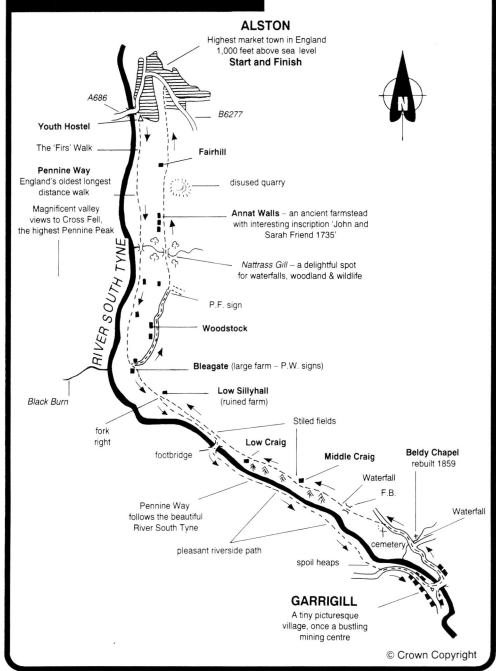

ALSTON
Highest market town in England
1,000 feet above sea level
Start and Finish

A686

B6277

Youth Hostel

The 'Firs' Walk

Fairhill

disused quarry

Pennine Way
England's oldest longest
distance walk

Magnificent valley
views to Cross Fell,
the highest Pennine Peak

Annat Walls – an ancient farmstead
with interesting inscription 'John and
Sarah Friend 1735'

Nattrass Gill – a delightful spot
for waterfalls, woodland & wildlife

RIVER SOUTH TYNE

P.F. sign

Woodstock

Bleagate (large farm – P.W. signs)

Black Burn

Low Sillyhall
(ruined farm)

Stiled fields

fork
right

footbridge

Low Craig

Middle Craig

Beldy Chapel
rebuilt 1859

Waterfall

F.B.

Waterfall

Pennine Way
follows the beautiful
River South Tyne

pleasant riverside path

cemetery

spoil heaps

GARRIGILL
A tiny picturesque
village, once a bustling
mining centre

© Crown Copyright

118

27. Alston

Location: Alston, highest market town in England, is 22 miles from Middleton in Teesdale, 46 miles from Darlington, 23 miles from Hexham and 10 miles from Penrith.
Route: Alston – Bleagate – Low Sillyhall – Garrigill – Low Craig – Low Sillyhall – Bleagate – Woodstock – Annat Walls – Alston.
Distance: Short walk 4 miles; long walk under 9 miles. Easy. Allow 3 or 5 hours.
O.S. Maps: Landranger 87 Hexham and Haltwhistle; 88 Haltwhistle. Pathfinder 569 NY 64/74 Alston; Outdoor Leisure 31 Teesdale.
Parking: Limited parking on Alston's cobbled main street. Alston Railway Station.
Public Transport: Wright Bros. Newcastle – Keswick; Haltwhistle – Nenthead; Alston – Nenthead. Check timetables.
Refreshments: Hotels, pubs, cafes, tearooms, fish shop in Alston. The George and Dragon in Garrigill.

Alston is the perfect place for tours afoot in the South Tyne Valley. This all-field walk follows the famous Pennine Way south of Alston and takes you along the South Tyne Valley to the tiny village of Garrigill, once a bustling lead mining centre. There are fine views including Cross Fell, the highest Pennine peak. The return, like the outward route via fields and farms, includes the little wooded valley of Nattrass Gill, well known for waterfalls and wildlife.

From Alston's old Market Cross, go down the cobbled main street and turn left along the A686. Pass the garage (J.H. Henderson), go down Brewery Bank and just before the bridge climb the stepped Pennine Way path up to Alston Youth Hostel. A plaque reads: 'The Firs. This woodland walk belongs to the people of Alston Moor June 1946.' Follow The Firs Walk high above the River South Tyne and at the end of this local walk you get your first view of Fiends Fell, better known as Cross Fell. Proceed along the Pennine Way southwards by the wall and down the stiled fields to the valley bottom of the South Tyne with the river a field or more away to your right. Cross the footbridge over Nattrass Gill. Go up the field through an open gateway and pass the whitewashed Low Ness Farm on your left. The route is straight ahead through stiled fields and when you pass a clump of pine trees on your left, swing left through the ruined wall, turn right along the same wall and cross the corner stile.

Proceed southwards via stiled fields and pass Low Cowgap Farm to reach Bleagate Farm with a bird's eye view of the River South Tyne below. Cross a waymarked stile and go up the farmyard to a double Pennine Way signpost where you can halve the walk by following the return route back to Alston. For the main route, turn right and follow the Pennine Way via marker posts to Low Sillyhall. As you approach the ruined farm, bear half right and cross a stone stile by a gate. Turn left along the wall and when the farm is on your left, look for a narrow path that leads you down by the tree covered craggy outcrops where white waymarks guide you along the River South Tyne. Cross the footbridge, turn left and follow the right bank of the River South Tyne for two miles. Leave the river, climb the pine-covered ridge and walk along the embanked path by the mine spoil heaps. At the road turn left, pass the former Girls School AD 1850 and enter the tiny village of Garrigill. The George and Dragon welcomes walkers.

Stronger walkers can add a 4 mile circuit (Walk 28) to this walk and see the impressive Ashgill Force. Leave the Pennine Way and Garrigill by the Nenthead road, cross the road bridge over the South Tyne and follow the quiet road past Beldy Chapel (rebuilt 1859) and note the landscaped waterfall. Just beyond the cemetery, turn left through the gate (signposted Bleagate), go down the slanting path and turn half right (check map), aim through an open gateway and keep straight ahead by the wall. Go over the footbridge with a little waterfall and cross the corner stile. The route now hugs the walled wood on your left for the next mile via a succession of 11 stiles to pass in front of Low Craig Farm. Fork left, follow the track to a roofless ruin and turn left, keep by the walled wood through the stiled fields to the ruined Low Sillyhall Farm. Rejoin the outward route and follow the Pennine Way back to Bleagate.

For the last leg of the walk, turn up the farm road, pass the white washed Woodstock and stride out along this elevated route with valley views of the South Tyne dominated by Cross Fell. Where the road turns right (footpath signs) fork left through an inset blue gate to a Public Footpath sign 'Alston' and turn right across the field with High Nest to your left. Cross a stile and veer right downhill over another stile into the secluded wooded Nattrass Gill, once a favourite spot with Victorian visitors. Go down the stepped path, cross the white-railed footbridge and see the single drop waterfall below. It's a glorious place with a wide variety of flora. Take your time as you climb up the stepped path and at the top cross a stile. Go along the next two stiled fields, join a gated track and pass the ancient farmstead of Annat Walls with an interesting inscription 'John and Sarah Friend 1735'. Follow the walled track northwards for a mile past the disused quarries and old the Fairhill Farm to complete a satisfying walk back into Alston.

28. Garrigill

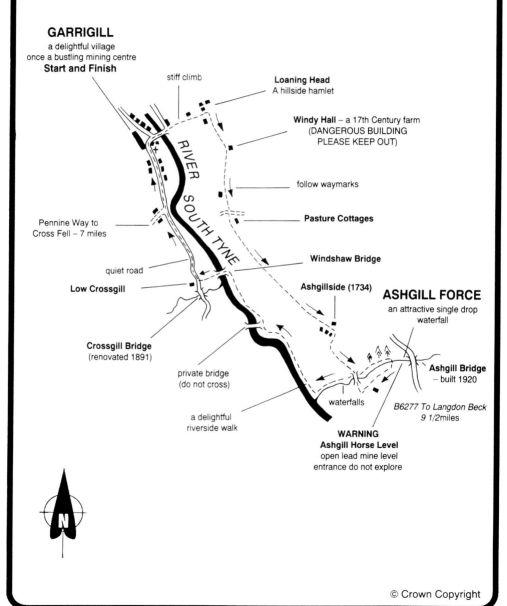

GARRIGILL
a delightful village
once a bustling mining centre
Start and Finish

stiff climb

Loaning Head
A hillside hamlet

Windy Hall – a 17th Century farm
(DANGEROUS BUILDING
PLEASE KEEP OUT)

RIVER SOUTH TYNE

follow waymarks

Pennine Way to
Cross Fell – 7 miles

Pasture Cottages

quiet road

Windshaw Bridge

Low Crossgill

Ashgillside (1734)

ASHGILL FORCE
an attractive single drop
waterfall

Crossgill Bridge
(renovated 1891)

private bridge
(do not cross)

Ashgill Bridge
– built 1920

waterfalls

*B6277 To Langdon Beck
9 1/2miles*

a delightful
riverside walk

**WARNING
Ashgill Horse Level**
open lead mine level
entrance do not explore

N

© Crown Copyright

28. Garrigill

Location: *Garrigill, a delightful Cumbrian village, is 4 miles south of Alston.*
Route: *Garrigill – Loaning Head – Pasture Cottages – Ashgillside – Ashgill Force – Windshaw Bridge – Garrigill.*
Distance: *Over 4 miles (6.5km). Allow 2/3 hours.*
O.S. Maps: *Landranger 87 Hexham and Haltwhistle; Pathfinder 569 NY 64/74 Alston; Outdoor Leisure 31 Teesdale.*
Parking: *Limited parking in Garrigill. Do not park on the village green.*
Public Transport: *Wright Bros, Alston Nenthead. Infrequent service. Check timetables.*
Refreshments: *The George and Dragon, Garrigill. None on route.*
Warning: *Do not explore the old lead mine entrance of Ashgill Horse Level.*

Save this short stroll in the South Tyne Valley for a rainy day if you want to see Ashgill Force in full spate. It's the finest force in the Alston area and one of the best in the North of England.

Leave Garrigill by the Nenthead road, pass the village pub and cross Garrigill bridge over the River South Tyne. Do not turn left along the road, but walk forward by Bridge End House and climb up the unsurfaced track for a steep start. As you climb steadily up the walled track, look back for fine views of Garrigill and South Tyne Valley. Near the top pass 'The Cottage' dated 1661 on your left, used as a religious meeting house in 1700. Enter the hillside hamlet of Loaning Head. At the footpath post marked 'Pasture House', turn right through the wooden gate and follow the path through a couple of fields with waymarked stone wall stiles. You pass on your left the ruined Windy Hall, a 17th century farmhouse with warning notices 'Dangerous Building Please Keep Out'. Aim half right for a waymarked telegraph pole near the far bottom corner of the third field. Turn immediately right, go down through a concealed wicket gate by the farm buildings of Snappergill. Turn left through the farmyard, follow the farm road and exit over a stile by a gate to reach a rough track. Go over the track, cross the wall stile opposite and pass below the single terrace former miner's cottages called Pasture Houses.

Continue southwards through the pleasant pastures (waymarked/stiled) and admire the superb views of the South Tyne Valley. Aim for a rusty corrugated barn with a yellow arrow and cross over a stile into the former farming hamlet of Ashgillside. Turn left in front of the only remaining farm (door lintel dated JAR 1734), go right along the track and pass a house on your left. Walk forward, cross the short stiled field, go over a track and cross a waymarked wooden stile. Go up, cross another stile and turn right down the field edge with a house on your right. Note, this path is by permission of the landowner and is not a right of way. Cross the stile by the gateway, turn left, hug the wall to the point where the path converges with a track overlooking the delightful Ashgill. Go downhill to a four way footpath signpost near a railed footbridge. Turn left, cross the stile and walk up Ashgill by some lovely little waterfalls. As you continue, the single drop

Ashgill Force by Robert Maddison

waterfall of Ashgill Force, spanned by the B6277 Ashgill Bridge at the head of a dramatic amphitheatre, comes into view. Cross the stepping stones over the stream. Spend some time at this secluded spot, which was a busy place 170 years ago when lead ore was extracted from the Ashgill Horse Level seen on your right, as you scramble for a better view of the waterfall. Do not explore the old mine, it's dangerous.

For the return, follow the miners' track by the loading bays for a high level stiled route above Ashgill to Waterfall Cottage known as Birds Nest. Turn right through the gate by the cottage and follow the track downhill where, at the bottom, turn right and aim for a wicket gate. Cross the footbridge over Ashgill, turn left and follow this lovely gill to reach the infant River South Tyne. Turn right, cross a stile and follow the fast flowing river with abundant wild flowers downstream for 880yds. On the way, you will pass a farm footbridge marked 'Private'. Do not cross, but continue downstream for 440yds to reach Windshaw Bridge. Cross the bridge over the South Tyne, note the mini gorge below and follow the walled track to come out opposite Low Crossgill. Turn right and follow the quiet road back to Garrigill. **N.B.** Walks 27 and 28 can be combined for a 13 mile circular walk.

121

KIRKOSWALD
A pretty red sandstone village

The College

Raven Beck

To Alston 13 miles

Kirkoswald Castle-13th century
(meagre remains)

Map navigation needed

B6314

Eden Bridge
built in 1762 at a cost of £768.16s 8d

bell tower

busy road

Pond

Follow yellow waymarks

Sundial memorial (private) to the writer and broadcaster Romany

Old Parks

To Carlisle

RIVER EDEN

Daleraven Bridge

excellent views of the Lakeland Fells

stiff climb

Settle – Carlisle Railway
Opened in 1876

Alternative short walk

Force Mill
A former cornmill

Tib Wood

GLASSONBY
A pleasant little village

Lacy's Caves
Five manmade caves named after Lt. Colonel Samuel Lacy of Salkeld Hall in the 18th Century.

To Little Salkeld

Long Meg Viaduct
5 arches, 137 yards long 60 feet high. It took four years to build.

Weir

Throstle Hall
ruined sandstone building dates from 1880

Addingham Church
dedicated to St. Michael, with its medieval history of disaster.

Long Meg and her Daughters
One of the largest neolithic stone circles in the country.

N

LITTLE SALKELD
A tiny hillside village
Start and Finish

The Watermill
Fully working watermill

To Settle

To Langwathby

29. Little Salkeld

Location: Little Salkeld, a small red sandstone village in Cumbria, $6^1/_2$ miles north-east of Penrith.
Route: Little Salkeld – Lacy's Caves – Daleraven – Eden Bridge – Kirkoswald – Old Parks – Glassonby – Addingham Church – Long Meg – Little Salkeld.
Distance: 7 miles (11.5km) or under 9 miles (14.5km) Fairly easy. Allow $3^1/_2$ or 5 hours.
O.S. Maps: Landranger 90 Penrith, Keswick and Ambleside; 91 Appleby; Pathfinder 577 (NY43/53) Penrith North; 568 (NY44/54) Southwaite & Kirkoswald.
Parking: Limited roadside parking by the small triangular green at upper end of Little Salkeld.
Public Transport: No regular daily service.
Refreshments: The Watermill, Little Salkeld. (Shop & Tearoom – Open daily: 10.30am-5.00pm). Pubs in Kirkoswald.
Warning: Lacy's Caves 'Dangerous path with sheer drops. Please take special care of young children. Proceed at your own risk'. Path by permission of landowner.
Note: Carry the relevant O.S. Map. Please keep dogs on lead. Expect plenty of mud. Stout footwear advisable.

This popular walk, packed with history and mystery, is one of the best in the Eden Valley. It offers an invitation to visit the remarkable man made Lacy's Caves and provides a fine introduction to Long Meg and her petrified daughters.

Leave Little Salkeld by walking west along the 'No Through Road' past the walled Salkeld Hall to the point where the lane splits at the double signs: 'Public Footpath' – 'Lacy's Caves/Daleraven' 'Private Road. No unauthorised vehicles. Footpath Only'. Turn right, follow the private road above the Settle-Carlisle railway to reach a barrier notice 'Long Meg. Private. Keep Out' and turn sharp left along the fenced signposted path 'Lacy's Caves/Daleraven' to pass the electricity sub-station. Turn right by the faded railway notices relating to the Long Meg railway sidings. Follow the fenced path by the remains of Long Meg Mine which closed in 1973. Enter Throstle Hall Brow Wood, where the path follows an old tramway and note the loading bays and shored up rock outcrops. Pass above the weir which once powered the old corn mill called Force Mill on the opposite riverside bank.

Carry on through Cave Wood and follow the riverside path upstream to Lacy's Caves, carved out of the red sandstone cliff overlooking the river. The man made caves are named after Lieutenant Colonel Samuel Lacy who owned Salkeld Hall in the 18th century. Their purpose is unclear. Some believe they were created as a fashionable grotto, while others say they were used as a cold store for wine and food. It is said that a man was employed to live in the caves pretending to be a hermit. If you explore these caves, proceed with care as notices warn you of the dangers along the narrow path with a steep drop.

Rejoin the main path and go up the stepped cliff path above the caves with good views downstream. The path leads down to the riverside for a delightful walk through Tib Wood. This stretch of the walk is always muddy and it has been improved with new

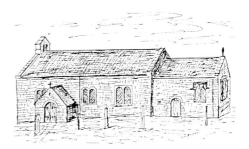

Addingham Church

drainage, small log bridges, and stiles undertaken by a Community Enterprise Scheme. At the end of the wood, cross a stile and follow the pleasant path by the River Eden. Climb up Kirk Bank above the wooded riverside and cut across the corner field to straddle a stile and go down the stepped plantation to Daleraven Bridge. To shorten the walk, turn right up the steep road for a mile to Glassonby village, where you rejoin the main walk. Admire the views of the Eden Valley, the Lakeland Hills and North Pennines. For the longer walk, turn left, cross Daleraven Bridge and go up the road for 100yds with the hidden footpath sign ('Eden Bridge') on your left. Go through the gate, walk forward by the field edge to reach the River Eden. Turn right upstream and at the field end, cross a stile and follow the farm track at first by the river. The track veers right through a couple of gateposts and hugs the fence on your right. Go through a gate, cross a small stone bridge and keep by the water channel until you turn left through a waymarked wooden gate. Turn right and pass a clump of trees to come out by the arched

(Continued on page 124)

123

(Continued from page 123)

Eden Bridge. Turn right along the busy B6413 and as you enter the attractive village of Kirkoswald note the 17th century manor house called The College, the name recording a college of priests who occupied the site until the Reformation of 1542. Opposite, the fine 13th century church of St Oswald built on the site of a sacred well is worth a visit. At the crossroads, there is an unusual bell tower sited away from the church and perched on the nearby hill. From Kirkoswald, take the Alston road uphill to the footpath sign marked 'Glassonby' and turn right through the gate and follow the track past the remains of the 13th century Kirkoswald Castle.

Go through a gate, walk forward and the path curves left below a fenced hillside. Keep on the level green path, pass the old oak trees and hug the fence on your right. At the field corner, turn right through a gate, follow the enclosed path by a pond and exit through a gate. Note, the route is waymarked with faded yellow arrows. Walk forward, pass a conical hill on your left and the path drops through another gate for a rough walk along the field edge with a wood on your right. Cut across the next field and converge with the same wood on your right, where the uphill path leads you out through a corner gate. Follow the track and as you approach Old Parks Farm, admire the westward views to the Lakeland Fells. On a small knoll in the cultivated field below there is a sundial memorial to Bramwell Evens, better known as Romany, who was one of the most popular of all children's broadcasters from 1933 to 1943. Go through the gated farmyard of Old Parks, turn right and follow the farm drive to reach the road. Turn right and follow the road uphill to the hillside village of Glassonby, where at the second road junction, turn left and take the road in the direction of Little Salkeld. Pass Glassonby Hall and 880yds beyond the cottage dated AD 1604, turn right by the barn signposted 'To Addingham Church'.

Follow the lane to the church dedicted to St Michael of the former village of Addingham which was washed away by the flood of 1350. This little church is well worth a visit. At the rear of the church, leave by the churchyard path and proceed south along the centre of the field and exit through a gate. Cross over the lane, go through the waymarked gate and follow the path down the field edge and where the wall ends, turn right and cross a waymarked stile in the fence. Proceed along the path by the small plantation and follow the waymarked route down the edge of the next two Lakeland Fields. In the third field you have reached the highlight of the walk – Long Meg and her Daughters, one of the finest Neolithic stone circles in the country, second only to Stonehenge. There are about 66 stones with Long Meg the tallest, a 15ft column of sandstone outside the oval of stones. Leave Long Meg by the farm road and head south down the lane which becomes unsurfaced and take the second turning on your left to reach the Glassonby/Little Salkeld road. Turn right and return to Little Salkeld.

30. Appleby

Location: Appleby is ten miles from Kirkby Stephen and 8 miles from Brough.
Route: Appleby – Flakebridge Wood – Greenhow Farm – Dufton – Brampton – Keld Farm – Appleby.
Distance: Over 8 miles (13km). Moderate. Allow 4/5 hours.
O.S. Maps: Landranger 91 Appleby; Pathfinder 578 (NY62/63) Appleby (part route); Outdoor Leisure 31 Teesdale (part route).
Parking: Chapel Street car park; The Butts; The Sands; Boroughgate and Appleby Station yard.
Public Transport: O.K. Travel X74 Bishop Auckland-Darlington-Carlisle. British Rail Settle-Carlisle.
Refreshments: Pubs, hotels, cafes, Appleby; Stagg Inn, Dufton. New Inn, Brampton.
Warning: This walk crosses the busy A66 dual carriageway. Exercise great care.
Note: Pathfinding needed between Flakebridge Wood and Greenhow Farm. Outdoor Leisure Map recommended.

Explore the Eden Valley with an attractive walk around Appleby via Flakebridge Wood to the pretty village of Dufton at the foot of the Pennines. From Appleby Station walk up Station Road and where it bends right, fork left up the path signed Hunriggs. Cross with great care the dual carriageway of the Appleby bypass (A66). Cross two stiles and a short field to reach Hunriggs Lane. Turn right along this lane with extensive views of the North Pennines. Once through a metal gate, turn left and follow the enclosed, stiled Stank Lane. The route ahead is waymarked with white painted stiles/posts. Go along the field edge, pass an isolated gatepost and fork half right across the same field. Cross the corner stile and, yards along the next field, turn left over a waymarked stile.

Skirt the edge of pretty Stank Wood and at the bottom of the wood, cross a stile and walk forward along an embanked path to reach a cart track. Turn left along the track and a waymarked post points the way alongside an enclosed wood. Go through a gate and follow the track which crosses the tiny bridge over Murton Back and curves right into Flakebridge Wood. Turn right up the track and on reaching the terraced Flakebridge Cottages, turn left along the track to a gate marked Private Road. Do not be deterred, it is a right of way. Cross the adjacent stile and ascend the track by the extensive cleared area of woodland. When the track levels out, take the second track on your right, pass the pond on your right and you might be lucky enough to see a red squirrel. Exit through the waymarked gate and, as directed, bear half left up the hillside and cross a stile by the sycamore tree.

At the top of the next field, cross another stile and head down the third field with the wood on your left. At the bottom, turn left through a hidden stile and cross the footbridge over Burthwaite Beck. Turn right and follow the path which contours the base of the tree-topped hillside and heads north westwards along the field by the wall on your right. Pass through a facing ruined wall. Reference to the O.S. map is essential as the right of way goes

The Pump, Dufton

through a gate in the upper left corner of the same field. The route westwards is easy to follow through a succession of fields over stiles and through gates to Greenhow Farm. Note: In the field with a large stone barn, go through the lower of two gates. From Greenhow Farm, turn right along the track and pass through a gap stile on your left. Follow the path by the stream and climb the signposted stile to reach the road. Turn left and opposite the cottages go through the handgate signposed Gyhll and Dufton.

Follow the path along the delightful Dufton Gyhll which is owned and managed by the Woodland Trust. It's a superb wooded ravine, carpeted with wild flowers and dotted with abandoned quarries. Cross a footbridge and climb the track up to Dufton village with its tree-lined green, drinking fountain and sandstone cottages. The Stag Inn offers refreshments. For the return route, leave Dufton by

(Continued on page 127)

125

30. Appleby

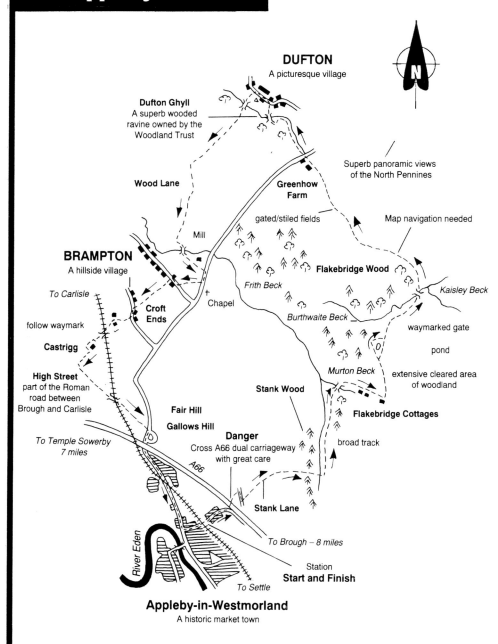

© Crown Copyright

126

(Continued from page 125)

the signpost 'Footpath to Brampton' located at the west end of the village. Go between the cottages and follow the path back down into Dufton Gyhll. Cross a footbridge and climb steeply out of the ravine. Go over a cross track and climb again via a stile into Wood Lane. Follow this lovely walled green lane southwards which twists and turns down to Brampton Beck. There are fine views of the distant Lakeland Fells. Fork left, cross the footbridge over Brampton Beck and bear left along the track that bypasses Brampton Watermill. Turn right along the road and cross the signposted stile on your right. Go up the field edge to come out by Brampton Hall. Turn right along the road and unless you need refreshments at the New Inn, do not enter the hillside village of Brampton. In yards, go through the signposted gate, go diagonally over the short field and cross the corner stile. Head up the long field,

watch out for the bull, and bear right through a gate by the black barn and out through the farmyard of Croft Ends. Turn left along the road and opposite some cottages turn right along the track (signposted Long Marton) to the whitewashed Keld Farm. Yards beyond the farm, cross a waymarked stile on your left and go diagonally over the field to cross the bridge over the Settle-Carlisle Railway. Cross a facing stile, go up the field edge and at the top cross another waymarked stile and go left down the track to pass Castrigg on your left. Once through a facing gate, turn left and right down the same field edge and at the bottom cross a corner stile (blue arrows) into a broad lane. Turn left along this lovely hedgerowed lane called the High Street, part of the Roman Road from Brough to Carlisle. Cross another bridge over the Settle-Carlisle Railway and you come out opposite Gallows Hill or Fairs Hill where the annual Appleby New Fair is held. Turn right along Long Marton Road via Station Road back to Appleby Station.

127

Index

128